The Malign Legacy

PENN ADAMS

THE MALIGN LEGACY First edition January 20, 2021.

Copyright © 2021 Penn Adams. Written by Penn Adams.

Edited by Simone Ford (IPEd) Australia

Cover Design by Rob Williams, www.ilovemycover.com

ISBN: 978-0-6488080-2-2 Ebook

ISBN: 978-0-6488080-3-9 Paperback/Print-on-demand

For Chloe and Amelia who light up my world

Chapter One

In the darkness of space far beyond the planets of Altan and Autabron, the small spaceracer *Teg-Kanish* limped in the void, floundering, like a wounded bird, its one uncharred wing struggling to keep it on course for home. First officer Decker Finn winced as he stretched across the navigator's console to punch in a set of coordinates. His cracked ribs and the lacerations on his face and shoulder were taking their toll, but he had injected the last of the yargon an hour ago and grimaced at the thought that he would have to go without the drug's sweet relief in the few hours before they re-entered the Altan system.

The *Kanish*'s encounter with the meteorite had been brief and lethal for most of the crew, including the captain. He and their sole passenger, the Altani ambassador, had been lost, blasted into space along with the starboard wing and with no hope of being recovered. Finn couldn't think about that now. Two other crew members were badly injured and needed him to get them back home as soon as possible. He assumed that their craft had been reported unaccounted for once they had not arrived at the Rakuumna Spaceport – what, now nearly thirty-six hours ago?

The comms had been taken out by the impact, so they hadn't been able to send a distress signal. But they would have been deemed missing and a search of galactic space would surely be underway by now. It was just a matter of waiting for help to arrive and, in the meantime, Finn guiding the vessel as best he could towards home space.

Finn reflected on this, his latest posting since joining the Galactic Union's fleet. He had been excited to leave his native Earth and explore the outer reaches of the galaxy. As a child he had soaked up every snippet of information about the distant planets of Altan, Dasnir, Hutho and Autabron and their peoples, so like humans yet with subtle differences, such as the pale green skin of the Huthons and the lace-like webbing of the hands and feet of the Dasnirians, all adaptations to their environments. He was amazed that the mountains on Altan, the high Ksas, were twice the height of the Himalayas on Earth and, consequently, remained unconquered. And although Earth was seventy percent water, that was as nothing compared to the vast oceans of Dasnir, where cities had been built both over the water and under it.

Once he graduated from the academy in Novatlanta as a pilot-navigator and had clocked up the required one thousand hours on raptors, he quickly signed up for the Galactic Union's spacefleet and was immediately sent to Genkarah, one of Altan's major cities and the Union's administrative base. There he had expanded his training to include weapons and security systems, additions to his portfolio that he hoped would one day lead to a promotion to captain of his own craft.

But, to his surprise and despite his arms training, he had been posted to the Diplomatic Corps and had spent nearly four years ferrying important personnel from one planet to another. It was uneventful work, but he had built a name and reputation for himself as a dependable and discreet man who could use his initiative.

From there he had transferred to the military wing and, finally, a chance to put his training into practice. The next three years were spent at outposts on Autabron and Hutho, training local security teams. Not that the Huthons grasped the importance of weapons and personal security. They were, by nature, a peaceful people, masters of the arts and music. They were just not interested in how to use a xelex cannon. But the Autabronis, they were a different breed altogether. Fiery, quick to anger and physically strong, Finn soon learned that if anyone did *not* need to know how cannon or field mortars worked, it was them. An irate, armed Autabroni was not a good thing – not ever!

Now, at the age of thirty-four, he had enough experience and expertise to apply for a captaincy, and Finn had hoped to hear of his success on his return from this journey. It should have been a swift run to Autabron to drop off the ambassador, but the meteorite had come out of nowhere. They had been running without a force-shield because it took too much power and slowed them down. Captain Milak had decided to sacrifice safety for speed, because the ambassador's mission in the light of the unrest at the Autabron mines was top priority. Apparently the meteorite had been too small and fast to be picked up on their screens and so, when it smashed into their starboard wing, the impact had been catastrophic. The hull was breached in at least three places and it was only Finn's quick thinking that saw those sections shut their blast doors and preserve the rest of the ship, but not before both the ambassador and the captain were lost. Finn had had enough nous to take control of what was left of the vessel and set the coordinates for the nearest planet, Altan.

Now, nursing his wounds and relishing the relief of the painkillers, he closed his tired eyes and prayed he would live long enough to see the sparkling lights of the city of Genkarah again. All they could do now was wait and hope that they would make it home or be rescued before anyone else died.

The stillness in the Cavern of Gunda was almost tangible. Although a thousand men and women of Guznon, true sons and daughters of Autabron, kneeled on the solid ground, there was not a movement nor a sound in the vast stone space. Their silent breath rose in the chill pre-dawn air, forming a mist that draped and curled over the prone body at the centre of the gathering.

Naked save for a loincloth, the young man's muscled torso was relaxed and his white-blond hair hung down the sides of the stone altar upon which he lay. His clear blue eyes stared upwards as he waited for the ceremony to be completed.

The silence was pierced by the deep and growing reverberation of the Horn of Gurkat, then by the guttural curling screams of the multitude. The noise rose like the thundering rumble of a rockslide. He sighed once, then filled his lungs to exhale his own cry of power.

In an instant, all noise ceased. He rose from the altar and stood facing the horde.

His natar, Mira, dressed in a flowing crimson robe, stepped forward holding a bowl of melted silver bergu, the precious extract of the bergussian ore that made her home planet envied by all in the Galactic Union. She dipped a sliver of red rock into in the hot thick liquid and drew it down the centre of the young man's chest. The baptismal streak would be burned into his flesh, an eternal reminder of who he was.

Her voice did not betray her great age as she spoke. 'Kalik Denkaun! Son of the twin suns! Bearer of hope! Shield of faith! Take up your spear! Lead your people out of cursed oppression! Your time has come!'

The crowd echoed her call. 'Your time has come!'

Denkaun smiled at Mira, the woman who had raised him since his mother's glorious sacrifice twenty-five years earlier. His birth mother, the little Altani witch Ko-Makum, had died a noble death so that his adopted people, the Guznon, might one day be free of the repression of the off-worlders, the mine owners who forced them to such labour. It was a destiny he must fulfil, he *wanted* to fulfil.

He stepped forward and touched his forehead to Mira's in a mark of love and respect before turning to face the mass of expectant faces. 'My time is *now*! I am the son of the twin suns, Lau and Uzno! The A'bat! Our struggle begins this day and I shall not fail!'

His body trembled with the power of his words and the crowd cheered in response.

'A'bat! A'bat! A'bat!'

The chant lifted the coils of mist through the cavern as one by one men and women stepped forward to bow, then touch Kalik Denkaun's bare feet. One among them caught his eye. The daughter of Dokau, Wika by name. Her white hair tumbled over full breasts as she bowed low before him. She lifted her head and her dark eyes looked directly into his, a provocative glance that promised much and sent a ripple of pleasure through his loins.

Mira gazed at the strong muscles of her adopted son's back that had suddenly tensed with the arrival of the Dokau girl. *Pah! She is not for him. Impudent fool!* Mira would speak to Kalik later about it, remind him of his destiny. Wika must stay a plaything, but never a wife! That was reserved for a special consort, and Mira had not spent all these years planning and scheming to see all her and Lyr's work lost on some foolish whim.

Her now dead husband had been sceptical when they first found the little witch at the spaceport near Euta Makaan. The tall blonde woman had come to them seeking refuge from her enemies and paid them well. She and her brother had caused much trouble in the Union by kidnapping the Ki of Altan, the proud queen Linnayen Genara. They had thought to rule through the brother, Durroc Navarr, who had once been the Ki's paramour. *Fools!* They dreamed too quickly, thought Mira. Such plans need time and patience. It had taken twenty-five years but she was now so close to achieving all they had wanted for their people, the Guznon. *A return to the true faith!*

Lyr Denkau had not seen what she had – that the little witch was pregnant. But, more importantly, that she was carrying her own twin brother's child. Over the months while they gave her sanctuary in the caves and tunnels of the Beshwuk mountains, the little witch had bleated on to Mira of her great love for her brother, who had been killed by Linnayen and her husband, the hated Kevor Jax. Far from condemning her unnatural passion for her twin brother, Mira was secretly thrilled. For had it not been predicted that only a son of twins would lead them out of oppression and hardship? Only a son of the twin suns of Autabron, Lau and Uzno, would bring them back to faith and power. The little witch – and the child she carried– were the fulfilment of the prophecy.

It had come to pass. The child, a boy, was named Kalik. The mother, Balisel Navarr, had died in the full glare of the twin suns on the Sill, a sacrifice – though not a willing one – that would fulfil the destiny of the first peoples of Autabron. Mira remembered the morning on the Day of Grunkaar, on the high ledge when the screen lifted to admit the rays of the twin suns. The little witch's body had begun to blister and shrivel in the immense heat. She had screamed that her son would avenge his father's death or she would haunt Mira to the end of her days. The little witch need not have worried for it was always her and Denkau's plan to make the most of the great gift of Kalik Navarr, known to the world as Kalik Denkaun after his adoptive father. For had not Mira foreseen what was to happen? A destiny was already written and the old woman knew that no ghost of the little witch would ever come to plague her.

'Please, Seti. Give it back.'

Calin Genara pleaded with her recalcitrant older sister one more time. Setiyan had snatched up the younger princess's journal and was dancing around the room while Calin chased lamely behind.

'If it's that important to you, you'll agree to do my tasks,' Setiyan returned, not bothering to hide her grin.

'That's not fair and you know it. Really! You're too old for this behaviour. Just give it back!'

Calin's voice had an edge of anger now. It was not that there was anything especially secret or important in the journal, but it was hers and at twenty-three years of age and a grown woman, she was entitled to her privacy. Setiyan was just being her usual boisterous self and, had Calin not been up in the early hours of the morning studying Huthon biology, she might have been less riled. She resumed her seat at the fine marble table in the centre of the room.

'Come and get it!' Setiyan's words danced across the room, but Calin folded her arms resolutely. 'What? Oh, I can keep it then, can I? Fine. Let's see …'

Her blonde head tipped forward as Setiyan began to scroll across the pages of her little sister's journal, though at such a speed it was impossible that she was reading the contents. In truth, she was not interested in Calin's innermost thoughts, mainly because she believed there was nothing worth knowing. Her owns thoughts and dreams were of far more importance to her – specifically, what was to be her destiny? Would they marry her off to a handsome Earthan, someone like her father, who had so swept her mother off her feet? Please, not a Huthon! Their pale green skin and serious demeanour did nothing to stir her blood. And how her aunt, Evica Genara, could have fallen in love with the Dasnirian Tariik Min, who was more fish than humanoid, defeated her. *No thanks!* Anyhow, she was young and there was plenty of time for romance and adventure before settling down into a boring political marriage.

Not that her mother and father's marriage – completely arranged from day one – had been unsuccessful. It was obvious that Linnayen and Kevor Jax loved each other, and she thought it might be nice to feel like that about someone *and* have them feel the same for you. Only not just yet. She glanced at a couple more screens then sauntered back to Calin.

'Mmm … On second thoughts, really, sister, you need to have some fun.'

With a careless wave, she threw the journal down onto the table in front of Calin, who pulled it back into her safe grasp.

'Thank you.' Her muted reply was swallowed up by the opening of the double doors and the noisy entrance of her father, Kevor Jax Bashir, formerly a prince of Earth, now Ki-consort to her beautiful, raven-haired mother, Linnayen Genara. Jax's eyes quickly swept the room and took in his two daughters, one with hair the colours of autumn, imperial and contained just like her mother, and the other a blonde whirlwind with terrifyingly blue eyes and a wide grin that was so often aimed directly at him.

'Papa!' Setiyan ran straight over and threw herself into his open arms, almost toppling his tall frame.

'Ho! Seti! Steady on. You'll knock me down one of these days.' He laughed as he collected her up and swung her around, her skirts flying out in a whirling arc.

'I missed you. Why did you take so long? You mustn't do that. Going away for weeks at a time. What about us? What about me?' Setiyan was insistent and the questions poured out of her like a torrent. Once back on the ground, she took hold of his jaw and looked him straight in the eye. 'I mean it. Stop going away.'

'Even if I come back bearing gifts?' he teased her.

'Oh! What have you brought me?' She scrutinised his face then began pulling at his pockets. He skipped away and went over to the smiling Calin, who sat patiently waiting for her sister's onslaught to subside.

'It's always all about her, isn't it?' he asked his younger daughter. He kissed the top of her head and sat down beside her. Calin rolled her eyes and smiled. It had always been thus. Seti was demanding of everyone's attention – except her mother. And most people eventually succumbed to her powerful personality, and mostly with good humour. Seti was never intentionally unkind or unthinking, but her own desires often leapt to the fore ahead of others in the room.

'Oh sorry, Papa. I've done it again, haven't I?' Setiyan's contrition was genuine. She took a breath and promptly kneeled before him. 'It's good to have you home. How was your trip?'

'That's better. That's the princess I know and love. The one who cares about other people and their feelings. The one who is all heart …'

'Yes, yes. I said I was sorry,' she interjected.

Jax laughed, shaking his head in despair. The girl – no, woman now – was a conundrum. Beautiful with long fair hair, azure eyes, a strong fit body and a mind as bright as the stars in the Genkaran night sky. He had probably spoiled her growing up and this had led to a certain streak of self-absorption. Whereas Calin, so much like her mother, was as different as the moon to the sun. Calm, intelligent, with a loving heart and a desire to please that was intrinsic.

'Enough!' It was time to rope the wayward daughter in and get to the matter of his visit. Seti crossed her legs and sat in front of him. 'Daughters, I'm actually home earlier than planned and there's a special reason. Now, listen ...'

He began to recount his visit to Earth and how his discussions with the representatives of the Earthan spacefleet had raised concerns over the supply of bergussian ore from Autabron. There had been delays in shipments recently and a worrying decrease in the quality of the ore, which had led to a greater need for processing. All this had meant an increase in costs for the fleet which, in turn, impacted on their ability to maintain security outposts on the Jarunei Strand. In all the years of mining the precious ore there had never been such concerns, and it needed investigating. The mine owners were looking into it which was, apparently, ruffling the feathers of the workers. If there was one thing the Union did not need it was angry Autabronis, who were quick to take offence. There had already been protests at mine sites. Jax and the other Galactic Union members felt it needed a lighter touch.

'I don't see what we can do, Pa,' Calin commented. 'Surely we have experienced diplomats who could take this on?'

Jax concurred. 'We do. But your mother and I agree that playing the "royal visit" card often loosens lips and breaks down walls. In all your mother's years of statecraft training and experience, she has shown time and again that a sympathetic ear and a willingness to explore solutions often avoids bigger problems.'

'So what do you want us to do?' Setiyan was engaged. She had been on visits before, mostly to commemorate events or open medcentres or school campuses, all of which bored her to tears. This sounded more challenging. An investigation. Digging to find out what was going on. This was much more the sort of enterprise she was keen to try. A real chance to test her statecraft skills.

'You should also know that Ambassador Sen-Latisian has been sent to Autabron to take stock of the atmosphere there, but – I'm sad to say – we've lost contact with the spaceracer he was travelling on,' Jax related.

'A deliberate target?' Setiyan asked quickly.

'Don't know. Too soon to jump to conclusions.'

'But you want us to be aware that this might be a dangerous mission?' Calin queried.

'Again, too soon to say. There are tensions and both your mother and I feel that it's time for us to become involved,' he concluded.

'Shall we both go to Autabron?' Setiyan fired off. 'We went as children but I have almost no memory of it. I'd love to go again. So would Calin.' Setiyan looked up pleadingly.

Jax raised his hands in an effort to hold back his eldest daughter's enthusiasm. 'To be decided.'

Setiyan furrowed her brow. She jumped up and turned away, swishing her long skirt behind her. Calin smiled at her sister's enthusiasm for what she saw as a dangerous mission and shook her head. 'Don't worry, sister. If they have to choose between us, I'd rather you go anyway. I have too much to do here. I've my thesis on Huthon parasitology to finish by the end of next month.'

Jax smiled at the dedication his youngest child showed to her studies and stroked her auburn hair.

'As I said, to be decided. We need to find out what's happened to the *Teg-Kanish* first. Meanwhile ...' He left the words hanging in order to tease Setiyan even more. She rushed back to his side.

'Meanwhile what?'

'There's the matter of your mother's party.'

Setiyan's face fell. She and Calin had been tasked with organising the entertainment for Linnayen's fiftieth birthday only a week away now and, to be honest, she'd not contributed much apart from ideas. She looked nervously at her sister.

'All in hand, Papa,' Calin assured him. Setiyan threw her a querying look.

Jax smiled. 'So, what are we to expect? Some fine Latis-mei choral singers? Earthan interpretive dance? Please, not a Huthon poetry recital!'

Calin giggled at his mock despair. 'I thought you loved poetry, Pa? No, don't worry. It will be lively and fun and everyone will have a wonderful time, won't they, sister?'

Setiyan nodded enthusiastically, 'Absolutely!' She instantly faced her sister with a questioning look.

'I guess I'll just have to trust you, then,' he concluded. He stood up.

'Wait!' Setiyan dashed over to stop his exit, laying a hand on his chest. 'You said there were presents?'

Jax raised an eyebrow and the corners of his mouth lifted in a warm smile. He threw an arm around her and moved towards the door, beckoning for Calin to join them. She placed her journal in a drawer of the table before running to join the fast-retreating duo.

'Wait for me!'

Jax led them to a balcony overlooking a granite-pillared atrium from where they could see two grooms, each holding a small furry animal. They were struggling to control the wriggles of two small red pandas, native to Earth, who were munching a long stalk of bamboo each.

The gasps of delight from the princesses could be heard all through the upper rooms of the Genara palace and they almost tripped each other over as they rushed down the stairs to take possession of these, the latest in their growing menagerie of pets.

'Oh, Pa! You're the best!'

'They're adorable!'

Jax beamed at his daughters. He knew he spoiled them, Linnayen warned him of it often enough, but he was lost. His heart belonged as much to them as it did to their mother, and he knew that there was nothing he would not do for any of them.

The excited squeals and laughter reached Linnayen Genara at her desk. She shook her head and the hint of a smile curled the corner of her mouth. Would there ever come a day when Jax would stop treating them like girls instead of the grown women they now were? She reflected that she had been younger than even Calin when she inherited the Ki-ship from her father. Only twenty-one years old and so much responsibility on such young shoulders. But thanks to Yenshar Genara's foresight, she had been trained well. So when the time came, she was completely prepared – almost too prepared. Her demeanour then was highly formal and distant. She was reserved and held her emotions in check so much of the time – except when it had come to Navarr.

Even now, more than two decades later, she still found it hard to reconcile those feelings for the man who had been firstly her emissary to Earth and, later, her lover. She had adored him, worshipped him. She had subjugated her every thought to his will and would have become his puppet had it not been for the accident on board the *Jensa Kadenx* as they travelled to Earth for her sister Evica's wedding. When the psytro-ion storm hit the ship she had smacked her head so severely that she was in a coma for many days. After she finally regained consciousness, she had no memory of anything.

She was like a newborn baby, opening her blurry eyes, seeing the world for the first time and struggling to decipher how it worked. She still recalled the fear and confusion that only the kindness of Jax and the understanding of her family had helped her to conquer. Finding out that she was an important person, a planetary leader, no less! Then discovering that she was married to Jax, had a devoted sister and mother – it was all so confounding. It was only the old counsellor Sen-Beoraan who she recognised, and his presence gave her some assurance that she would eventually remember everything.

And she did – in time. It all started to come back to her. But not before Navarr, her former lover, had tried to resume his position with her. She had been horrified and disgusted at his attempt to seduce her in the quiet of her hospital room. Luckily, Evica and Tariik Min, now her sister's husband, had heard her screams and come to her rescue. Linnayen had seen Navarr's confusion as they pulled him off her, his eyes uncertain and then angry as the realisation dawned that she wanted no part of him. The woman she had been was no more and, from then on, all her attention was turned towards her husband.

The laughter from the atrium rose like a wave breaking onto her thoughts. It made her restless and she stood to stretch her aching back. Linnayen moved over to the window, its carved wooden sash framing the city far below. Dusk was settling over the spires, walkways and gleaming towers of Genkarah, and with it came a rich purple hue, fractured by a thousand tiny specks of light as people prepared for the coming evening.

Jax never talked about how she had made him feel in those many months after their wedding. She had paraded her paramour in front of him and turned to Navarr for guidance and affection, snubbing the man who truly loved her. Jax had adored her from the start. Theirs was a political marriage and, whilst she felt little for Kevor Jax at the beginning, the same was not so for him. Seeing his wife with his one-time friend was torture and he had distanced himself deliberately.

She could only imagine the pain she had caused him and had spent many years making it up to him – not that it was hard. They had long since been reconciled, especially since the birth of Setiyan. As she gazed out of the palace windows over the darkening city, she knew that was why he was so devoted to Seti. Her birth had sealed their happiness, so how could Linnayen blame him for loving her as much as he did?

Her reverie was broken by a sharp tap at the door. She spun around, expecting to see one of the girls with a squirming animal. But it was Lady Li-el Dacas, her mother.

'I would have sent ahead but I know you would have made an excuse not to see me. So here I am.' The older woman spoke with her usual regal manner.

Linnayen crossed the space between them and took Li-el in her arms.

'Don't be silly, Mother.'

'I'm not being silly. You've been avoiding me. You're always avoiding me. I've seen you duck away on my approach. It's very rude!'

Linnayen lowered her head and gave a small grimace. It was true. She *had* dodged her mother's company from time to time.

'I'm sorry, Mother. I haven't meant to, but with the birthday ball coming up, I've had so much to do.'

'Rubbish!' Li-el snorted. 'The girls – well, Calin – have been organising everything. And the menu was set weeks ago, as were the decorations. And that's why I'm upset.'

Ah, here it comes, thought Linnayen.

'You know that's my expertise. I've organised hundreds of balls and functions, both in your time and in your father's. Why haven't you asked me to assist? It's completely … completely … Oh, what's the word?'

'Untenable?' Linnayen offered.

'Yes, untenable. And impolite!'

Li-el sighed, shoulders slumping as she sat in the chair at Linnayen's desk and smoothed the folds of her blue silk dress. She stiffened her back and then picked up a stylus, twirling it furiously between her fingers. Linnayen knew that the storm was not quite over.

'It wouldn't have happened ten years ago … Even five years ago! You think I'm too old, don't you? Think I'm losing the pot, don't you?'

'Plot,' Linnayen murmured. 'Not pot.'

'There, you see? That proves it!'

'Oh, Mother.' Linnayen swiftly moved to Li-el's side and kneeled to encircle her in a warm hug, stroking her greying hair. The contact seemed to calm the older woman and Linnayen spoke soothing words into her ear. 'I didn't want to exclude you. I wanted to save you the work and the worry, that's all. I wanted you to focus on the nice things, like what gorgeous creation you're going to wear, and how to style your hair. Who to dance with. These decisions are much more enjoyable.'

Li-el nodded. 'Mmm. Maybe you're right.'

'So, what *are* you going to wear?' Linnayen bounced up and perched on the edge of the desk. 'I can't wait to see.'

Li-el looked up at her daughter through hooded eyes. 'You think to placate me by diverting my thoughts. Nice try, daughter, but it won't work.'

Linnayen stood and shrugged. 'Think what you must, Mother, but I assure you that we only have your best interests at heart.' The look on Li-el's face told her that her mother was not convinced, so she went on. 'And Jax wanted to give the girls more to do, something different. They've been so good with attending to the usual rounds of ceremonies. But they must be bored stiff by shaking all those hands and giving endless speeches. We thought organising a party would be more interesting. And it would test their skills.'

'Calin's skills. Not Seti. She's as flyaway as a plinka,' Li-el countered, referring to the beautiful indigo night-moth of Hutho. 'And she thinks she's as pretty as one too.'

'Now, Mother, don't start on that.' Linnayen's tone was frosty. She had heard the same complaint so many times from Li-el as the girls were growing up and hated for them to be judged on their looks. In her eyes, both her daughters were beautiful, one with long golden tresses and crystal eyes, the other with russet hair and peridot green eyes. Both were bright and had excelled at their statecraft training. Both were considerate of others and, more importantly, empathetic. And for that she was eternally grateful.

Li-el sighed. 'Very well, daughter. I'll say no more.'

She put her weight on both arms of the chair as she pushed herself up. Nearly eighty years old now, she had begun to notice too many small aches and pains.

Linnayen reached towards her. 'Here, let me help you, Mother.'

'I'm fine.' She waved her away and began to walk towards the door. She stopped midway and said over her shoulder, 'I thought the Dasnirian sea-silk in pale vermillion with the waterfall pearls your father gave me.'

Linnayen smiled. 'Gorgeous! You'll make the rest of us look drab.'

As Li-el continued on her path to the door, she lifted her chin and replied, 'That was my intention.'

Kalik Denkaun's eyes scanned the dark red horizon. In the far distance, the low hills of Camdru lay sleeping in the pre-dawn chill, yet to be burned by the rising of the twin suns in an hour or so. The once high peaks had been eroded over the centuries by the infernal heat and intense cold that each day and night on Autabron brought. That, at least, was natural and as it should be, the path of natural elements that none could change. The destruction the mines brought was the complete opposite. Denkaun's planet was being raped of its riches by the greed of the Union. Bergussian ore had brought the raiders to his homeworld many centuries ago. The planet was a seemingly never-ending source of the material that had built thousands of space vessels. Could they have known that there would come a day when the ore would be exhausted? *Of course they could!* Had not the same pattern repeated itself on many planets before? But did it stop them? Did it even slow them down? *No! Not by even a breath.*

Denkaun tried not to let his anger spoil this morning. It had been a good night. The ceremony had been long and he should have been tired. But when Wika Dokau had pulled aside the tapestry to his chamber and dropped her cloak to reveal her full, luscious beauty, he found new energy. His response was primal and immediate.

She had crossed the floor silently and, sweeping aside his loincloth, took hold of him. He smiled into her dark eyes then allowed his gaze to travel the length of her naked body. Her breasts were full, their nipples erect. He dropped to his knees, the better to smell and taste the secret part of her. She was moist and, as he touched her soft heart with his tongue, she moaned with pleasure.

His hands had reached up to cup her breasts and he squeezed her nipples hard. She did not mind. He had long since gathered that

Wika was willing to endure almost any level of agony as long as it brought her the sweet surge she craved.

He knew when she was close – he always knew. Her gasps deepened and she gripped his head, pushing him into her body. At just that moment he pulled away and pulled her down onto the rug-covered floor. She squirmed and groaned, begging him to enter her and he wasted no time, thrusting his engorged penis deep into her cleft. Within a minute their bodies exploded in a surge of pleasure, their warm breath mingling in the chamber's steamy interior, their guttural cries filling the spaces of the rock walls.

Wika had pushed him off her body as she struggled to control her breathing. Kalik was a big man, strong with a broad chest and thighs that nearly tore her apart when he was taking her. He was the finest of the Guznon, brave and powerful, and she would have no other. He had allowed her to thrust him away even though he felt an uncommon desire to stay on top of her, crushing her into the stone floor until she was no more than a patina of dust.

Now, in the early morning calm, leaning against the casement, he turned his gaze from the dips and rises of the skyline to the curves of her sleeping body. Wika gave him pleasure, but he knew Mira was unhappy with this liaison. She had other plans for him and had made it plain that he may take as many concubines as he wished, but he must not offer marriage. Mira had her reasons and he knew not to gainsay her in this matter. It had been his foster father's wish – nay, command – that he comply with their long-held dream of uniting the Guznon people and restoring their freedom.

And he wanted that too. Even though his blood was not Guznon, they had raised him, nurtured him, cherished him, and he was as bound to them as Lau is to Uzno. For was he not the A'bat? The one foretold. The warrior of hope who would free his people and right all wrongs. And Mira was wise and all-knowing, and whatever she had foreseen would come to pass, as surely as the Day of Grunkaar brings the replenishing rains.

A muffled sound emanated from the sleeping woman. She was waking. He strode over to the bed and shook her shoulder.

'Get up. You must go now.'

Wika mumbled a complaint. 'No, Kalik. A few more minutes.'

His voice was stone. 'Now!'

Resignedly, Wika swung her legs out of the bed. His eyes narrowed. Wasn't it enough that she enjoyed an honour that many woman wanted? To be chosen by the A'bat. Why must she always tarry?

She rose from the cool sheets and took up her cloak from where she had dropped it last night. Denkaun had returned to the window, his gaze on the distant hills, not her.

Wika walked over and sank to one knee before him. 'My lord, my love.' Still kneeling, she bowed her head.

He glanced at the tumbling tresses and sighed. 'Why are you still here?'

Wika's head dropped even lower as she stood and backed away. Denkaun did not see the retreating woman or acknowledge her subservience. His mind was already back in the deep caverns of Euta Sakek, the once beautiful array of carved halls and sacristies that had crumbled into dust a mere three months ago. The mine had come too close and, despite all the warnings from the workers, the orders had been to keep drilling. It was inevitable that his people's most sacred site would be damaged in some way. Little did they think the destruction would be so complete. Two thousand years of history and devotion crumbled to nothing in less than a day. Once the collapse of Euta Sakek had started, it could not be stopped.

Mira, Denkaun and thousands of Autabronis had stood dumbly in front of their vidscreens showing live footage of the rubble that was once their underground cathedral. As they witnessed the brown clouds of broken rock rising, curling and finally settling on their treasured carvings and statues, their anger grew until, like the swirls of sacred dust, it soared to the heavens. The mine owners, the GKD company, had expressed sorrow and wrung hands in so-called grief, and the Union had sent emissaries to foster talks between the miners and the company. But all knew that there could be no retribution rapid or painful enough to pay for this act of destruction.

Until today, thought Kalik Denkaun. *Until today.*

Chapter Two

In the end, Decker Finn's dose of yargon had lasted just long enough to save him from the pain of his cracked ribs, although the gash in his shoulder had burned for many hours. The agony of trying to breathe had just started to return when he had seen the signal of an approaching vessel on the bridge screens and that the call sign was Union. They were still a day out of the Altan system when the search vessel had found them stumbling blindly towards home. The vessel's captain, a petite, dark-haired Dasnirian with strikingly aqua eyes, explained that the *Teg-Kanish*'s signal had shown up as being off course and, given the news from Autabron, she had been sent to find them forthwith.

'What news?' he had queried.

'It's not good. There've been attacks and explosions all over Autabron. To be expected though,' she replied. 'That's why we were so worried about you.'

'A terrorist attack?' His eyes widened and he shook his head. 'Nothing so exciting. Just an unexpected meteorite strike.'

'That's to be determined.'

The captain cocked an eyebrow at Finn and her gaze travelled the length his body before she swirled away and returned to her duties piloting them home to Altan.

Now, in his room at the medcentre in Genkarah, Finn reached for the clikon. He frowned as he watched the vidscreen relaying the late-night news from Silbaraz-Re, the planet's largest city. There were riots on Autabron at the Euta Makaan processing plant. Two compactors had been obliterated by what the investigators thought had been turgex devices, and the transporter lines had all been torn down and smashed by a mob of around a thousand Autabronis, thought to be from the Guznon tribe. The damage was extensive and would take weeks to repair, but Finn was not surprised at the anger of the crowd. When the news of the destruction of Euta Sakek had come out, he reasoned it was

17

only a matter of time before something would go wrong – badly wrong. It was why he'd been escorting the ambassador. There was hope that his intervention and a promise of a full enquiry into the disaster would forestall such action.

But the Dasnirian captain's words had planted a seed of doubt. It *had* been a meteorite, hadn't it? Not sabotage, surely. The ship would have been checked for explosives before they left dock – wouldn't it? The captain had said 'to be determined', and he cursed that he'd be facing a thorough investigation. *Damn!* It could have him grounded for weeks. And then what if he was a suspect? This could ruin his career.

Finn slammed the clikon into the folds of the sheet, then winced with the pain in his torn shoulder as the screen went black. He exhaled loudly. *Come on. You have nothing to worry about.* But in those three years on Autabron he'd made many friends. That was not going to look good. There was a storm coming his way and, as he drifted into sleep, he wondered if it would do as much damage as that damned meteorite.

Mira waited, her eyes closed and head resting against the cool rock wall in the shadows of the tunnel leading to the most holy of the Guznon sanctuaries, Kadis Sakek. In the distance she could hear drops of water bouncing onto the surface of the smooth reservoir. The Kadis, a vast artesian lake of ancient water fed by all too infrequent rains, was both sacred and necessary to her people, for it held life. The tagirp fish had fed her people for centuries, long before the despised off-worlders had brought their so-called cuisines. *Pah!* Food that was slowly killing the once strong and proud men and women of Autabron, making them sick and fat and slovenly. *No wonder we have lost our faith!*

She was alone in the darkness. Her people had gone forth and done their work. The destruction at Euta Makaan meant that the huge plant would be processing nothing for many months. The precious ore would remain where it belonged and the Galactic Union could rot in hell.

Kalik had been awe-inspiring: fierce, strong, his voice powerful in the dark. His rallying call had been relayed throughout the tribes, a compelling whisper here and there that had surged to a war cry. Within weeks, all the peoples of Autabron – the Guznon, the Gaksi, the Konkanaw, the Graan and the No'os – had gathered and united in their mission to reclaim their lands. A new dawn was coming. The A'bat would lead them to freedom and self-determination, no longer to be governed by the greed and deception of off-worlders. *Curse them all!* Kalik would take back their lands and they would live under the blessings of Lau and Uzno as it was always meant to be.

A gust of cool air stroked her face. Instinctively she turned towards it and her hand moved to the razor-sharp dagger in her belt. She heard the dull thud of feet and drew further into a cleft in the rock. Suddenly, a soft hiss broke the moist air and the light of a glow-globe filled the space.

'Natar?'

She stepped forward out of the gloom, blade unsheathed and ready to strike at the exposed neck of the figure behind Denkaun.

'Please don't kill him, Natar. I'm not quite finished with him yet.' Denkaun's voice betrayed a sardonic smile as he laid a gentle hand on her arm. 'This is Hanashi. He led the raid on the transporter lines – very successfully, I might add.'

Denkaun released another glow-globe and let it float above the trio. Mira bowed her head to the compatriot.

'You are welcome, Hanashi.'

'My natar, our shaman, Mira, has been looking forward to meeting you, my friend,' Denkaun explained to the still startled Gaksi leader. 'Although her manner might make you think otherwise today.'

Mira lifted her chin. 'I make no apologies for my caution. There is much at stake.'

Hanashi concurred. 'Indeed, Shaman-Mira. We have much to lose if we are caught. Already, hundreds of Guznon have been detained. It takes only one to talk.'

'*My* people will not speak to the ganak scum!'

'And neither will mine!' Hanashi fired back.

Mira spat at the ground. The Gaksi had as long a history on Autabron as the Guznon. But resentment had built over the centuries as the northerners boasted of their husbandry and hunting skills. They had chased the bika and lived off their hides and flesh and milk and had become self-sufficient with ease, while her people had had to survive on and beneath the planet's harsh surface. The Guznon could only farm the paltry feir fungus in their dusty caverns and they had been forced to kowtow to their off-world overlords. But their subjugation had made them strong and fuelled their anger in a way that the pampered Gaksi could never understand.

Even so, these times called for all the tribes to work together to rid themselves of the hated ganaks who sucked their planet dry. The A'bat had spoken of this, of his hopes and dreams that one day they would regain their lands and live as Lau and Uzno always intended: in faith, in moral strength, in the sure knowledge that a green and glorious world awaited them after death.

Denkaun was quick to still his foster mother's temper. 'Natar, Hanashi means no disrespect. I am thankful to him for his people's help, as should you be.'

Mira snorted. He was right, but it was hard to let go of prejudices that had existed for centuries. The Gaksi, so fortunate, had always looked down upon her people, thought themselves so much better. If it were not for the prophecy she would never countenance working with them, or the other tribes, to get rid of the off-worlders. She must put aside old hatreds for the sake of the prophecy.

'Come!' Denkaun had already moved away towards Kadis Sakek. 'Follow me.'

The trio moved along the passageway, the air cooling their cheeks as the plinking of droplets became louder. In a few minutes they turned the last curve in the tunnel and the roof rose away. Their breath twirled in the soft light of the glow-globe and rose into the unknown space above. Ahead lay a mirror-smooth, seemingly endless expanse of black water, an occasional ripple reflecting a golden arc by the light of the orb.

Mira smiled and looked at the stunned Gaksi. 'This is why we struggle.'

Denkaun's eyes narrowed as he looked down at her wrinkled face. 'It's why we must win.'

The trio stood in silence, taking in the glory, the incomprehensible fact that there could be so much free-flowing water on their scorched planet. Suddenly, Hanashi dropped to his knees and bowed his head.

'By the blessed twin suns, I vow before the waters of Kadis Sakek that my life is forfeit if we fail in our task.' The Gaksi leader's words hung in the still air.

Denkaun placed a firm hand on his head and tilted it upwards until their eyes met. His words, when they came, were both fire and ice. 'We will not fail. So I will not have to kill you, my friend.'

Linnayen Genara studied her reflection in the mirror, brow knitted as her gaze ran up and down her body. The years and two childbirths had thickened her frame, and despite her husband's assurances that she was still as beautiful as the day he had first seen her, she could not help but feel dissatisfied with the changes. There had once been a time when she could go fall-flying on Hutho, revelling in the thrilling rush as she leapt away from the waterfalls and plunged hundreds of metres before landing feet-first on a raft, slowed only by the flaps in her wingsuit. She always left it until the last minute to deploy the brakes, a feat that gave her immense pleasure as she so often beat her opponents to the pontoon. But that was another time, a time when she had been her 'old' self and before the accident on the *Jensa Kadenx* that had wiped so much of her memory. A time when she had been in love with Durroc Navarr, the man who had said he loved her too but who only wanted to possess her. And he had. He had possessed her heart and soul and body for a year or more and she had burned for his love.

After the accident, though, it had all changed. When she finally awoke after the tumbling fall that had put her into a coma for nearly a week, she was not the person she had been before. Regaining her memory had taken many months, and her personality had changed from an imperious, proud queen to a softer, more insightful leader. She had no recollection of Navarr – or anyone, for that matter, except old Sen-Beoraan, her trusted counsellor. There had been many weeks and months relearning her role and rediscovering her family and, of course, Jax, her husband, the man she had cheated by her affair with Navarr.

As Navarr's light faded from her world, Jax stepped into it and she had fallen truly and deeply in love with him. Even now, after twenty-five years of marriage, his was the only touch she wanted, the only kiss she needed. His smile warmed her heart, and one look into those midnight blue eyes brought on a fiery passion that so often needed to be quenched immediately, much to their mutual delight. When the mood came upon her, she would send a glance his way and, before anyone knew it, the important meeting or ceremonial dinner was over and they would disappear to their rooms, restraining the impulse to touch each other's body until they were out of sight. She wondered if it would be so tonight.

Her fiftieth birthday celebration. The girls had worked hard to make it a glorious evening and, although it was not a milestone she was particularly glad to commemorate, she was happy to have her family and friends there and vowed to enjoy herself. Her mother was especially pleased that Evica, Linnayen's older sister, and Tariik Min, Evica's husband, had made the trip from Dasnir to be with them, leaving the srif farm in the capable hands of Tariik's mother and father. They were bringing with them their twin boys, Yudar and Kenis, who Linnayen remembered only as adventurous ten-year-olds. But Seti and Calin were excited to be seeing their cousins again and had many trips and outings planned before they returned home. Tonight was just the start of the family reunion and all matters of state were on hold for a few days.

'You look stunning, my lady.'

A soft voice interrupted her reverie followed by a small, mottled hand smoothing a crease at her shoulder. Her maidservant, Nen, passed behind her to gather her evening cloak from the gilt chair next to the mirror. Handing the cloak to her mistress, she noticed the look of studied concentration on her face.

'Why the frown? Tonight will be fun. Your daughters have planned many entertainments and, knowing them – especially Seti – there'll be surprises galore!'

'Mmm, I know,' she mused.

'You sound worried.'

Nen took one of Linnayen's hands in her own and stroked it, a gesture familiar for more years than Linnayen could remember. Nen had joined the royal household as a shy, slender eighteen-year-old when the little princesses were just out of babyhood. The three-year-old Linnayen had taken to her immediately and, as the years passed, their bond strengthened. Then, when the twenty-four-year-old Linnayen had been taken by Navarr, it was Nen, her wisp of a maidservant, who had hefted an ion-laser onto her tiny shoulders and shot the kidnapper, thereby saving Linnayen's life. This was but one of the many reasons she had to trust and love the ageing servant.

Linnayen put her thoughts aside. There was much to be grateful for, not least of which was her faithful Nen, more a friend than a servant. 'I'm so glad you're coming to the party, Nen.'

The old woman's face creased into a doting smile. 'How could I miss it?' She paused and raised an eyebrow. 'Besides, you need me to keep an eye on your mother, no?'

Linnayen's face broke into a wide smile. 'And you are possibly the only person able to do that. Even Jax can't always control her and she adores him.'

'Ah, but she listens to *me*.'

Laughing, the two women made their way to the door. It was true. Li-el Dacas, always so stately and proud in the presence of almost everyone outside of her immediate family, melted like butter in the presence of Nen. Perhaps it was because they were of a similar age. But Linnayen knew that a bond had also been forged the moment that Nen killed Navarr.

The Altani queen shook her shoulders, stretched her neck and lifted her chin. She turned to leave her rooms and begin her descent into the sparkling ballroom, where a mass of guests waited to celebrate her birthday. The past had no place in her mind tonight. Tonight was for joy.

There were few dark corners in which a party guest could hide that night. But Avad Jarkoo, the operations controller of Gunashey, Kuth & Dor, managed to find a spot from where he could survey the Genara clan and their guests. An alcove between two immense pillars of Huthon mahogany, inlaid with the swirling opaline colours of kalendarium, provided the perfect cover. From here, the Autabroni's black eyes scanned the room, noting only the most important, the most influential and the most beautiful.

The Ki herself was a superb being, he concluded. Her long black hair, crystal green eyes and sumptuous curves were enough to make every man desire her. Indeed, Kevor Jax was a lucky man. But it was her daughter who drew his attention. The Princess Setiyan was as lively as the waters of a mountain stream, dancing and cavorting around the ballroom with a succession of willing young partners. Even her laughter tinkled gaily above the hubbub of chatter and music. Her body was as enticing, with its round hips and full breasts, a shape that was only further enhanced by the drapes of cobalt sea-silk that fell from her shoulders. Jarkoo determined that, should the opportunity arise – and he very much hoped it would – he would one day enjoy the princess's many charms at greater length.

Did the girl's father even suspect that the seeds had already been sown to bring the girl to Autabron? He thought not. *Kevor Jax is too trusting.*

'My goodness! I didn't see you there.' A man's accented voice broke his reverie and the Autabroni started. 'Sorry, old man. Almost tripped over you.' The man held out a hand, a friendly gesture and something Jarkoo was not used to. 'Duncan McCrae. Pleased to meet you.' The sandy-haired man's smile was engaging.

Jarkoo recovered quickly and took the proffered hand. 'Avad Jarkoo.'

The Earthan looked him up and down, noting the pale ruby hue of his skin and his blond hair, worn very short. 'So you'll be from Autabron, am I right?'

'Correct. I am with the GKD company, in charge of operations.' Jarkoo's voice was without inflection.

'An important man then. And what brings you to Altan?' Duncan asked.

'This celebration, for one thing, and to meet with some of our customers and suppliers.' Jarkoo had not spoken this many words to anyone all evening and he swallowed nervously when the man's silence and raised eyebrow clearly expected him to say more. 'It's not the first time I have been here, of course.'

'Really? When were you here last?'

'About five years ago.'

'Five years. A holiday?'

Jarkoo wondered how many more questions this stranger would throw at him. He was not used to being engaged in small talk and he could not help but feel that he was being interrogated. 'A holiday? Ah, I am not so lucky.'

'Then this time you must take the opportunity to look around. It's a beautiful place.' Duncan warmed to the topic and continued. 'The Ksas Mountains are spectacular, even now in summer. In fact, better, because you get to see more of them. Not so much snow. I often hike there. Do you play golf, by any chance?'

'Um … I don't think so.'

'Never heard of it, eh? Then I'll have to teach you. What are you doing tomorrow?'

Jarkoo fidgeted and cleared his throat. 'Well, I have meetings in the morning and …'

'So your afternoon's free, perfect. I'll send a windshifter to your lodgings –'

'No!' Jarkoo hadn't meant it to come out quite so loud. 'I mean, no, I can't. My afternoon is busy too. I'm meeting a work colleague.'

'Really? They can come too.' Duncan was not going to be put off.

'It's a woman. I don't think she would be –'

Duncan broke in. 'Fantastic! I know lots of ladies who love a round or two. Golf, of course!' His laughter at his own joke would have been infectious with anyone else. But Jarkoo's mouth fell open and his eyebrows knitted. 'Just joking, old boy. Now, off you go and enjoy the party.' Duncan slapped the confused man on the back and, laying an arm over his shoulders, almost pushed him out into the room. 'I'll see you tomorrow.' Duncan shook his hand again and walked briskly away.

Jarkoo quickly lowered his head. He had no desire to be seen. He was the watcher. But he could not spin himself back into the shadows now because someone else was making their way towards him, someone for whom he would gladly remain visible.

Although she had spent much of the evening dancing and chatting with her peers – mostly the male ones – Setiyan was a creature of her upbringing and not unaware of the need to forge links and uphold her family's favoured position. Since her father had warned of the possibility of a journey to Autabron, she had familiarised herself with the guest list and made a mental note of who she needed to speak to. One such person was the GKD operations chief, Avad Jarkoo. She had been trying to find the man all evening and, finally, she spotted her father's old friend Duncan McCrae in conversation with him. She wondered if her father had sent Duncan to probe the man. It wouldn't have surprised her given her father's gift for statecraft learned over twenty-five years of political manoeuvring. Now was her chance. She strode purposefully up to him and noted the lift of the Autabroni's chin and the smile in his dark eyes.

'Director Jarkoo. What a pleasure to meet you at last.'

She stopped a couple of metres from him and waited for the traditional bow that was a mark of respect to the royal family. Instead, he nodded his head and placed a hand over his heart. It was enough to mollify her expectations.

'Princess. I am honoured.'

'May we talk, Director Jarkoo? Somewhere quieter perhaps?'

'Of course.' His eyes widened.

They walked through a pair of ornate doors that led to a balcony overlooking the city. Far below, thousands of lights twinkled in the purple haze of the evening. The spiralling metallic towers, opaque crosswalks and torchlit gardens lay beneath them, home to over three million souls. In the distance, the hazy foothills of the Ksas encircled the city like a mother's arms around a child.

'Stunning, isn't it?' she observed. 'I've seen this all my life yet it never fails to take my breath away. I hope you're enjoying your visit to our home? It must be so different on Autabron.'

'It is. We have mountains too, but our cities must be below ground. Pretty views are limited.'

'The heat must be terrible. I'm told that the ground temperature at midday is so hot that flesh blisters in three seconds. Is that true?'

'More like thirty seconds. People often exaggerate the conditions on my planet,' he corrected, a twitch of a smile at the corner of his mouth. Jarkoo continued. 'Most of our external operations take place close to sunset and again at sunrise. But our polar regions are bearable.'

Setiyan leaned in, her eyes wide. 'How so?'

'The extremes of hot days and freezing nights are much less. We even have stunted forests and grasses on which the bika herds feed.'

'I've seen bika on screen,' she replied. 'They're a strange creature. Six legs and that flat bony plate on their head. But such adorable eyes.'

'You know we eat them? They are our main source of protein.'

Her smile froze. 'Needs must, I suppose. Anyway, that's not what I wanted to talk to you about.' She gestured for him to follow her to a low seat in the recess of the balcony. 'Please, sit. Now then, my father tells me that there has been much trouble at the mines. Euta Makaan in particular. What can you tell me about that?'

He flinched briefly. 'What do you want to know?'

His attempt to compose himself was not quick enough to escape detection. Setiyan picked up on the micro-expression and the deflection in his response. What few outside the Genara and Dacas families realised was that Linnayen and Li-el had raised the girls to be extremely sensitive to body language. Whilst both Seti and Calin had the inherited ability to read minds with their mentantism, protocols largely forbad its use without the express permission of the target. Consequently, the reading of micro-expressions had become second nature to them all.

She pushed on. 'Everything. Everything you know – and suspect.'

He swallowed before commencing. 'Well, yes, there have been some explosions and tampering with equipment. Hydraulic lines punctured so that they still operate, but at reduced efficiency. It slows output. So far, we estimate that ore extraction is down by nearly twenty percent.'

'And the quality of the ore? That's been affected too?'

'Yes, but that's more about the location of the ore leads. We're reaching exhaustion of existing seams. We have had to expand into previously untapped areas.'

'Is that why you destroyed Euta Sakek?'

Jarkoo shifted uncomfortably and cleared his suddenly dry throat. 'That was unfortunate.'

'That it collapsed? Or that you found no new reserves of ore?'

Jarkoo's eyes bore into hers as his brow furrowed. 'It was an accident, I can assure you. It was –'

A loud crack from inside the ballroom cut off any further explanations, the noise followed by a series of bellows and shouts and the pounding of footsteps.

Seti jumped up and ran towards the balcony doors, Jarkoo tracking close behind. The scene that met their eyes was one of pandemonium. Chairs were overturned. Tables knocked askew. People were diving to the floor and screaming as doors were slammed shut and guards rushed to block anyone's exit.

The princess scanned the chaos, looking for the people she loved. Where was Calin? Her mother? Where was her father? A group stood near the dais at the far end of the room, the place where her mother and father had been sitting when she had moved onto the balcony with Jarkoo. In a blur, she saw Calin dashing towards the group. A dark pit opened in her stomach and the sound of her own blood pumping through her veins crashed inside her head. She picked up her skirt and ran the length of the room, all thoughts of the unforthcoming Autabroni gone from her mind.

It was as though everything was happening in slow motion. But what *had* happened? She could see three or four guards, their weapons raised, pounding towards a fleeing man who was holding a laser. The guards screamed at him to stop and people quickly skittered away as the barrel of the assassin's gun wavered around. Finally he stumbled over an upturned chair and the leading guard tackled him to the ground.

As she skidded to a stop, Calin's eyes met hers. There was worry in them, but her sister's steady hand placed on Setiyan's arm comforted her in the midst of the horror before them. Jax's body lay crumpled on the floor in a slowly growing pool of deep red blood, but already a medic was pushing people out of the way in order to treat him.

'Stand back! Please!' The order was barked out and the onlookers shuffled back to allow the doctor through.

Seti saw her mother buckled on the floor next to her father's head, her face drained of all colour. She was stroking his hair and shaking her head while a low moan escaped her lips. Seti could see she was struggling for breath, her eyes glassy.

Meanwhile, a stretcher arrived and her father's limp body was lifted gently onto it. Though unconscious, Seti detected the rise and fall of Jax's chest above the gaping wound in his lower abdomen. The relief swept through her. *He's alive!* In the company of the medics and now Duncan MCrae, the stretcher hovered towards the exit. Seti was torn. Should she go with her father? Should she stay here? In the end, Calin made the decision for her.

'Seti, Mother needs us. As does our grandmother. We need to look after them. Duncan is with Father.'

She nodded slowly. Her head felt heavy as a hammer. With Calin, she lifted their mother from the bloodstained polished floor and led her towards Li-el Dacas, who was seated at a table a few metres away with a shivering Nen beside her.

'Grandmother, are you alright? And you, Nen?' It was the controlled voice of Calin that carved through the sobs and anguished cries of the guests.

28

Li-el's tear-filled eyes went from one granddaughter to the other as they seated Linnayen next to her. 'Why? Who would do this?'

Seti kneeled and took her hands. 'We'll find out. Don't worry.'

Calin cast a glance over her shoulder to see that the guards had pinned down the suspected assassin and were clamping restraints on him. 'They have the man, grandmother. He'll be interrogated,' she assured the women. 'We must go to Father.'

'No!' This was Linnayen, now suddenly recovered. Her eyes were as sharp as needles and fixed on the retreating party of guards who were dragging the man away. 'I will question him. He can tell no lies to me!'

Li-el nodded to her daughter. They both knew that the niceties of asking permission before invading another's mind were to be put aside in this case. Interrogation by a mentante, especially one as skilled as Linnayen, would be highly effective.

'Tell the guards,' the Ki instructed Setiyan. She looked down at her hands and dress, the glittering rose silk now smeared with her husband's blood. Her voice was firm. 'I'll do it now.'

Chapter Three

It felt as though he had been waiting for an hour or more. But when he checked the time, it had been a mere twenty minutes. Finn paused in his pacing of the stark white hallway and stared blankly out the tinted window, hands spread wide against its frame. The shining towers of Genkarah city, with dozens of small windshifters darting between them, sparkled in the late afternoon sunlight. At any other time he would have appreciated the view, so like his home city of Novatlanta back on Earth. But not today.

It had been a week since he had told them everything he knew: what he thought had happened and how he was sure the tragedy on the *Teg-Kanish* was an accident. But the looks on the three inquisitors' faces had been harder than steel. They had given no hint of their musings and, when their questions turned to his friends and other contacts on Autabron, he felt he had reason to be concerned. Yes, he had made friends at the Euta Makaan plant, but only in the transit bays – drinking buddies, no more than that. And yes, he had explored caverns in the Camdru hills with a group of Guznon academy students. But that was part of an exchange program sanctioned by his commanding officer – an attempt to improve community relations – and no, he wasn't still in contact with any of the participants. They hadn't seemed convinced.

His reverie was broken by the flat tones of a stiff-backed attendant.

'Lieutenant Finn. Would you come through, please?'

He cleared his throat and nodded to the pale-skinned Huthon, who stood next to the open doorway with his hands lightly clasped. Inside the room were the same three inquisitors who had interviewed him previously, but they were joined by a fourth, a woman with long wavy russet hair and piercing green eyes. Calin Genara. She stood to one side of the table. He recognised her from vidscreen capture of functions and gatherings she had attended. His first thought was that she was far prettier in person, and taller. He could not imagine why she would be at this hearing.

'Lieutenant Finn. Please don't be alarmed.' Her voice was rich and deep and oddly reassuring. She walked towards him, gesturing for him to come further into the room. 'I am not here to interrogate you. That has already been accomplished by others more qualified than I.'

What did she mean by that? Finn was finding it hard to be calmed. His nerves were on a fine edge. The results of this hearing could see the end of his career and he could not begin to imagine what else he could do in this universe. Spacefleet had always been his dream and he dreaded having to let it go, especially as he had done nothing to bring it on.

The lead inquisitor, an Altani counsellor, spoke. 'Lieutenant. Please sit.'

Finn's eyes travelled to the chair placed in front of the oval table and he took his place. Calin took a seat at the farthest end.

The counsellor looked askance at his fellow questioners and the princess before continuing. 'A thorough examination of the *Teg-Kanish* has now been made and I have to tell you that, as we suspected, there *is* evidence of sabotage. There were traces of an explosive compound known as sauconium in the oxygen filtration conduits. This is not a naturally occurring compound and, therefore, could not have been produced as the result of a meteor strike, which was your explanation.'

There it was. The accusation was now bound to follow. *My explanation was what I thought was the truth!*

'Now then …' The old Altani stopped to check a note on his screen. 'Our investigation into whether or not you played a part in this sabotage has led us to two conclusions.'

Finn was desperate for the man to speak. *Come on. Get it over with.* The old counsellor looked across to Calin Genara. Finn could read nothing in her face. At a nod from her, the Altani continued.

'Firstly, that you are cleared of all implications. It is our finding that you had no knowledge of any sabotage and you acted in accordance with emergency procedures following such an event.'

The sigh that escaped from Finn was audible to all in the room. He closed his eyes briefly and lifted his chin. He knew he was innocent but the relief of hearing that others knew it too was overwhelming. When he opened his eyes, he saw that the Genara princess was smiling at him.

'And secondly ...'

Finn snapped back to attention.

'That you acted with bravery, intelligence and compassion for your fellow crew and brought your ship home, despite your own severe injuries. As such, this panel instructs that you be awarded a commendation on your record.'

Finn could hardly believe his ears – a commendation! He shook his head in disbelief. When he refocused on the three inquisitors, they were smiling, then each stood and came over to shake his hand. Calin Genara was the last to come to him as the rest of the panel members began to exit the room.

'Well done, lieutenant.' She too held out her hand, smiling. 'You look a bit stunned. You didn't expect this result?'

'Frankly, no. I thought they wouldn't believe me.'

'It was obvious you were telling the truth.' The woman spoke with a maturity that belied her years. Finn knew that she was a good ten years younger than himself and yet, at that moment, he felt that they were contemporaries.

'Yes, but how did you know?'

'Well, I'll be frank. A couple of the panel were not convinced at first and ordered an extensive background check. But I'm happy to say that Sen-Bodek – the woman who interviewed you after you were discharged from the medcentre – was very confident.' Calin placed a calming hand on his upper arm and continued. 'She is a mentante and we have learned that when Earthans are excited or anxious, they are very easy to read.'

'I was an open book?'

'That's a quaint expression. Fits perfectly,' she replied. 'Sen-Bodek called me in to confirm and, when I reviewed the feed, it was also obvious to me. You'll be happy to know, Lieutenant Finn, that you are not a terrorist.'

Her laughter was warm and genuine and he could not help but join in. Vidscreen footage gave the impression that she was reserved and unapproachable. It was good to see that she was much less stiff in real life.

'That's a relief.'

Suddenly, she stopped laughing and her tone became serious. 'And that's also why I have a special favour to ask you.' She began to walk towards the doorway but, noticing that he had not followed, she stopped and looked back. 'Please. It's nothing too onerous or unpleasant,' she assured him. 'Well, maybe on second thoughts ...'

The frown lines on his forehead deepened.

'It's my sister. She's to go to Autabron and she needs a bodyguard. So you see, Lieutenant Finn, it's like they say on your home planet: no good deed goes unpunished.'

Two days had passed since the attempt on Jax's life and he had drifted in and out of consciousness. The wound from the ion-laser had cut deep into the right-hand side of his middle torso and, although healing well, a part of his spleen had had to be removed and he had lost a kidney. The replacement universal biogro organs would take a few days to emplace themselves fully into his body. In the meantime, it was important for him to rest.

Linnayen sat slumped over one arm of a low sofa in Jax's hospital room, her body folded into its upholstery so that, in the dim evening light, she was almost indistinguishable from the fabric. A sudden sigh followed by a cough brought her out of her sleep. She sat up and stretched her arms, yawning as she moved to Jax's bedside.

'I was wondering when you'd wake up,' she said.

She stroked the side of his face with cool fingers and brushed dark hair out of his eyes. He smiled, then tried to swallow.

'Wait. I'll get water.'

She brought a flask from the side table and held its thin fleximetal straw to his mouth. He drank greedily, his eyes closing with the relief the cool liquid gave.

'Better?'

He nodded. 'Much – and for seeing you.'

She leaned down and kissed his lips, the force of her love in that touch causing his breath to quicken.

Linnayen pulled away. 'It's all right now. You'll soon be up and about,' she assured him.

'Everyone else? Are they –'

She stopped his question with a finger to his lips. 'We are all fine. No one else was hurt. You were the target, my love.'

'But why? We must find out.'

33

Linnayen sighed and hung her head. 'And we would have, had he not killed himself.'

'What! How?'

'He was being restrained in the ballroom. He'd been disarmed and I was going to question him when he collapsed.' Linnayen tried to hide the anger but her cheeks flared red and her lips tightened. 'His heart stopped. The guards tried to revive him and they applied a reviv, but nothing.'

'Damn! Autopsy?'

'It's being done now. But I'd say it's poison, or maybe an implant activated by a remote device.'

'In which case,' Jax finished for her, 'the real killer was possibly in the room.'

'Indeed. Seti has a team going over the guest list. He was Altani, though. We have his name and they're going through his history right now. I'm sure we'll find something.'

'Let's hope so. We must get to the bottom of this.' He paused and studied his wife's features. Still so beautiful. But the thought that they could so easily have been clouded with the grief of his death was frightening. They'd had twenty-five years together. But for him and, he knew, for her too, that would never be enough.

'And Calin?'

'Calin has stepped up in exactly the way I would expect her to. With my approval, she is making plans for Seti to fulfil your mission to Autabron. Obviously, you can't go.'

'Nonsense! I'll be fine. She can't go on her own.'

'She'll have bodyguards.' Linnayen tried to sound reassuring.

'It's not that. I'm sure she'll be safe in that respect. It's the division of the mission. My plan is to each take a stakeholder. I'm to connect with the mine management and she's to talk to the workers.'

Linnayen sighed again. 'You're a stubborn man, Kevor Jax.'

'Would you have me any other way?' He grinned.

'Yes! But why take the risk? Stay here and recuperate. I can go in your place.'

'And have you both away from me? I think not.' His jaw set firm. When he got like this, she knew it would be hard to shift him. 'I will go. You and Calin will stay safe here and I will keep a very keen eye on my eldest daughter. Now then, about those other kisses you promised me.'

'When did I –'

A knowing smile played on her mouth as he reached up and tugged gently at the embroidered collar of her blouse. As he brought her down to his lips, hers were already parted, ready and willing to receive him.

Avad Jarkoo reasoned that his visit to Altan could have gone better, but not much. Although the assassination attempt on Kevor Jax had failed miserably, it had not detracted from his intended goal. Doubtless, he should have chosen a more experienced assassin. But thankfully the implant, underlain in the skin behind the hapless fellow's ear and sold to him as a personal communicator, responded immediately to his signal, and the poison had swum through his veins without pause. Jarkoo had queried the need to kill the Ki-consort at first, but his instructions had been clear. The interfering father must be removed and the mother, normally so dominant, must be neutralised by her uncontrollable grief. In this way the princess would be primed to accept the comfort and support of a new friend such as the A'bat, who, as the leader of the Guznon people, would travel to Altan to attend the state funeral. That was now impossible, of course.

Then he had heard the news that morning that the royal party would undertake a diplomatic mission to his homeworld and that Setiyan was excited to be included. They would be leaving later that month, by which time he would already be home. Whether or not her meddling father was to accompany her was not mentioned in the vidcast. But, if the fates determined that he should join the delegation, Jarkoo assessed that he could be permanently removed once on Autabron. In fact, he had explained to the old shaman, it might turn out better that way.

A delicate morning mist clung to the spires of Genkarah city, coating the cool metal towers with a fine dew. Soon the sun would rise high enough to evaporate the droplets. *Such a waste!* On his home planet this liquid bounty was as valuable as Altan's famed blue mineral ambicinite and would not be squandered to the heat of the day. Long before the twin suns of Lau and Uzno rose more than a few degrees above the horizon, the fine spray was sucked from the dej-nets and channelled down into the depths below the Beshwuk Highlands. His people, the Guznon, had farmed water for as long as they had existed, ensuring it was safe in tanks below the red-brown surface. Without their husbandry the planet would have been uninhabitable, and Jarkoo was more than proud of his people's achievements.

As he took his place on the spaceracer, destined for home, he wondered briefly if he was as committed to their cause as he should be. Was this the way to achieve their destiny? Mira had said it was so – the only way, according to the prophecy. They must do whatever it took to free their people from the tyranny of the off-worlders, even if some should suffer in the process. As Mira had said, all great enterprise involves great sacrifice.

And when he thought of all the treasures torn away from his planet, making the men and women of Altan and Hutho and Earth phenomenally rich, it made him sick to his stomach. Every day since he had trained for this job, he'd swallowed the bile of his complicity. Having to pretend he was one of them, a boss, keeping the mine working efficiently, sometimes made him physically ill, especially when he saw transporters fly away carrying the refined bergussian to the other Galactic Union planets. But he had taken a pledge many years before as a student that he would work to tear down the constructs of greed. It was his sworn mission.

That he enjoyed an easy life in the better corners of Zaz-Rakuum, with filtered air, comfortable furnishings and cool water on demand, was of no consequence to his undertaking. For wouldn't he still have all that when the off-worlders were sent packing? Only then, he would own it. It would belong to him and his people completely and there would be no more need for his gross deception.

As the spacecraft lifted away from the Genkarah transit tower, he smiled, then closed his eyes. He had no need of the sight of Altan's green forests and snow-tipped mountains, nor its wide golden grasslands. Pictures of Autabron's magnificent flame-red peaks and vast orange deserts filled his mind's eye and he allowed a single precious tear to track down his cheek.

'I do *not* need a bodyguard! It's ridiculous.' Setiyan folded her arms across her chest and set her lips in a firm line. 'I can take care of myself.'

Linnayen watched her daughter swirl about, noticing her smile as she caught her reflection in a gilded mirror that hung on the far wall of the large reception room. Her daughter saw little of the sumptuous furnishings around her, many of which had been wedding gifts. The mirror, whose gilt frame was of myriad sea creatures diving through foamy waves, was from the Dasnirian ambassador and the crushed velvet couch she now sat on had come from her husband's family home in the floating city of Elidian back on Earth.

Seti had thought her summons to her mother's rooms shortly after breakfast meant an important briefing about the Autabron trip. She knew Linnayen had tried to talk her injured father out of going, but Jax had been resolute. His wound was healing quickly and he insisted it was his duty to go. Nothing would stop him. So it was just the two of them and that's all it needed. Her mother's suggestion of taking a personal bodyguard, let alone a cohort of some thirty others, was silly and completely unnecessary.

Linnayen raised an eyebrow and kept her voice calm. 'Maybe you can. But after what happened with your father, we need to take precautions.'

'We don't know that was connected to Autabron.'

'And we don't know that it wasn't,' Linnayen retorted. 'But we *do* know that your father's inquiries into the disruption of ore production on Autabron have met with some resistance. Even the operations director was less than forthcoming when your father interviewed him and he, surely, would've wanted answers.'

'He's an odd character,' Seti mused. 'I tried talking to him at the party. He seemed defensive.'

'When I met him, he was reluctant to meet my eyes,' Linnayen recalled. 'There was something …'

'Off,' Seti finished for her. 'I felt it too, but not danger. Which is why I don't need a bodyguard.' She turned away and went to leave the room when Linnayen stopped her.

'Not so fast, Seti!' Linnayen stood and raised a hand to halt her daughter's progress. 'Come back here, please.'

Seti's shoulders slumped and she let out a loud sigh, but there was no gainsaying her mother when she used that tone. She spun around to see Linnayen making her way to the desk, a fine piece of carved Huthon pine inlaid with a smooth sea-glass panel. Linnayen pressed a hidden switch and the far edge of the glass lifted until it was nearly perpendicular. It revealed an image of a brown-haired man with high cheekbones and a strong, clean-shaven jawline.

'My nanny, I presume?'

'Lieutenant Decker Finn. Earthan. Weapons expert. Pilot-navigator. Newly commended for bringing home what was left of the *Teg-Kanish* after it had been destroyed by suspected Autabroni terrorists.'

'I'm sure he's wonderful, very skilled. But I don't need him.' Seti stood firm, hands on her hips and blonde head tipped to one side. She gave the screen a sidelong glance before glaring at her mother.

'And he has an extensive knowledge of Autabron geography, history, customs and culture having spent three years stationed there.'

'Great! So he's good with guns *and* he can bore me to tears.' Seti began to pace in front of her mother's desk, puffing out her chest as she began her rant. 'Not only can he shoot people I might want to talk with but he can also patronise me with his vast knowledge, most of which I'll have already learned on the two days it will take to get there. Oh, I can't wait!'

She saw her mother's eyes shift to a point behind her back. Seti had not heard the door slide open.

'Well, that's good, sister. Because he's here right now.' Calin's eyes were smiling as she spoke, but the man standing next to her had a confused look on his face. He shifted his weight from one foot to the other. 'Let me introduce Lieutenant Decker Finn,' Calin continued. 'And this, lieutenant, is my sister, the Princess Setiyan Genara.'

Finn looked from the one – so cool and calm – to the other, a whirl of blonde tresses sending daggers at him from her stunningly blue eyes. He lowered his head in a bow, hoping that it wouldn't get chopped off at the neck.

'Welcome, lieutenant,' said Linnayen, who had come from behind her desk to stand next to her eldest daughter. 'I've heard good things about you.'

'Thank you, my lady.' He cleared his throat. 'You too.'

Linnayen and Calin smiled. The familiarity of the Earthans never failed to both amuse and, occasionally, shock. Luckily, being married to Jax for all these years and with two half-Earthan daughters, Linnayen had grown used to these instances of informality and was not offended.

'Oh ... I didn't mean to ...'

'Please,' Calin interjected, 'we welcome your honesty. It's one of the reasons you've been chosen for this mission.'

'My daughter is right. Although ...' Linnayen frowned and moved towards him. She took his arm and led him over to the couch, gesturing for him to sit with her. Once they were settled, she continued. 'It's not the least of your attributes. We hear that you're extremely proficient with a range of weapons.'

'I am. But I hope I won't have to use them.'

'Again, refreshingly honest. It's my experience that aggression rarely solves anything,' Linnayen concurred.

Setiyan looked on at this interaction with mouth agape and chest pounding. She shot an angry glance at Calin but her sister was busy watching her mother calm the nervous man.

In the glass-domed, two-man windshifter from his quarters to the palace, Calin had had more time to get the measure of this man. As they had sat facing each other, the towers of the city passing by far below, his body language told her as much if not more than his words. Yes, he was nervous, but also confident in his skills and experience. He had talked of his homeworld, growing up in the deep south of Amerimex, a land of lush fields and green mountains. It sounded a little like the grain fields of Hashaniq on Altan and she longed to see Earth again. He professed it was always his dream to explore the galaxy and had studied hard to win his place at the academy in Novatlanta.

The sisters had been twice to Earth as children to visit their grandparents, Sheikh David and Lady Thea Bashir, but had only visited the countries of Eurotania and the Makassan Republic. The memories of mountains and rainforests had fast faded and Calin vowed that evening to take out the travel journal that her mother had insisted they keep. It would be enjoyable to relive the memories. Meanwhile, Lieutenant Finn also spoke of his time on Autabron and Hutho. For nearly three years he had instructed local security personnel in the use and maintenance of a range of weapons, including mid-range xelex cannon, personal ion-lasers and qasar-mortars. He had spent much of his time transiting between the two planets but had been based in Zaz-Rakuum, the large underground city near the Euta Makaan mine. This had given him a good insight into the Autabroni people, he had told Calin, especially the Guznon tribe.

'I'll be frank. They're not an easy people to like. Very serious. Don't play cards with them,' he had warned.

Calin had laughed. 'They sound fierce.'

'More that they have no sense of humour,' he explained. 'A punchline is usually more punch than line.'

She could not help but smile. This no-nonsense soldier certainly had a way with words. And his face was not unpleasant, either. Laugh lines scored his tanned skin and his eyes were a rich warm brown. Apart from a few silver hairs at his temples, the thirty-four-year-old had a full head of nut-brown hair. She wondered how he would cope with her sister, though if he could survive three years with the fiery Autabronis then surely he would manage Setiyan's occasional outbursts.

Seti nudged her sister out of her reverie with a sharp prod in the waist.

'Ow!' Calin turned and glared into Seti's angry eyes. 'What was that for?' she whispered.

'You brought him here. You could have warned me,' she hissed.

'Oh, Seti. He's here to help. Don't be such a …'

'What? Pain? Nuisance?'

Calin's mouth was a straight line. 'All of the above!' She pulled Seti towards the balcony, out of the range of her mother and Finn's hearing. They were talking amiably on the couch and hardly noticed the movement of the two girls. 'Don't be such a grouch. This is for the best. He's really experienced and a good man, if you give him half a chance. Pa is going with you but he's still recuperating, so he can't protect you as he'd like to.'

'As I said to Mother, I can look after myself,' Seti replied.

'But *he* can look after you better!' Calin snapped back. 'So get used to it. Either he goes with you or you don't go at all.'

Seti stared at her sister. Since when had she become so dominant? It was almost as though she was acting like a parent. Her brows knitted together and she folded her arms across her chest.

'Very well. If I have to.' Her concession was delivered between gritted teeth. She cocked her head, turned on her toes and stomped back to the centre of the room. Calin smiled and followed.

Finn and Linnayen were still talking. He was nodding at something her mother was saying when Seti marched up and planted herself in front of them.

'Lieutenant Finn,' she began, interrupting Linnayen. 'Oh, sorry, Mother ...'

Linnayen brushed aside the intrusion. She was only too pleased to see her daughter finally engage with the man. Calin had obviously worked some magic – or some threat.

Finn quickly stood up and bowed his head.

Seti's frown was still etched into her features as acknowledged his gesture. 'Yes, quite. So, you'll be coming with me to Autabron, but I want you to know that I am perfectly able –'

Linnayen jumped in. 'What my daughter is trying to say is that she is perfectly able to learn from you, Lieutenant Finn, and happy that you'll be looking after her.' She looked up at the still bristling frame of her eldest daughter, her eyes checking any smart remark Seti might have thought up. 'And she can't wait to hear all about your experiences on Autabron, which, I am sure, will be crucial to her mission. Isn't that so, Setiyan?'

Seti's returning smile did not stretch as far as her eyes. 'Of course, Mother. Absolutely. Now, if you'll excuse me, I have some studying to do.'

With that she trounced out of the room, leaving all three with awkward smiles on their faces. The silence sat between them like a piece of fine crystal on the verge of shattering.

Linnayen was the first to speak. 'My apologies, Lieutenant Finn. My daughter can be a little – what do you say on Earth? Headstrong?'

'She's stubborn, lieutenant,' Calin added, 'but she has a good heart. She'll come around.'

'Well, we've two whole days together on the journey,' Finn replied. 'I'm sure we'll get along just fine – eventually.' The look on his face was one of hope mixed with anxiety, and both Linnayen and Calin nodded their agreement with this sentiment.

Finn bowed to take his leave. He was halfway to the door when he turned with an engaging smile. 'There's another saying we have on Earth: what doesn't kill you makes you stronger. Don't worry. I'll keep her safe.'

Once he had left the room, Calin turned to her mother with a hopeful look. 'Do you think she'll be all right?'

Linnayen took her daughter's hand and patted it softly. 'Seti will be fine. But as for that poor lieutenant, that's anyone's guess.'

Chapter Four

Denkaun surveyed the mass of Autabroni mine workers before him. The crowd had not appreciated the sentiments of the plant manager, Avad Jarkoo, as he pleaded with them to remain calm and allow their representatives to engage in talks that would lead to better pay and improved work practices. Did they not know that even as he spoke, the Ki-consort and his daughter would soon be there to meet them and hear their concerns? These were important people, Jarkoo assured them, who would undoubtedly listen with open hearts and minds.

But, unsurprisingly, the patience of the mine workers had worn thin. The sea of roseate-skinned faces glared at Jarkoo. There had been no increase in pay for nearly three years, yet prices for food and rents had almost doubled in the same time. And what about the company's profits? GKD made 60 billion keks last year, one of their best trading years ever, but none of that good fortune had been passed on.

Denkaun could not have hoped for a more satisfactory set of circumstances. The fomentation of unrest and disquiet suited his purposes perfectly and he wondered how much Mira had had to do with these unsettling days. As ever, his natar kept her thoughts much to herself. But his trust in her was implicit. Whatever schemes she had devised, he knew they would ultimately lead to the fulfilment of the prophecy. He must let her have her way, though it would be hard to give up Wika Dokau when the time came. He had become so used to having her available to him whenever he wished and she had learned exactly how to please him in so many regards, and not just sexually.

He found himself enjoying her company. Her voice was mostly quiet and soothing, her presence like a calming drug in the face of the tension brought by their great enterprise. From childhood, Mira had made it clear that he was destined for greatness, that he would lead the people out of darkness. This was the prophecy of the great witch, the Ko-Makum of Rundak, who had given her life to bring on the sorely needed rains on the Day of Grunkaar three hundred years ago. Her eyes were the crystalline blue of the mineral zorcuum, just like his own and his mother before him. That he was not Guznon by birth did not matter. He was born of twins, just as the prophecy said. But there was more to the Ko-Makum's prediction. She foretold that the A'bat, the warrior of hope, would begat a line of great leaders who would return the Guznon to their rightful place as the most powerful tribe of their homeworld. There was but one essential condition and Mira had already taken steps to bring this about: the A'bat must procreate with one of his own blood.

Denkaun knew that he was the only progeny of his mother. But Mira had said that his father, Durroc Navarr, had a daughter too. Mira would find her and bring her to him. They would marry and make many children, and he would have no time to waste his seed on a concubine. Wika would have to go, Mira had insisted. Even so, that day was far in the future, surely? He would not have to part with the comely daughter of Dokau too soon.

The image of her white-blonde hair falling across her bare breasts roused him from his musings and he took a deep breath. Jarkoo was looking at him, pleading with him to speak to the crowd. The rumbling of disquiet among the workers was taking hold and Jarkoo knew he could not hold them much longer.

Denkaun nodded to the frightened mine manager and stepped forward to the edge of the dais. He raised his muscled arms and glowered into a thousand pairs of eyes. It took no more than a minute for silence to spread around the hall to allow the A'bat to speak. Denkaun brought his arms down and clenched his two hands together in a symbol of both prayer and unity.

'Brothers! Sisters! My people! Your trials are many, your faith is strong, but I see your spirit is flagging. And why should it not? You work hard, you care for your families and you make the bosses rich by your endeavours. Why should you not share in the proceeds that flow from the rape of our homelands by the greedy ganaks?'

Denkaun could feel the rumble of the crowd, like the first stirrings of an earthquake. They were primed and ready to explode, but he knew he could hold them back – for now. He took a deep breath and, scanning the faces once more, waited for complete silence before continuing.

'Yes, rape! They rape our ore fields! They rape our gas fields! And if we had fields of rich grasses, they would rape them too!'

Thousands of heads nodded their agreement as a cry went up among the crowd. *Kill the ganaks!*

He looked across to Jarkoo and Mira, the former's eyes pinched and panicked while the latter's were calm and smiling. He raised his arms once more and the yells diminished to whispers until silence was regained. It was time to bring his people to heel.

Denkaun lowered his voice, forcing the crowd to bend their heads towards him. 'My friends, we need not kill. We need not even fight. There is a better way, a way that will bring us complete control not only of our mines but of our whole planet. I am the way! Yes! I – am – the – way! Have faith in me! I am the A'bat, the warrior of hope!

Now, looking down at the multitude of faces, he saw smiles. He saw hope in their wide dark eyes.

'Yes, my people, I have a plan. I will meet with the Ki-consort and demand he not only listen to our grievances but also resolve them! He will force the bosses to give us what we want, what we need. And what do we want? What do we need? Our freedom, brothers and sisters! Our freedom!'

The cheer that went up rebounded from the rock walls of the meeting chamber like the shockwave of a dirratin gas blast. Denkaun felt it smack into his chest. He took another deep gulp of air and called out to the crowd one last time.

'I am the way! A'bat! A'bat!'

As the crowd took up the chant, a fine cloud of dust drifted in the arid air. Mira came and stood behind his left shoulder. She placed a wrinkled hand upon his warm skin and, as she gazed at the tumultuous crowd in front of them, her eyes sparkled like two black diamonds.

She whispered into his ear. 'Well done, my son. It has begun.'

If Decker Finn had had any illusions about building a friendly relationship with Princess Setiyan, they were soon dashed. By the end of the first day on board the spaceracer *Teg-Koorym*, she had made it clear that his presence was decidedly abhorrent to her. He knew, of course, that Altani customs and manners were different to those on Earth. They were a more formal people given to traditional ways and he had to accommodate these variations. His years in the Diplomatic Corps had certainly taught him that. But the princess's degree of reserve was bordering on rudeness and it had not gone unnoticed, either by him or by her father.

Finn had seen the look of pity in the older man's eyes when Setiyan had flung yet another barb at him about something he had said, or something he did. It seemed the princess had strong views about every aspect of Lieutenant Finn's speech, skills and mannerisms and she neither liked nor approved of any of them. He wondered how on earth he was going to be able to protect her if she would not let him get close.

On the second day out from Altan, Jax called a final meeting to go over their schedules on Autabron and confirm the approaches they would be taking. Other diplomats had accompanied them on the mission. There was Kalisa Caspiran, the Altani minister for trade, Rutak Birkaan, the Galactic Union's industry secretary and an Autabroni, and lastly, Pieter Serekunda, the Earthan head of the Eco-ethics Council. Each of them would play a vital part in the examination of GKD's operations and were experts in their fields. Caspiran, who was a cousin of Linnayen's, had been working in the Union's commerce and trade division for over twenty years since she graduated from the university in Silbaraz-Re. Birkaan also had a long association with the Union's industrial enterprises and was respected for his many academic dissertations. As for Pieter Serekunda, he was an unknown. None of them had met him before their departure. But given the recent catastrophic destruction of the sacred site at Euta Sakek, it was necessary to have an ethics expert on the team. Serekunda had been on Altan at the time and, therefore, available to join them.

As each member entered the cabin, Jax nodded a friendly welcome, as did Setiyan. She obviously had no problem with all of them, thought Finn. But when he had entered and was being introduced to each team member, Setiyan had kept her head down and perused her notes, ignoring him.

Jax spotted the discourtesy and cleared his throat loudly, causing Seti to look up and catch the glint of steel in his deep blue eyes. She straightened her back and put her notes to one side.

They took their seats as Jax began. 'Welcome, everyone. I think we're all agreed that we have a difficult task ahead of us, which is all the more reason for making sure we're organised before we arrive at

Autabron. I think we're all agreed on the split into two teams to begin with –'

The Earthan, Serekunda, interrupted. 'I expected to be working alone.'

'Not possible at this stage. Tensions are running high and I can't risk anyone being on their own. It's going to be hard enough for you to look into the Euta Sakek incident without stirring up more trouble.'

Serekunda shook his head. 'Surely that's an exaggeration. I'm going to hear their concerns. And decreased mine outputs and a few protests by the miners hardly seem dangerous.'

Birkaan jumped in. 'Have you ever been to my homeworld, my friend?' Serekunda frowned and began to reply, but Birkaan was ready. 'I thought not. So you obviously have no idea of the Autabroni character. We are a proud people with strong emotions. A simple protest, as you call it, can soon disintegrate into a mob. You would not want to be caught in such a gathering.'

'Rutak is right, Pieter. We can't take chances. Remember – all of you – we are on a fact-finding mission. We're here to build relationships with our hosts so that they feel comfortable in opening up to us,' finished Jax.

Setiyan could not resist the urge to comment. 'And that's going to be hard enough with a cohort of guards around us.'

'The guards are necessary.' Jax's voice was firm. They travelled with twenty crack security personnel – a necessary protection for them all.

His eyes scanned the group. Serekunda had been nodding his agreement with Setiyan. But Birkaan and Caspiran remained impassive. The latter's voice was softly persuasive. 'Princess, I know I will feel safer and, given our shared heritage and skills in statecraft, I'm sure that you and I will have little trouble in assuring our Autabroni hosts that we come with open hearts and minds.'

Setiyan smiled and gestured her acquiescence. She wondered if her mother had deliberately chosen Caspiran to spy on her.

Jax began speaking once more. 'Thank you, Kalisa. You're quite right. We don't want to ruffle any feathers while we do our work. Even so, we must find out the source of all the unrest. Our intelligence has discovered that the raid on the transport feeder lines was conducted by a group of militants from the Gaksi tribe.'

'That's ridiculous!' interjected Birkaan. 'The Gaksi are a northern tribe who have little to do with the mines or its operations. They even still live a traditional life, herding the bika and living in pakirans on the surface.'

Setiyan was surprised. 'On the surface? I would have thought that was impossible.'

'Not so,' Birkaan said. 'The climate at the poles is less severe. The temperature drops enough so that grasses can grow. That's what the bika feed on. It's actually quite pleasant.'

Finn smiled. 'In a Sahara sort of way.'

Jax guffawed at this reference to their mutual homeworld and Setiyan shot a look at him that would have withered a lesser soul. She clearly did not appreciate the bond of friendship that Jax seemed to be forging with the odious lieutenant.

'Even so, the Gaksi leader, a man called Hanashi, seems to be involved,' Jax continued. 'After intercepting some suspicious transmissions between Hanashi and a maintenance worker at the mine, our intelligence chief decided to have him monitored more closely. We'd actually been surveilling the worker, not Hanashi. But after the contact between them, we began monitoring his movements.'

Jax depressed a command on his tablet and a three-dimensional image of the Gaksi leader appeared in the midst of the table. The group studied the man's features, the typical reddish skin tones, the white hair worn in a traditional plait and the black eyes so common among the Autabronis.

Jax went on. 'Then, two weeks ago, he came to Zaz, apparently to visit a distant uncle. But, unusually, he then made a trip out to the Beshwuk Highlands – Guznon country – and it's unlikely he would have been welcomed there. The two tribes have a history of animosity.'

'This is true,' Birkaan added. 'For over a thousand years these tribes have barely spoken. The Guznon see the Gaksi as having all the best land, all the wealth, and the Gaksi think the Guznon are low-born and ill-mannered.'

Serekunda frowned. 'Couldn't this Hanashi just have been, well, a tourist? The highlands are said to be quite spectacular. The sunset colours on the cliffs are renowned …'

'Ah, my friend, the sunset colours on the Beshwuk cliffs might be the last thing he ever saw if he were found there,' said Birkaan.

Finn nodded his agreement. 'But he went and, presumably, came back to Zaz?'

'Indeed he did, which leads me to suppose that he met someone there – someone important enough to risk his life,' Jax replied.

'Do we know who that might be?' asked Setiyan.

Kalisa Caspiran took over. 'We have an idea, yes. And if so, it would be a worrying turn of events.'

The tall woman straightened her back and touched a panel on the table in front of her. An image of a young man appeared on the vidscreen at the far end of the room. His features were symmetrical and his blond hair was twisted into a long plait that hung over one shoulder. The image was blurry, though, and it was hard to make out the details of his visage.

'I apologise for the visual. It's all we have. Taken by an operative who attended a recent rally. He's Kalik Denkaun, the adopted son of the now dead Guznon leader Lyr Denkau. Though his mother, Mira, still lives and is regarded as something of a holy woman. A shaman. They say she can see the future. Denkaun is not Autabroni, as you can hopefully see by his skin tone. He could be Altani or Earthan, we don't yet know. The fact that we know so little about this man is in itself of concern.'

'Why?' Setiyan's eyes were narrowed and drawn together. 'What does he have to do with the Gaksi leader?'

Jax turned to her. 'We're hoping you'll be able to find that out, daughter.'

Her eyes, now wide open, glared at her father. 'Me?'

'Yes. I'm sending you to the Beshwuk Highlands to meet this Kalik Denkaun. Find out if he met with Hanashi. Denkaun spoke at a recent workers' rally and our reports say that he was extremely well-received. Inspirational is how he was described. It appears that he is emerging as their new leader. Think you can handle it?'

Setiyan was in no doubt. 'Of course, if you think this is the best use of my skills.'

'If I may,' interjected Birkaan, 'Beshwuk is dangerous territory for an off-worlder. You must be invited.'

Caspiran spoke, her voice clear and calm. 'We have already sent a request to the Lady Mira and it has been accepted. Indeed, her reply was most gracious.'

The doubt on Birkaan's weathered face was obvious, but he remained silent.

Jax continued. 'Seti, you and Doctor Serekunda will make the journey. Lieutenant Finn will, of course, accompany you. His knowledge of local customs and tradition will be useful.' Jax smiled at the Earthan. 'As for the rest of us, we'll be travelling between Zaz-Rakuum and Euta Makaan and meeting with the mine staff and managers. I've prepared a list of personnel for each of you. There's an organogram on your files too, so you can get your heads around the company structure. Rutak, can you lead the briefing tomorrow? You know more about operations than the rest of us.'

Birkaan concurred and Jax stood, indicating to the rest of the group that the meeting was now over.

'And me, sir? Have you anything for me?' This was Serekunda.

'Yes, of course. A background memo is in your file too, Pieter,' Jax returned. 'It's not much, but I'm sure you'll be able to fill in the gaps once you've met the Guznon in their home territory. Should be quite fascinating.'

'Mmm. If we survive.'

Setiyan laughed as she rose from her chair. She placed a reassuring hand on Serekunda's shoulder. 'No need to worry. We have our brave lieutenant to save us.' She threw a cold glance over her shoulder to Finn, who bowed and saluted with an index finger to his head.

'I'm commissioned to save one of you. I've yet to decide which.' He smiled wryly and walked away, leaving Setiyan with a murderous look on her face. *Yes, indeed*, thought Finn. *Things couldn't be better.*

Whilst her eldest daughter was fuming with resentment on board the *Teg-Koorym*, Linnayen, her mother and Calin had relocated from the palace in Genkarah to the Dacas family chalet in the Ksas foothills. The grey stone base of the five-hundred-year-old building was cut into a steep, grassy slope, encased by scented rilo pines at the rear and sides. Their dusky blue needles framed the old buildings perfectly against the rose-tinted sky, a product of the traces of jekarion gas present in the Altan atmosphere. A mere two hundred metres away, deeper in the forest, could be heard the gush of a tumbling waterfall that was in full spate after the recent rains, and it was this noise that held Linnayen as she stared into the space outside the open window.

Her meditative state was interrupted by the entrance of her youngest daughter. Calin glided across the polished wood floor to stand next to her mother, leaning her head on the older woman's shoulder. She cupped an arm around her waist.

'Did you sleep well?' Linnayen asked. She had been up since before dawn, always a light sleeper when Jax was away.

'Sure did. I'd forgotten how the mountain air does that – knocks you out. But not you, Ma? How long have you been up?'

'Not long,' she replied, stroking her daughter's cheek.

'Liar,' Calin countered with a brief smile. She knew only too well the bond her parents shared. You only had to look at the way they were together, how they would fix their eyes on each other and could not resist holding hands when close enough. Neither rested easily when apart and the recent assassination attempt on her father had given her mother even more cause to worry. 'Pa will be fine. You don't need to fret.'

Linnayen gave the briefest of smiles then moved away from the window over to the low table, where a jug of fresh cuya juice had been set earlier by Nen. She took a seat, spreading the long folds of her embroidered dressing-gown over her legs.

'Come sit with me,' she ordered, and patted the sofa next to her.

Calin poured some of the juice into an ornate polished metal chalice. The furnishings and accoutrements of the chalet were not to her taste, nor her mother's. But Li-el loved these relics of her family's past and insisted on using them when they were visiting.

'It's so good to be up here, Mama. I sometimes wish we could just live here all the time, away from all the noise and bustle of the city.'

'I don't think your sister would agree,' Linnayen declared. 'And I'm not sure living with your grandmother all the time would keep either of us sane.'

Calin grinned and her green eyes sparkled. 'I won't tell her you said that.'

'I'm glad you like it here, but …'

'Ah, there had to be a but,' Calin sighed in resignation. It was too good to be true that they could just be in this mountain paradise for a holiday. Duty called. Duty always called. Their rank brought them many privileges but it also came with responsibilities.

Linnayen took her daughter's hand and continued. 'We have a job for you, your father and I. We are the only ones who know about it and you must keep it secret too.'

Calin drew her eyebrows together and put down her juice. Her voice was uncertain. 'Go on.'

'There's a person in Genkarah – newly arrived – that we'd like you to get to know.'

Calin rolled her eyes. 'A new friend for Calin. How nice.'

Linnayen laughed. 'Not like that. I'm sure you're capable of finding your own friends. No, this man is different.'

'How so?' The lightness in her tone belied her intense interest.

'His name is Hasler. Adrik Hasler. He's a professor of biogenetics at the university. Earthan. Very bright, so I'm told.' Linnayen shifted in her seat and reached across the table for a tablet which she then proffered to Calin. 'Take a look.'

As she tapped the screen, various data sped by: his picture, university record, birth and upbringing details and current location, plus a list of research projects on which he had worked. Her eyes scanned the information. It all looked very ordinary, a typical academic's life.

'And what makes him the object of our interest, Mama? What dirty deeds has he been up to?'

Linnayen sighed. 'Well, nothing so far – on Altan. But he spent the last year on Autabron working at the university in Zaz. Look again.'

Calin complied and returned to the latter entries. 'Let me see … Er, yes, set up a project on Autabroni physiology … Special reference to gastrointestinal pathogens. Seems pretty normal.'

'Except that in the course of his time there, his laboratory took possession of a consignment of urthrengo. Knowing of my past experience of the drug, it was flagged to me by the Dean at Genkarah University.'

'What? How much?' There was genuine surprise and concern in Calin's voice. This extremely dangerous drug was one that her mother had had first-hand experience of years earlier, before her marriage, when Linnayen had been drugged by the would-be usurper, Durroc Navarr. It was a powerful inhibitor that induced compliance in its victims and only a handful of laboratories were permitted to store it. Too much and it was lethal.

'Enough to cause concern. Fifty units.'

'Wow! That's enough to flatten an army.'

Linnayen nodded. 'Exactly. The lab has permission to store it. But why would a biogeneticist need any at all? Especially if you're studying the Autabroni intestinal system. I can't see a link. But, since the troubles on Autabron and the attempt to kill Jax, I can't help feeling that there's a connection. It may be nothing.'

'But you sense something? And you want me to find out what it is.' Calin smiled and kissed her mother's cheek. 'Not a problem. I'm kind of glad to have a distraction.' It was true that since Seti had left for Autabron with her father, things were quiet and, frankly, Calin had been hoping for something to do other than study Huthon biology.

Linnayen frowned. 'Be careful. This is not just a distraction. Things have felt strange lately. Even your grandmother feels it.'

'Like a puzzle where the pieces don't quite fit.' Calin nodded.

'Ah! You've felt it too.'

It was true. Even up here in the mountains, away from all the drama of the city, Linnayen still sensed a change in the status quo, like a ripple in the fabric of the atmosphere. One of the aspects of mentantism that she, her daughter and grandmother shared was a sixth sense, an awareness of thoughts and feelings at a macro level. Yes, they could all read people's minds if they chose to, and with permission, even Setiyan to a lesser extent. But it was more. Linnayen tried to describe it once to Jax. *It's like I can feel people's thoughts all together, like a choir of voices. The tone can be joyful, like being completely at peace. Harmony. But if it's discordant then I feel anxious, because the world's not quite right. It's out of kilter.*

Calin shifted her seat and rose, stretching to release the tension in her shoulders. 'Yes, for weeks now. I didn't realise you'd felt it too.'

Linnayen's eyes contained a mixture of sadness and hope. She stood and held her daughter's hands. 'What we have is a gift. But we must use it wisely. And you must use it to find out what this professor was up to and if there's a link to the troubles on Autabron.'

Calin opened her mouth to object and her brow furrowed. But her mother squeezed her hands to silence her. 'I know it isn't right. But these are challenging times. Do what you must, Calin. We're relying on you.'

The young woman sighed and her shoulders dropped. These were special times. Of that there was no doubt. She extracted her hands and moved them to hold her mother's face.

'Of course. I'll do what I can.'

With a final kiss on both Linnayen's cheeks, she turned towards the door and waved a goodbye as she walked. Only a day to enjoy the mountains and she would be off again.

'I knew I shouldn't have unpacked so quickly ...'

The Right Honourable Harriet Sophia Oenone Whitton-Blake tapped a pearl stylus against the perfect bow of her pursed lips as she read the notes on the polished desk in front of her. The shadow flitting back and forth, disturbing the light, was that of Avad Jarkoo. She lifted her chin and, from under the fringe of her bobbed red hair, her grey eyes glared at him.

'Do sit down, Jarkoo!'

He stopped, cleared his throat and took a seat to one side of the desk, his frame still creating a shadow. The woman shifted her position in order to get the light.

'Well?' Jarkoo asked.

'Wait,' she instructed.

Harrie Whitton-Blake was not one to be ordered around. The only daughter of Sir Anthony Whitton-Blake, third son of the Earl of Lindrick, was a woman who was used to taking command. Jarkoo had read her file. She had risen at breathtaking speed up the ranks of Covert-7, the Earthan intelligence agency, and was now deputy chief of strategic affairs. Part of her rapid elevation was due to her father's influence, of that he had no doubt. But her talent for discerning information and organising complicated projects certainly kept her at the top of her profession. She had no inkling of her gifts when she was a lowly history and politics student in New York all those years ago when she had met the twenty-three-year-old Kevor Jax Bashir and had become his first love.

'Mmm, you'll have to manage them carefully. Caspiran especially. Likely to have her family's trait – mentantism.'

'I can't do it alone!' Jarkoo burst out. 'You need to back me up.'

'Not possible. Can't be there.' Harrie had a unique clipped style of speech, a product of growing up listening to her father. He had spent over twenty-five years in military intelligence and his speedy reportage had rubbed off on the whole family.

Jarkoo shook his head vigorously. 'I'll meet them, of course. And I'm happy to take them on rounds of the plant. But I really think you need to speak to them. Make it look like the Earthans are just as worried about the disruptions as us.'

'Which we are!' Harrie fired back.

'Yes, of course. I didn't mean ...'

'Thought you had it under control,' she snapped. She pushed her chair back against the red stone wall and walked to stand behind him. She bent down and, tracing a finger down his neck, she whispered into his ear. 'You made promises, Jarkoo.'

He looked up at her defiantly. 'And I've been keeping them.'

'Not lately.'

He shrugged her away and stood up. This was not the time to fall prey to her, no matter her desirability. He moved swiftly to the thick tinted glass window through which could be seen a vast bronzed plateau of baked rock, shimmering under the glare of Lau, the only one of the two suns now visible above the horizon. It was late in the day and he was annoyed with the Earthan woman who treated him with such contempt. *She will pay too! Damned ganak! Once I've had my fill of her.*

'I assure you, the workers will come back into line as soon as the new batch is processed and applied.'

'Make it stronger. The effects are wearing off.' She barked her order, as if he were some servant.

'I can't do that. It could kill them. Or we'd be caught.'

'You. *You'd* be caught.'

'You're complicit. You've as much to lose,' he warned.

Harrie's face was as hard as the stone of the walls surrounding them. She waited a full minute before replying. 'Dear man, I'll be long gone. But you ... You're poisoning your own people. I might get a slap on the wrist. *You'll* be torn apart, like a pack of dogs on a bloody carcass.'

He shook his head, not wanting to admit that she was right. The urthrengo distillation had worked wonders since he'd started feeding it into the water system over a year ago, the dosage increasing little by little. The workers had become more compliant, easier to manage. They obeyed orders and had not complained about their pay or conditions anymore. Even Mira thought this would work in their favour. For when his people found out how they had been duped by the ganaks, their anger would shake the very rocks to dust, and at their helm would be the A'bat, glorious warrior of hope!

It had been straightforward to plant a few explosives – after all, he knew of the best locations to cause damage, but not too much. Sabotaging the machinery in the processing plant had been a little more difficult, but Mira had been insistent. They had to slow down the flow of ore and introduce a few impurities. Otherwise the Galactic Union would take no notice. Naturally the red-headed Earthan woman did not know of his secret alliance with Mira Denkaun – and could not find out. *We all have our agendas in this.* Hers was profit for the Union. But his? He had a dream that one day his planet would be free, that all the ganaks would be gone and the Autabroni people would control their fate. They would once more own their lands and return to the way of faith.

The Earthan woman, though, was right. If his people found out what he had been doing to their water supply, they would tear him limb from limb. They would not wait for explanation of how their sacrifice was needed to bring about change. That the end would justify such terrible means. He had long since decided that, if it came to it, he would be willing to lay down his life.

'No one will find out. But we need to make sure the Union mission doesn't discover the truth. You can ensure that.' Jarkoo was insistent. 'You can steer the investigation. Don't tell me you're not capable of subterfuge.'

Harrie walked over to where he stood and took in the expanse of the rocky desert plateau. Some people found this arid landscape mesmerising. But for her, it was a godforsaken hell and she would much rather be on her way back to Earth, with its lush forests and deep blue oceans. The posting to Autabron over this past year had been a necessary evil. But maybe – just maybe – the thought of seeing Jax again after all these years was intriguing enough to keep her here for a few more weeks.

She lifted her chin and looked into the Autabroni's black eyes.

'Very well. Subterfuge it is.'

Chapter Five

'You cannot have him! Marriage is out of the question!'

The old woman's words stung her like ground rock in a sandstorm. It was not fair. She had been with Kalik for many months now. She had given him freely of her body. She had bathed him, massaged his limbs, fed him and, when it came to lovemaking, she had entertained his every need. And all this was done willingly and most gladly, for she was in love with the shaman's adopted son. It didn't matter to her that he was Altani. His white-blond hair, so like her own people's, was soft, and Wika loved to comb and dress it. That his skin was pale and not reddish toned like her own, coupled with the piercing blue of his eyes, made him even more attractive. How could she give him up? *Impossible!*

'I do not ask for marriage, even though my father wishes it.' She fought hard to keep her voice soft but also strong.

'That's as well,' Mira replied. She shook her head and sighed. 'Wika, you should not have allowed yourself to become tied to him. I warned you months ago.'

A tear crept into the corner of her eye. She was already tied, bound in a way that Mira could not yet see. 'I could not help it. He is …'

'Destined, for someone else. Not you.'

The woman's words cut like a knife. She knew about the prophecy. Hadn't all Guznon children been raised on the story that one day a son of the twin suns would come to free them from their oppression? That from the A'bat, their warrior of hope, would spring a line of kings? But only if he too coupled with a daughter of the twin suns. And that was not her. Though who the daughter was, Mira would not say. Only that she was coming, that she was near.

'I know,' Wika conceded. 'But the daughter of hope is not come yet.'

Mira sighed once more and she shook her head. 'But she *will* come. She is close. You must step away.'

Suddenly a heavy tapestry on the far wall of the rock-lined room was pushed aside and Denkaun entered. Both women jumped to their feet, but only Wika bowed her head. Denkaun acknowledged them with a lift of an eyebrow and took the seat Mira had just vacated.

'What's this? Why are you here, Wika?'

'Mira asked for me, Kalik.' Her reply was delivered with a hint of reproach. It was not *her* fault that she was in his private chamber without his consent.

He turned his head slowly. 'Natar? What have you been saying to my sweet Wika?'

The old woman bristled. She had every right to speak to the daughter of Dokau, especially in the light of the princess's imminent arrival on Autabron. 'I have been reminding her, my son, that she will have to step aside for the daughter. She is in orbit now and will be with us in only a few days.'

'And why should Wika step aside?' He stretched the words out and darkness clouded his eyes. At this, Wika's eyes lit up.

Mira's brow creased. Surely he understood the importance of these next few days. Nothing could come between him and his coupling with the Aun'bat, the daughter of hope. The prophecy was too important. 'Kalik, my good son, there must be no impediment to your marriage. Wika must not be present once the Aun'bat is here in Beshwuk. You must not be distracted.'

Denkaun rose and went to his foster mother. He stroked her wrinkled cheek fondly and kissed her forehead.

'Dearest Natar. I know my purpose. I will not veer from my path. Neither Wika nor even you will lead me from my destiny.'

Wika allowed herself a sly smile. So, the old crone was getting her just desserts.

Mira raised a hand as if to protest but Denkaun took and kissed it, then placed it back down to her side.

'Wika will stay,' he commanded.

'But –'

'I have spoken.' His voice was soft, low and hard as stone. 'Leave me now.'

He returned to his seat as the two women nodded their acquiescence and turned towards the tapestry-covered doorway.

'Not you, Wika.'

Mira froze and cast a look at the girl that spoke of nothing but pure malice. Wika flung her long fair hair back from her lovely face. There was no denying the look of triumph in her black eyes. She had won. The old woman's power over him was waning. Kalik would keep her and she would ensure that he would never want to let her go. She turned and crossed the space to kneel at his feet.

From close orbit, Autabron was a swirl of browns and reds and oranges. With the lack of any strong cloud formations in its atmosphere, it could almost be mistaken for a gas planet. But the occasional gashes in its barren landscape – the result of both earth tremors and ancient water courses that had long since disappeared – gave lie to that assumption. This was a hard, stone planet, its twin suns having baked the landscape to a crisp but for a hint of green at its north and south poles. Here the land could maintain a thin vegetative cover that transpired enough moisture to produce the scrawny grasslands grazed by the prized herds of bika. The Gaksi tribe knew they were fortunate in holding these lands and over millennia had fought to keep them, while the sway of the poorer Guznon and other red-land tribes had diminished. Trapped in their warrens, the rock tribes were forced to live off feir fungus and tagirp and whatever resources the ganaks in their mercy gave them. It was humiliating and, thought Decker Finn as he watched the planet crawl by beneath them, explained so much about the Autabroni temperament. Anyone would be tough and quick to anger given such a legacy. This was a planet where you had to fight to survive.

'Glad to be home, lieutenant?' The voice was mocking and he did not need to look around to see who was trying to bait him.

'Glad to be at the end of this journey, princess.'

His tone was clipped and the way he emphasised the word 'princess' made Setiyan bristle. He never called her 'my lady' as he should. It was disrespectful. 'If only the whole mission could be over. I'm sure that would make us both very happy,' she snapped back.

He shook his head and spoke with a wistful sigh. 'Indeed it would. Personally, I can't wait.'

'How dare you! Why must you be so rude?'

This was the first time she had genuinely lost her temper with him. It was also the first time they had been alone. All prior encounters on board the *Teg-Koorym* had been in the company of the other mission members or her father and they had both been forced to act with a degree of courtesy.

He glanced at her over his shoulder. 'Apologies, princess. But I thought you'd be pleased to see the back of me.'

'Oh, I will be. I don't need you.' She sneered at his insolent look. 'A bodyguard! As if I can't look after myself. I'm fully trained, you know. Even hand-to-hand combat.'

He nodded curtly. 'I can believe that.'

He returned to the view out of the porthole. It was safer not to look at her. Not that he didn't want to. *Damn it!* She took his breath away. He'd tried not to take in the high cheekbones, the crystal blue eyes and the shining blonde hair. Even her lips were near as perfect as a woman's could be, and she had a perfume that seared his senses. Standing this close, he could not stop the reaction of his body.

'Don't test me, lieutenant. I'm not someone to mess with,' she spat back.

'Don't worry, princess. I won't be messing with you.'

He pushed away from the porthole, intending to go back to his quarters. But she was blocking his way and, in an attempt to step around her, he stumbled. He put out a hand to break his fall and it touched her waist, forcing his face in towards her neck. For a split second, his mouth was inches away and he felt a primal urge to kiss her skin. She did not move and she did not push him off her.

He quickly shook himself back to reality. 'Whoa, sorry. I didn't …'

She stiffened and stepped away from him. 'Don't let me keep you, lieutenant.' Her glance went upwards and she flicked her hair off her shoulder before walking smartly away towards the bridge.

As he looked at her retreating back and the curve of her hips, he sighed. *No. This can't be happening. Not her.* It had been a couple of years since he'd felt anything like this for any woman. He shook his head, groaned and turned back towards his cabin. This was going to be a tough job as it was. He did not need any more complications.

Calin searched the university's directory for the location of the biogenetics department. It took up three levels of the Injago Tower on the main campus and, as it was only a short walk to the vatortube, she did not feel the need to hurry. Professor Hasler was not expecting her for another twenty minutes which gave her time to go over her thoughts.

She was too well known to pretend to be anyone other than herself. So she had decided to feign an interest in his work because of the research she herself was conducting into the origins of the genetic link between Earthans and Altanis. This similarity had been uncovered twenty-five years earlier by Doctor Ullan Ropar. It had always been believed that the humans of Earth and the similar species of hominids on Altan and the other Union planets had evolved entirely independent of each other, a serendipitous sparking of life on different but similar planets. But Doctor Ropar had found that this was not so, that the two species, and indeed all other hominid species, shared the same paleo-genesis. How far back in time and by what means the various branches of the family had been separated or dispersed had not yet been established, but it was an intriguing question and an arm of research that was in its infancy. Adrik Hasler should be a mine of information on the subject – if he wasn't investigating the effects of one of the nastiest toxins on the human body.

That was a puzzle. Why urthrengo? What possible link could there be between it and the professor's supposed field of research? It didn't make sense. But the possibility of the drug escaping into the wider community – and so much of it – was too risky a situation to ignore, and she was determined to use whatever means to get to the bottom of it.

As Calin and her two security aides stepped from the tube onto the uppermost of the three levels, she was met by a young Huthon woman who smiled, bowed and greeted her.

'Welcome, Lady Calin. We are most honoured by your visit today,' she said, her voice soothing and almost too quiet to hear.

'That's kind of you. But I hope I am not disrupting your work?' Calin replied.

The woman, like all Huthons, was reserved of manner and kept her head lowered as a mark of respect to the young Altani princess. 'Oh no. Of course not. We like to have visitors and please feel free to ask any questions, either of myself or Professor Hasler.' She beckoned her to follow as she walked towards the main doors of the laboratory.

Calin signalled to the aides to wait then walked alongside the genial woman. 'And you are?'

'Doctor Amanie. I specialise in haemochromatosis in the Kaeliep people of the northern forests on my homeworld.'

'Not sure I know what that is,' Calin replied.

Amanie smiled and led her towards a large opaque screen, which slid to one side as they approached, revealing a laboratory behind. 'It is a condition where too much iron is absorbed into the blood. A genetic disorder. If it is not discovered early it can lead to many complications of vital organs such as the heart and the liver,' Amanie explained as they walked past a bench cluttered with trays and glass pipettes.

'And is one of the reasons for the premature demise of so many Kaeliep!' A male voice piped up behind them. 'Doctor Amanie's work is going to change all that, though. She's made great strides.'

Calin swivelled to see a man with a mop of honey-coloured hair grinning broadly at her through a full beard. He held out a hand for her to shake in the traditional Earthan style of greeting. The informality was not appropriate and, at a sharp glance from Amanie, he quickly withdrew it and gave a short bow instead.

'Oh, please. There's no need …' Calin began, reaching for his hand. 'Professor Hasler?'

'Sure am,' he replied, the smile returning to his face.

His hair flopped across his eyes which, Calin noticed, were a warm light brown. But most noticeable was his youth. Calin had done her research. She knew he was in his early thirties but she expected him to look older, more haggard and even a little doddery and forgetful. Instead, Adrik Hasler looked even younger than her and his Earthan skin was pale and smooth. She could not help but stare.

Suddenly aware of her scrutiny, she spoke. 'I am so sorry. I didn't expect you to be so young. Most of my professors at university were at least a hundred.'

He laughed out loud. 'Same! Yes, I often get asked for my ID at conferences, even when I'm the keynote speaker.'

Calin felt herself being drawn to him. He was like a cheeky schoolboy and there was an obvious glint of mischief in his eyes.

'I was a prodigy. That's all. Graduated at seventeen. No stopping me after that.'

'Your parents must have been very proud.'

He hung his head. 'Ah … Not really. Dad's a quantum physicist and my mother is Adanita Hasler …'

She gasped. 'The composer? Who wrote the Damerdown symphonies?' At his shy nod, she continued. 'That is some of the most beautiful music I've ever heard. My grandfather took us to see her. She was conducting – oh, about ten years ago now – in the concert hall in Elidian. I've never forgotten it. It was a magical evening. The music was so uplifting. I was thrilled to be allowed out so late too.'

'I'm glad you had the opportunity,' Hasler responded. Calin noted that his tone was flat, all trace of his former good humour had disappeared. Was there some discordance in this talented family? 'Anyway … Would you like to see around the lab?'

'Of course.'

'Amanie here will be your guide. I just have a … er, calls, things to do. You know.' He pushed a hank of hair out of his downcast eyes. The change in his demeanour was so sudden that her puzzlement must have shown. He realised it needed addressing. 'Perhaps you can stay for lunch?'

'Er … yes. That would be great.'

With that he turned and walked quickly away.

'The professor may be young but he has all the hallmarks of quirk, yes?' Doctor Amanie, too, studied the fast-retreating frame of the biologist. 'We have become used to his Earthan ways.' Her smile was one of both sympathy and understanding.

Calin grinned. She wondered if this might be a good time to probe the young woman. 'Indeed. What is he currently working on? Must be important.'

'I'm sure it is. But Professor Hasler's research is classified. I am afraid I'm not free to tell you anything more.' Then, realising that she may have given offence, the Huthon added, 'Oh, I am so sorry. I actually do not know exactly.'

'I was given to understand that he was continuing Doctor Ropar's early research into paleo-evolution in primates and hominids,' Calin said, trying to sound both well-informed and casual at the same time.

Amanie led her through the laboratory, manoeuvring between lab benches and workers, all of whom had their heads down, hard at work.

'You know of this?' The woman sounded surprised.

'My mother met Doctor Ropar when she was first made Ki. She formed a favourable impression of him and funded his research for many years.'

'Of course. Forgive me.'

Calin decided to push her advantage. 'Tell me, Doctor Amanie, is there anyone here working on the effect of toxins?' She kept her tone light and her eyes innocently wide.

The scientist's pale green skin seemed to flush and a frown passed across her brow. 'Toxins? Why would *we* need to study such things?'

'Oh, I thought you used toxins to produce vaccines.'

Doctor Amanie recovered her calm. 'Ah. I see. Yes, that does happen.'

'And are any of you working on that now?'

'Not that I know of,' Amanie answered. 'Why do you ask?'

There was a look of genuine puzzlement on the woman's face. Calin had been reading the woman's body language since they met and felt safe to push ahead. Either Doctor Amanie knew something about Hasler's activities or she didn't and Calin was sensing enough discomfort to know that she would be able to read the truth in the woman's response to her next statement.

'Because a significant quantity of urthrengo was delivered to Professor Hasler when he was on Autabron a year ago and –'

She did not have time to finish as Amanie put a finger to her lips and pulled her towards the opening that led back into the foyer. Calin tried to draw away but the Huthon, who was a few centimetres taller and surprisingly strong, retained her grip.

'Not here!' she hissed and, as she pressed a panel in the wall to call for the vatortube, she turned. Her green eyes drilled into Calin's. She flicked a glance over Calin's shoulder as if to check that they were not being followed then took her elbow and spoke loudly. 'Let me show you the gardens. They're quite stunning at this time of year.'

The tube doors slid open and the two women entered, followed smartly by Calin's aides. They did not speak another word in the confines of the building. Calin was going to have to wait for her questions to be answered.

As the *Teg-Koorym* descended slowly through the Autabroni atmosphere and approached the docking chamber, a whirlwind of brown dust flew upwards, temporarily blocking Setiyan's view of the surface. But as they came closer to the spaceport she saw that its entrance was set on a low, bare plateau. The haze soon cleared and once the spaceracer had dropped below ground level, she was able to see the clean lines of the modern port, shining walkways cut into the red rock and glass viewing panels giving glimpses of the vast underground city beyond.

Zaz-Rakuum was not the first of the mining cities on Autabron but it was the biggest. This upper level, closest to the surface, stretched into a warren of carved tunnels and avenues for five kilometres. The lower residential levels sank into the bedrock to a depth of nearly five hundred metres, each level with its artificial parks, shopping villages, hotels and offices. The atmosphere was continually filtered not only to provide clean air but also to extract the eternal red dust that would otherwise consume the city. The two suns, which revolved slowly around each other, every full revolution taking a year to complete, made the surface an inferno for much of the time. Life in these mid-latitudes was tough and it was only the polar tribes who had the good fortune to be able to survive outside of the underground mining settlements.

Even so, many Gaksi had traded in their simple livestock farming lifestyle for the comforts of Zaz and the other underground cities. Who wouldn't? Food was plentiful. There was time for leisure and GKD and the other mining companies had invested trillions of keks into making this place modern and cosmopolitan. There could be no doubt that the rewards from the bergussian ore and other minerals sucked out of the crust had made it all worthwhile, both for the mine owners and the workers.

Setiyan could understand why there had been protests, though. The destruction of the sacred site at Euta Sakek had been a real disaster and she was keen to talk to the tribe leaders about this tragedy. She also wanted to know how such a stupid mistake could have been made. Was it genuine error or had it been deliberate? In the meantime, she would have to suffer the company of the ridiculous Earthan bodyguard, who had the good sense to stay out of her way while they completed their descent.

Why he kept popping into her thoughts was a mystery. He had been unforgivably rude and she should have told her father. What stopped her? She shook the uncomfortable thoughts away. Whatever she felt about Decker Finn would have to wait. There was a new city to explore and adventures to be had.

'Seti!' Jax called her to attention. 'Over here. The reception party are ready for us.'

She stepped quickly over to where Jax stood at the head of their group, the other team members lined up to each side of him and their attendants at the rear.

'Here. Next to me,' instructed Jax. He smiled at the excited glow in her eyes.

She had to squeeze past Finn, who stood slightly behind her father. He did not even step back to give her room to pass. *Imbecile!* She took the chance to throw a look of venom up to him, but he seemed not to have noticed.

The outer hatch doors swung open and some twenty paces away stood Avad Jarkoo and a group of six or seven others, all either Altanis or Earthans. They were dressed in the traditional Autabroni style of red robes with orange sashes worn across one shoulder, each showing the logo of the GKD company. Jax stepped forward, as did Jarkoo, and they both held out a hand to the other in greeting.

'Avad. So good of you to meet us in person. I know you are a busy man.' Jax's voice was warm. You would never know of his reservations about this man, thought Seti. Her father, though Earthan, had learned well the Altani ways of statecraft and the ability to hide true feelings.

'My lord, it is an honour and a pleasure to see you again – and looking so well,' Jarkoo replied. 'Let me introduce my colleagues.'

One by one, each red-robed member of the party stepped forward and offered their welcome. In return, Jax introduced Sen-Caspiran, Pieter Serekunda and Rutak Birkaan and outlined their expertise. When he came to Setiyan, Jarkoo's smile stretched across his face.

'Ah, your beautiful daughter! Welcome to Autabron, princess. A pleasure to see you again. This time, I hope, we will have more time to talk.'

'Thank you, Director Jarkoo,' Seti returned. 'I hope for the same, though my stay in Zaz may be short as I am to spend some time with the Guznon in the Beshwuk region.'

Jarkoo face froze. 'Beshwuk? I am surprised. Things are unsettled there. I would not –'

'My daughter will have Doctor Serekunda and a bodyguard, Lieutenant Finn, with her,' Jax interjected.

Seti fought to keep the grimace off her face, though the presence of Finn's body at her back made her breath come a fraction quicker. 'And I have been invited by Mira Denkaun, who I am told is a shaman of the Guznon people,' Seti added.

'Lady Mira? Well, in that case, I will be happy to organise your transport.' Jarkoo's manner was snakelike and Seti felt a ripple of dislike run through her.

Suddenly there was a noise at the rear of the GKD assembly and a woman's voice could be heard apologising to those in front of her. The accent was very obviously Earthan, its tones polished and clipped.

'So sorry. Got held up.'

Seti felt her father stiffen beside her. He was fixed to the spot, staring at the stunningly pretty woman who had appeared, and the look on his face was anything but warm.

The woman smiled, her grey eyes cat-like under a short fringe of red hair. 'Hello, Kev.'

He nodded in return. 'Harrie.'

At the one-word reply, Seti turned to look at her father, bewilderment on her face. He obviously knew this woman, who now turned her gaze from the father to the daughter. She approached with her hand outstretched.

'Harriet Whitton-Blake. Call me Harrie. Pleased to meet you.'

'Um, hello,' Seti replied, eyes wide. She shook the proffered hand.

Her father's stilted reaction to this woman was odd. She had called him 'Kev', the diminutive of Kevor, her father's proper name. Even her mother did not call him that because, she had once told her, he disliked it. But he must have once been good friends with this woman for her to be so familiar.

Jarkoo interrupted the moment and spoke to Jax. 'I see you know Miss Whitton-Blake.'

'We've met.' Again, Jax's response was less than effusive.

'Bit more than that, Kev.' The woman grinned and spoke to Jarkoo. 'College together. Back home. Yonks ago.'

Seti smiled. 'An old friend? How nice, Father.'

Jax's glance to Seti was delivered with the merest turn of his head. He remained silent.

'Miss Whitton-Blake is here on behalf of the Earthan security agency Covert-7. They, too, have been investigating our situation,' Jarkoo explained. 'We'll be working together.'

Jax's frown at this news did not go unnoticed. His look to Harrie was as dark as a storm cloud.

'Don't worry, Kev. Won't get in the way. Here to help.'

'Indeed,' Jarkoo said, then smiled broadly. 'We're glad of any assistance. Isn't that right?' This last part was delivered to Jax, who had not yet taken his eyes off Harrie.

Seti nudged her father in the arm, conscious that he did not seem to have heard Jarkoo. At her touch, he recovered himself. 'Absolutely. Happy to hear any insights from – what was it? C-7? I'm sure your talents are well suited to their work, Harrie.'

The red-headed woman raised one perfectly plucked eyebrow and smiled. 'Spot on.'

Was she saying that his assessment of her character was correct, wondered Seti, or was it about the nature of her work, that she was good at it? There was clearly history between these two and she couldn't wait to ask her father about it.

Jarkoo cleared his throat. 'Let me show you to your rooms. If you'll follow me.' He beckoned their group to follow him along the raised walkway and out of the docking chamber. Jax took a place next to Jarkoo, followed by Caspiran, Serekunda and Birkaan, while Seti was left at the rear of the group. Suddenly, she caught the aroma of a rich, floral perfume as Harrie Whitton-Blake fell in step with her.

'You're very pretty,' she said.

Seti was used to getting compliments, but not often from women, and it took a couple of seconds for her to reply. 'Thank you.'

'From your mother … Looks.'

'Ah, yes. So people say. Though I have my father's eyes.'

Harrie stopped walking, which caused Seti to stop, too, then look over her shoulder with a look of concern on her face. The Earthan woman suddenly held Seti's chin with a light but firm grip and stared into her face.

'Yours are paler.' She perused Seti's eyes for a further moment before striding away.

'Wait!' Seti called. Her father and the others had moved on. But Decker Finn heard her and waited, a silent sentinel at the chamber's exit.

Chapter Six

As the lights went up, the audience began to murmur and stretch out stiff limbs before gathering cloaks and bags and moving towards the theatre exits. Linnayen always loved this moment at the end of a performance, a collective warmth where every soul was usually smiling, depending on how good the play had been. She thought of it as the visual and audible satisfaction of creative work well done and well received, and she was more than pleased that she and Jax's good friend Duncan McCrae had been a part of it.

She took her mother's arm as they stood and made their way to the reception rooms to meet and thank the cast. Though some formal duties could be tiresome, like policy discussions and chamber ceremonials, she had always enjoyed meeting the everyday people who worked hard and gave so much to the community. Her support of the arts, though, had only happened because of Jax and Duncan. She had had little time for them as a pampered young Ki, mesmerised by the hateful Navarr and bound by her own arrogance. Thank all the fates that that part of her life was over and would not intrude on her happiness ever again.

'Did you enjoy it?' Li-el asked over her shoulder as they passed their security guards in the doorway. 'No, don't answer. I can tell you did.'

'Mother! Stop it. I can tell when you're in my mind, you know.' Her voice was a soft warning.

'Oh, don't be so precious,' the older woman snapped back. 'It just saves time.'

'To know what I'm thinking?' Linnayen shook her head and rolled her eyes. This was not an uncommon experience. Her mother had used her mentante abilities to read her daughter's and others' minds on many occasions, even though it was incredibly impolite. She and her sister, Evica, had got used to it over the years, but they still felt the need to object in the hope that one day she might stop.

'Just ask me, Mother. Use your words and I'll tell you the truth.'

'Mmm, maybe,' Li-el replied, raising a single eyebrow. 'But where would be the fun in that?'

Li-el walked ahead to meet the play's director, who bowed reverentially. It was not often that the dowager Ki-consort and the Ki herself graced his theatre. The cast and some of the crew were lined up to be presented to the honoured guests and, one by one, each received a handshake and a few complimentary words about some aspect of the performance: how well they captured the pathos, how their timing had been amazing and learning the lines – how *did* they do it?

Linnayen grinned on hearing her mother ask this last question. Everyone knew that each actor's lines were uploaded onto an implanted sonochip. Had Li-el forgotten this? Or was she just trying to make conversation? Linnayen felt that twinge of unease yet again.

Once the formal greetings were done, Duncan came up to her side and planted a quick kiss on her cheek. Apart from her family, he was the only other person in the known universe allowed this familiarity and she rather enjoyed it.

'My darling Linnayen!' he exclaimed with as much dramatic grandeur as he had displayed on stage only thirty minutes earlier. 'I still can't believe that oaf of a best friend got to you before I did. There's still time to change your mind and run off with me.'

Linnayen laughed. Duncan was such fun, always making jokes. But she knew that deep down, his loyalty to her and Jax was rock-solid. He would do anything for them. Why, he had even come to her rescue all those years ago when she had been kidnapped – and he was not a fighter. He and his father, Joe, had also worked to uncover the plot to destroy the peace treaty she had devised. She would always be grateful to him.

'I'll think about it. I might enjoy making him a little jealous.'

'Clever as well as beautiful. He's a lucky man.' Duncan took her arm and led her towards a balcony overlooking the city. They pushed through the pale green silk drapes to take in the lights of Genkarah spread before them. It was refreshing after the stuffiness of the warm theatre.

Linnayen leaned on the balustrade and breathed in the night air. 'But I couldn't take you away from your first love, Duncan. What would the theatre be without you?'

'Hopelessly dull, of course,' he fired back, the usual mischievous glint in his hazel eyes.

They chatted about family and friends and, more interestingly, Duncan's love-life while taking in the coloured lights reflected from the spires and the speeding windshifters zooming between them. Suddenly, the curtains parted and an attendant informed Linnayen that she had a transmission from her daughter on Autabron.

'I'll take it here,' she said, then turned to Duncan who had moved as if to leave. 'No, stay. Seti will want to say hello to you too.'

The attendant returned with a small screen from which a holographic image of a smiling Setiyan was projected.

'Mama ...' she began, then on seeing who she was with, 'Uncle Duncan!'

He groaned. 'Please, not "uncle". Makes me sound so old.'

'Well you *are* old,' Seti responded with a wide grin. Duncan acted out being stabbed in the heart with a knife, making them both laugh.

Linnayen jumped in. 'Seti, how is it going?'

'Well, I think. I'm off to meet the Guznon leaders the day after tomorrow and see what we can find out about the Hanashi visit. But everyone's been very helpful so far.'

Linnayen knew her daughter well enough to sense the hesitation. 'But?'

'A couple of things. Nothing too urgent.'

'Go on.' Linnayen's tone had changed from interested mother to concerned Ki.

'Well, it's Lieutenant Finn. He wants me to have a tracker injected. I said no. It's over the top. Ridiculous.'

Linnayen looked to Duncan. She did not need her mentante abilities to read his thoughts. *Like father, like daughter.*

'The lieutenant is just doing his job, daughter. He is, after all, your bodyguard. And how can he guard your body if he doesn't know where it is?'

'Mmm. That's what Pa said.' Seti's brow furrowed. She had been hoping her mother might understand that she was perfectly capable of looking after herself. Finn was overstepping the mark.

'Where you're going is dangerous territory –'

71

Seti interjected, 'But I've been invited! I'm an honoured guest. Nothing is –'

'Anything can happen, Setiyan! You don't know.' Linnayen was only too aware of the dangers her daughter might face, for hadn't she also lived through such uncertainties? *No. Anything to keep her daughter safe.* 'The lieutenant is right to be worried. He knows these people and you must accept his judgement on this. I agree with your father and I will send through my order on this matter.'

'But, Ma ...'

'No buts.' Linnayen voice was stone. Seti pursed her lips and nodded her defeat. Linnayen continued. 'You said there was another matter?'

'Yes. It's probably nothing. But I've asked Pa and he just clams up.'

Linnayen moved to sit on a bench, beckoning Duncan to join her. 'Go on. What is it?'

'There's a woman here. She's part of the investigation team. I think she might be a spy. She's pretty cagey. I don't know what to make of her.'

Linnayen shook her head, nonplussed by her daughter's concerns. 'And how is this affecting you?'

'Not so much me. It's Pa. He obviously knows her. He goes quiet around her. Like maybe she's a threat ...'

This was worrying. After the assassination attempt, this was the last thing Jax or she needed. 'In what way? Physically?'

'Not sure. I just have a bad feeling about her. Her name's Harriet Whitton-Blake. Could you check her out for me?'

Linnayen froze, mouth open. Duncan reacted instantly and took the screen out of her hands.

'Leave it with us, sweetheart. We'll get back to you *prontissimo!* Bye for now.'

He clicked Seti's image closed and reached out for one of Linnayen's limp hands. She looked into his eyes, his sympathy and understanding meeting her fears and questions. She did not want to face the truth. *Could it be the same woman? Of course it was. Who else could have that name? What was she doing there?* Then the doubt crept in like a writhing morning frost across the valley of her heart. *Why hadn't he told her?*

72

The call from Calin was a welcome diversion and Jax was relieved to get out of the same space as Harrie Whitton-Blake. They had been in the middle of a tour of the facility at Euta Makaan, led by Avad Jarkoo, when an aide tapped Jax on the shoulder and whispered in his ear. He made his apologies to the group and walked back to the quiet office from where they had begun their visit. As he passed her, Harrie ignored him and for that he was thankful. He had been keenly aware of her presence since they met in the docking chamber two days earlier, his unease not helped by the waft of her distinctive perfume whenever she came close.

There was no avoiding it. She was still a beautiful woman. Those pearl grey eyes drew him in just as they had done twenty-five years ago and her lips were still full and enticing. He tried to stop himself but he remembered the feel and taste of them. He recalled too the soft curves of her body, the way she would offer her neck to his kisses and the way she crooned his name, breathless and in a voice as rich as velvet.

She had been his first love and, after only a few months, he had been ready to propose. When he discovered her deception, with what she had called 'just a fling', he was heartbroken. She was a cheat and a drug-taker. How could he have been so wrong? The pain went to his core. So when he fell in love again – this time with the young Altani queen, Linnayen – he was at first cautious. Their courtship had gone well and, although she seemed shy and reserved, he put that down to nerves and the formality of Altani manners. He hoped she would come to love him as he had begun to love her. But, yet again, he was deceived. She had been Navarr's lover for months. It was only the head injury from the accident on board the *Jensa Kadenx* that caused an amnesia so deep that she forgot her lover and began to fall for her husband. It had been thus ever since. Linnayen and Jax had become deeply devoted to each other, their relationship as enduring as the high Ksas Mountains.

He put all such thoughts away as he concentrated on Calin's image on the screen. Seeing her animated face, he reminded himself that but for the disaster that had been Harrie Whitton-Blake, he would not have met Linnayen and would not have these two amazing daughters.

Calin filled him in on her meeting with Amanie and Hasler at the university.

'So Hasler was pretty much impenetrable. He was friendly at first. But later, over lunch, he just shut down. You know how it is with Earthans. We find them difficult to read when they're in control of their emotions.'

Though Calin was a gifted mentante, it had proved the case that Earthan minds could not be read as easily as Altani ones, unless they were in a state of distress or anger. Their more extreme emotions allowed mental barriers to drop. But despite Calin's gentle probing, which was of course quite improper, Hasler had remained cool and calm in their meeting and she picked up nothing. She had felt distaste at having to use her skills in such a way, but the danger of the drug urthrengo outweighed the disrespect.

'I couldn't ruffle so much as one feather, and I didn't want to push it too far in case I made him suspicious,' she continued.

'No, I agree. So? A dead end?'

'No. And this is where it gets interesting.'

Calin almost sounded like her sister. It was Seti who usually loved intrigue.

'I was taken to the university gardens by one of Professor Hasler's colleagues, a Doctor Amanie, who refused to talk until we were outside the building. She told me that though she wasn't on Autabron when the shipment of the drug arrived at Hasler's lab, one of her co-workers, Mikel Piek, was. They'd been at a research lab together on Hutho years earlier. They'd become good friends and kept in contact regularly.'

Jax interjected. 'Until something happened?'

'Well, she just doesn't know. Amanie said that Piek mentioned something strange going on at the lab in Zaz-Rakuum – they had had visits from the GKD mine security chief and this was unusual. He couldn't understand why security people from the mine would have any reason to be interested in their research. I mean, biogenetics? Piek said that it didn't make sense and Amanie agreed with him.'

'I'm getting the feeling that something bad happened,' Jax commented.

'And you're right.' Calin sighed heavily, remembering the quiver in Amanie's voice as she told Calin that her friend had asked Hasler what was going on but that he had snapped at him to mind his own business.

The Huthon woman's voice had shaken as she recounted the events. 'Mikel was – is – a dedicated scientist. He meant no offence. It was just an honest enquiry. He was really upset by the professor's response. Then, a few days later, he had been working late and as he was leaving, he saw Hasler at the loading dock. Mikel saw him take delivery of some small cases from a driver who wore a GKD uniform. He told me that he asked about it the next day – just an offhand comment. But Hasler was furious. He wouldn't answer.'

The tears had fallen from Amanie's eyes as she continued. 'He called me later that day. He was upset and said he was sure Hasler was up to something and he was going to find out. And then I never heard from him again. I've asked Hasler, the local authorities and his family, but – nothing. Hasler told me that Mikel resigned and he presumed he went back to Hutho. He says he hasn't heard from him since.'

As Calin relayed the story of the missing scientist, Jax's brain worked hard to assess the information. How did this fit into plant sabotage and the mine workers' unrest? He couldn't see how the pieces went together – for now. But he was certain they would. They would just have to do more digging, and one of the first steps would be to discover what had happened to Mikel Piek.

'I'll see what I can find out,' Jax concluded. 'Well done, sweetheart.'

'Let me know what else I can do. So how's Seti doing? Is she all right?'

Jax had to smile. Indeed, the thought of his daughter's behaviour over these past days exasperated him yet warmed his heart at the same time. She had behaved perfectly in front of Jarkoo and the other mining and local community representatives, had been welcoming and friendly. But for poor Lieutenant Finn it had been a different story. She had kept herself aloof and distant, and he had even begun to question the sagacity of his and Linnayen's decision to bring him along. But on balance, and even though his daughter was a formidable force of nature, she was just as mortal as the rest of them. His resolve did not falter.

'Oh, she's excellent, Calin,' he replied with a long sigh. 'A perfect princess in every respect.'

Calin smiled. 'That's my sister. Good luck, Pa. Let me know if you find anything.'

Decker Finn's thinking matched Jax's. He had hoped that, as the days passed, Setiyan would stop being such a princess and calm down – accept her fate, accept that no matter what, he was going to do his duty and protect her. But she wasn't making it easy and it didn't help that he found himself questioning his emotions. She was so damn difficult and yet, every so often, when she was unaware of his presence, he found himself studying her profile, the fall of her hair, the curves of her body, and he was acutely aware of his own body's response.

They were due to leave for the Beshwuk Highlands in less than twenty-four hours, so this would be their last day in Zaz, and he had asked her for her proposed itinerary for the day. She had deliberately obfuscated when he asked for the third time.

'How can I know where I'm going, Lieutenant Finn, until I get there?' Her voice was testy and she shrugged her shoulders.

'I have to know. There are security checks I need to make,' he replied.

'Yes, yes.' She flicked her hand at him. 'I'll be fine. What harm can there be in a little shopping?'

He clenched his mouth and tried not to blurt out what he wanted to say. *What harm? Crowds. Confusion.* It would be nigh on impossible to ensure her safety in such an environment.

'Can you at least tell me what shops you intend to visit?'

Seti shook her head and for the first time looked up into his eyes. It was a look of pure sufferance. She put down the breakfast pastry she had been eating and brushed the crumbs from her rose silk blouse. 'Sorry, no.'

'As in you can't tell me or you won't?'

She jumped up and strode towards him, eyes like ice, and pushed manicured fingers into his chest. 'How *dare* you question me? Who are *you* to speak to me like that?'

She flicked blonde hair back from her face and moved to turn her back to him when he grabbed her arm. This was the last straw for Finn. His eyes drilled down into hers.

'I'm the one who will save your spoilt, entitled backside when you get into trouble due to your own stupid actions, that's who! But trust me, princess, if you're happy to die on an assassin's blade then go for it. Don't let me stop you!'

His breath came hard and fast. As suddenly as he had gripped her, he released his hold on her arm, swivelled on his heel and strode away. He stopped at the doorway and, without turning, spoke through gritted teeth. 'I'll be back in twenty minutes to escort you while you shop!'

If Finn could have seen the look on Seti's face at that moment he might have rethought the timeline. Now was not a moment to be leaving her to her own devices. The cogs inside her beautiful head were spinning wildly and he could not have known where they would end up.

Linnayen tapped on her desktop and tried to focus on her schedule for the tenth time that morning. Her eyes scanned the room listlessly. *I must focus. I must not get distracted. But why did he not tell me?*

She flipped the ornate drawer handles distractedly then traced the lines of the dark woodgrain, her eyes following the whorls and streaks in the timber. It was a massive piece of furniture, hand carved by Huthon craftspeople out of the deep brown wood of the purguna tree, which grew close to the Genara family lodge on the floodplains of the Utieku River on Hutho. The lodge had been gifted to them many centuries ago and was a treasured retreat. She had taken the girls there a few times as small children but had brought Jax there only once, and only because he had insisted. The lodge held a memory of Navarr, one of the few that had crept back into her mind over the years. It was their first meeting. She had stepped from the carved rock pool in the central atrium in a flimsy muslin bathing dress, unaware that he and old Sen-Beoraan had entered. Her reaction to him then had been visceral and, at the memory of it now, she felt her stomach lurch. Later she had been repelled by him, but not then. Then she had been drawn to him like a ksari moth is pulled inexorably to a moonbeam. She had not wanted Jax to visit, had not wanted him to be contaminated by her memories – at least, that's what she told herself.

After twenty-five years, the past seemed to be pulling them back and she could not make sense of the world. There was a darkness growing. She could feel it. Both Li-el and Calin sensed it too. But she could not tell what it was, or where it was, or why. She had not felt so unsettled in many years and this business of Jax's former lover only added to her unease.

It was only a month or so after they had reconciled, once they were back home on Altan, that Jax had told her about Harrie. It was his first serious relationship and he imagined himself deeply in love. He had even thought about proposing marriage. Then, on a surprise visit, he had discovered her with another man. She had also been using narcotics, and all the while he had suspected nothing. It was as though Harrie had a secret life, was another person. The dishonesty damaged him deeply and went a long way to explaining why Linnayen's own deception had hurt him so badly. But, at the time of his recounting, he was completely over Harrie Whitton-Blake and devoted to Linnayen. His wife was then and – he swore – would always be the love of his life. And she believed him. So why had he not told her about Harrie being on Autabron?

At that very moment, the console on her desk buzzed with a call. It was Jax! *Had he been reading my mind?*

'Hello, my love.' His deep tones broke her reverie and reminded her of how much she loved the sound of his voice. The screen came to life and she saw the warm smile on his handsome face. 'Have I caught you at a busy time?' he asked.

'What? No, not at all.'

'You looked faraway. I hope you were thinking of me?'

Again, that smile and those familiar midnight blue eyes that always made her breath come a little faster.

'Fishing for compliments at your age, husband. Really ...' She shook her head and smiled back at him.

'If a man can't expect a good report from his wife then he's in a bit of trouble,' he rejoindered easily. 'But anyway, I have news. Firstly, Calin briefed me on her meeting with Professor Hasler and, quite frankly, there's reason to be concerned. Has she filled you in?'

'Yes. He seemed reluctant to give any information and I just can't see a link between his research into Doctor Ropar's work and this awful drug.' She could not bear to think about the time when Navarr's twin sister, Balisel, had used urthrengo on her to make Linnayen compliant. There were many hours when she was in captivity – maybe even a couple of days – when she had no memory of what had happened to her. The thought did not sit well.

'I agree,' Jax continued. 'There's none. But the missing scientist? That's another matter. I'm in touch with the local police force here, trying to find out if they know anything. Their investigation into his disappearance was only sparked when Doctor Amanie contacted them, and that was two weeks after she had last heard from Piek.'

'That's unfortunate. I take it the trail had gone cold?'

'Sure had. But it's not hopeless. I'm looking over their interview notes and travel manifests. Maybe he left and went back to Hutho. Maybe he's still here somewhere – perhaps sick or in hiding?' Jax shook his head and sighed loudly. 'Between you and me, I don't have a good feeling about this, and neither does Calin.'

'No. Do what you can.' Now was the time to mention it. She decided to give him the opportunity. She just could not bear the indignity of having to raise it herself. 'How is everything else? Are you healing well? And how are your meetings with the mine people going?'

Jax's frown deepened. 'Mmm. That's a bit tricky.'

'How so?' She tried to keep her voice light.

'Well, there's a problem, something you should know,' he began. 'One of the investigation team is an old, well, not friend as such … Harriet Whitton-Blake. You remember her? I told you about her ages ago.'

'I remember the name,' Linnayen replied innocently, a frown of ignorance crossing her brow. Then, as if it all came flooding back, her eyes opened wide. 'Oh! She was your first …'

'Yes, first love, I suppose.' He shifted in his seat. 'It was such a long time ago and, honestly, it feels like that was another me. Twenty-five years of loving you, well, I'm toast for anyone else these days.'

This must be one of those Earthan expressions that he often used, though she'd never heard this particular one before. 'Toast?'

He grinned. 'Sorry, sweetheart. It means I'm useless to anyone else. You have my heart and soul. Always will.'

He placed his hand over his heart and Linnayen, usually so perceptive, mistook the gesture.

'So she's tried to seduce you?'

'What? No!' He struggled to regain his composure and get back to the light-hearted vein of two seconds ago. But it was hard not to sound defensive. 'She's kept her distance, and that's fine by me. As I said, I'm all yours …' Then, more softly, 'Linnayen, you know I love you.'

There was no denying the sincerity in his voice and in his eyes. He had the look of a penitent kareek, begging for forgiveness from its mistress for having stolen a sweetmeat from the table.

'And I you. But still … Stay away from her,' she ordered. With a toss of her long black hair and a smile at the corners of her mouth she added, 'She's probably old and ugly now anyway.'

Jax laughed out loud. It was not often that his beloved wife showed her feelings so openly and he was secretly pleased at her jealousy. 'She is. Hideous,' he confirmed with a mischievous smile. 'No competition.'

Linnayen's green eyes flashed at him. 'You're making fun of me.'

'No, my love. I speak truth. I'm the luckiest man alive.' Jax looked over his shoulder and nodded his head. Someone had obviously entered the room and he was being summoned. 'I have to go now, sorry. We'll talk later, yes?'

She nodded and put her hand on her own heart before raising her fingers to her lips and kissing them. *So, he is true to me.* Her fears calmed, she turned back to the much-neglected daily schedule and gave it her full focus. All thoughts of Harrie Whitton-Blake were put aside – for now.

Closing the companel, Jax breathed a long sigh and rubbed his forehead. He hated not being completely honest with her and, without doubt, the sick feeling in his stomach was karma for this small deception. Thank goodness Duncan had warned him that Linnayen knew about Harrie. Now all he had to do was figure out how to deal with her.

She had been what he could only describe as playful with him, using suggestive language and throwing him sultry sidelong glances that he presumed were intended to stir his passions. If so, it was not working. Whilst Harrie was still a beautiful woman, with silky red hair that showed no sign of grey and almond-shaped eyes that still sparkled, the fact was that he was in love with his wife. Linnayen was his lifeblood and he hated being away from her. Harrie Whitton-Blake was a mere distraction, a remnant of his youth, a reminder of his naivety and, quite frankly, a time he'd rather forget. Getting that message across to her, though, was proving awkward.

He recalled the debriefing they had all attended last night. In the company of Avad Jarkoo, Sen-Caspiran, Serekunda, Birkaan, Harrie, his daughter and, of course, Lieutenant Finn, they had gone over everything they had found so far regarding equipment malfunctions, ore contamination and the residue of the explosives used on the transmission lines. Birkaan had worked on the detonation devices and reported that they were somewhat primitive but entirely effective.

'It's a simple heat-controlled mechanism,' he had related. 'Once a pre-set temperature is reached, the coil melts and the explosive is activated. The transporter lines are switched off for two hours in every seventy-two for routine maintenance. Once they'd cooled down, the explosives and their detonators were placed. Within ten minutes of the lines coming back up, the friction causes them to heat and, well, you know the rest.'

'Which means that our saboteurs must be part of the maintenance crew,' Jax had concluded.

Harrie shook her head. 'Not necessarily. Any number of possibilities. They could be crew or could have broken into the plant, even days beforehand. Could even be paid mercenaries.'

'Have all engineering and maintenance personnel been screened?' This had been Caspiran.

'That's nearly complete,' said Jarkoo, 'There's still a few more to go. We've found nothing so far.'

Birkaan had continued. 'And it's my belief that the footage from the on-site scanners has been compromised. It looked too ...' His black eyes glared under his dark brows. 'How can I describe it? Normal, ordinary. Nothing unusual appeared to have happened. I've asked for it to be checked.'

'Also underway,' Jarkoo had confirmed. 'Maintenance logs for the crushing plant are being re-examined as well to see if the malfunctions could have been predicted. You know, normal wear and tear.'

'But you do not think so, Director Jarkoo?' Caspiran had remained quiet for much of the meeting. Her role was largely to observe and, only if strictly necessary, use her mentante abilities. The director's behaviour and body language had caused her concern. She had the feeling that he knew more than he was telling them and, when she had broached it with Jax over dinner, he had authorised her to shadow Jarkoo.

'Frankly, no,' Jarkoo had replied. 'We have a strict policy of parts replacement here at GKD and, according to the logs, that schedule has been maintained.'

'What if the new parts were themselves damaged?' Harrie had asked.

'That would mean some sort of interference at the parts production facilities – and we have those on all the planets except Dasnir,' Jarkoo had countered. 'That would be a massive operation –'

Birkaan had interjected. 'No. We know which parts have malfunctioned. So we know where they were produced.'

'Birkaan's right,' Jax had concurred. 'So, Jarkoo, can you contact those suppliers and brief local inspection teams? Let's check for quality control before we start suspecting sabotage. Now then …' He turned to Setiyan and Lieutenant Finn. 'As for your mission – and you too, Doctor Serekunda – I take it transport has been arranged?'

'Yes, Father. Director Jarkoo has us travelling to the highlands the day after tomorrow. We'll be leaving before dawn.'

Jax had nodded. 'How long is the journey?'

'Just under two hours,' Jarkoo had supplied, then turned to speak directly to Seti. 'Lau and Uzno will have risen but they'll be low on the horizon by the time you arrive. You'll be quite safe.'

His reference to the danger posed by the twin suns did not go unnoticed. Working on Autabron was difficult at the best of times, but travel on the surface at these mid-latitudes once the suns were higher in the sky was impossible.

'We will have a support flier, too, my lord. Just in case,' Finn had added.

'I'm sure we won't need it, though.' Once again, Setiyan had to have the last word and it was, as always, dismissive of Finn. Jax had sighed and looked under his lashes at his recalcitrant daughter. His mouth had been tight as he spoke.

'The lieutenant has taken a sensible precaution. Thank you, Finn. Thank you everyone.'

The meeting ended and all had risen to return to their quarters. Seti had kissed her father on the cheek and wished him a good night. As she turned to leave, he had taken her hand and pulled her back.

'Stop it. Stop baiting him.' His voice was low and clipped.

Her blue eyes had sparked defiantly. 'I don't know what you mean.'

'You have a choice to make, Seti. Back off or go home. I can send for your sister instead.' He didn't often speak to her like this, but his tone had sounded a warning that she knew to be serious.

'No!' She had let out a long sigh and her shoulders sagged in defeat. 'Very well. I'll try. But –'

'No buts. Do it.'

With a final shake of his head, he had released his grip and kissed her briefly on the forehead before bidding her goodnight. It was only once he had turned to gather his jacket and briefing notes that he had spotted Harrie still seated at the table. She was smiling up at him.

'Firm … I like that.' Her voice was like silk. 'Very attractive in a man.'

Jax did not move and he had refused to speak.

'You know, Kev, I would have behaved if –'

'If what?' he had barked. 'If you hadn't found someone with deeper pockets and a supply of your favourite hit?'

She had tucked her bobbed hair behind her ears. 'Darling …'

'Don't call me that.'

'Sweetie …'

'Or that!'

'Very well.' Finally she had seemed to show some recognition of his demeanour. She had taken a breath and stood up before continuing. 'Kev, I apologise. Sorry for being a bad girl. But all that – long time ago. Let's be friends. We've got to work together. May as well be pleasant.'

He had put on his jacket before speaking. His head was lowered and his eyes closed as he recalled the night he had discovered her deception. Suddenly, he had felt her hand on his arm and smelled the familiar spice of her scent. His nostrils had flared as he turned to face her.

'You're right. We must work together. But it doesn't have to be pleasant, and it won't be – for me.' He shook his head and brushed her hand off his arm. 'Why are you really here, Harrie? Why is C-7 involved? Did you know I was coming? Come to think of it, how long have you been on Autabron?'

'So many questions! Let me answer them over a drink.'

Unperturbed, she had swung away from him and sashayed towards the door. Without turning her head, she had said, 'Meet you in the bar in twenty minutes.'

Chapter Seven

Wika Dokau rose from the soft folds of Kalik Denkaun's bed and stared reflectively into the light of the glow-globe that hovered in the corner. The rock walls of the room emitted enough warmth to keep her from dressing and, besides, she gloried in her nakedness and knew her man did too. If Mira found her here, though, she would be angry. But Kalik would protect her. Of that she had no doubt, especially now.

She slid her feet into a pair of bikaskin sandals, one of the gifts to Kalik from the Gaksi leader Hanashi. They were too large but having the freedom to purloin his possessions was a privilege, a freedom even Mira was not allowed. Since becoming his concubine, Wika's position in the tribe had risen significantly and her father was immensely proud, despite the lack so far of the traditional formal bond of marriage. She was heart-sworn to Denkaun and marriage would surely follow.

'You bring honour to our family, my daughter,' he had said as her stroked her long white-blonde tresses. 'Even though he is not blood, he will be our leader and our family will rise with him. Do nothing to change this!'

And she would not. She would tread carefully around him – would not anger him. For his ire was as powerful as his strong hands that often pulled and squeezed her flesh when they made love. Yes, there was pain sometimes. But the surge of pleasure at his softer caresses, especially when he touched the most private places of her body, overwhelmed her. His fingers would find her and make her wet for him, make her crave him until he pushed open her legs and pumped his life-water into her. This was his gift to her and she greedily accepted it.

She went to the nightstand and poured warm water into the carved onyx bowl, adding a few drops of scented oil. It was a light floral perfume made from the blossom of the Huthon larka tree which she knew her man liked best. She cupped the water in her hands and let it trickle down her neck and breasts and belly, watching it puddle on the polished stone floor.

Suddenly, the door slid open and Kalik stood there, a silhouette in the glare of the light behind him. She could see a retinue of followers over his shoulder and moved her hands quickly to cover her nakedness.

'No! Let them see,' he barked. Her eyes widened, questioning his command. 'Let them see a true woman of the faith. A woman of belief!' His voice was deep and cavernous.

He walked across the room and stood behind her. His hands took hold of her arms and pulled them behind her back. She shook her hair forward to cover her breasts but he also swept up the tresses and would them around his fingers. She was completely exposed to the men and women of Guznon, who stood agape. Some of the women turned their heads away to lessen her shame, even some of the men. But most stood staring at her like hungry beasts at a mound of flesh.

'My lord, please,' she began. Then in a whisper, 'Kalik, my love …' She tried to twist her body around. This dishonour was too much! 'Please … Let me go,' she sobbed, the tears beginning to fall from her eyes.

'Why do you weep?' His voice boomed in her ear but he was talking to the crowd. 'You should be proud of who you are! Of what you will become! Of your dedication to me, the A'bat! For I am everything. I am the way. I am the hope. As this woman does, so shall you all.'

With this he pushed Wika down to the floor. She landed heavily on her knees, slipping in the water still there. It gave her the chance to at least use her hair to cover her body.

'So shall you all!' he repeated.

At this, the crowd took note and slowly, one by one, each man and woman dropped to their knees and bowed their heads. They began to chant: 'A'bat, A'bat …' The crescendo rose until Denkaun lifted a hand to stifle the noise.

'Enough! Go now!'

Wika could see the faces of the women now looking askance at her as they got up and moved away. Some showed pity, some disgust, but others – just a few – displayed envy. Indeed, they wanted to be where she was. Did they imagine they would gain power? Had she? No. But she would. When she told him her news, of what his life-water had created inside her belly, he would not treat her with such humiliation. She would never be on her knees before him again.

The door slid to a close and, finally, they were alone. Denkaun picked up a towel from the nightstand and threw it at her.

'Cover yourself.'

'My love,' she began, rubbing the soft fabric over her cold and wet body, 'may I speak?'

Denkaun walked over to the bed and pulled off his tunic. She saw the ripple of the muscles in his chest and arms as he stretched to remove his undershirt.

'About what?' he replied. His mood has changed. A few seconds ago he had been a ranting, domineering leader. But now it was as though all the breath had gone out of him. His shoulders sagged and he ruffled his fingers through his hair as if to shake out a great weight.

'I have news,' she started. She rose carefully and, gripping the towel, moved to stand before him at the bedside.

'So do I,' he countered. 'The Altani woman will be here soon. Tomorrow is your last day with me.'

Wika gasped. 'No! Please don't send me away.'

'It must be. You cannot be here.' His voice was matter-of-fact.

'No, my lord! I must be where you are,' she pleaded and instantly kneeled before him. She turned her face up, eyes wide. 'Please don't send me away. I must be near you. I love you.'

He shook his head and, as he stroked her hair and cupped her chin, he spoke soft words. 'Wika … Sweet Wika. It's impossible. You know what Mira has said, how important it is to bind the princess.'

'Alien bitch-queen! I hate her!' Wika spat the words back at him.

He grabbed her jaw, all softness now gone. 'The alien bitch-queen who will bear me a son! A son to follow me. A son to lead the Union. The prophecy cannot be tainted.'

'A son? Is that what you want? Is it?' Her voice rose, and although she knew she risked his anger, this was her last chance to stay by his side. 'Then *I* will give you a son.' She leaned back, further revealing her stomach. The bare mound below her waist showed the first signs of growth. She took one of his hands and pulled it down towards her belly. 'Here is your son! He grows within me.'

Denkaun froze. He had not expected this. His eyes, so tired and almost closed moments earlier, now flew open and his breath came fast.

He reached down and, placing both hands under her armpits, lifted her until she stood upright. Now level with his gaze, he stared at her abdomen, then ran his hands over her skin.

'It's true, lord.'

'How long have you known?'

'A month maybe,' she replied.

'And it's a boy?'

She nodded her confirmation. 'The mawkaan tested my waters. It is male.'

He sat on the bed. Wika could not hide her smile. The child inside would secure her place next to the A'bat. Even Mira would not try to banish her now and her father's faith in her would be validated. She reached down and tilted his chin so that she could see his face. 'I must stay, lord. You cannot risk the safety of your son.'

A cloud passed across his eyes and his shoulders dropped. There was a decision to be made. If Wika stayed in Beshwuk, she could threaten his plan to enthral the Altani princess. But if he sent her away, she might be at the mercy of his enemies, and he was not naïve enough to suspect he had none. Although he was the A'bat, the chosen one, there were always those hungry for power and riches who would take his place at any opportunity. The killing of his concubine and his child would be an enormous blow.

He rose from the bed. Pushing his fingers through her pale hair, he gripped the back of her head in his hands. His eyes drilled into hers. 'You will stay.'

She wanted to shout her triumph to the heavens. Mira would be furious, but she would be powerless against the A'bat. Kalik's word was law.

'But you will not be seen,' he added. 'You will be covered. Mira will bring you a parab tomorrow to wear in public.'

Wika's chin sank to her chest and her mouth was a tight line. The thought of being shrouded was intolerable. She had committed no crime. Parabs were worn only by those wicked men and women who had broken the law – thieves, adulterers and the like. Why such humiliation? What would her family think of such treatment?

'A parab? No! How can you say this? I have done nothing wrong!'

'I know this, but it is the only way I can keep you with me at this time. Your choice.' His words were so cool and offhand.

The stinging in her eyes took hold and tears fell across her cheeks. *Did he not see the pain his words caused?* But what were her options? Stay here, hidden from the world but close to him. Or banished to another settlement, never to see her man for who knows how long. He may even forget all about her in time as the months of her pregnancy passed. No. She needed to stay close, and if wearing the hated parab must be the price, she would pay it.

He had removed his pants while she considered her position and then sat down on the bed, naked in front of her. He pulled back the coverlet and patted the space next to him.

'Well?'

She brushed away the tears and swallowed as she nodded her submission. He reached across and pulled her towards him. She made only a token show of resistance, all of which dissipated with the first kiss he placed on her belly. He licked the skin of her stomach, then her breasts. His tongue circled her nipples and sucked them into his mouth. She still bore the traces of the fragrant oil she had used to wash earlier and its scent worked to arouse him. He pulled her closer until she could lift her knees onto the bed in order to straddle him.

'That's good, sweet Wika.' His voice was now as soft as the warm morning winds that greeted each new day. 'You will stay with me. You will be my secret love.'

He said 'love'! She could hardly believe it. He had never spoken thus before. No matter what the alien bitch-queen would come to mean to him, she, Wika Dokau, was his love! And as he plunged himself deep inside her, she threw back her head and cried for sheer joy.

Whilst Setiyan had had to submit to the emplacement of a tracker under the skin of her lower arm – her father had been immovable on this – she did not have to let Lieutenant Finn have it all is own way. Still smarting from his rebuke, calling her spoilt and entitled – *how dare he!* – she snapped a last bite of the breakfast pastry and threw it down. She would show him how capable she was of looking out for herself. The intriguing underground city of Zaz was waiting to be explored and she was going to have fun. *He wouldn't understand fun if it jumped up and smacked him in the face!* Although she had to confess that he had quite a nice face – and really nice eyes. Even so, the thought of it being slapped was quite energising.

The day was running on and, if she was to miss his dreaded return, she had to get moving. Given the familiarity of her profile in the media, she decided to use a holomask to cover her face and chose to project a three-dimensional file image of a thirty-something Autabroni woman. In this way she could go about the city unrecognised, although disguising her accent would be impossible. She looked forward to finding new clothes and trinkets and maybe jewellery – presents for her mother and grandmother and, of course, Calin, who she knew would have loved to be with her. No matter. She would make up for it by buying her something gorgeous to wear.

Within minutes of Finn's departure, Setiyan had thrown on a knee-length blue cloak with an attached hood, essential for hiding her wavy blonde hair. Though such colouring was not unusual among Autabronis, her curls would be noticeable. The long black pants and gloves she donned also hid her pale skin. She was confident she would appear just like any other traveller passing through the city.

The door slid open and, as luck would have it, the Autabroni escorts who had been stationed at the end of the passage were in the middle of a game of opponetix on their screens. So engrossed were they that they did not see her slink towards the emergency hoverplate at the other end of the level. Within seconds she had mounted the plate and zipped quietly away and upwards to the next level in the hotel's atrium. Jumping off, she walked to a glass exit panel through which she could espy a row of stalls and shops with throngs of people passing by.

Although the city was almost completely underground, natural light was filtered down through the levels via mirrors and skylights set into the surface that were kept free of the desert-blown sand and grit by means of a regular mechanical pulse. As a newcomer to the city, Seti looked up every time she heard the slight thumping noise of the pulses, but no one else seemed to notice them. The crowds were busy looking in windows, walking briskly or stopping to talk. In Genkarah, where there was so much more space, you would never see groups so close together. The people here were smartly dressed; they walked confidently and quickly. But she was keenly aware of the lack of diversity. There were no dark-haired Dasnirians or tall, green-skinned

Huthons here. Even Altanis were few and far between and she'd spotted only one Earthan – a woman – looking at a café's menu screen. The people passing along the balconies and verandas that surrounded the central atria nearly all had shades of red skin and with elegantly styled blond hair, even the few children.

She suddenly realised that she had hardly moved from the glass doorway. If Seti wanted a little freedom she would have to get moving or Finn would easily catch up to her.

She strode to the end of the level and jumped onto a public veyor that was about to leave the platform. She had not seen where it was headed but that was unimportant. In fact, the more mysterious and unknown the better.

There was almost too much to take in. She had never seen so many people in such a confined urban space before, and a variety of doorways and cave-dwellings sped past so quickly that she could barely glimpse into them. The veyor spiralled deeper into the city and others passed it, returning towards the surface. All at once, she saw what looked like a park coming up. It was set high up on a central plinth fifty metres or so above the base level of the city. The idea of a green, open space four hundred metres below ground was so compelling that she decided to get off and explore further.

A flower-covered walkway led from the platform to the park. People hurried past, some even giving her a brief nod before continuing on their way. A delicious smell of rich, tasty spices wafted from a squat kiosk up ahead. She had to try whatever it was they were selling.

'Morrow, good woman!' The vendor was an old man, his head swathed in a cream cotton headdress and his black robes held back by a shimmering apron of opalescent fabric. 'My wares tempt you, eh?'

'Indeed they do,' she replied, smiling. 'What are these?' She pointed to some sausage-shaped delicacies that sat behind an opaque shield.

'Ah! My speciality. Karokaran dumplings served with a feir dipping sauce. You will love them. Only two keks!' he pronounced.

'And these?' She pointed to red strips of what looked like grilled meat.

The old man's eyes lit up. 'Oh ho! You are an adventurous traveller to ask for prized bika slivers. How about you try a little of both? I give you a sample.'

Seti was about to agree when she realised that she would have to disable her mask in order to eat. 'Ah ... No, but I will buy the dumplings and one sliver to take home.'

'Good, good. But eat here in the gardens before they go cold is my advice.'

His smile revealed some missing teeth and Seti wondered if years of eating tough bika meat had contributed to the gaps. With a returning grin, she raised her left hand to have her credits scanned. The old man quickly plated her food and proffered it, all the while exclaiming his gratitude and imploring her to come again.

She waved her thanks as she walked away further into the gardens before disengaging the holomask and lifting the meat to her mouth. It was a little overcooked but tasty and, after skimping on her breakfast to dodge Lieutenant Finn, its goodness and flavour were very welcome.

The trees in the park were like nothing she had ever seen, small and squat, barely three metres high, but perfectly formed. One took her interest, its blossoms bright orange and shaped like a spiral shell of the kind she and her father had collected on the beaches near his family's home in Elidian back on Earth. She reached up to touch one but, as she drew a finger over the bloom, it emitted a shrill squeal and snapped itself inside the nearest leaf. She laughed and reached for another.

'It's a deego. Most people call it the screaming tree.'

Seti swivelled round and saw that the voice belonged to a young Autabroni seated on a bench. His eyes were shrouded by a heavy brow, but his height when he stood allowed her to see his face quite clearly. He smiled without showing his teeth, strands of hair stuck to his clammy-looking skin. His sunken cheeks made her think he might be ill.

'The neighbours around here won't thank you for making such a noise.' He came and stood next to her.

She shrugged. 'Then I apologise. I'm a traveller here.'

The smile, such as it was, disappeared. 'That is obvious. You should not be here alone.' His voice was emphatic, almost scolding. She did not need another Lieutenant Finn telling her what to do.

'Thank you for your advice.' She nodded and turned to walk away.

'I will accompany you … For safety.'

She stopped and faced him. 'Thank you but no. I prefer to walk alone.'

He took a step closer. 'This is a dangerous neighbourhood. The park harbours thieves and vandals. I will come with –'

'I said no!' she interjected. Did this man think she was unarmed? If so, he was much mistaken. She moved her hand closer to the small dirk tucked into the waistband of her pants.

He raised his hands as if in supplication. 'My apologies, good woman. Go in peace.' From any other lips, the salutation would have sounded submissive. But there was an edge to his voice that made her skin crawl.

She turned on the spot and walked away. In the near distance was a small pool with a fountain and people nearby. Safety. Even so, she had to pass through a pergola of vines some fifty metres long. She looked over her shoulder – the man had gone and she allowed herself a deep breath. He had been right about one thing: this was not a nice neighbourhood. She noticed now that the gardens were unkempt, plants untrimmed with weeds between cracks in the path. Perhaps she should make her way back to the veyor platform. After all, she had presents to buy.

She shook off the feelings of unease and had pressed on towards the tinkling fountain when suddenly her arms were wrenched behind her back. In front of her stood the heavy-browed Autabroni, his eyes glinting with disgust. Before she could call out, a filthy hand smothered her mouth and her head was pinned tight to the chest of the man's accomplice. She couldn't even swivel her head to see who was holding her.

'You should have heeded my warning, woman,' the Autabroni snarled. 'A bad neighbourhood.'

She struggled against the restraining arms of her captor, but he must have been a full two heads taller than she and his hand across her mouth felt like an iron plate riveted to her face.

The black eyes scanned her from head to toe as though weighing her worth. But she could tell that he had not recognised her.

'Oh, what treasure we have found. Here's a pretty thing.' He spoke to his partner but his eyes focused on her

He came closer, so close that she could smell the fetid breath from the slit of his mouth. He pulled apart the folds of her cloak and murmured a low growl at the rise of her breasts under the pink silk blouse.

'You seek to tempt me, woman,' he drawled, 'and if I had more time, I would let you. I want only your credits – today.'

With that he withdrew a scanner from his pocket and yanked her wrist from behind her back. She tried to pull her hand away but his grip was too firm. As he held the device his dark smile grew wider.

'Oh! We caught a tasty morsel today, Niraak.'

The man holding her laughed as he too saw the scanned credits loading. 'In more ways than one, Liem. Let's take her.'

Seti tried to scream. The robber's hand held firm and only pitiful gurgles came from her throat.

'A pleasant thought, my friend. But no. We have all we need,' Liem replied.

Seti was relieved that the terror would soon be over. At least they weren't going to kidnap her – or worse. Then the unthinkable happened.

'But you're right, my friend. Why not take a little pleasure?' Liem looked around. No one was in sight. Suddenly he ripped open her blouse, licking his thin lips at the sight of her naked breasts. 'Oh … So good …'

Seti tried again to scream and struggled wildly. She raised her right leg and slammed her heel back down as hard as she could onto her captor's foot. With a yelp, he wrenched her head back hard into his chest. The pressure on her jaw and mouth was unbearable and tears fell from the corners of her eyes.

Liem laughed. 'You have spirit, woman. Yes, I think we should like to ride this alien bitch, eh, Niraak? Bring her!'

He turned on his heel, gesturing for his partner to follow, when a sudden crashing noise came from above. A dark figure fell through the vines of the walkway and slammed a punch like iron into Liem's lower abdomen, toppling him to the ground. He screeched with pain. The attacker swung a leg to kick the Autabroni and, at the same time, withdrew a laser from his belt and pointed it squarely at the head of Niraak.

'Let her go and you live!' Finn's voice was pure steel.

Through the gap in the vines, Seti saw a windshifter hovering and another figure dropped to the ground, landing lightly with weapons ready. Niraak's eyes flew back and forth. Outmanned and outgunned, it would be stupid to resist. He released his hold on Seti, who instantly fell to the hard-packed earth. She flipped over immediately and raised a leg to deliver a kick to his left shin. Niraak yelled and instinctively went to kick her back, but a finely aimed shot from Finn's laser to his thigh toppled him.

Finn signalled to the guard to bind Liem's hands, who was still lying prone and trying to regain his breath. Then Niraak was restrained and left in a sitting position, still groaning from the injury to his upper leg.

Finn moved over to Seti. 'Princess ...' He held out a hand to raise her from the ground, which she accepted. 'Are you all right? Here, let me ...' She was trying to pull the flaps of her cloak to cover her torn blouse. As she rose, Finn averted his eyes.

This was the time when he should have been gloating, Seti thought. Had she not proved his point that she needed a bodyguard, just as he said? But instead he held her safely in his arms while he gave orders to the guard and spoke into his comms for the local police to hurry.

'Don't worry, it's over now. We'll soon have these two put away.' Did he realise that he was stroking her hair as he said this? 'We'll get you back to the hotel and cleaned up. It'll be all right.'

It was ridiculous how comforted she felt by these small actions and strange that the warmth of this man's arms around her made her heart skip a beat. Only now that it was over did she remember that she had been shaking with fear. She could breathe again, and the relief that the worst had not happened was overwhelming. She felt her knees give way and would have fallen except for the lieutenant's powerful arms. He swept her into the windshifter, which had now landed on the adjacent lawn. Guiding her to a rear seat, Finn issued a final order to the first guard to wait for the police then took the controls.

They ascended slowly, following the same rising spiral that the veyors took to return to the surface. As the levels went past and they rose higher, more crowds appeared. Finn noticed her gaze and spoke gently. 'Maybe this afternoon some shopping. When you're feeling better.'

She nodded weakly and tried to smile.

The rear dock of the hotel came into view and Finn settled the windshifter back into its bay. He took Seti to her room with a promise to stay outside until she was ready to leave, sitting on a bench in the passageway.

As the door closed behind her she recalled the touch of his hand stroking her hair and the tenderness of his strong arms encasing her. She had felt his breath on her neck and she wondered if he had felt the pounding of *her* heart as surely as she had felt the drumming of his.

Avad Jarkoo downed the last of his wine. It was a vintage directly imported from the Yeljo vineyard in Hutho's Esor Valley, very expensive, very delicious and the perfect accompaniment to the bika fillet they had just enjoyed. He twirled the empty crystal goblet in his fingers, watching the light play over its facets before placing it delicately back onto the table.

'That was a good choice. 'S there anymore?' he asked his companion. His words were slurred.

Harrie grimaced. 'Not for you.'

The evening had not passed quickly enough and Jarkoo's behaviour had struck her as increasingly tedious. Her relationship with the mine's director had been entertaining when she had first visited Autabron over a year ago at the start of the mission. But she had found its resumption on this second visit to be a little flat – and that was even before Kevor Jax's arrival.

'You think I'm drunk? Well, I'm not,' he insisted. 'At least, not drunk enough. I know why you're here, lady spy. I know what you're up to. You can't fool me.'

Harrie's face was a mask as she allowed the man to rant on.

'You're watching me. Do you tell your bosses I'm incompetent? Will you tell them I'm drunk tonight? Yes, I think so. I think you will tell them I'm the wrong man for the job. But too late! I'm the *only* man, and whether you like it or not, you're stuck with me.'

Her smile was indifferent. She flicked a speck of fluff from her skirt and sighed. 'Oh, how you do run on, Avad.'

'Stuck – with me. No one else to do your dirty work, lady spy. Just me!'

'If you say so.'

The ravings were becoming tiresome. Harrie stood and dipped down to collect her wrap, a luscious red silk embroidered with dark fuchsia flowers.

'Oh, so now you've had enough of me? You've got what you wanted and now you walk away.'

'Tired. Need sleep.' Her voice was flat. He was such a bore these days. Once he had become C-7's operative all those months ago he had lost his fascination. The sex had become much the same as it always was after the first few weeks.

It hadn't been like that with Kev. He had been so damn good-looking with a body to die for, and the sex had been amazing. It was true, though. She had blown it. Her father had been furious. She could have been the wife of the only son of the United Democratic Nation's president. *Think of the power that would have brought!* But Harrie had always been honest, if only with herself. She knew that even with Kevor Jax Bashir at her side she would have tired of him eventually, and he was too noble to entertain her need for the odd lover or two. Then there were the drugs. The escape was so delicious, but Kev had never felt the need for them. He already had such a charmed life – wealth, influence, a great job and a family that loved him. What would be the point in seeking the forgetfulness of a narcotic world?

And now, here he was. Age had almost improved him. With a few silver hairs at his temples and flecked through his stubble, he was still an attractive man. His body appeared to be rock hard too, so he obviously looked after himself. It seemed such a shame that he kept himself for his wife. After all these years, she realised that she more than wanted him. She craved him, just like a drug. Avad Jarkoo was now nothing more than an irritation, and once this mission was over, she would dispose of him – permanently.

'Stay! Come on. I'm sh-orry,' he pleaded with her. 'Don't sleep. Let's have sex. I'll make it good for you. I promise.'

'Don't make promises you can't keep.' She drew the folds of the wrap around her cleavage. Jarkoo frowned.

97

'I will keep … I promise,' he cajoled. Then, seeing the stony look on her face, he changed tack. 'Can't go yet. We must speak of dosages.'

'Go to bed, Avad.' Her interruption was final. 'We'll talk in the morning.' With that, she swung away and moved swiftly to the doorway.

'What? Not even a kiss goodnight?'

She stopped dead and, without bothering to turn her head, she sighed heavily and pressed the door control panel. 'Bed!'

The door slid closed behind her. As she walked along the balcony towards the veyor, she reflected on the compact she had made with Jarkoo. It was her father who had come up with the idea of drugging the workers' water supply. Since joining the Galactic Union over twenty-five years ago, Earthan resource companies had taken an increasing slice of mining industries on the other four planets. Even the monolithic GKD company had been slowly eaten up by the Earthan minerals giant Millien Inc., which now owned slightly over thirty-five percent of its shares. When her father had been approached by Millien's chairman, Natesha Koskinen, he had been unsure about getting involved. She had voiced her strong concerns about the growing anger of the workers, but its impact on output at the mines on Autabron, whilst important for Ms Koskinen, had been of little interest for him. However, Anthony Whitton-Blake, soon to retire as the head of Covert-7, listened while she spoke of the connection between irate workers and political instability on the remote planet. Such disturbances had a habit of spreading and, whilst C-7's purview was the monitoring of unrest on Earth, she had evidence of correspondence between the respective workers' unions. Trouble was brewing. It was spreading like a cancer and, she put to him, what could be done to cut it out before it grew too big?

Whitton-Blake came up with the idea that if you couldn't remove the anger by giving the miners what they wanted – an increase in pay and better conditions, something Ms Koskinen was dead against – then another means could be employed. Drugs were often used to control mood on Earth. Even the formal behaviours of the Altanis were relaxed by the use of fre-gath, a recreational drug. Unfortunately, this had only a short-term effect. It was also easy to detect in the bloodstream. However, a few days of research proved fruitful. Of all the thousands of toxins he studied, urthrengo, a compound developed on

Hutho, was the most effective in controlling both mood and behaviour in the longer term. It was, as he put it, the ultimate truth-serum.

His next problem was in how to administer it to the workers on Autabron so that its effects were continuous and useful, and that brought him to the ways various efficacious drugs were given to the population of Earth. It could not be given as a vaccine, the potency of which could result in severe illness or death. And the workers could not be guaranteed to take it as a medicine on a regular basis, even if they believed any public health message associated with it. But then, Whitton-Blake mused to himself, did the miners need to know they were receiving it? Especially if the dosage was low enough to be virtually undetectable? Then he came across the history of fluoride, a chemical added to drinking water on Earth to improve dental health over a millennia ago.

All that was left to do was find a source of the drug, get it to Autabron and find someone to be complicit in its delivery into the water supply. The fact that not only workers would be subdued by its relaxant effects but *all* men, women and children in mining communities across the planet did not faze him. It was well known that Autabronis were a feisty, temperamental people. It would do them all good to calm down.

Harrie agreed to set up the project. She'd targeted Jarkoo and used sex to recruit him. Then, on finding a nasty skeleton in Professor Hasler's closet from his school days involving an accusation of rape – the girl having been paid off by Hasler's mother – she secured his cooperation in importing the urthrengo, his lab being the only facility with the necessary approvals. Jarkoo, in turn, suborned a manager at the utilities department to drip-feed the drug into the water system, telling her that it was an additive that promoted muscle growth. What Autabroni man or woman did not want greater physical strength?

It had all gone incredibly well. Within weeks, workers' protests had tailed off, production had increased and things appeared to be returning to normal. Then, a few months ago, with the destruction of the sacred Euta Sakek, new anger flared and old grievances resurfaced. Harrie deduced that the Autabronis may have built up a tolerance to the drug. Did they need to up the dosage? It looked likely.

Enough for tonight. She was tired and needed to sleep. The Princess Setiyan would be gone by the time she woke in the morning and poor Kev would be missing her. His darling daughter out there in the Beshwuk wilderness where anything could happen. She had already had a skirmish with muggers that morning. Danger lurked everywhere and Kev would worry. He would need someone to comfort him. And who better than his old friend and lover?

Chapter Eight

A full hour before the first of the twin suns, Lau, rose above the horizon, they were called to the docking chamber. Finn had hardly slept the night before, both from restlessly rehashing the dangers of Seti's mugging and thinking about his response to her. Every nerve and muscle warned him not to get involved. Why couldn't his heart feel the same?

Over dinner last night she had talked enthusiastically about leading her own team into the more remote regions of Autabron and her eyes had sparkled every time they connected with his. Did they hold a promise of something more, or was he imagining it? Either way, he'd be a fool to let his guard down and especially not in the next few days. Seti had spoken animatedly about the Guznon, displaying her breadth of research. But was this for his benefit or her father's? Even so, they knew little about these areas where people lived a traditional life, so unlike those who had come to work in the mines. Finn had reminded her and Serekunda of the need to be watchful during their visit and she had not responded with her usual disregard, which surprised both he and Jax.

As for Finn, the return to the Beshwuk Highlands was not altogether unpleasant. Although his earlier time there had been brief, he appreciated the landscape. Raw red mountains spiked into the clear skies like shards of burnished metal forced through swathes of deep orange sand. His hosts back then had taken him to a viewing platform that revealed the full, treacherous beauty of the desert. As the suns had risen higher in the sky, the heat haze made the land shimmer and broil. He imagined that he, Setiyan and Pieter Serekunda would be shown such a sight once they arrived. But for now, the ninety-minute journey by aerporter lay ahead of them and he hoped to pass the time in contemplation of the pre-dawn scenery, rather than the physical attractions of the young princess.

'Lieutenant Finn! Good morning.' Pieter Serekunda jumped up as Finn entered the docking chamber's anteroom.

'Good morning, Doctor Serekunda.'

'You look a little sleepy, lieutenant. Late night?' Serekunda's smile was accompanied by a wink.

'More restless than late. Going over equipment and schedules.'

'Very diligent of you,' Serekunda offered. 'I, on the other hand, slept like a baby.'

Finn smiled. He had had reservations about the social scientist at first. Serekunda seemed too quick with his opinions and, in Finn's experience, it was better to hold your tongue until you knew enough to make a useful comment. But Serekunda jumped straight into any conversation and did not shy away from asking questions. It was, Finn now believed, borne of a desire to know as much as possible rather than arrogance.

'That's good, because where we are going, the beds are not as comfortable,' Finn replied with a quick smile.

Serekunda grimaced. 'Once you've experienced the delights of living with the D'nongra people on Hutho – sleeping in hammocks five hundred metres above the forest floor – anything is comfortable. Trust me, turning over in your sleep was not an option.'

As Finn laughed out loud, the door panel slid open and Setiyan entered. On seeing her his smile faded as quickly as his heart began beating faster.

'Good morning. What's the joke?' she asked, smiling.

'Oh, nothing, my lady. Just remembering a project I once visited,' Serekunda responded. 'Did you sleep well? I heard about your terrible experience yesterday. I hope you're not hurt.'

'No, I'm fine. And I slept well enough, thank you for asking.' At this she looked directly at Finn, but he was busy fixing a strap on his pack.

'A bad business. Thank goodness the lieutenant here was able to get to you so quickly.'

'Yes. Very fortunate,' she replied, still looking at Finn.

This time he caught the friendly glance but did not trust himself to speak.

'Thank you, Lieutenant Finn. I might not have said it enough yesterday but I am truly grateful for your intervention.'

He put the pack down and nodded to her, a fleeting smile on his lips. 'All part of the service, princess.'

As they walked along the metal walkway leading to their aerporter, Finn scooped her case out of her hand. He instantly pretended to drop it, looking up at her with a grin on his face as he did so. 'You know, there're already a whole heap of rocks on this planet. You didn't need to pack more.'

He was rewarded with a smile that took his breath away.

As the closest of the Union planets to her homeworld, Calin and Setiyan had visited the family's lodge on Hutho many times over the course of their childhood, most often in the company of their mother. But when Calin's grandmother, Li-el Dacas, the dowager Ki-consort, suggested she accompany her to Hutho, she was more than a little surprised. Grandmother rarely left the palace in Genkarah these days, preferring its comfort and closeness to all the delights and amusements of the city. One thing they could always be certain of, though, was Li-el's ability to shock and bemuse.

'I always loved the lodge,' Li-el pronounced while sipping her dish of sinnsey tea.

'Excuse me?' Linnayen's eyes flew open. 'Since when? I recall you complaining to Father that the place was cold and draughty.'

'Well, yes, it is in winter,' the older woman conceded. 'But in springtime ... Ah, the blossom! The fresh air! Very invigorating.'

The mottled shade of the flower-decked palace balcony was pleasant. Far below, Genkarah bustled in the midday sunshine. Windshifters glided smoothly between the glass and polished metal towers and, below these, tiny figures wove through the dark green parks and along pathways. Calin had invited both her mother and grandmother to take tea with her before she set off on her journey to Hutho that afternoon. At her mother's suggestion, she was going to investigate the source of the urthrengo that had been shipped to Professor Hasler's laboratory and see if she could find out more about the controls on its production.

'Another memory, Mother. After all these years, things still come back to you,' Calin noted.

Linnayen's eyes opened wide with surprise. 'So they do!' A flash of her dead father's laughing face came into her mind. Yenshar had been so stiff and formal in public, but not with her and Evica. She smiled wistfully. 'Though not often. Just snatches here and there.'

'Even so, it must be good to find those missing pieces. To remember what you were like when you were younger and first met Pa.' Calin's smile contained the simple hope of the young.

Linnayen glanced at her mother and Calin could not help but see the private signal that passed between them. Not all the memories were happy and some would be better left alone.

Li-el reached across the table and took Calin's hand. 'I remember meeting your grandfather for the first time. I didn't take to him.'

Linnayen laughed.

'It's true. I didn't like his looks. If I'm honest, he looked a bit rough. Unkempt. You see, I had been brought up to expect a certain level of nobility. All the young men I met were from good families. They had impeccable taste and good manners and they always looked so handsome.' The old woman smiled at the retelling of a story that Linnayen and Calin had heard many times before. 'I was quite a catch. The Dacas line had three Kis in its history, you know. The Genaras only had one – before Yenshar, of course.'

'But you came to love Grandfather, though.' This was more statement than question and Calin smiled at her mother. They knew Li-el would take up her story.

'Love? More like than love at first. And respect, yes. Most definitely. Indeed, it was my respect for him as a statesman and a military leader that led me to love him.'

'And, I've been told, the intervention of a certain woman,' Linnayen interrupted.

'Oh, she was nothing!' Li-el brushed the thought away with a sweep of her hand. 'The women of the Shayra family are known for their loose ways. Unara got nowhere with him!'

'Be honest, Mother. She made him more attractive to you.'

Calin found herself giggling quietly at this interchange between her two favourite women, both so regal in the outside world yet so familiar within the family.

'Well, she made me see his potential, shall we say.'

Calin couldn't resist faking a swoon. 'And his handsome green eyes. And his strong arms. And his –'

'That's enough!' Linnayen admonished with a grin.

'Needless to say,' Li-el continued, 'love blossomed and for a few short years we were happy. But the war … His duties took him away from me, you understand. We never meant to drift apart, but …'

Linnayen reached across and stroked her mother's cheek, feeling the soft near-translucent skin beneath her fingers and hoping that her touch brought some comfort. 'That's all right, Mother. I'm sure he knew you loved him.'

'Did he?'

The look in the older woman's eyes could have crushed a lesser soul. It was difficult to witness these changes in her mother. This once powerful, imperious woman, so self-assured, was becoming ever more uncertain and reflective. Linnayen could not help but be worried.

'Yes, Mother. He did,' she replied softly. 'As do we all. Which is why I don't want you travelling to Hutho.'

'But I could be company for Calin …'

'Thanks all the same, Grandmother, but I'm fine. I'll be busy. And, no offence, but –'

'You'll slow her down, Mother,' Linnayen interjected. 'She has a job to do. It's not a sightseeing trip.'

Calin nodded her agreement. 'And I don't have much time. I've got to find out who made so much of this drug *and* who commissioned its production.'

'And if it's still going on,' Linnayen added, before turning back to Li-el. 'It's not a place for you at this time, Mother. And Calin will be perfectly safe. She'll have security and one of her Min cousins, Falvii, will meet her on Hutho. She'll be well looked after.'

The old woman did not look convinced. Her eyes, still fierce, bored into Linnayen's. 'Do I know him? Can we trust him?'

Calin laughed and moved to kneel in front of her grandmother. She took the woman's hands in hers and kissed them gently. 'Yes, we all met him at Aunt Evica and Uncle Tariik's twentieth wedding anniversary. He's the son of Tariik's older brother, Odar.'

'He was quite dashing as I recall,' said Linnayen. 'Do you remember him, Calin?'

'Not really. My mind was elsewhere.'

'You were finishing your studies at the academy, I remember.' Linnayen smiled fondly at the memory of the quiet little girl who so often had her head buried in a vidscreen while her elder sister was going to parties, mountain climbing and flying fast windshifters. Calin was perfectly happy in her reclusive way. It was understandable that she might have no memory of her flamboyant Min cousin. Linnayen only hoped that he had matured and settled down, as Evica had vowed to her.

'Trust me, sister. He's a different young man these days,' Evica had said. 'He did very well at the cadet school and he graduated with honours at university in political science and philosophy, of all things!'

Evica went on to tell her that Falvii Min was now teaching at the senior academy in the city of Ruk on Hutho and seemed to be doing very well. He would look forward to seeing Calin again, she was sure, and he had taken leave from his work to accompany her over the next few weeks. Linnayen had been mollified by this news. Perhaps Calin and Falvii would get along after all.

She was shaken from her reflection by Calin announcing that it was time for her to leave.

'Stay safe, my sweet,' Linnayen ordered as she stood and took her daughter into her arms for a final hug. 'Don't do anything reckless.'

'It's me, Mother, not Seti. I'll be fine.'

'And report back every twelve hours. You remember?'

Calin rolled her eyes, smiled and gave her mother a kiss on the cheek. 'I'm sure you won't let me forget.'

She dipped down to kiss Li-el and gave another quick hug to Linnayen. With that she left.

Linnayen collapsed back onto her seat. The two women sat looking at the view before them, mute in their thoughts. Linnayen had never had both her children away from her at the same time before. It seemed unnatural. And they were both in positions that could put them in danger. News of Seti's encounter with the thieves on Autabron had been deeply worrying and she had never been more glad that she had insisted on the presence of a bodyguard. But would Falvii Min be able to look after her gentle Calin if there was trouble on Hutho? A teacher-cum-political scientist was hardly a bodyguard. But it was done now. Jax had agreed on this course of action and had said that he had faith in Evica's summation of the man. Time would tell.

Li-el stood up and laid a hand on Linnayen's cheek. It caught a tear that had tricked from the younger woman's eye.

'If you're that worried, daughter, perhaps you should go yourself.'

Linnayen's sigh shuddered through her whole body. 'Oh, Mother,' she moaned, 'They're all away. Jax. The girls. I hate being alone.'

Li-el stroked her daughter's long black hair and said with a happy smile, 'Then it's just as well I decided not to go with Calin, eh?'

At first, flying from Zaz with just starlight to guide them, she could make out nothing of the landscape. The deep navy above sprinkled with crisp white stars and the complete blackness of the ground below made the first sixty minutes or so of the journey uninteresting. But gradually, a pale light began to creep across the barren brown wastes and, as more features became apparent, Seti moved closer to the windows of the aerporter. A mere two or three thousand metres below she could make out flat rocky plains, mostly featureless apart from the occasional puff of dust. Off in the far distance, the silhouettes of sharp mountains rose like dog's teeth against the dark indigo of the night sky. But, within minutes, the peaks picked up the first rays of Lau and glowed with a golden brilliance.

'Look at that!' Seti called across to Finn and Doctor Serekunda. 'It's so beautiful. The colours!'

'Wait a few more minutes and you'll see another phenomenon,' advised Finn.

'What?' asked Serekunda.

'The dew-rise. Every morning, without fail, what little moisture there is in this godforsaken land is trapped in the lowlands and deep valleys,' Finn explained. 'Before the suns' rays can reach into them, the mist sits in the crevices. But once the warmth is felt, they dissipate in bubbles of steam. Keep watching. It's quite a sight.'

Seti returned her gaze to the window, as did Serekunda. He was the first to comment.

'Ah! I see it now. Look, lady. See the mist everywhere.'

'Yes! Like ribbons. Like it's alive.' Seti's voice rose with wonder at what they were seeing.

Finn laughed. 'That's about the only thing that *can* live on this surface. And then only briefly.'

'Such a shame. It's so beautiful like this,' she replied.

'As is the nature of beauty. So often fleeting, so rarely found.' The doctor was in a contemplative mood. Seti smiled at him, then Finn. *How had she never noticed those warm brown eyes?*

Before much longer they were a mere thirty kliks from the Beshwuk dock and the dew swirls were long gone. The corona of the second sun, Uzno, had just clipped the horizon. The jagged outline of the highlands was fast approaching and the now rust-coloured sand plains were left behind.

Coming closer to their destination, the aerporter swung around an arm of the nearest mountain and, suddenly, they were plunged into deep shadow. Only the lights of the vessel picked out the open doors of a dock. With decreasing speed, they glided smoothly into the rock-walled bay and the pilot set the craft down on one of four raised metallic pods. Immediately, the dock doors slid closed behind them. It was clearly important to keep the warming air out as much as possible.

Through the window Seti could see Guznon tribesmen and women in their orange robes gathered to meet them. At the head of the reception party she made out an older woman with pure white hair and a deeper red tinge to her skin. She wore a headdress of polished stones that sat like a crown across her forehead. Could this be Mira, she wondered, the shaman who had invited them? If so, she was not surprised the people followed her. She was stately and her black robes, trimmed with white felt, fell in many folds down to the ground. She held a staff, but her majestic bearing belied any need to use it for support.

'Coming?' Pieter Serekunda asked, before lightly tapping her shoulder.

Seti was still transfixed by the scene. 'Right. Yes.'

'Big moment, eh?' Serekunda smiled.

She returned the smile with a nod but the frown lines between her eyes said it all.

'There's no need to be nervous, princess.' This was Finn.

'I'm not,' she retorted. 'I just want to make a good impression.'

'Then don't speak,' Serekunda advised.

'Excuse me?' She had been used to such rudeness from the lieutenant. But Serekunda?

'Don't speak *first*,' he explained. 'Their custom is to spend some moments in ceremonial greeting during which time you say nothing. And you must let one of us speak first ... because we are male.'

Finn was grinning. This was clearly the highlight of his morning so far.

'So when *can* I speak?' Her hands went to her hips.

Finn supplied the answer. 'When you're spoken to, princess.'

If she could have wiped the grin off his face right then and there she would have done so with immense pleasure.

The vessel's doors sloughed open and the warm dry air pushed into the cabin. Pieter Serekunda took the lead followed by Seti, then Finn pulling up the rear. They stepped off the ramp and onto the platform where Mira and a host of Guznon men and women waited silently for them. As they drew closer to Mira, a low chant began. The crowd hummed and then began to sway in unison in a circular motion. It reminded Seti of the shoaling of the kipr'aa fish in the lake back home on Genkarah. She and Calin often used to run down to the lake shore as small children and paddle in the blue water. They would squeal with pleasure as hundreds of the opalescent fish swam back and forth between their legs, weaving a slow single-minded figure-of-eight as their scales caught the sunlight. She couldn't help but smile at the recollection and then briefly wondered what Calin was doing at that moment.

Serekunda stopped in front of the shaman. Seti drew up to his right and Finn joined them so that she was flanked by them both. Mira's black eyes, with barely a trace of white in the sclera, were fixed on her as the old woman began speaking in the Guznon tongue. Her words were like the chant – mesmerising – and Seti had no clue what they meant. So she kept her face impassive, trying to meet the old woman's gaze, even though she desperately wanted to look all around. Finally, Mira raised her hand and the crowd stopped its noise and motion. She slammed her staff onto the ground in front of her and the metal tip drew a spark from the rock floor. Then, at last, she moved her gaze from Seti to Serekunda.

'Our greetings to you, Doctor Pieter Serekunda. You are welcome in our hearts.'

Serekunda bowed his head and laid his right hand upon his chest as a mark of respect. Mira repeated the same words to Finn, using his full title, and he copied Serekunda's response. Then she came to Setiyan and waited a full minute just looking at her before speaking.

Seti raised her chin as though about to speak when, suddenly, she heard Finn cough – a signal to stay silent.

'Great princess! Setiyan Genara of Altan. Daughter of the Ki Linnayen, most gracious Lady of Light. Long have we waited for you! You are welcome in our hearts. Our A'batau!' With which words and using her staff for a scaffold, she kneeled in front of Seti and bowed her head.

Before Seti could respond, the crowd took up the chant once more, only this time louder. Its sway became more pronounced. In her mind she repeated the word that Mira had used, 'A'batau', and wondered what it meant.

Seti threw a questioning look to Finn whose eyes were as round as her own. *What should I do?* He shook his head, obviously as nonplussed as she was. She nodded her acknowledgement and Mira, now standing, once more struck her staff on the ground. The chanting immediately ceased.

'Great princess. Come with me. We have a chamber prepared.' The old woman spoke clearly and slowly. Her Guznon accent was strong but Seti had no difficulty making out the words. Remembering Serekunda and Finn's earlier instruction, she now took the opportunity to reply.

'Thank you, lady. You do me and my companions much honour with your kind welcome. I will follow you.'

Apparently it worked. A toothy grin spread across the old shaman's face. 'Gracious as well as beautiful. This bodes well for your stay with our people.'

Seti smiled in return. Mira raised her hand as she moved to walk away and the crowd parted obediently to let them pass. Over her shoulder, Seti saw Finn and Serekunda fall in step behind them, both giving the other a questioning look. Finn shrugged his shoulders and Serekunda exhaled a breath which he seemed to have been holding for the last five minutes.

The introduction had gone well indeed and she could not help but wonder why Lieutenant Finn had been so worried. He had called the Guznon 'abrupt' and 'insular', 'easily riled'. But Lady Mira had been charming. Seti was encouraged by this start to their mission and saw no reason why it would not meet with every success.

Sen-Caspiran and Birkaan had spent a couple of days poring over a pile of GKD production reports, trying to match dates to shift workers' names and plant locales. They had put the information through every variable and algorithm they could think of: time, place, person, amount of ore, concentration of ore, and so on. Nothing had jumped out so far. All they could faithfully report was that over the past year, the amount and quality of the ore had dropped by around six percent, with no significant spikes or even dips, just a steady decrease.

'From this data, we can only conclude,' Sen-Caspiran said, 'that this is a natural phenomenon and it's continuing. Ore seams have been worked out.'

'So, in effect,' Birkaan added, 'the company cannot produce bergussian at the same level because the ore just isn't there anymore. At least, not in the existing mine sites.'

Caspiran nodded. 'Meaning that all we can recommend is that the company explores new areas, undertakes new surveys to locate profitable locations.'

Jax frowned. This was what he had feared. Had they reached the tipping point of production? And, if so, how much longer could they continue to dredge the strata of Autabron for its riches?

'We may have to conclude, both to the company and the Union, that Autabron has entered the last phase of its profitability.' Jax shook his head sadly. 'A shame, but it forces us to develop other resources.'

'Costly.' This was Harrie. She reclined languidly in a chair at the far end of the conference room table and, as always, never spoke more than she needed to.

This latest show of negativity needled Jax. 'But important! And, ultimately, necessary.'

'Just saying.' Harrie batted away his comment as if it were a bothersome fly.

Caspiran spoke again. 'GKD will not like our conclusion or recommendations. But we can't tailor facts that are not in evidence to suit their expectations. Unless you have uncovered anything in your investigation, Ms Whitton?'

'Not a sausage. Workers' demeanour went from unpleasant, to improved and back to grizzly again. Can't find a cause.'

'Apart from the lack of a pay-rise for the last two years and a reduction in annual leave entitlements by a day,' Jax put in.

'But the improvement in attitude happened around nine months ago at a time when there'd been no pay rise for more than a year and the holiday allowance had already been cut,' Birkaan pointed out. 'If anything, they should have been angrier *then*.'

'And no trouble until the destruction of Euta Sakek three months ago. That was a spark,' agreed Jax. 'An unforgiveable breach. Birkaan, did you find out what really happened there?'

The Autabroni's face darkened. He was not of the Guznon tribe, but the destruction of any sacred site on his homeworld affected them all. 'I got nothing but excuses. A culmination of stupid mistakes is how Jarkoo explained it. Most reprehensible, he said, and the offending personnel are to be prosecuted.' Birkaan spat out the words like a bitter poison. It seemed that Birkaan's opinion of Avad Jarkoo, like Jax's, had been sinking as the days passed. Why this Autabroni man had not been more distressed about the desecration of Euta Sakek puzzled him. And he was a Guznon too! It should have maddened him as much as it did his workers.

'Thank goodness for that at least. But there *is* something going on and we need to dig deeper.' Jax leaned an elbow on the table and rubbed his forehead. The frustration of not finding anything conclusive was getting to him, and the undercurrent with Harrie had not helped. His testiness with her was becoming more obvious, and it had not improved with their collaboration on the workers' psych reviews.

'We'll keep going,' Caspiran assured him. 'We're talking to the site supervisors tomorrow. That might throw up some ideas.'

'With your abilities and Birkaan's knowledge of his own people, that might give us something,' Jax replied.

'Forgive me, lord, but I cannot probe as you suggest, can I? That would be most improper.'

'No. But no one can read people better than a mentante,' he elucidated. 'Between the two of you, you'll know if someone is lying.'

'We have drugs for that,' Harrie uttered under her breath to Jax.

His return gaze was a dagger. 'You have drugs for everything, Harrie.'

He quickly stood up from the table and thanked them for their work before dismissing them for the night. Harrie was the last to make it to the door and, while he shuffled documents into his portfolio, she turned back to him, frowning under her short fringe of red hair.

'I really *am* sorry, Kev. I was a complete idiot – cruel and selfish. And, well, just unforgivable.'

Jax remembered something. When Harrie spoke in full sentences, when she wasn't being flippant and making damn silly off-the-cuff remarks, she was usually telling the truth. She took a few steps towards him and laid a finely manicured hand on him arm. He froze. Her perfume filled his nostrils and he was conscious of his heart beating a little faster. *How could she still be so desirable?*

'I didn't have the sense to see that I had everything I ever wanted in you,' she finished.

She squeezed his arm and gave a remorseful smile. With a shrug and a sigh, she turned to leave the room.

As she drew nearer to the door, Jax called out. 'Wait!'

She halted and looked at him quizzically.

'Join me for dinner tonight.' It was both a command and a request. He saw the slow, warm smile creep across her face and he was conscious of another memory – of a time when he would often see that smile on that flawless face and be gloriously happy.

Sure enough, once all the greetings were over and they had been given a light breakfast of warm kiska bread smothered with salty tagirp paste, they were taken to a high platform overlooking the flat lands below. From the force-shielded viewport, Seti could see for herself the carnage that was mid-morning on Autabron: the baking rust-coloured sands, the whirling twists of dust and pulverised rock that raced across the plains, and the heat haze that distorted all she saw. She, Serekunda and Finn had been taken through various passages, twisting and climbing ever higher through the mountain's blood vessels. Thankfully, some contained vatortubes to lift them; as fit as Setiyan was, she knew that if she had had to traverse the thousands of stairs it would have taken to reach the viewing platform she would have been exhausted.

'This is amazing!' she exclaimed, then turned to Mira. 'How can anything live out there?'

'Nothing does. But it was not always so, great princess. Our ancestors tell of a time when rain fell on the plains and grass grew and bika grazed in herds of thousands.'

Seti shook her head in disbelief. 'How long ago was this?'

Mira sniffed at the girl's lack of knowledge. Had she not been briefed on the history of Autabron? But then, why should she? Why should any of the ganaks care about her homeworld? All they wanted – all they saw when they looked on these plains – was profit. She would have to be educated on all this, and she would be – in time.

'Around two millennia.' This was Finn. 'But the orbit around the two suns has changed. It's getting shorter. The days on Autabron are now four minutes less than they were a thousand years ago.'

Seti frowned. 'Such a small thing can make such a huge difference? Lady Mira, I am so sorry. I didn't know this.'

'Why should you, great princess? Why should anyone who is not of our people?'

The reprimand was gently delivered, but it stung enough for Seti to lower her head before speaking again. 'Then I promise to find out while I'm here. I want to know everything.'

They looked out again at the view, protected both by a tinted fabric awning that jutted out from the edge of the cliff and, more importantly, the translucent force-shield running from the floor to the rock ceiling of the platform. The high viewpoint, known as the Sill of Makum, was only ever fully open to the elements at pre-dawn and sunset. At all other times, the shield was necessary.

'There's something I'd like to know right now,' Serekunda piped up. 'The stone chair. What's that for?'

In front of them and protected by the force-shield stood a magnificent, marbled throne some two metres wide. The white rock, so different from the dark reds and rusty browns of the highlands, shone even in the muted sunlight as if with an inner glow. Its smooth surfaces were carved with frescoes of mountains and valleys and animals grazing, as well as the shapes of men and women in traditional cloaks.

'Yes, I was wondering about that too,' said Seti.

'It is reserved for a ceremony, the Day of Grunkaar,' Mira replied.

'You still celebrate that?' Finn asked, his confusion plain on his face. 'I thought that hadn't happened for centuries.'

114

Mira did not look at any of them as she spoke and her face was a stone wall. 'Our ceremonies are precious to us, as is our history. We keep the chair as a reminder of our culture.'

Finn cleared his throat. 'It was used to offer a human sacrifice to the twin suns,' he began, turning to Seti and defying Mira's stare. 'On a day chosen by the tribe's seer, a volunteer would be strapped into the chair before dawn. The tribe would all gather – in the place where we're standing right now – and, as the suns rose, the victim would be cooked alive.'

Seti tried hard to contain her gasp of horror as Mira, with a look of steel at Finn's presumption, took up the story. 'And, at sunset on that same day, clouds would roll in from the north and it would rain so hard that the wadis would sing with joy. This one sacrifice would save our people. We must never forget the gift we are given on the Day of Grunkaar.'

'And you believe that this death will bring the rain?' Serekunda queried.

'Do you not have similar beliefs and practices among your own people, Doctor Serekunda? I have heard of human sacrifice on Earth,' Mira countered.

'Yes, but all that died out thousands of years ago. Scientific knowledge has long replaced blind faith. And much the better for it – well, for the most part anyway. There's a certain tribe in the polar region who still kill one beluga whale every year to honour one of their gods. Heaven knows why. Completely inedible.' Serekunda's amusement at his own statement was shared by Finn. The look on Mira's face told them she was not as charmed. She diverted her gaze to Seti.

'Great princess. We must leave now.'

'Of course, but … Please, just call me Setiyan,' she pleaded. On seeing the look of horror on the old shaman's face, she added, 'Or lady, if you feel that's too informal.'

Mira nodded her assent, then held out her hand to gesture them towards the exit.

They descended back through the passageways and vatortubes and, against the background of Serekunda and Mira's chatter, Seti could not stop smiling. Everything was going so well and the visit was off to a good start. So why Lieutenant Finn's brow was so furrowed, she could not understand. Their mission would go well. Of that she had no doubt.

Chapter Nine

As Calin disembarked from the spaceracer, she could see Falvii Min waiting on a wide balcony that overhung the spaceport. Even at this distance – a good hundred metres – she could see that he was tall and with the usual mop of black hair common among Dasnirians. He waved and she returned the gesture. They had spoken only briefly before she left Altan twenty-six hours earlier and all of it pleasantries – nothing about the main purpose of her visit. Her mother thought it wise not to be explicit over open comms.

Falvii stood at the top of the ramp as she surfaced onto the balcony level. A broad grin lit up his tanned face and he threw open his arms for a hug as she approached. 'Cousin! How great to see you again! Wow, you're even prettier than I remembered.'

Calin shook her head and tried not to smile. 'Charming as ever, Falvii.'

She allowed herself to be swept into the tall man's arms. He almost lifted her off the ground. Her security officer, Lukas, a burly Earthan, moved a hand to his concealed weapon but relaxed on hearing Calin laugh.

'And you smell good too,' he added, sniffing her auburn curls. 'Why is it all the women in my aunt's family are so beautiful?'

Calin grinned. 'You haven't seen my third cousin – on the Dacas side, of course. Perfectly hideous.'

'Ha!' he guffawed. 'And with a sense of humour too. Careful with my heart, Calin Genara. You could break it!' His laugh was infectious.

If the next few days were to go on like this, Calin pondered, this mission could turn out to be fun. She would have to remind herself that her mother and father expected news and a full report about the illicit drug production. Then again, she thought, as she followed her handsome cousin out of the spacedock and onto a windshifter, there was no harm in admiring the scenery.

She had already seen a couple of female heads turn to look at Falvii, as well as one male. He was a striking specimen, with dark hair, sea-blue eyes, a long straight nose and a smile as wide as the ocean. But he seemed to be unaware of the stir he caused and focused all his attention on Calin, eager to get her away from the crowds.

He entered their destination into the shifter's console and took a seat next to her.

'You'll love it here,' he assured her as the craft ascended over the trees. 'You'd think I'd miss the sea, eh? But not so. This is a beautiful planet with many forests, lakes and rivers. Hidden treasures. I hope to show them to you.'

'If there's time, Falvii. I have work to do first.'

'Yes, of course. And I will help you. I've been here long enough now to know my way around a bit. We'll make a good team, you and I.' He patted her knee affectionately and the warmth of his touch suddenly made her feel a little breathless.

There was no doubt about it. This man had charm oozing out of his fingertips. She wondered if it worked on everyone as well as it seemed to be on her.

'I booked us into the Rekkushu Gardens Hotel. When they heard it was for you, they gave us the Canopy Suite,' he crowed. 'Nothing's too good for a princess, eh?'

'Oh, Falvii. No! I'm supposed to be here on a quiet visit.' She was horrified. How could she run an undercover investigation when everyone on Hutho knew she was here? The expensive hotel would alert the media and they'd end up being followed everywhere they went. 'I know you meant well. But you must cancel it. We're supposed to be staying with you – at your home.'

'Oh no! My place is a dump,' he retorted, shaking his head. 'Trust me, the Rekkushu is better, and anyway, the word is already out.'

Seeing the deep frown lines cross her forehead, he added brightly, 'Don't worry. This is Hutho. People here fall over themselves to be respectful. You'll have complete privacy and, most important, security.'

She had to admit to the truth of his words. Huthons were different. They were a peace-loving people brought up to be humble and honest and loyal, traits that she wished more Altanis would adopt. Arriving on most other planets, the media would have been present in droves at the spaceport. But not on Hutho. The media were so unobtrusive that if anyone *had* been there she probably wouldn't have known.

She looked to Lukas for confirmation and he nodded confidently. 'Very well. The fancy hotel it is.'

Falvii's reception of this news was effusive. 'Fantastic! You'll love it there and it'll make a nice change from my digs.'

So Falvii was going to stay with her? A 'suite' implied more than one room and, once they had checked in and entered the Canopy Room, she saw that it not only had two bedrooms each with bathrooms but also a large tastefully furnished lounge and a wide shaded balcony. The view across the lush forests to snow-tipped mountains in the distance and the immaculately manicured gardens below took her breath away. It was like an illustration from a travel guide. Perfect symmetry, perfect colours, all under a cloudless pale green sky.

'Wow!' exclaimed Falvii as he plonked himself down on the damask silk of the large sofa and stroked the smooth fabric. 'This is pretty good, eh? Beats sleeping on my spare bunk and fighting off the bugs.'

Calin laughed. 'I'm pretty sure my Aunt Evica and Uncle Tariik wouldn't allow their nephew to live in such conditions.'

He grinned. 'It's true. My place is fine. But it's nice to treat myself – and I am on leave, you know.' He patted the sofa and gestured for her to sit with him while Lukas took the bags to the bedrooms. Falvii sat up straight and his grin faded. 'Now, tell me more about our mission. Aunt Evica told me that I was to help and stay close to you – although that won't be hard.'

Once again there was that flirtatious look in his eyes and Calin suspected that he used it often to get his own way. 'You might rethink that when you know what I'm to do.'

'Ah, now I'm intrigued. Are we to face danger? Will there be thieves and villains and cutthroats –'

'Falvii, be serious,' she cut him off. It was important not to trivialise their mission. 'Now listen … and try not to interrupt.'

He sat in amused silence, enjoying being chastised by his lovely cousin with the dark flame hair and the peridot green eyes as she explained their mission. Her research had turned up only two laboratories on Hutho that could have produced significant quantities

118

of the drug in question. Their job was to investigate the supply chain back to its roots with their cover story being that they had been commissioned as part of the Union's regular five-yearly check into the production and storage of toxins. Their permission came from the Institute for Drug Control in Silbaraz-Re, where Calin was a board member, and under the authority of the Ki herself, Linnayen Genara. This would, hopefully, be enough to get them past locked doors and, given that Huthons were naturally trustworthy, they hoped to get honest answers to their questions. She also wanted to find out if Mikel Piek had returned home or been in touch with his friends and family. Doctor Amanie's crestfallen face came to mind as she had told Falvii of his sudden disappearance.

He asked a few pertinent questions about their mission, and it was a relief that he seemed to have moved on from their flirtatious start. She was not used to drawing attention; that was Seti's domain. But without doubt it was going to be more difficult than she imagined to concentrate on her task with such a handsome man at her side.

'My lady, I wish to take you to a special place.'

Mira had returned to Seti's quarters after they had rested from the morning's tour of the Beshwuk caverns. They had been taken through broad tunnels and vast open caves wherein people gathered to greet the off-world visitors with warmth and friendliness. Some had invited them into their homes to meet their families and, for Seti, the idea that these people lived primitive lives was soon dissipated. Many homes had views across the Beshwuk plains, their windows protected by the same sort of force-shield they had seen up on the Sill. Air was filtered, cooled and pumped into every corner of the multi-level town. She was amazed to find that the settlement of nearly ten thousand Guznon men, women and children lived in well-appointed cave-dwellings and had their own avenues of shops, workshops and services such as schools and a medical centre. So when Mira came to find her, she wondered what more wonders this place could hold.

'Should we bring the others?' she asked as they passed the door to Finn's room.

'No, lady. This is just for you.'

At the look of concern that passed the young woman's face, Mira added, 'There is no need to worry. You have my word you will be quite safe.'

Seti nodded her acquiescence and followed Mira to the end of a passageway and then into a vatortube that descended quickly below ground level.

'My goodness!' she exclaimed to Mira. 'I didn't realise your city went so far down.'

'We are an industrious people, lady. Centuries ago, as our lands dried and parched, we began to construct the burrows,' Mira explained. 'With the technology brought by the mining companies, we are now able to live above ground level inside the mountain. But our heritage lies down here, in the bowels of the rock.'

'Like at Euta Sakek.' Seti's voice was subdued. 'That must have been a terrible blow.'

'When the gan ... When the miners blew it up? You can't imagine the pain.' The old woman shook her head slowly and Seti sighed sympathetically.

Finally, the tube slowed and its doors slid apart to reveal a long tunnel lit by glow-globes. The floor was of rock and the walls roughly hewn, a far cry from the smooth sophistication of the community above their heads. Seti could not help feeling a little claustrophobic but quickly swallowed her fears when she saw Mira turn and smile warmly.

'Just a little farther, lady.'

Suddenly, the tunnel widened and she became aware of a change in the air. A light sweat beaded at her temples and her nostrils expanded to take in what smelled and tasted like moisture in the air. They turned a corner and, without warning, glow-globes lifted themselves and danced into the void of a large chamber, the floor of which was a lake. The reflected light of the globes dappled the surface of the water and some also shone from beneath it. Where they illuminated the scene, Seti could see that the water was crystal clear. Indeed, it was hard to tell how deep it was. One metre or ten? It was impossible to know.

She gasped. 'Oh! This is ... This is amazing! Mira, I'm overwhelmed.'

The shaman watched the play of emotions on the young woman's face with satisfaction. 'This is a most holy place for our people.

Kadis Sakek. A lake that stretches underground in tunnels and caverns for a thousand kliks, as far as the northern plains. Even the Gaksi, who are so blessed already, revere these waters. There is not one thing more precious to us.'

Seti picked up the emotion in the woman's voice. 'I can see why.' She touched Mira's hand and gazed into her eyes. 'It's so beautiful. Stunning.'

'I'm glad you think so.'

A man's voice broke the stillness. The figure rose out of the shallows to her right and took a few steps towards them. Seti's eyes were wide with both shock and a little fear as the stranger approached. He wore a short loincloth, but his legs beneath it were muscled and well-defined, as was the rest of his body.

'Kalik, my son,' Mira began. 'You startled us.'

'My apologies, Natar.' He placed his hand on his heart and bowed his blond head. When he lifted it, Seti saw that a smile played on his mouth and there were laugh lines at the corners of his azure eyes. He stared directly at her and a heat ran through her body, nipping at her senses and causing her to gasp.

'You must be the Princess Setiyan.' He picked up a towel and dried his hands before offering one to her. 'I'm Kalik Denkaun, Mira's adopted son.'

She stumbled over her words. 'Oh … Yes. Pleased to meet you.'

He threw the towel casually over his shoulder and pressed her hand between his two. His grip was warm and firm, his skin surprisingly soft. 'I had not expected to meet you like this, lady. Please forgive me.'

As Seti fumbled for the right thing to say, Mira interrupted the exchange. 'Kalik, please go and dress. You should have been ready an hour ago.' She then turned to Seti. 'I am so sorry for my son's impropriety. He was to be presented to you at our formal luncheon.'

Seti shook off the apology with a smile. 'It's not a problem. With a lake like this, anyone would want to swim.'

Denkaun laughed out loud as he continued to dry himself. 'So true, lady. Perhaps you'll join me next time?'

She did not dare speak. A picture flashed inside her head of them, mostly naked, swimming in the crystal water, and her heart pounded as a lightness rippled through her body.

121

'The princess will see you later, Kalik,' Mira insisted, and with a final flash of a smile he turned and walked away down the passage towards the vatortube. Seti could not help but look over her shoulder to see if the rear view was as good as the front. It was.

Mira shook her head in despair. 'My son is disrespectful, lady. He shall be admonished for his behaviour.'

'Oh, please … Don't. I'm not offended.' She felt the need to steady herself and get back to her mission. 'Tell me,' she began, 'about the lake.'

Mira recounted the history of the Guznon and the significance of the waters, explaining that the lake system flowing under much of the surface comprised water that had fallen as rain thousands of years ago. The Beshwuk community drew very little from the lake itself, depending instead on water piped to them from Zaz, paid for by the mine owners.

She tried to concentrate, but Mira's words mostly sailed over her head. Her nods were those of an automaton and all she could think about was when she would see Kalik Denkaun again.

Harrie was beginning to question herself. Normally so assured, so professional, she could rein in her emotions with a snap of her fingers. It was one of the things that made her such an excellent operative for C-7. But these last few days with her old flame had tested her resolve. Jax had a way of disarming her with just a look. It was one of the things that had drawn her to him all those years ago when they were students together at the Diplomatic Corps in New York. That and his openness, his honesty, his lack of guile. After all the lovers she had toyed with, he was a breath of fresh air, and the fact that he was so well-connected, being the son of the president of the Council of the United Democratic Nations, made him even more fascinating. Now, of course, he was powerful in his own right as the Ki-consort to Linnayen Genara. But he still had the air of integrity and goodness that had attracted her in the first place.

At dinner the previous evening they had reminisced over the few months they had been a couple: the weekend skiing in the Catskills, the surprise trip to Bora Bora and the time she and her father had come to Provence to meet his parents, Thea and David. Meeting them was tantamount to getting the seal of approval and she had played her part in charming them. Could she honestly blame her deception all on her father? True, he had encouraged her to get close to Jax, but that had been more about the Bashir family's money. At least, that's what she had thought then. Now she saw it with the eyes of a spy. It was always about influence and power and secrets, and the more Anthony Whitton-Blake had of all three, the better.

As expected, Jax had been a perfect gentleman at dinner. If she had hoped their private meeting might lead to something of a romantic nature, by the end of the evening she was almost glad they had ended as friends. He spoke so lovingly of his daughters and, more especially, of his wife and his pride in their mutual achievements that the thought of trying to pull all that apart was an anathema to her. Even under orders, she would be more than loath to undertake such a mission. Thankfully, for now all she was tasked to do was continue to enthral Avad Jarkoo and ensure that the contamination of the drinking water in Zaz-Rakuum continued at levels necessary to keep the workers compliant. And that brought her to another problem.

She went to Jarkoo's office and as the door slid open, he stood to greet her. He dropped a hand to cup one cheek of her bottom in its tight tan skirt, at which she smiled before lifting his hand free as though it was a soiled rag.

'Really? Here?'

'But you are so delicious. And I've missed you,' he complained, one finger stroking her neck. 'You're always with them.'

She pulled away. 'Because I must,' she insisted, her mouth tightening. She did not feel inclined to pander to the man's whims right now. He must learn to control himself or he would give the game away.

Jarkoo shrugged. 'I suppose I'll have to share you – for now.' He kissed the top of her head and turned to walk back to his desk. He did not see her grimace at his touch.

'Hurry them along if you can, my sweet,' he finished.

He punched in a command at the console on his desk. Instantly a three-dimensional image hovered above the desk. It was a plan of the city showing all the levels. Three red dots were evident, two in the offices of the main plant and one at the police headquarters on level one, closest to the surface.

Jarkoo began. 'Here are Caspiran and Birkaan.' He pointed to the two dots furthest from the city centre. 'They are interviewing our supervisors and, of course, this will serve them nothing. But can you tell me why the Ki-consort should be with the police? What does he hope to discover about falling ore production there?'

'Nothing, I'd say,' Harrie returned. 'But sabotage? Possibly a great deal.'

'Ridiculous! The investigation was thorough. The police found nothing.'

Harrie sighed. The man's stupidity was beginning to irritate her. 'It's his job to investigate.'

'Agreed. But keep him away from the water plant.'

'No reason to go there,' Harrie countered.

'Make sure it stays that way.' Jarkoo resumed his seat at the desk. 'Now then. The dosage.'

Finally! 'Wondered when you'd get around to that. Got to be upped.' She perched on the edge of the desk and leaned across to switch off the holoimage, conscious that the angle improved Jarkoo's view of her cleavage. It paid to keep him sweet – for now.

'D'you want to kill them?' Jarkoo seemed genuinely shocked. 'It's already at the maximum.'

Harrie nodded. 'But it's not working. We must calm them.'

'In that case, GKD shouldn't have destroyed Euta Sakek!' His voice had risen a notch.

She shrugged. 'Water under the bridge. Mistakes happen.'

'So you seriously want to increase it?' His face changed, sweat beading at his temples and on his upper lip.

Was he losing his nerve? She stood up and walked around the desk to position herself in front of him, lifting the hem of her skirt. The dark space between her legs drew his eyes like a magnet and his hand followed. 'Seriously,' she replied. 'Do it. Twenty percent.'

His gaze returned to her face as his fingers stroked the moist darkness at the top of her legs. She licked her lips, sighed, stretched her neck languidly and leaned back on the desk. His eyes widened and his chest heaved. His response was primal and he would not be stopped.

If this is what it took to secure the man's compliance, she would have to succumb. Enjoying the invasion was too much to hope for. *But if only it were Jax.*

Penn Adams

'I honestly thought you were over the running away thing. Obviously, I'm an idiot!' Finn was furious. 'Your first day in an unknown place with unknown people – often *angry* people, I might add – and you're gone. Did you learn nothing from yesterday's experience?'

Seti pushed past him and entered her quarters where she flopped onto a low sofa. The image of Kalik Denkaun still floated in her mind, but any feelings of goodwill it gave her were dissipated by her bodyguard's testy attitude.

'Don't speak to me like I'm a child! I was perfectly safe.'

'You couldn't know that!'

'I was with Mira. Just us. No crowds.' She rolled her eyes. 'Really, lieutenant. And anyway, you could track me.'

The door to the rock-walled room slid to a close behind Finn. But he remained in the doorway to block to any attempt she might make to leave.

'Actually, I couldn't. Wherever you were, your signal was lost,' he countered.

'Oh … I didn't realise. Sorry.'

The look of contrition on her face seemed quite genuine and Finn found it hard to stay angry with her. He shook his head and exhaled a long breath. 'Apology accepted. So where were you? Just so I know where to look the next time you take off.'

Seti's eyes widened as she told him about the underground lake and how Mira had described that it wound its way through layers of bedrock as far as the northern polar regions. She jumped up from the couch and went over to the window, beckoning Finn to follow her. 'I mean... Look at that.' She nodded towards the red-brown plains far below, pockmarked by moving whirls of dust. 'So dry. You just wouldn't imagine that there's water here, would you? But I saw it. So much of it!'

'In all the time I was here before I never heard about that.' Finn's brow creased and his eyes narrowed.

Before Seti could comment, the door to the chamber slid open. It was Pieter Serekunda.

'Ah! The wanderer returns. We thought we'd lost you – again.'

Once more Seti apologised, then regaled him with her new-found discoveries. Like her, Serekunda was enthused, but when it came

125

to the reasons for the secrecy surrounding Kadis Sakek, he was more erudite.

'The name gives it away. Sakek means "holy", and it's this tribe's experience that anything they hold precious – or sacred, even – is taken away from them. Or destroyed. I can see why they wouldn't want the water's presence to be widely known.'

'Then why show it to the princess?' Finn folded his arms across his chest.

Seti glared at him. 'And what are you implying?'

He cocked his head. 'Well, you *have* told two people already.'

Serekunda laughed. Instantly the glare came his way instead. 'Sorry. I'm sure there's a good explanation.' Undaunted by Seti's irascibility, he continued. 'Meanwhile, I've been sent to get you two. It seems we are to be honoured with a formal luncheon. Mira's attendants are waiting outside. So come on. Shake a leg.'

The wide passage wove steadily downwards. There were no windows here, no glimpses of the parched Beshwuk plains below. Just brown rock walls and the interminable dust that accompanied every step they took. Seti wondered if she should have changed her clothes. She was still wearing the tunic and pants she had travelled in from Zaz and she couldn't remember when she'd last brushed her hair. If this was the event where she was supposed to meet Kalik Denkaun properly, she hated the thought that he would see her so dishevelled.

Once again, her thoughts turned to the man she'd seen less than an hour ago. Handsome did not do him justice. He was striking and, she realised now, he was not from Autabron. Not even a hint of red skin, although he did possess the typical white-blond hair. Mira had called him her 'son'. But where was he from? And how had the old shaman come to have taken him in? She should have been concentrating on the questions arising from their mission – to find out the causes of unrest – but the only thing in her head at that moment was the thought of meeting him again.

Finally, they came to a large meeting hall lit by a hundred or more glimmering glow-globes. Its roof was supported by many pillars, each of which was more than a metre in diameter and finely carved with scenes of people and mountains and the twin suns. Every fresco on every column was painted in bright primary colours, and between them hung gossamer-thin fabrics in shades of orange. At the far end of the hall was a U-shaped stone table filled with platters of food and jugs. Mira stood at its centre, and as they approached she gave them the traditional welcome, hand on her breast.

'My greetings to you all. You are welcome in my heart.'

Seti led them closer and Mira gestured with a sweep of her arm to proceed to the half-dozen or so seats on the outer edge of the table.

'Lady, please sit here.' She indicated a chair to one side of the centre. Finn sat next to her, leaving the central place empty. Mira and Serekunda filled in on the other side of the empty chair. Looking at Seti, Finn's brows lifted, questioning the reserved space. She smiled. Seti had a good idea who would be joining them and the thought that he would be sitting beside her made her stomach flutter.

Sure enough, as soon as they had been served some wine by the attendants, the sound of a horn played from the back of the chamber and a low hum of chanting voices filled the space. As the volume increased, a pair of tall drapes was pulled apart and Kalik Denkaun entered the chamber. To either side of him came the men and women elders of the Guznon tribe wearing blood-red robes of office overlain by gleaming metallic sashes into which were slung curved scabbards. Finally came a group of some twenty or so acolytes dressed in orange robes and each banging a round flat drum. The whole procession was stately and, for Seti, Finn and Serekunda, quite unexpected. While the two men gaped at the gathering, Seti had eyes only for the man at its head. Denkaun's chest was bare, crossed by two cloth-of-gold sashes that were studded with gems of many colours. Below the waist he wore a loose sarong of a deep crimson trimmed with gold thread, and his feet were bare. His blond hair was worn loose, falling in waves over his shoulders. But there was no getting away from his eyes. The ice-blue orbs drilled into Seti, who was transfixed. It was only when Finn nudged her arm that she broke away with a sharp intake of breath.

'Who's that?' he whispered.

'Kalik. Mira's son,' she replied, trancelike.

'But he's not –'

'Shh!' Even as she quietened Finn, she did not take her eyes off Denkaun and he did not take his eyes off her either.

Denkaun and the elders stopped when they came close to the inner curve of the table and, within a couple of seconds, the chanting and drumming stopped. Denkaun lifted his chin and raised his arms out to either side before bringing his gaze back down to the off-world guests.

'Greetings, Princess Setiyan of Altan. Greetings, Doctor Pieter Serekunda of Earth. Greetings, Lieutenant Decker Finn of Earth. You are welcome in my heart.' With which he paced his hand on his chest and bowed low before them all.

Mira rose from her chair. 'Friends, this is my adopted son, Kalik Denkaun, the A'bat of the Guznon people.'

Finn shifted uncomfortably in his seat. His brows drew together. 'The warrior of hope?'

Mira eyes flashed. 'Not warrior in the literal sense, my friend. More like someone who struggles to give our people a better future.'

Denkaun smiled at him. 'My natar speaks truth, lieutenant. Every day I try to bring hope and security to my people.'

'And how do you do that?' This was Seti, finally able to speak.

He turned to her and the warmth in his eyes caused her breath to come a little quicker. When he spoke, his voice was honey. 'By my teachings, lady. I speak to my people. I calm their fears. I explain their world and give them hope.'

Finn glowered. 'You say *your* people, but you're not Autabroni.' The suspicion in his voice was obvious.

'Lieutenant!' Seti admonished.

'I'm just curious,' Finn shrugged, returning his gaze to Denkaun.

'It's a terrible Earthan habit, friends. Wanting answers,' Pieter Serekunda interjected. 'Please forgive us.'

'Naturally,' Denkaun responded cheerfully. 'And I will happily tell you more over lunch.' With that, he came around the table and took his place between Seti and Serekunda.

The smile never left his face while as he began to tell his guests about his genesis, and his eyes, when they settled on Seti, glowed with an icy fire.

'My mother was Altani, a beautiful woman deserted by her lover, cast out by her family. She came to Autabron, pregnant and alone, and was taken in by my natar and my father, Denkau,' he explained.

Mira took up the story. 'She was young and so helpless. Denkau and I could not refuse her sanctuary. She was like a daughter to us. We could not have children of our own. We called her Ko-Makum in honour of the revered Witch of Rundak.'

Finn's brows puckered again. 'That means little witch, doesn't it?'

'It does, for she was most bewitching. Her hair was white, like ours. But her eyes and skin, so pale. I often joked to my husband that we should have called her Ka-Jinn.' Mira smiled fondly at the memory she had just that minute conjured.

'What's a Ka-Jinn?' asked Seti, enthralled by the story. She wanted to know everything about this man.

'It means ghost or spirit in our language,' Denkaun replied. 'My mother was like a fairy.'

'So you remember her?' Serekunda asked.

Denkaun shook his head. 'No. I have no memory of her.'

Mira's head dropped to her chest and when she lifted it, they could see that her eyes were glassy with unshed tears. 'Our poor daughter was so troubled, so sad. She always felt the shame of being rejected by her family, even though Denkau and I gave her love and kindness. One day when Kalik was only a few months old, a madness came over her. Before the dawn, she stole up to the Chair of Grunkaar and waited for Lau and Uzno to appear.'

Seti gasped and both Finn and Serekunda sucked in their breath. Mira continued with the tale.

'We searched all day for her, but no luck. We assumed she had gone to the city. But, that evening, clouds formed on the horizon and a great rain swept in, the like of which we had not seen in twenty years. The Day of Grunkaar was upon us without warning. We rushed to the high Sill. As soon as we could retract the shield we found her. Her poor body.'

'How terrible!' Seti exclaimed. 'It's hard to believe she would take her life in such an awful way.'

She looked at Finn who nodded his agreement.

'The only comfort was that Kalik was so young, he did not suffer the grieving as we did.' Mira returned.

'Not a day passes when I am not thankful that Mira and Denkau took me in and raised me,' Denkaun added, keeping his gaze for Seti

129

alone. 'And, although I'm saddened by my birth mother's story, I don't mourn her. I look upon Mira as my mother and the Guznon as my people. I consider myself blessed.'

'But aren't you interested in where she came from? Her family? I could try to find out for you,' Seti offered gently.

Her attention was drawn by a sudden cough from Mira. 'How kind of you, lady. Perhaps we may talk of this later. But, for now, please enjoy the feast.'

Once the princess and her entourage had retired after lunch, Mira came to see Denkaun in his rooms. The broad smile on her face told him all he needed to know.

'It went as you hoped, Natar?'

'Better.' She laid a bony hand on his bare chest. 'We may not even need the drug, and the pheromone oil is working well. She is taken with you. Even a blind man could see it.'

He grinned and kissed the top of her head. 'But you *did* use it?'

'Of course. We haven't come this far to make a mistake now.' The old woman stroked his pale cheek but, to her dismay, he quickly turned away. Did she detect a growing arrogance? *Pah! Just like the mother!*

In truth, Kalik's birth mother, Balisel Navarr, had been imperious and haughty. Her time with them was a chore that had to be undertaken in order to obtain the child she bore. The son of the twins – Balisel and her twin brother, Durroc – was all-important to the prophecy. If Mira had to contend with Kalik's ego too then so be it. No matter how much she cared for him, it was his legacy that was important.

Chapter Ten

It had been a long day and, for Falvii and Calin, a fruitless one. Their visits to both pharma processing plants – as far as they knew, the only places where urthrengo could be produced – had yielded nothing. Neither had apparently even made the drug in the last five years, and as for having had orders for such excessive amounts, that was an impossibility. Both plants were run by Huthons and they were freely given access to all records. After two days of scouring every document, they had to admit defeat.

'Are you sure the drug we're looking for *is* urthrengo?' Falvii asked when they got back to the hotel on the second evening. 'Could it be something else?'

Calin shook her head. 'No. There's no mistake. That's what Hasler took delivery of when he was on Autabron, and the autopsy on the man who tried to kill my father showed it was in his blood too.'

She sighed heavily and looked at Falvii who had flopped down onto the couch. The day had been warm and the humidity had risen steadily. Even now, looking out of the windows of their suite, dark clouds filled the horizon, occasionally lit by flashes of lightning.

'Well, there's nothing more to do today. I'm going for a shower,' she stated, crossing the polished floor towards her bedroom. She began to pull off her thin jacket.

Falvii called, 'If you need me to scrub your back, just whistle.'

She stopped in her tracks and returned to the sofa. She placed her hands firmly on his shoulders and leaned her body towards his. A broad grin broke out on his face.

Calin's lips were pursed and she cocked her head to one side. 'The only scrubbing I need you to do is to the inside of your mind.' With that, she pulled back and turned away, but not before throwing her jacket over his head.

Under the thin fabric, Falvii laughed before taking a deep draught of her body's perfume. He couldn't help but enjoy the scent.

Yes, they were cousins, but not by blood. There was nothing wrong in pursuing the beautiful Calin. Even her name sounded like music inside his head. In these last two days he had found it hard to stop looking at her. But she had just laughed off his attentions or treated him like a fool. There had to be a way to win her heart – before she broke his.

They had already decided to explore the parklands next to the hotel that evening and dine wherever took their fancy. Falvii wanted her to try some of the traditional Huthon savouries that were sold at stalls and kiosks in the park courtyards. After that he planned to take her to the pools in the Kushaan Canopy Park which was part of the hotel's complex. The swimming and spa pools were set high up in the trees, each with a glass bottom through which you could look down on the gardens far below. The unique attraction was popular with visitors, but Falvii was hoping that there would be fewer people to disturb them so late in the evening.

He must have nodded off, Calin's jacket still over his head, when he became conscious of a slight rustling noise. It sounded as though it was coming from outside and he rose and went to the balcony to investigate. Leaning over the balustrade, he saw nothing of interest other than the view across to the wooded hills, now smothered by ominous grey clouds. Few people wandered in the gardens below, it being late in the day and nearly dark. He took a gulp of fresh air, yawned and stretched before returning to the main room. Hearing the gushing sounds of Calin's shower, he decided to wash and change before their evening too. He went to his bedroom and undressed, completely unaware of the figure some fifty metres away on a branch of a gari-oak tree who tracked his progress through field glasses.

Their first afternoon in the Beshwuk settlement was spent meeting with the heads of the main Guznon families. The gathering of twenty or so mainly male elders was at first a little frosty, but Setiyan responded by using her training in statecraft to bring them around. She asked many questions and listened intently to their answers without interrupting. She apologised for her lack of knowledge but expressed how very eager she was to know more. She complimented them on their settlement and stated her wonder at the comforts it held. They should be proud, she said. They had honoured their forebears with their skill and devotion.

By the end of the afternoon, the elders were smiling and nodding and praising the young woman's intellect and understanding of their troubles. Indeed, as Finn put it later in their quarters as they debriefed, she said and did all the right things, a true diplomat.

'I have to hand it to you, princess, you were pretty good,' he conceded.

'Thank you, lieutenant,' she replied, pouring a glass of water.

'They certainly seemed to warm to you,' Serekunda agreed. 'I wasn't expecting these people to be so open.'

'They're not normally. Keep themselves to themselves. It feels odd.' Finn's brow was dark.

'So what did we discover?' Serekunda brought them round to the business at hand. He began to list his impressions. 'Firstly, I heard their disquiet at the way their sons and daughters have gone to work in the mines and been lured by the better standard of living. They appear to have disdain for the luxuries of city living. But was that more to do with the break-up of the family unit? I know that since my son left home, I hardly ever hear from him.'

'That's pretty normal,' Finn added. 'We all leave home eventually.'

Seti ignored the glance he had thrown her way at his last remark. 'I think it's more. No one complained about the lack of contact and, let's face it, life here has all the comforts of Zaz and, I presume, the other mining cities too. I picked up an underlying anger. Hard to say exactly …'

'They're always angry. That's just them,' Finn countered.

'No, it was something else.'

'Something they're not telling us?' Serekunda queried.

'Maybe.' Seti took a sip and continued. 'One of the elders, a woman, talked about the way the decisions were made by the mining bosses. She called them ganaks. She said years ago, the workers' council was always consulted. But not nowadays.'

Finn's eyes flew open. 'Ganaks? Strong words!'

'What does it mean?' Serekunda asked.

'It started as just a term for off-worlders. But, well … Let's just say your mother would make you wash your mouth out for using it these days.'

'Yes, I picked up the hatred as she said it,' Setiyan stated. She went over to a low couch and sat down, slipping off her shoes. 'Then someone else complained about the lack of religious devotion in their young people.'

'I heard that too. Not attending the ceremonies, that sort of thing,' Serekunda said.

Finn pulled off his jacket and threw it over the back of a chair before sitting on a high stool by the window. Behind him, the suns were now low on the horizon and a purplish red glow filled the clear sky beyond the mountains. The plains were already in deep shadow, their features blurred by the encroaching dusk. 'What about their leader, this Kalik Denkaun? Is it just me or does anyone else think it strange that an Altani should be their chosen one, their "warrior of hope"? And what does that even mean?'

'It's not unheard of,' Serekunda replied with a shrug. 'There've been tribal societies that selected their leaders purely because of some aberration, like albinism, for example, or a physical deformity.'

'He's certainly not deformed,' Seti chimed in, a light blush immediately flooding her cheeks.

'Really?' This was Finn. He cocked one eyebrow as he looked at her.

Seti glared back at him. 'From what I could see.'

Instantly the image of the near-naked, powerfully built man rising out of the clear waters of Kadis Sakek flooded her mind. Did her breath come a little quicker? She shook it away. 'Anyway, he's their choice. And they seem devoted to him.'

'And how! He's revered like a god,' Serekunda commented.

'Almost like a cult,' Finn added.

Seti frowned. It was true. From what she'd seen so far, the Guznon people – even Mira herself – had a godlike respect for Kalik Denkaun. She could see why. There was something about him – an aura maybe – that drew you in. At least, it was affecting her, and it was confusing. In the last few days she had begun to think about Decker Finn. However much he irritated her, she also found him attractive. Those warm brown eyes and the way his smile transformed his face. And there was no denying that when he had held her after the mugging, her heart beat a little faster. She had even thought about how his lips would feel on her own. But then she had seen Kalik Denkaun. Whatever chemistry had been in the air, it had worked to make her forget the handsome lieutenant.

Finn stood up and grabbed his jacket from the back of the chair. 'I'm off. Need a shower. Let's talk after dinner.'

'I'm with you,' said Serekunda. 'See you later, my lady.'

The door panel slid open and two men left the room. Seti got up from the couch and went to the window. Through the force-shield, she saw the last vestiges of light had left the sky and stars had begun taking over the void. She felt light-headed and sleepy. It *had* been a long day. Would there be time for a short nap before meeting Mira and Kalik and the elders again at dinner? She finished her water and decided. Yes, time to rest.

Laying down on the bed, she pulled the coverlet over her and was not surprised to find that, as she closed her tired eyes, the image that came to mind was that of Kalik Denkaun's smiling face and piercing blue eyes.

At the desk in his room, Jax reflected on his visit to the police headquarters. The commander had assured him that an extensive search had been made for the missing person, Mikel Piek, but turned up nothing. Every manifest for every departing vessel had been checked for a month following his reported disappearance with no outcome. Every contact of his had been spoken to and they had no news to offer, except that he was a private person. Likeable. But reserved. There were few Huthons living on Autabron so if he was still in the community somewhere, the commander said, he would certainly have been discovered by now.

'You can't mistake that green skin, eh?' he said, and he had laughed derisively.

'How about Professor Hasler?' Jax had asked. 'Anything on him?'

'Not that I can recall,' the commander replied. But he had offered to search their database. 'One thing I can tell you, though, his apartment was in the best area of Zaz. If that's what they earn, I'm going back to college!'

This had puzzled Jax. He was of the same opinion as the policeman. Surely professors didn't earn that much.

Meanwhile, Kalisa Caspiran and Birkaan had made progress. After interviewing some twenty supervisors at the Euta Makaan plant and ruling them all out of their enquiries, there was only one other left to interrogate, a woman who had been transferred to the mine at Te'kaan two days after the explosions. Avad Jarkoo was organising an aerporter and they were to leave that evening to speak to her.

Jax had not yet heard from Setiyan, although Finn had relayed their safe arrival. He reported that they had received a formal welcome and that the natives were behaving in a rather more friendly manner than he would have thought likely. But Jax, like Finn, found the warmth of their reception unusual.

His thoughts were interrupted by a signal from the vidscreen. It was Harrie. She was outside and wanted to speak with him. He buzzed her in. She sauntered into the room and perched herself on the corner of his desk. She was dressed in a dark green satin jumpsuit with a neckline that plunged almost to her waist. At her neck was a string of diamonds tumbling into her cleavage.

'Dinner? Thought you might like company.'

There was no doubt about it, she was an attractive woman and some part of him was stirred, especially when he saw the shadow of her breasts beneath the fabric. He sighed heavily.

'Thanks … but no. I'm tired.'

Harrie pouted and a frown crossed her smooth forehead. 'Oh no, surely you're not going to make me dine alone?'

'Sorry.'

She stood and placed a finely manicured hand on the side of his neck, caressing it before lifting his chin so that he could look at her. She leaned over him and her other hand travelled down towards his groin. He took a deep breath, trying hard not to respond. Her perfume filled his nostrils. He felt an unmistakeable movement below his waist.

'You *will* be, darling. *So* sorry.'

He pulled away sharply and stood up. She stumbled back but quickly regained her balance.

'Stop it, Harrie! Enough!'

She sighed and rolled her grey eyes. 'Really? Okay, I'll behave.'

She walked towards the door then stopped, turning and tilting her head to one side in a childlike gesture. 'I suppose I should've known.

Won't bother again.' Her voice was soft. She took a last look at him and lifted her chin defiantly before turning away.

That was close. How could he still feel so enticed by this woman after all these years, and especially after having been madly in love with his wife for over two decades? Maybe it was time to go home. After all, he was making no progress here and both Caspiran and Birkaan could continue the investigation. Seti had Finn, Serekunda and their guards to look after her, and she'd only be in Beshwuk for another couple of days. No one needed him here. He would call Linnayen and tell her he was coming home as soon as possible.

After a quick dinner with her travelling companions and an early night, the next morning Seti felt revived. So when Kalik Denkaun came to her quarters and proposed an outing for the day, she was excited at the prospect. It helped that he was still pleasing to the eye when fully clothed in a crisp blue shirt and tan pants.

'Where are we going?' she asked.

He raised one eyebrow and a smile crept into the corner of his mouth. 'Ah, now that would be telling. But I think you'll like it. Indeed, I know you will.'

She smiled in return. This was the sort of adventure she had expected and hoped for. She asked Denkaun to wait while she gathered a jacket and, as she put an arm into a sleeve, she remembered Lieutenant Finn's warning that he had not been able to get her signal yesterday when she had left with Mira. If she did it again, he would be furious – and so would her father. Finn would be bound to tell him.

'I'm sorry to hold you up but we'll need to bring Lieutenant Finn with us.'

Denkaun's smile froze for a second. Just as quickly, his brows knitted together and he shook his head. 'Oh, that won't be necessary. It's perfectly safe where were going.'

'I'm sure it is. But I can't run off on him again. It wouldn't be fair,' she insisted. Before Denkaun could say another word, she went to the companel and punched in the code for Finn's room. He answered immediately.

'Lieutenant, hope you've had breakfast. We're off on an adventure. You, me and Kalik Denkaun. How soon can you be ready?'

Had she secretly wanted to catch him off guard? If so, it didn't work.

'Be right there.'

Seti looked up and smiled into Denkaun's eyes. 'He's coming.'

Denkaun's returned a tight smile. 'Wonderful! Let me help with your jacket.'

He moved behind and held out the jacket for her to slip her arms into. Once on, he squeezed her shoulders. His hands were strong and she was conscious of a ripple of pleasure at the back of her neck where she felt his warm breath.

'There.' He left a hand on the small of her back. 'Oh, don't forget your water bottle. No one goes anywhere here without water.'

'I can believe that,' she concurred and went over to the chill unit and took out a metal flask of cold water. *If he keeps that up I might need it – and not just to drink.*

Finn was already waiting outside and greeted them both as they made their way to the nearest vatortube.

'I trust you slept well, lieutenant?' Denkaun asked.

'Like a baby.' Finn nodded to Seti. 'And you, princess?'

'Fine, thank you, lieutenant.'

'And did you speak with your father last night?' The slight emphasis Finn placed on the word 'father' was enough to both annoy her and make her feel guilty at the same time.

'No, I thought I'd wait until I had more news,' she fired back, flicking hair out of her eyes. 'That all right with you?'

Finn held up his hands in a gesture of compliance. 'You don't need my permission, princess.'

'Correct. Now shall we get going?' She turned on her heel.

Denkaun led the way down a series of vatortubes and stairways chiselled into the red rock. The steps were wide and worn, suggesting that carving them out of the belly of the rock had been the work of many over centuries. Finn estimated that they'd descended maybe two thousand metres in all, which, taking in the elevation of their rooms within the mountain itself, meant that they were at least a klik underground. It was a complex warren and, thought Finn, it would be more than easy to get lost down here.

'You obviously know these passages well,' he commented to Denkaun after they'd been traversing them for nearly ten minutes.

138

The blond man laughed. 'Not so well that I haven't got lost down here a few times. Mira and my father were often called out to find me.'

'You were a mischievous child then?' Seti queried.

'Independent, let's say.'

'Did you never wonder about your heritage, though? I mean …' Seti hesitated. 'Well, you obviously knew you weren't like other Autabroni children.'

'I didn't need to ask. Mira and Lyr told me everything. They held nothing back.' His tone was so matter-of-fact. Her brows lifted in both surprise at his candour and admiration for his honesty. He continued. 'I think it's important for everyone to know who and what they are, don't you?'

'Of course,' she agreed. 'Where I come from – in my family, I mean – it goes without saying. Both my parents can trace their lineage for many generations. Apparently I have many brave and interesting ancestors. Some, according to my mother, it's best not to talk about in company.' Seti's laugh was relaxed.

Denkaun grinned. 'What about you, lieutenant? Any bad apples in your line?'

Finn scowled. His family was, compared to the princess's and even Denkaun's, completely ordinary. 'No way. My mother is a cosmonic engineer at the Monas spaceport and Dad is in finance.'

'He's an accountant?' This was a sneering Denkaun.

Finn glared back. 'A socio-economist. He works for the Treasury. Devises policy.'

'Still sounds dull.' Denkaun threw back his head and laughed loudly. 'Don't worry. I'm sure it skips a generation.'

Seti laughed along with him. But before Finn could retaliate, they had turned a corner and stepped onto a flat platform of rock at the side of a long tunnel. Finn made out a faint rumbling noise coming from the dark shadows off to his right. It sounded both familiar and odd and the air was warm.

'What is this place?' Seti asked, craning to better see the scene.

Denkaun replied with an unmistakeable note of pride in his voice, 'Something special, as you're about to find out.'

Seti's puzzled look matched Finn's. A few seconds later, they detected a change in the airflow. Finn moved closer to Seti, ready to pull her back from the platform's edge to the confines of the rock wall as a tube-like cylinder flew out of one end of the tunnel and pulled up level to where they stood. Its nose was pointed like a bullet and its fuselage built of a glistening metal that sat beneath a translucent roof. *An underground railway!* They even still had some of these on Earth.

'My goodness!' Seti exclaimed. 'What is this?'

Denkaun's face was all smiles. 'This, Lady Setiyan, is the q'ist, a subsurface transport network we built with our friends the Gaksi and No'os tribes,' he explained. 'The off-world miners arrived with their technology two centuries ago now and our forebears employed it to create these underground tunnels. They connect the tribes. We can't travel easily above ground. But down here ... Well, as you can see.'

'I've heard about this,' Finn added. 'When I was stationed here. But I was told that the system had broken down and wasn't in use.'

'You were misinformed, my friend,' Denkaun countered. 'How else could we keep in contact with the other tribes?'

'This must be very useful to your people,' Seti said.

Finn raised an eyebrow but said nothing.

'So, let's climb aboard,' Denkaun suggested, touching a panel on the metal skin of the q'ist. At once a door flew open to reveal rows of seats wide enough for two in the rounded interior. He gestured for them to enter. Finn placed himself behind Seti and Denkaun sat next to her, taking hold of her hand and bringing it to his lips. When he kissed it, Finn saw a pink blush colour Setiyan's neck and caught the hint of a shy smile. At that moment the door snapped shut and the inertia of the rapid forward momentum pushed Finn back into his seat. It put paid – albeit temporarily – to his overwhelming desire to strangle Kalik Denkaun.

Calin had never experienced such a thing. Raised high up in the branches of a stately ksarpi tree, she could see the twinkling lights of the hotel's gardens through the bottom of the pool. The many hues – pinks, blues, greens, yellows – refracted through the glass and, without the aid of a dive mask, were a brilliant, blurry abstract of colours when she looked down. She popped back up to the surface for more air.

'This is amazing!' she exclaimed to Falvii, who sat at the pool edge while her security officer, the stoic Lukas, kept watch from a discreet distance.

He smiled. 'If there's one thing the Huthon people appreciate more than their trees it's water. So why not put the two together?'

'Well, whoever had this idea, I'd like to thank them. A cool swim at the end of a long hot day suits me.'

'I'm glad you like it.' He got up and crossed the wooden deck to a side bar. 'Can I get you anything?'

But Calin had already plunged down again. He could see her body spreadeagled on the bottom of the pool, still taking in the view beneath, her dark red hair floating like a swathe of seagrass. He smiled again, remembering back to his visit to Altan. *Was it nearly five years ago now?* She had been in her first year of university and was more interested in her studies than men. Despite his efforts then to get to know her, including inviting her to go hiking in the mountains and, once, to dance with him at his aunt and uncle's party, she had mostly resisted with a nervous smile. 'Ask my sister,' she had said to both requests. So he did, and he and Setiyan had had a fun time. But for some reason he could not quite put his finger on, she did not intrigue him in the same way her younger sister did. He'd had girlfriends at school and, later, at university. He was not inexperienced. Setiyan was typical of many of these early paramours, high-spirited and independent. But, at twenty-five and with a serious career path ahead of him, he had begun feeling the need to settle down. Then there was the inescapable fact that Calin had changed from a shy, skinny girl into a beautiful woman. If anyone could be described as having come out of their shell it was her.

A sudden splash interrupted his musing. Calin had come up for air.

'Aren't you coming in?'

He put down his drink, ran the few steps to the pool's edge and launched himself into the air.

Calin screamed with laughter as the splash went over her head. 'You could've just said yes,' she cried.

'Ah, but where would be the fun in that?'

He dived under the water and swam in wide circles around her. Being Dasnirian and having lived as much in water as out of it, his eyes refocused automatically and he could see her shape clearly. He was also fast underwater. His people had evolved to adapt to their watery environment and the webbing between their toes was very efficient at propelling them at much higher speeds than all the other hominid species. Finally, he came up for air.

'Very impressive,' Calin commented. 'Obviously I'm not going to challenge *you* to a race.'

'I'd let you win,' he replied hopefully. His grin was infectious. Calin laughed and turned to pull herself out of the pool. 'Hey, not so fast!'

His hands went around her waist and before she knew it he had picked her up and thrown her to the middle of the pool. She screamed with laughter.

'Falvii! Just you wait,' she warned once she had resurfaced.

'For you? I will, I promise.' He said it with a smile but he couldn't hide its truth. He would wait – for as long as it took.

Suddenly, she stopped laughing and he could see that she was focused on something over his shoulder. The sudden silence drew Lukas's attention, too, and a hand went to his weapon.

Falvii turned and saw the lights of the pool reflected in a pair of eyes huddled within a leafy branch. Someone was watching them. He pulled himself out of the pool and crossed the distance in a couple of seconds, beating the security officer to it. As he swept back the leaves, he saw a small figure – a child - blinking back her tears. Falvii was stopped in his tracks. Calin climbed out of the pool and stood close behind him, nodding to Lukas to step back.

'Oh, don't cry. It's all right,' Calin said soothingly. 'Falvii, help her down.'

He stretched up his hands and gently lifted her from the tree. 'There you go, little bird.' He set her down on a cushioned bench. 'Here's a more comfortable perch, I think.'

Her eyes widened and she pulled up her legs, throwing her arms around her knees.

Calin kneeled before her without touching the frightened child. 'It's all right, we won't hurt you. Are you lost?'

The girl said nothing but shook her head.

'Were you just wanting to have a swim? Are you staying at the hotel?'

She shook her head again. Calin glanced up at Falvii but he shrugged his shoulders.

'Maybe we can find your parents for you?' he offered.

'No, thank you, sir.'

Calin smiled. Huthon children were raised to be polite and respectful. It was a refreshing quality. 'Then how can we help?' she asked.

'Mistress, I am sent with a message.' She paused and took a nervous breath. 'Go to Xaca.'

Calin and Falvii looked at each other, brows creased.

'Xaca? I don't understand,' Calin said.

'Who sent you?' Falvii asked.

'That is the message. It is all I know, sir. Go to Xaca.'

The child looked just as perplexed as they did. Falvii put out a hand to help Calin up and spoke again to the girl. 'How can you not know who sent you? Was it someone you know?' His voice was gentle but the child's eyes welled again and her chin sank towards her chest.

'I am sorry, sir. I do not remember.'

Calin sat next to the child and risked putting an arm around her shoulders. She responded well, snuggling into Calin's side.

'I think she's been mindheld,' Falvii mused.

Calin's frown quickly turned to anger. 'Seriously?' The thought that this small child could have been manipulated by a mentante was horrendous to her. It broke every code in the book.

'Must be,' he replied. 'I can't see how else … Someone wants us to go to Xaca but they don't want to reveal their identity.'

'So a trap?'

'Or a tip-off.' He reached over and gently patted the child's head. She lifted her chin to look at him and smiled. 'Either way, we'd best get this little bird back to her nest.'

Chapter Eleven

Finn estimated that they had travelled at lease a thousand kliks. The q'ist shot them along through tubes and tunnels and occasional partly covered bridges that gave them glimpses of high brown mountains across sweltering dusty plains. All the while, whenever they were above ground, the twin suns were never seen. But Finn conjectured from the lengthening shadows in the distance that they were heading towards one of the poles – the northern one, in fact.

'You're right, of course,' Denkaun confirmed. 'We're heading towards Hiresh. But we'll be getting off before there.'

'Hiresh? In the Gaksi lands? And we'll be welcome there?' Finn could not keep the surprise out of his voice. *Since when do the Guznon and Gaksi cosy up to each other? Could this explain Hanashi's visit?*

'Of course,' Denkaun replied smoothly. 'We have always traded with them.'

'Yes, but –' Finn began.

'Why would they not welcome us? Besides, we'll not venture far into their country.'

Denkaun turned his attention back to Seti, who had said almost nothing since they left Beshwuk. This worried Finn. It was not like her to be so quiet. He saw over the back of the seat that Denkaun had edged himself closer to her and was, even now, holding her hand. She neither objected nor pulled away!

'I want to show you how beautiful my home can be. All you off-worlders know are our deserts and our mines. There is so much more.'

Seti looked into his ice-blue eyes and smiled. 'I'd love to, Kalik.'

Since when had she started using his first name? This was odd, disquieting, but he felt at a loss to stop it. Finn wondered if he should contact Jax.

'We're nearly there,' Denkaun announced. 'Make sure you have your flasks.'

Seti lifted her water bottle and took a quick sip as the q'ist began to slow down. By the time Finn had fixed his pack on his back they had come to a stop and the doors slid open.

They stepped out onto another platform like the one back at the Beshwuk settlement and Finn saw two powerfully built armed guards standing at the entrance to a narrow gash in the end wall. As soon as Denkaun led them through the gap, the guards resumed their places. They strode along an ever-widening, ascending passageway. Finn could feel the air becoming warmer. He vowed that if the so-called warrior of hope was leading them into a furnace he would have no hesitation in blowing his brains out, no matter how important he was.

After a hundred metres or so they saw daylight ahead. It was bright, but not the glare Finn had expected. They exited into a sheltered, rounded valley surrounded by high red peaks. The rays of the twin suns were completely excluded from this place, the height of the mountains blocking them for what Finn guessed might be most if not all of the day.

'Wow!' Seti stood at the exit, trying to take it all in. This was her first time on the surface of Autabron and, Finn had to admit, it was spectacular. There was even vegetation here, with low-lying bushes and what looked like grass in the bottom of the bowl-shaped valley.

Denkaun had started down a path. He looked back up at Finn and Seti, a grin stretched across his face. 'Well? Aren't you going to join me?'

Instantly, Seti set off after Denkaun, who was now leaping down the rocky steps. They were both whooping and hollering with delight and it was all Finn could do to keep up with them.

The path led them through dusty green shrubs, under which grew a tough grass, and towards a larger clump of trees set right at the bottom of the valley. Denkaun and Seti disappeared into the trees and Finn suddenly heard her gasp of wonder.

'Oh, amazing! Unbelievable!'

Denkaun's voice was warm and velvety. 'For you, my princess. A special place.'

A breathless Finn quickly caught up to them. Within the trees was a clear pool reflecting the cobalt of the sky, the whole surrounded by deep green tree ferns.

'How is this possible?' Finn turned to the smiling Denkaun.

'This is Adnat'olak. It means heavenly spring.' Denkaun swept a hand towards the idyllic scene. 'The elevation here is actually below ground level, so far below that the groundwaters of Kadis Sakek seep into the space. It only survives because of the mountains around us and the higher latitude we have now travelled to. Have you noticed how much cooler the air is here?'

'Yes!' This was Seti, still gazing wide-eyed at the oasis. 'I wouldn't have believed such a place could exist.'

'My home has many wonders, lady, and I want to show them all to you.'

There was that voice again. So smooth, almost snake-like. Finn's face darkened.

'Come!' Denkaun stirred them out of their trance. 'I have another surprise.'

He led them along the edge of the pool some hundred metres or so until they came to a tented pavilion. The sides and roof were of a thick, white canvas and Finn could see that a deck jutted out from it over the water with a small, covered gondola tied to it. Denkaun lifted a side flap of the tent and they passed through. Inside was a scene fit for a palace. A luxurious quilted couch sat against the back wall with a view out across the lake. Around the edges of the pavilion, large cushions sat on top of richly woven carpets and, in the middle, jugs of wine and platters of fruit and other foods Finn could not identify were placed on a low table.

Seti's eyes and grin couldn't get much wider. 'Oh, how wonderful!'

'Sure is fit for a princess,' Finn couldn't help commenting.

'No more than you deserve, lady.' Denkaun took her hand and led her to the couch. 'Come sit with me.' Once seated, he looked up at Finn, who still stood at the entrance carrying his pack. 'Ah, perhaps a cushion, lieutenant? My apologies. I was not expecting there to be three of us.'

Finn grimaced. *I'll bet you weren't.*

'This food looks delicious,' said Seti.

'Then let me tell you all about it.' Denkaun proceeded to regale her with where each morsel came from and how it was prepared, all the time feeding her little pieces. He reminded her to drink either some water or wine, stressing the importance of keeping hydrated. 'You too, lieutenant. Please help yourself. I'm sure you'll like this wine, though I confess, it's imported. From Earth, actually.'

Finn wasn't to be tempted. Duty first. He would protect the princess even though she looked like she needed nothing from him. Seti had curled herself towards Denkaun's muscular body and all her focus was on him.

Finn couldn't help but notice that the two of them seemed to be getting closer, and not just physically. The usually fiery, arrogant princess was like putty in this man's hands. Whatever he said, she agreed with. He had never seen her like this and, frankly, he didn't much like it.

Suddenly, Denkaun jumped up and pulled the giggling princess to his side. 'So now you've tasted our local delights, let me offer you something more.'

She laughed and allowed herself to be led down to the jetty where Denkaun helped her into the rear seat of the gondola. Finn got up to join them, but as soon as he set foot on the planking, he saw that the vessel was only big enough for two people.

'I'm so sorry, lieutenant. You'll have to guard your princess from the shore.' The smirk that accompanied these words was almost more than Finn could bear. 'I promise to take good care of her, though. There's no danger.'

No physical danger. Of that Finn was fairly sure. But what was the woman getting herself into? This change in her demeanour was most discomfiting and it had all happened so quickly. As soon as they had arrived in the Beshwuk settlement she had changed, but for the life of him he could not fathom why.

There was nothing to be done at that moment but sit and wait for her return, and as he did so, his face belied his darkest thoughts.

Seti couldn't explain it. Whenever this man came close to her, whenever she saw him, she was instantly drawn. She became breathless and her heart beat faster, as though it would jump out of her chest. His eyes fascinated her. They were so similar to her own – the same glacial blue, as clear and unblemished as the very water they were now passing over. Then there was his touch. His hands were warm and soft, yet strong.

Every time he touched her she felt a shiver run through her body like nothing she had ever felt before.

There had been suitors, of course. Young men from good families had been presented but ultimately rejected. Some she had met at formal ceremonies and engagements, some serious and well-educated, others funny and charming. They all could have been perfect matches for her. But Kalik Denkaun was different. He was electricity! He made her feel alive.

And alive was exactly what she felt as Denkaun swiped a glass panel in the bow and the gondola pushed away from the jetty. He sat next to her and his eyes never left her face. He spoke but she had no idea of what he was saying. The soothing vibration of his voice was mesmerising and when he laid his hand on her leg she gasped with pleasure.

'Lady, I wish to know you – in all ways,' he breathed into her ear.

'Kalik … I …'

'Don't speak.' He took her chin and turned her face towards him. His eyes travelled over her features as his fingers traced the outline of her cheeks and lips and then her neck. Her breathing quickened and a warm radiance flooded her body. Suddenly he stopped and looked over his shoulder. Finn was still standing on the jetty some two hundred metres away. His arms were crossed and his gaze fixed on the gondola.

Denkaun turned back to her. His satisfied smile reached his eyes. He returned his fingers to her face and, as they came to her mouth, her lips parted and he traced a moist line around them.

'My sweet princess …'

Her breath came harder. She raised a hand to touch his face, to pull him closer to her.

'Tonight,' he whispered, 'I will come to you.' He pulled away and punched a command into the gondola's control system.

She could not speak, did not need to speak. Her eyes glowed with happiness and, as the craft took them back to the jetty, only one thought consumed her mind. *Kalik, my love!*

In the hotel lobby a Huthon woman stood with the manager, who spoke to her in a serious and soothing tone. The woman's eyes were nervously scanning the space around them. As they entered, the little girl wrenched her hand free of Calin's grip and hurtled towards the woman. She was instantly swept up into the woman's arms and a firm kiss was placed on the child's forehead before being set on her feet.

'Enni! Why did you run off? I was so worried.' The woman stroked her fair hair.

'I'm sorry, Mama. But the man gave me a message. He made me go.'

'What man?' Falvii asked. The woman looked to him questioningly and he now addressed her. 'Sorry, I should explain. Your daughter – Enni, is it? – found us at the pools and gave us a message. But she has no memory of why.'

'We think she was mindheld,' Calin added quickly. 'But now we know it was a man.' She smiled encouragingly at the girl. 'You remembered, Enni.'

'Yes. Yes, it *was* a man!' The child's grin was more of relief than anything.

'Mindheld? What are you saying?' The woman pulled her daughter closer to her.

Calin explained how some people cultivated skills to control the thoughts and actions of others by hypnosis. It had originally been developed as a form of psychotherapy, but to use it on a child was a shameful action. The mother looked horrified and immediately nestled her child even closer.

'Can you tell these people more?' she asked Enni. 'Who did this to you?'

The girl's face was a picture of concentration and she closed her eyes. When she opened them again, she spoke clearly. 'He was Huthon and about this tall.' She jumped up, trying to reach a point in the air above Calin's head. 'And he had a beard.'

'Anything else?' Falvii queried.

Enni took a few seconds to think. 'He had a scar, just here.' She drew a line from the corner of her right eyebrow to the top of her ear.

So now they had a description of the messenger, but what about the message? They had thanked Enni and her mother and returned to their rooms. Lukas scanned the suite, checked the windows, then went to bed while she and Falvii searched the hotel's tourist database for 'Xaca' – whatever he, she or it was.

They soon discovered that it was the name of a village near the headwaters of the Utieku River, and the only way to get there quickly was by air. The database said that the Xaca region had once been the centre of logging for the precious hakana hardwood. It was now a reforestation area and welcomed tourists to its many walking trails and natural pools.

'Doesn't sound too dangerous – or a location for an illegal drug lab,' Falvii commented.

Calin yawned. 'Let's just see when we get there.' The swim and the excitement of the evening had taken their toll and she was ready to turn in. 'We'll order a windshifter in the morning. I'm off to bed.'

Falvii went to a glass-fronted cabinet and pulled out a bottle of honey-coloured liqueur. 'Nightcap? It's the finest Huthon sherry.'

The evening – although interrupted – had been going so well. He hoped they could continue.

On her way to her bedroom, she paused and lay a hand on his shoulder. 'Tempting. But I need sleep. Thanks anyway, Falvii. See you in the morning.'

He nodded and blew a kiss to her retreating frame. She may have been exhausted but Falvii knew he would struggle to sleep as images of the beautiful young woman in the clear waters of the pool flooded his mind.

They set out at dawn the next morning with Lukas taking the helm. Despite Falvii's desire to hold off until they could get a contingent of armed guards from the local police, Calin was keen to follow the lead they'd been given – and without fuss. He insisted, though, that they lodge their flight plan with both her mother and the Rekkushu police.

The sky was clear and, by leaving early, they missed the rising humidity. Along the way they caught glimpses of the river's raging waterfalls between the trees. After an hour of flying low over the treetops, mist was beginning to gather and they were happy to put down at a landing area on the outskirts of the village before the clouds got too thick.

The noise of the shifter's engine died away and was replaced by the sounds of birdsong and the chattering of kaypak monkeys. Insects whirred in the warm moist air as Falvii led the way along a path towards the village. They had only been able to see a few buildings from above due to the gathering mist and the cover provided by the rainforest. But when they got to a clearing, the structures that had looked solid from the air turned out to be ruins. Fragments of water-stained stone walls had tumbled to the ground. Green-tiled roofs were cleaved in two atop the remains of buildings, and grass and saplings had begun to fight for dominance. There was no one in sight.

Calin and Falvii looked at each other. Whoever once lived at Xaca was not there anymore.

'Some village,' Falvii said resignedly. 'Looks like no-one's been here for years.'

'The phrase wild goose chase springs to mind,' Calin remarked with a tired sigh.

'I can't believe that someone went to all the trouble of sending us that message for nothing. It just doesn't make sense.' Falvii frowned and scanned the surrounding trees. 'I'm going to look around. There might be more beyond the trees. Stay here with Lukas.'

Calin grimaced. 'Don't go too far.'

'I won't.' He checked his laser pistol in the belt at his waist then nodded and walked into the forest.

Calin stepped gingerly over the collapsed walls of the first building while Lukas walked the perimeter, gun at the ready. There were remains of what looked like a child's cot and an overturned metallic chair partially obscured by weeds, so she guessed it might have been a private dwelling. It was hard to make out what had caused the destruction, though. She could see no traces of scorch marks or ion-laser striations.

The next building she examined was the same. A collapsed roof, its tiles smashed overlying wooden beams that were splintered and askew. Here she found a companel with its screen caved in, like someone had taken a hammer to it. Again, a couple of creepers had begun their journey to re-establish supremacy over the rubble. But given how quickly everything grew in this heat and humidity, Calin guessed this devastation was recent.

Suddenly a bird screeched and she was forced to duck, its talons nearly raking her head as it swooped. The motion threw her off balance and she fell, landing hard on her tailbone.

'Ow!' she cried.

'Let me help you up.' She started at the voice behind her and turned to see a bearded man with a scar on the right side of his head. 'I think your companion startled the bird.'

Despite the pain in her back, Calin tried frantically to shuffle away. The man loomed above her, blocking the dappled light through the trees.

'It's all right,' he began, 'I won't –'

Suddenly, he toppled lifeless onto her, pinning her to the ground. The breath shot out of her lungs as she groaned under his weight. Above her, a triumphant Lukas appeared. He bent down to lift the man's body off her.

'Are you okay?' he asked.

Calin grimaced. 'Yes, but ... Oh, I hope you haven't killed him.' She scrambled to the side of the unconscious man and checked his neck for a pulse. *Relief! Out cold, but still alive.* 'You've stunned him. That's all.'

There was the noise of bushes being pushed back and Falvii was suddenly at her side. He took in the scene before sweeping the hair back from the man's forehead to reveal a scar above the right eye. 'So this is our secret messenger.'

'It appears so.' She stretched out the taut muscles of her neck. 'Let's hope he wakes up soon.'

No sooner had the words left her mouth than the stranger's face contorted in a spasm of pain and a breath escaped in a rush from between his lips. He opened his eyes and squinted up at them. Falvii instantly raised his weapon at which the man shook his head.

'Not necessary ... No threat,' he grunted, raising a hand to rub at his left shoulder.

'Explain yourself!' Falvii commanded.

'May I sit up first?' The man coughed and pushed himself onto his elbows. Calin jumped up to stand next to her cousin.

'Speak! Who are you?' she barked.

'Please ... My name is Mikel Piek. I am – or rather, *was* – a scientist. I mean you no harm.'

Calin sucked in a breath at the name but remembered that this was a man prepared to use mentante powers to control a child's mind. 'Doctor Piek? You worked for Professor Hasler on Autabron. But I thought you were …'

'Dead? I might as well be,' he acknowledged sadly. 'And I might still be if you won't help me.'

'Doctor Amanie told me you had disappeared,' Calin said. 'She thought you might have been harmed.'

The man's eyes lit up. 'You saw Li-kah? Is she well? Oh, please tell me she is safe.' The words spilled out of him like water. 'I've been so worried for her.'

'She's fine. I saw her in Genkarah at the university ten days ago.'

Piek's eyes closed and he cupped his cheeks in both hands in the traditional Huthon gesture of prayer. 'Thanks be to all the gods!' He turned a doleful gaze on them. 'The Earthan woman said she would kill Li-kah *and* her family if I didn't comply. I had no choice. Even Professor Hasler is being coerced. I can't believe he would do this otherwise.'

Falvii looked at Calin to see if any of this was making sense to her but her brows too were knitted together. 'Would never do what?'

'Mind control a child, perhaps?' Calin snapped, a hint of venom in her voice.

Piek shook his head sadly and drew his hands together in a gesture of supplication. 'Please forgive me, my lady. When I saw how you reacted with Enni, I knew you were here to help. I'm happy to show you my lab. I'm sorry.'

Calin scowled at him. 'You were watching us?'

'Since two days ago. One of my suppliers told me you had called at the pharma-plant asking questions.'

'Suppliers!' Falvii's face began to redden. 'What is going on here? And who's being coerced? Speak plainly!'

Piek's shoulders dropped and he exhaled a long breath. 'To supply the drug, the one you were asking about. To send it to Autabron. I make it here. These ruins are a cover for an underground laboratory.'

Calin interjected. 'Wait – are you telling us that *you've* been making urthrengo and sending it to Autabron?'

'Yes.' Piek's head hung even lower.

'But why? What for?' asked Falvii.

'Oh, I assumed you knew. To put into the water supply.' At the joint looks of confusion on their faces, Piek went on. 'You know that the drug reduces resistance, induces compliance? Well, they are using it to make the mine workers more amenable, less irritated. They were becoming agitated with the demands for increased output and no rise in wages. So the mine owners –'

'Drugged them, to keep them quiet,' Calin finished.

'Yes,' Piek said. 'But the effects wear off over time unless you increase the dose. But that runs the risk of death.'

Falvii scratched the back of his head. 'So let me get this straight.,' he began. 'You've been helping the GKD organisation to poison their workers.'

'It's biological behaviour control on a mass scale, yes. But no one has died from it,' Piek added sheepishly.

'Yet!' Falvii exclaimed.

'You mentioned an Earthan woman. Is she behind this?' Calin asked.

'She and Director Jarkoo.' Piek's voice rose. 'They're dangerous people. I've seen what they do. They beheaded my pet kareek and threatened to do the same to Li'kah! I had to comply so that she stays safe.'

Piek stood up cautiously and brushed down his clothes before turning to Calin. 'They've demanded I produce more of the drug. Twice as much. But I just can't … I can't see an end to it.' He shook his head despairingly and when he lifted his eyes to her again, Calin saw tears. 'I need your help, my lady, to end this. Can you make sure Li-kah Amanie and her family will be safe if I give myself up? And Professor Hasler's family too?'

Calin looked at Falvii, who gave a small nod of encouragement. 'Of course we'll help,' Calin said. 'But first, you have an apology to make to a little girl and her mother. And then be prepared for all hell to break lose.'

Finn's face was a stone mask. Setiyan suspected that there had not been a second when his eyes had not been on them as they had sailed lazily around the small lake, but her bodyguard's concerns were of so little importance now that she knew Denkaun felt as she did.

154

To be so close to the man and feel his touch on her skin was an indescribable sensation. She had looked into those aquamarine eyes and felt bound to him by chains of steel. And, in the gondola, when he had stroked her cheek and pushed back a strand of her hair, his fingers lingering softly on her mouth, she had had an overwhelming desire to place her lips on his.

Only a day! This was how long she had known this man and yet she could hardly wait until the next time she would see him.

They had returned to Beshwuk on the q'ist transporter late in the afternoon. Finn was a silent, brooding shadow and said not a word the whole time. But she had hardly been aware of his presence as her eyes never left Denkaun's face for more than a couple of seconds.

Denkaun returned them to her rooms and, with a light kiss on the back of her hand, left, vowing to see her later. Almost before the chamber door slid shut, Finn began.

'What was that all about? Going off in that boat –'

'Gondola,' she interjected.

'Without one thought for your safety.' He held up his hands in a gesture of despair. 'I just don't know. You don't seem to care.'

'Kalik would never hurt me. I was quite safe.' She could not say the words without smiling. The memory of his strong hands caressing her neck still made her breathless.

'You don't know the man. You've no idea of what he's up to.'

'Lieutenant Finn, please stop. I know enough about him to know he is being solicitous and a good host. That is all.' She moved to the closet and began eyeing her selection of dresses, taking a thoughtful look at each one.

'I have a bad feeling about him,' Finn insisted forcefully.

'And I don't.' Setiyan stopped perusing her clothes. 'Please leave. I have to get ready for dinner.' When Finn did not move, she turned an angry glare at him. 'I said leave ... please!'

With an angry scowl, Finn spun on his heel and left the room. Setiyan had already returned to her wardrobe by the time he exited. She settled on a shimmering indigo silk floor-length dress with a sapphire necklace – to bring out the colour of her eyes – before heading to the bathroom. If her hopes and dreams were to come true, tonight would be more wonderful and more exciting than she could ever imagine.

155

It took a couple of days for Jax to complete his meetings with the remaining GKD officials and miners' representatives and for a spaceracer to arrive for his journey back to Altan. But following his conversation with Setiyan on the morning of his departure, he felt sure he was making the right decision. She had reported that they had received a warm welcome at Beshwuk and that she, Serekunda and Finn were getting to know the people. They had established an excellent rapport, especially with the tribe's leader, Kalik Denkaun, who had been more than hospitable. He had spent a great deal of time with them and answered all their questions honestly and openly. The mission was going even better than they had expected and Seti went so far as to declare it a triumph of diplomacy.

Jax had made his apologies to Sen-Caspiran and Birkaan. He would return to Altan having completed as much of his investigation into the explosions and the missing scientist as was possible for now. He hoped they would find out more once they had spoken to the supervisor at the Te'kaan mine. Either way, whilst it looked like the plants were being sabotaged, evidence was hard to find and he questioned whether he had any further role here. Further investigation into Professor Hasler's sudden wealth could be done from home and, after this week away, he was anxious to see Linnayen again.

When the call came from Calin and Falvii that they had found Mikel Piek on Hutho and that he had startling news about the water at the mine sites having been contaminated, he was a day out from Altan. His ship was too far from Autabron to turn back and, if he was honest, he had set his heart on seeing his beloved wife again. But he relayed the news immediately to Caspiran and Birkaan.

Kalisa Caspiran's normally placid face darkened with the news. 'How could this happen? Who is responsible?'

'Piek accuses Director Jarkoo and spoke of an Earthan woman. I'm hoping that's not Harrie Whitton-Blake,' Jax replied.

'Though you fear it is,' Caspiran finished for him.

'It would make sense,' Jax continued. 'According to her, she's been on Autabron to monitor the tensions on behalf of Earthan security and government interests. One way to reduce the workers' anxieties would be to drug them.'

'If this is the case then Birkaan and I will take extra precautions.'

'Absolutely. Find out what you can and get samples of the tap water tested – independently, of course.'

Jax finished the transmission and massaged his aching head. This was all too much. So many questions flooded his mind. Did the people know that they were being drugged? He assumed not. But if they'd found out, that would explain their disquiet with the mine owners. Or was the destruction of Euta Sakek enough to fuel rebellion? How involved was Avad Jarkoo? Instigator or puppet? Had Professor Hasler been complicit? That would explain his ability to pay for such a fine apartment. As for Harrie, he didn't want to admit that she was at the heart of this deception, but he knew she was more than capable of it.

Sitting beside the captain on the bridge, as the sight of the blue-green hues of Altan hove into view, he thanked whatever fates had brought him to this home and this woman. Linnayen's arms were just a few hours away now and he would never be more relieved to be with her once more.

Chapter Twelve

It was past midnight and the settlement was finally quiet. Denkaun, naked in the chill of the evening, stood looking out of the viewport. Below him the folds of land lay like grey velvet swathed in the silver light of the moon, Aunis, and behind him stood Setiyan Genara. Her soft, warm flesh pressed into his as her hands encircled him. One lay on his chest, the other on his flat belly. He felt her breath on his back and heard a contented sigh escape her lips.

Such lips! Only a couple of hours ago he had enjoyed crushing them with his own before pushing them apart with his tongue. Though she had restrained herself over dinner, not daring to touch him in front of everyone, it was a different story when he had come to her rooms later. The door had slid open and she stood in the moonlight, waiting to receive him, her chest heaving with anticipation. In just two paces he had swept her into his arms and grasped her long, fair hair, pulling her head back to expose her neck. At the first touch of his mouth on her skin she had groaned with pleasure, and as he worked his way up to her lips he slid a hand down to remove her dress from one shoulder, exposing her breast. He had turned and twisted the nipple urgently until it was stiff and demanding of his mouth. He was amazed that he needed to do so little to overcome any resistance.

He could almost feel the pounding of her heart as her dress had fallen to the floor, and, as he had hoped, she was naked underneath. Only the string of blue gems at her neck remained. He pulled back, wanting to see the full beauty of his prize. His eyes hungrily devoured the sight of her firm, high breasts, the smooth curve of her hips and, most tantalising of all, the shadowed mound at the top of her legs where his fingers began to probe insistently. She had moaned with the pleasure he gave her and pulled his face to her own to receive her demanding kisses, all the while forcing her body into his, wanting to feel his skin against her own. Her hands soon stripped him of his tunic and then fought against the restraints of his belt. Her need had been immediate, as he knew it would be. The drug, diluted into every liquid she had tasted since coming to Beshwuk, combined with the pheromone oil smoothed into the skin of his neck was having the desired effect. Mira had told him to expect her submission, but her eagerness for him was unforeseen. Not that it was unwelcome. He had only ever had Wika and a few other women, all Autabroni. So it was a pleasurable change to have someone – something – different. And the princess was so compelling. For her, once was not enough.

Now, as he stood gazing at the midnight landscape, he counted that they had copulated three times. He had planted his seed deep inside her and he felt sure that it would not be wasted. Even so, one more time would not hurt.

He took hold of her encircling hands and turned to face her. One hand lifted her chin while the other descended to her breasts. The reaction was electric. Her mouth fell open and she gasped. Her arms flew up to pull his body closer to hers. He smothered her mouth with his own as he lifted her legs to fit around his waist and spun her around. He pressed her against the glass of the viewport until she was a mere silhouette beyond which he saw the silvern desert, its soft shadows glistening in the moonlight.

This was his land, his country. And, through this woman, he would take not only this world but all the other worlds too. It was the price fate said he must pay, but with such a willing partner there was no cost at all. He pushed his erection deep into her and felt her contract against it, stimulating him once more. His breath came hard and fast and his chest heaved. He would make it last longer. She needed to reach her climax too. Nothing must be wasted. Finally, with one final thrust, he felt her spasm and then melt with the glorious release of orgasm.

'My sweet princess ... You'll never know how much you mean to me. Stay with me. Stay forever. Stay ...' he crooned into her ear as he burst inside her.

Her answer came between his demanding thrusts. 'Yes ... Yes ... I'm yours.'

Setiyan's eyes were closed in the rapture of the moment. She could not see Denkaun's self-satisfied smile in the pale light and would never know how much it was a mirror image of the old shaman's, who sat watching them on a vidscreen two levels below. After years of waiting and planning, the prophecy would finally come to pass. The son of the twins had mated with his sister. The legacy was forged in the mingling of their seed.

The morning of their third day in Beshwuk dawned as it ever did. First Lau topped the horizon and a shaft of piercing golden light slammed through Finn's force-shield viewport. He groaned as it played on his closed eyelids, insistent that he open them and greet the day. There was nothing he wanted to do less. He pulled the quilt up over his head, inside of which a thousand tiny hammers smacked against his brain. This was the result of the two extra flagons of kooruk he had drunk last night after he'd returned the princess to her rooms. He should have known better, of course. He'd done the rounds of enough bars on Autabron on his past visits to know the dangers. But this brew was lethal. It had tasted so smooth, like drinking amber honey. It was only when he'd stood up to make his farewells that he realised its kick. He'd barely made it back to his room where he instantly toppled onto the bed like a collapsed chimney.

There was a knock on the door and the sound of the panel sliding open. 'Morning, my friend!' Serekunda's voice was as bright as the sunlight now pervading every nook and cranny of the room.

'Ugh.' Finn did not move under the quilt.

'I thought you'd say that. So I've brought you the perfect breakfast.'

Finn emitted a whimpering noise.

'Ah, don't be like that. Trust me. This is just the ticket, my friend,' Serekunda announced happily. 'Fresh sivakaan juice with a dash of spicy stukka.'

'Fuck off.'

'Did you know that curse is the same in at least twelve languages?' Finn's groan came louder as Serekunda continued. 'No? Mmm, well Elder Jakaanha warned me last night at dinner. He said the way you were going at it you'd need this if you wanted to be able to walk this morning.' Jug of juice in one hand, Serekunda stripped away the quilt covering Finn's tangled body with the other. 'I see he was right.'

'I still have legs?'

'Indeed you do, lieutenant, and, thankfully, they are still encased in your trousers.'

Serekunda poured some of the blue juice into a glass from the bedside table and handed it to Finn once he had pulled himself into a sitting position.

'We are tasked to meet with the representative elders of the Gaksi tribe today, if you recall,' he reminded Finn. 'We leave in about an hour, so I thought I'd give you a head start.'

Finn swallowed some of the thick juice. The taste reminded him of pineapples from back home and seemed to be having a calming effect on his stomach already.

'Thanks. Is the princess up yet?'

'Haven't seen her. But I'd be surprised if she's as bad as you. I saw only water in her glass.'

Finn took another slug of the juice and smacked his lips. 'Mmm. She's usually more palatable after a glass of wine.' A frown crossed his face as memories of the previous evening began to surface. 'Why'd she leave so early? I thought she was having fun.'

Serekunda smiled and raised his eyebrows. 'I think that was more to do with the young man at her side than any wine. He seemed to be claiming all her attention.'

Finn's frown deepened. 'Yes. There's something – I don't know. Something off about Denkaun. What do you make of him, Pieter?'

Serekunda sat on the bed next to Finn. 'Well, what I find hard to understand is the tribe's total acceptance of him. I know of examples in ancient societies on Earth where a stranger has been revered. But Autabron has always been such an insular place. There's hardly any inter-breeding between the tribes even. Maybe there's something about Kalik Denkaun's heritage that we don't know.'

'Or that we haven't been told,' Finn completed the thought.

'Well, we're not going to find out anything if we don't get you up and functioning.' Serekunda stood and proffered a hand to Finn. 'Come on, my friend. Get into that shower. If you'll pardon me for saying, you need a wash.'

Wika was waiting for him when he returned to his rooms. She sat upright on the end of his bed with her hands folded in her lap. She looked almost demure, except for the black fire in her eyes and the steel set of her jaw. Denkaun went straight past her and began disrobing as he walked towards the shower.

'What brings you here, Wika? I thought I told you to stay with your father. Indeed, I know I did.' Now fully naked, he came over to her and forced her chin up to face him. 'Why have you disobeyed me?'

'You know why I'm here,' she spat back. 'Did you enjoy the bitch-whore?'

His smile did not reach as far as his eyes as he spoke. 'Very much. Do you want the details of the many ways I took her? Would you like me to do the same to you?' He pushed apart her legs with his own, forcing her back onto the coverlet and raising the hem of her skirt as he did so. 'You would, wouldn't you?'

Though Denkaun was a strong man, Wika was Autabroni and more than his match. She raised her hand and slapped his cheek hard, then took advantage of his surprise to push him off her and roll to the side out of his grasp. He fell onto his back and lay there laughing. She stood up, panting from her efforts. *He finds this funny!* She stepped to the end of the bed and leaned over him, pulling her arm back. He caught her fist in an iron grip before she could connect with his face.

'Oh no, my love. That'll never do.'

'Oh! You ... I hate you!'

'No, you don't, my sweet Wika. You love me.' His voice was silken, tempting. He drew her down on top of him, but she struggled to pull away.

'No! Not after her! You reek of her!' She writhed in his arms and scrunched up her face.

'It's true,' he conceded. 'So I'll wash her off and you can join me.'

He rolled her off him easily then stood up, pulling her with him. She fought against his grasp, crying as he dragged her behind him towards the bathroom.

'Stop yowling, woman! You'll distress our baby.'

'As if you care!' she screeched. 'You think only of yourself.'

He stopped in his tracks, turning to face her. His body went rigid and she crumpled with the pain his grip inflicted on her wrist. She dropped to her knees.

'Let me go,' she begged. 'Please ... You're hurting me.'

'I think nothing of myself. Everything I do is for our people, for the Guznon, for Autabron. Do you still not see it?

'I know. I know –'

'I am the A'bat!' he interjected, his grip on her arm tightening. She squirmed and tears gathered at the corners of her eyes. 'Through me, the prophecy will be fulfilled. There is destiny here.'

'And you, child, will not interfere with it!' The old shaman's voice filled the room. They had not noticed Mira's entrance.

Denkaun instantly released Wika, who began massaging her crushed limb. He stepped over to Mira, face beaming, and kneeled before her. She stroked his white-blond hair then tilted his face up to her, leaning down to plant a kiss on his forehead.

'Oh, my son. Never have you made me happier. The seed is sown.'

'Natar, I have done my duty and will do so again until the outcome is assured.'

Mira laughed and shook her head affectionately. 'Ah! So you enjoyed your mission? And why should you not? The princess is a beauty.'

Wika scowled at the pair of them, the naked man prone before the old hag. It was unnatural, sickening. She loved Kalik but hated the old woman. *She takes control of him and I am as nothing! But I bear his child. Mine will be the firstborn! The first, the one who will inherit.*

The pounding silence filled her head. As she watched the hated woman touch her beloved man, an idea began to germinate. What cared she for the stupid prophecy? Her child, Kalik's child, would be born long before the bitch-whore's. *And who's to say hers would survive?*

The early morning sun threw shards of pink-tinged light through the glassware sitting atop the table on Linnayen's private balcony. Crystal slivers danced lazily across a bowl of fruit, kicked into occasional motion by a light breeze that pushed through the gold leaves of potted entaki bushes. Jax had only arrived home the evening before but Li-el could not resist joining her daughter for breakfast to hear the news firsthand.

'Granted, I know little enough about his first love. But Duncan's told me everything I need to know.' Li-el Dacas was firm. 'She's dreadful!'

'You don't know that, Mother,' Linnayen retorted, just managing to keep her voice neutral.

'I do. Actors are expert in studying people, all their little traits and foibles. I think Duncan's got the measure of her.' Li-el had got into her stride and was going to take full advantage of it. 'He told me that he never took to her. Very manipulative. Poor Jax, only a boy. Completely clueless! She ran squirrels around him!'

Linnayen tried not to laugh. 'Circles, Mother. Squirrels are small furry animals.'

'Really? Are you sure?' She harrumphed. 'Anyway, what he's discovered about her does not surprise me one bit.'

'He suspects. He's not yet sure,' Linnayen countered. 'Though how many Earthan women could there have been on Autabron at the time?'

Linnayen sighed resignedly. It had been wonderful to have her husband back at home, although his news was worrying to say the least. Could it be true that the workers in the mining settlements were being drugged to keep them malleable? What a despicable act if so. Calin and Falvii were bringing back the scientist, Mikel Piek, to Altan for further questioning and to be reconciled with Doctor Amanie. Piek had said he didn't know the Earthan woman's name and he had never seen her, but he might recognise the voice. As per protocol, Jax had recordings of the team's recent meetings in Zaz-Rakuum, and Harriet Whitton-Blake's distinctive accent was unmistakeable.

Deep down, Linnayen wanted the Whitton-Blake woman to be the antagonist. She had picked up the confusion in her husband's voice and demeanour when speaking of her and she had to admit to feeling a twinge of jealousy. She knew about Jax's first love affair, of course. He had been open about it shortly after they had been reconciled – after her affair with Navarr had ended. But he had also been dismissive of it. She later found out from Duncan McCrae that he had been besotted with the woman. Being Jax, he had planned out his whole future with her. Even Jax's parents, David and Thea, had liked her immensely and, Duncan had revealed, would have been happy for them to have married. What must he have thought on seeing her again after all these years? Had he still been attracted to her?

Lost in her thoughts and deafened by the early morning birdsong, she did not hear Jax enter the terrace.

'Aha! My two favourite women.'

He strode over to Li-el and bent down to kiss her cheek before turning to Linnayen and stroking her face affectionately.

'How do you manage to always look so beautiful in the morning?' he asked his wife with a broad smile.

'And how do you manage to come up with a new compliment each day?' she returned.

'It's a gift. But you bring it out in me.' He took a seat at the table and began to fill his plate. 'This looks good. Can I have the last piece of mushroom bake?'

Both women ignored him, though Li-el waved a hand giving her permission. They had already eaten and, before their discussion about Harriet Whitton-Blake, had been reading their schedules for the day. Linnayen returned to her list.

'I'm opening the new native language centre in Silbaraz-Re later this morning. So I can't meet Calin off the transporter,' she commented.

'Mmm. That's okay. I'll send one of my men. I've that energy symposium.'

'I can meet her,' Li-el piped up. Both stopped and looked at her, eyebrows raised. 'Well, I can. I'm not senile. I know where the transit tower is. Besides, I want to see Falvii Min too. I hear he's very handsome. Turned out well.'

'My sister says that Odar Min's boys are all very good-looking,' Linnayen agreed.

'I wonder what Calin thinks of him?'

'Mother!' Linnayen warned. 'Don't you go pushing her onto him. Calin takes her own time in these things.'

'Yes, but if I don't do something, I'll be dead before either of these girls are married.'

Jax choked on a mouthful of mushroom bake. A crumb landed on the warm brown tiles of the balcony and was quickly swept up by one of the purple-feathered belika birds that nested in the potted shrubs.

'They'll marry in their own good time, Li-el,' Jax spurted, trying to keep the rest of his food in his mouth. 'And if they marry, I'll lay a thousand keks that you'll be leading the procession.'

'Indeed I will,' Li-el retorted. She stood and smoothed the folds of her dress, a sumptuous emerald silk. 'I think the kala pearls today. I want to look my best. Young Falvii needs to see that our women retain their beauty well into maturity.'

As Li-el walked away humming to herself, the belika bird, famous for their mimicry, tried to emulate the sound. It's gargling interpretation made Linnayen laugh even more.

'I suppose we can't stop her, can we?' Jax surmised cheerfully.

'And I wouldn't want to. But now that she's gone ...' Linnayen raised an eyebrow and smiled seductively. 'Have you had enough breakfast, my love? Or do you have room for something else?'

Jax needed no persuading. He pushed his plate aside, wiped the crumbs from his mouth and jumped up. Bending down to capture his wife's cheeks in both hands, he kissed her passionately. As she rose and allowed him to sweep her into his arms, Jax smothered her neck with kisses and she groaned with delight. Whatever meetings and events they had planned for that day would have to wait and, Linnayen thought to herself, whatever memories Jax had of other women would soon be nothing but dried-up relics of an ancient past. She would make sure of it.

Finn could see that Setiyan was trying hard to concentrate. The Gaksi elders were regaling her and Pieter Serekunda with concerns over the loss of their traditional ways. Their ceremonies and rituals had become increasingly inconsequential to the younger generation, who, as they saw it, had been entranced by the ease of life in the cities and ubiquitous media intrusions into everyday life. More than one complained that the mine never gave their workers enough time off to come home for important events, so how were they to know their heritage if they could not partake in it? Another elder – a mother of two sons – bemoaned the fact that they had decided to choose their own wives, something that went completely against tradition. But what seemed to cause the most distress was an apathy among their people generally. Even a few of the elders who lived in the cities had, as one old man put it, 'become contaminated with indifference' and were not even concerned at the changes in the behaviours of their younger tribe members.

How could this be happening, they wanted to know. For two hundred years, the mine owners had enjoyed a relatively happy co-existence with the Gaksi, the Guznon and all the other tribes of

Autabron. They had been proud that their planet was so important to the Galactic Union. It was only in the last year or two that things had changed.

Setiyan listened and nodded and offered words of comfort and concern. But Finn could see that every so often, her eyes would glaze over. She might still be looking at whoever she was with, but she was not registering what they were saying. Was she tired, he wondered. She had looked pale when she met them at the q'ist transporter that was to take them to the Gaksi lands. Maybe she was sick? Mira joined the party as an ambassador, but Finn was relieved to see that Kalik Denkaun had absented himself. When Mira mentioned his name in order to pass on his apologies, Seti's eyes had opened wide with expectation. But, as the old woman explained his absence, they clouded over and her chin sank.

All through the journey and even since then she had been uncommonly quiet, which, given the fiery nature of the tribespeople, was quite useful. They respected the fact that she listened rather than proffered her own views. As for Serekunda, he was in his element. He engaged with both solicitude and understanding, taking notes and promising to do his best to find out what he could. The Gaksi elders were pleased that they had been consulted and, after a brief lunch, the Beshwuk group made their farewells and left for home.

Once on the q'ist, Mira congratulated Serekunda and Setiyan.

'I am so pleased, my lady and Doctor Serekunda, that this visit to the Gaksi has been fruitful. My fellow tribespeople have been honoured by your attention.'

'It was a pleasure, Mira,' Serekunda assured her. 'And I mean to follow up their concerns as soon as we get back to Zaz-Rakuum.'

'Which will be the day after tomorrow,' added Finn.

Seti shifted uncomfortably in her seat and her brow furrowed.

'We will miss you. Though you'll be looking forward to seeing your father again, my lady,' Mira commented solicitously.

'No!' Before she realised it, Seti had blurted out her rejection of the idea of leaving Beshwuk. At the sight of the surprised faces before her, she continued quickly, 'I mean, that won't be possible. Seeing my father. He's already left for Altan.'

Mira nodded. 'Oh, forgive me. I did not know.'

'Please don't apologise. In fact …' Seti paused mid-sentence and she swallowed before continuing. 'In fact, I won't be leaving for Zaz. I've decided to stay … a little longer.'

It was Finn's turn to speak without thinking. 'What! You … You can't!'

Pieter Serekunda's face was equally dark. 'My lady, our schedule …'

'I'm staying.' Her statement was delivered with a calm that Finn had never seen in the young woman.

'You can't,' Finn replied firmly. 'Your father has given me –'

'Orders, I know,' Seti interjected. 'But I'm staying anyway. There's more I need to know – *want* to know. I'm staying.'

With that, she turned away from them all and closed her eyes. Finn sat in shock. She was just being stubborn. *Being a bloody princess!*

He looked to Serekunda and was met with a helpless shrug and an expression that matched his own, confusion and concern in equal measure. But as he glanced at Mira he could have sworn he saw the hint of a smile.

Harrie emptied another drawer into a valise. With Jax having gone a few days earlier and her instructions passed on to Jarkoo, she saw no reason to stay on Autabron. It was a shame that Jax had gone scurrying back to his wife, but not unexpected. Twenty-five years was a long time, though she was sure that he had been tempted. No matter. She would be pleased to get home. There were new interests back on Earth that would keep her occupied. Autabron – and especially Avad Jarkoo – had become tedious beyond belief.

As she pushed down on the overfull case, the door slid open and the object of her distaste himself stomped into her room.

'Harrie, you can't go,' Jarkoo said. 'Something's gone wrong.'

She turned away from him and kept on with her task.

'It's Piek,' Jarkoo insisted. 'He's been found.'

At first the name didn't register, but within seconds she had stopped, swivelled around smartly and her eyes drilled into Jarkoo's.

'How?'

'I don't know but he went silent three days ago. I've been trying to get him on comms. Then this morning he was seen at the transit tower in Genkarah, apparently arriving with the younger Genara princess.'

'Explain.'

'Hasler saw it on the morning's feed. The princess was the story, of course. But Hasler said he saw Piek behind her . He was part of her group.'

Harrie's brain fired up. What did she need to know? Would Piek's capture – if that's what this was – affect her? Would he talk? *Of course he would. Probably already had. Cat's out of the bag.* Out of the corner of her eye, she saw Jarkoo nervously shifting from foot to foot. *Bloody idiot! So annoying.*

Within seconds, she had her course laid out.

'Did you increase the dosage as I instructed?'

Jarkoo was startled by the question at a time like this. 'Well, yes, of course,' he replied anxiously. 'But we needed more supply. That's why I was trying to get in contact with Piek.'

Harrie nodded. 'Makes sense. And you told no one?'

'Of course not.'

'Good.' She turned back to the suitcase on her bed and removed a small flick-knife from the side pocket. Her father had been right: it always paid to keep a weapon close by. She slid the blade into the sleeve of her jacket and swivelled to face Jarkoo. Without stopping for a breath, she punched him hard in the face. He staggered with the force of the blow, raising a hand to the site of his bleeding injury. His eyes connected with hers and were filled with confusion and surprise. She came at him again, this time a punch to the side of his neck. The soft tissue caved under the blow, pushing the air out of his windpipe. But in the few seconds he took to absorb the assault, he regained some sense of the danger he was in. It was time to fight back.

He ducked the next blow and dove into her stomach with his head, throwing her back onto the bed. His weight held her pinned and he slapped her face hard.

'What're you doing? Bitch!' he yelled at her. But all he got in return was a sick smile through the blood that had begun to ooze from her mouth.

She squirmed underneath him and got her hands up high enough to push him off, rolling with the grace of a cat to the side and shaking the knife easily into her hand. She would have plunged it into his abdomen there and then but Jarkoo had caught the movement and grabbed her wrists. He rolled back on top of her, pinning Harrie with his weight.

Pulling himself back onto his feet, Jarkoo dragged her with him. Immediately Harrie swung a knee into his groin and as he yelped in pain, he let go of her wrist. She immediately brought her arm down and the blade connected with his thigh. He cried out with the sudden tearing agony in his leg. She looked up at him, triumph in her eyes.

Jarkoo raised a knee and slammed it hard into her stomach, enjoying the sound of the wind escaping her lungs as she bent over.

'Bitch! Think to kill me? Fool!' He spat the words as he slammed a fist down onto the back of her head.

As Harrie groaned and slumped to the floor, Jarkoo turned her body over and kicked her hard in the stomach, but Harrie used the opportunity to wield her blade once more. She rolled towards him and plunged the knife deep into his heel. Jarkoo screamed and dropped to the floor, the strength in his legs leaving him.

Maybe she had been stupid to take on an Autabroni – even their women were strong – but another piece of Daddy's advice came into her mind as she watched the man fall, a look of anguish and surprise on his twisted face. Any fast-acting poison was as effective as brute force, and when applied to the tip of a blade was extremely useful in a tight situation.

Jarkoo was not quite dead as he tumbled, which gave her time to puncture his lungs and one of his kidneys as he lay on the floor. It was important to ensure the blood still flowed at the time these wounds were inflicted, she reasoned. She wanted no questions about his death. Everyone must be assured that she had been forced to kill him in self-defence and, without doubt, once they saw the many bruises and injuries she had received, they would be.

Chapter Thirteen

It was like smashing his head against concrete. He had tried to reason with the princess but she had sat there serenely, with an expressionless look on her face, affirming that she would be staying in the Beshwuk settlement for the foreseeable future. He had railed that this was not the object of their mission. They were there only to judge the temperament of the tribespeople, not live with them. Their stay was to be a few days, certainly no more than a week. But she would not be shifted.

'I will stay here,' she asserted. 'You may go back to Zaz-Rakuum if you wish. But I will stay.'

'You can't! It's not part of your brief to stay. We've found out what we need. So it's time to go.'

Seti removed her outer tunic, folded it and laid it across the back of a chair where she smoothed out the last of the creases. 'I don't know how many more times I need to say it, lieutenant – I am staying.' She sat in the chair and began to remove the fastenings on her shoes.

Finn was not giving up. 'So what am I going to say to your father? He'll be furious.' He paced the polished earth floor then spun back to face her once more. 'You have duties back home on Altan. You have to be there.'

'They're nothing. Calin can do all that.'

She tugged at the clasp on the second of her boots.

'Here,' Finn said, kneeling in front of her. He had not been this physically close to her since her mugging in the park in Zaz and he could not stop the extra beat of his heart as he touched her skin. The clasp came free and he pulled off the boot with a flourish.

'Thank you,' she replied.

Just then the door opened and Kalik Denkaun walked in, smiling broadly. 'Ah! You're home, my princess.'

Seti jumped up from the chair knocking Finn to one side in her haste to cross the space to Denkaun.

'Kalik! How wonderful to see you!'

Denkaun bowed low before her and Finn judged it was only this that stopped her from throwing herself into his arms. He rose from the floor. *So this was the reason.*

'My princess, how lovely you look today,' he exclaimed, his eyes travelling the length of her body. 'Superb!' He flattered with the smoothness of a frozen lake, but the meaning of his words did not extend to his eyes.

Setiyan did not speak but Finn knew enough about body language to pick up her yearning. She was straining to be as close to him as possible.

'I've come to invite you to dinner. There are some delicacies I want you to try, my lady. I think you'll – no, I *know* you'll like them. Will you join me? If you're not too tired …'

'Of course I'll come to you – I mean, join you. I'd love that,' she breathed and then swallowed her excitement.

Finn tried to hide his scowl. Did she think he was a fool? Anyone could see the lay of the land. Setiyan Genara thought herself to be in love with this man. It was going to be impossible to drag her back to Altan now and Finn was not looking forward to explaining it to Jax and, even worse, the Ki.

Denkaun smiled and took both of her hands in his to kiss them, his eyes never leaving her face for a moment. 'I'll send for you,' he said and started to turn away before stopping suddenly. 'Ah, lieutenant, I have not forgotten you. My captain of the guard and his men have asked that you and Doctor Serekunda and your men join them tonight. They have an exercise planned, to be followed by a regimental dinner.'

Finn smiled regretfully. 'That's kind, but I'm afraid –'

'Oh, please understand. Your princess will be quite safe. My natar, Lady Mira, is joining us, as are some of the other senior women of our tribe.' He turned his gaze from a speechless Finn back to Setiyan. 'Your princess will be in the best hands, I assure you. Indeed,' he laughed, 'I will be surrounded by chaperones!'

Setiyan smiled. 'I'll see you later.' She cast her eyes down as a flush of pink rose up her neck.

Smiling, Denkaun let go of her hands and walked out of the room. Seti swayed on the spot, looking at the closed panel.

Finn's mouth tightened and he folded his arms across his chest. 'So how am I supposed to explain this to your parents?'

Seti's back stiffened and she lifted her chin. 'Say what you like to them. I'm staying.'

'And now I know why,' he retorted, his mouth a thin line.

'You know nothing! How dare you presume to comment on my behaviour,' she warned, some of the old fire back in her voice. 'Leave me, lieutenant.'

Finn raised his hands in a gesture of defeat. 'Sure. You have a date to get ready for.' He walked across the room towards the door. 'Don't let me keep you, princess.'

Once the panel had slid to a close behind him, he heard the thud of something thrown against it. He smiled sardonically. *At least she can still get angry.* Then, just as quickly, he grimaced at the thought of having to explain the situation to the Ki-consort and his wife. *Could this day get any worse?*

Jax was going through the water sample report that had just come through from Sen-Caspiran and Birkaan when he was notified that Decker Finn was waiting to speak with him. He frowned, not wanting to be disturbed. But then Linnayen hurriedly entered the room and opened the companel.

'Can't he wait?' he asked, annoyed.

'He said it was important and needed to speak to both of us,' Linnayen replied, her tone tinged with concern. 'Please, put him through.'

Jax tapped the panel and the blurry visage of Decker Finn came into focus.

'My lord, my lady, I'm sorry to disturb you but it's urgent.'

'Of course, lieutenant. Please, what is it?' Jax asked.

'The princess has decided to stay in the Beshwuk settlement,' Finn began. But before he could continue, Linnayen interrupted.

'For how long?'

'That's just it, my lady, she won't say. But, er, I think she means for quite some time.'

Jax's brows drew together. 'Well what does that mean? Surely you've met all the tribes by now. Is there any special reason she needs to stay longer?'

173

Finn took a deep breath and plunged on. 'Well, no need exactly. But … She has formed an attachment with the leader here, Kalik Denkaun. You remember we spoke of him? The new leader of the Guznon tribe.'

Linnayen's face froze. What had happened to her daughter? Seti could be headstrong, even a little wild at times. What had she done now?

'Formed an attachment? In what way? Friendship?' she grilled Finn.

'Perhaps more than friendship,' Finn admitted. 'I've tried to reason with her, but …'

'I know my daughter, lieutenant,' Jax added resignedly. 'She's a person of strong emotions. I take it she's fallen in love with this man?'

Linnayen glared at Jax. 'What? No!'

Jax patted her hand. The gesture was meant to reassure her but Linnayen's eyes were a stormy sea green. 'You know how she is.' He turned his attention back to Finn. 'And Denkaun? What about him?'

Finn frowned. 'He's not Autabroni, for one thing. He's Altani by birth. His mother died and he was taken in by the shaman, Mira, when he was a baby. At least that's what we've been told. He's charismatic. Seems to be almost worshipped by the people here. They call him the A'bat, which means warrior of hope.'

'You sound unsure, lieutenant. What do you make of him?' Jax queried.

Finn sighed and shook his head. 'Personally, I don't like him. Though I can see why he's got them all running around after him. I suppose he's good-looking, has a powerful presence when he speaks. As I said, charisma.'

'And the Guznon people? You said they worship him, and he's a warrior. Should we be worried for other reasons?' Jax asked. The ramifications of further unrest on Autabron and his daughter being mixed up in it were beginning to take shape in his mind. Setiyan could be in danger and completely blind to it.

'Hard to say,' Finn responded. 'They have a small security force here. In fact, I've been invited to an event with them tonight. But this is one tribe among many. As far as I know, Denkaun's popularity is largely confined to the Guznon.'

'But that doesn't mean he's not known,' Jax concluded.

'I'm worried.' This was Linnayen. She looked at Jax. 'I think we must insist that she come home.'

Finn's face fell. 'Excuse me, my lady, but I've tried talking to her. So has Pieter. It's no good. She won't budge.'

'Then we'll speak to her directly. Don't worry, lieutenant. Managing our daughter's moods is something we're used to. Now, in the meantime, there's something else you need to know.'

Jax proceeded to tell Finn about the discovery of Mikel Piek and his part in the water-poisoning plot and the possible complicity of Jarkoo and Harrie. The results from the lab in Zaz-Rakuum showed concentrations of urthrengo in samples from every mining community they had tested so far. Kalisa Caspiran had asked for samples from other communities to be sent to Zaz as soon as possible.

'What about here?' Finn asked. 'Shall I send a sample to them?'

'Yes, please do. We need to know how widespread this is. In the meantime, say nothing to the Autabronis until we know more, and especially not to Director Jarkoo or Miss Whitton-Blake.' Jax hung his head. This was getting messy and he couldn't help feeling that he should never have left Autabron. 'My wife and I will speak to Princess Setiyan. And if she still won't listen to reason then I'll come back there and drag her home.'

'We both will!' Linnayen added.

They thanked him for his efforts and signed off, the companel sliding back into the desktop.

Linnayen reached across and took Jax's hand. 'I think we should go anyway. Right now. Something feels wrong.'

That Setiyan had fallen in love was not of initial concern. She had done so before with at least two young men that Jax could recall and her response had always been both passionate and short-lived. But to have done so in only a few days, and to be so far away, surrounded by strangers who may not have her best interests at heart, was more than disturbing. Jax knew his wife well enough to know that she was referring to more than just her gut feeling. This was her mentante sensibilities kicking in and he'd be a fool to ignore them.

He took her beautiful face in his hands and kissed her lips. 'We'll leave as soon as possible.'

175

Harrie woke up in the medcentre bed. *Surely a body was not meant to feel this stiff?* But when she tried to pull herself up to a sitting position, the wrench in her guts made her scream with pain and wish she'd stayed supine. Who brought her here, she wondered. The painkilling drugs must have kept her unconscious, but for how long? She was about to call for a medicant when she remembered what had happened.

There had been a fight, but what about? Why had Jarkoo come to her and why did he attack her? *No!* She attacked *him*. Because of the scientist, Piek. He'd been caught. They were exposed. Jarkoo had failed and she had to save herself.

There would be questions. Piek was on Altan – with the Genaras. He would implicate her. *Of course he would.* So what would her story be? That she had been commissioned by Covert-7 to infiltrate GKD and pretend to be – what? A co-conspirator. *Yes, that'd do.* She had been spying on Jarkoo and reporting back to C-7 the whole time. But she'd had to go along with the drugging scheme so as not to break her cover. A hateful mission but she'd no choice. Then he'd come to stop her from leaving. She couldn't take any more of his sexual attacks. Yes, she'd even had to endure that. When he pushed her down onto the bed, she had to fight back. Luckily, she had always kept the flick-knife handy – Autabron was, after all, a dangerous place. Never dreamed she'd have to use it! *Didn't mean to kill him. So sorry. But what else could a woman do?* Her bosses in C-7 would back her up. The call she'd put in to Daddy in the seconds after Jarkoo's life drained away would ensure it.

The translucent door slid open and a doctor entered. 'Hello, Miss Whitton-Blake. And how are you feeling?'

Harrie gave an obligatory groan and tried to shake a strand of her hair off her face.

'Here, let me.' The doctor pushed aside the offending wisp of red hair and smiled at her patient. 'You've taken quite a beating.'

Harrie's nodded weakly. 'Agreed. Prognosis?'

'Internal and external bruising and two cracked ribs, but there's no other damage to your internal organs, thankfully. You'll need to stay in bed for at least two days.' The doctor patted her leg reassuringly.

'Won't be hard. Feel wrecked,' Harrie rasped. She swallowed and indicated her need to drink. The doctor immediately brought a small flask of water to her and she sipped the cool liquid through a metal straw. 'Thanks.'

Once she had drunk her fill, the doctor returned the flask to the bedside table before speaking again.

'The police need to speak to you. They're waiting outside. Can I show them in?'

Harrie took a long breath and shrugged her shoulders, wincing just enough to make herself look like a martyr.

'Sure. Let them in.'

Her smile as she said these words was hopefully just sickly sweet enough to convince the world that she had been through a terrible ordeal but was plucky enough to survive. Confident of fooling everyone, only one niggling thought remained. Would Jax believe her too?

As Denkaun had promised, dinner was shared with the elder women of the Guznon tribe. Mira had been there too, seated to Seti's left. The women wanted to know about her upbringing and her family history. And especially her mother, the famous Linnayen. What about Altan? They'd seen vid images of its snow-capped peaks and wide fields of yellow grain and were impressed. Was she homesick? Or did she now see the beauty of the desert? Maybe she could stay a little longer. Would she? Could she?

Seti smiled and answered all their questions openly. Yes, her homeworld had much beauty but nothing as impressive as the vast deserts of Autabron. And, of course, growing up in the palace at Genkarah was a privileged existence, but her parents ensured that their daughters knew the value of hard work and devotion to duty. Yes, she was enjoying her time on Autabron and would stay as long as she could.

From time to time, beneath the table, Denkaun stroked her hand. His warm fingers played softly over her skin and occasionally the tips travelled onto her leg too, causing shivers of pleasure to consume her. She had chosen to wear loose-fitting lilac silk trousers with a thigh-length embroidered cream blouse. The fabric met with the demands of Autabroni discretion but was not thick enough to mask the touch of his hand on her body. It was as though she was naked in front of him – all the time – and she wanted to be.

As soon as the empty plates of the final course were removed, Mira stood and announced in a sober voice, 'Come, women of Guznon.

Pay your respects to our honoured guest and take your leave.' She turned to smile at Seti and Denkaun, her approval obvious to the delighted princess. *She sees my love for him – for her son.*

The last of the elder women left the dining room. Mira turned to follow them. But as she reached the ruby curtains concealing the doorway, she turned. 'My lady, I bid you goodnight and may the sweetest of dreams come to you and fulfil all your deepest desires.' She bowed, swept the drape aside and left the room, beckoning the remaining servants to follow her.

At a wave of his hands, the glow-globes dimmed and retreated to the edges of the space, tucking themselves into the bare earth lintels that surrounded the room. The silence of those few moments was broken only by the sound of Seti's heart hammering.

Still seated, they turned to face each other. He looked deep into her eyes and a trace of a smile moved his mouth. Then, without warning, he slowly but forcefully pushed apart her legs. Her breathing became ragged as she felt his hands move over her thighs. Suddenly, they seized the flimsy fabric at her waist and ripped it apart. His smile was cat-like when he realised that there was no further barrier to her flesh. She had worn no undergarments. His eyes never once left hers.

'Oh, my love,' she sighed, reaching out to him, wanting his mouth on hers. But he held back. Instead, he dropped to his knees and began to kiss the inside of her thighs, all the while drawing nearer to her centre. She massaged the fine blond hair of his head and pushed herself nearer to the edge of the chair so that he could taste her more easily. Feelings coursed through her body such as she had never had before. This was love beyond her wildest dreams. As Mira had predicted, her deepest desires were becoming a reality.

A warm surge began to devour her body. She had to have him inside her. Pushing his head away, she rose from the chair and lay on the table. As he stood to survey the semi-naked woman before him, her eyes pleading with him, he needed no prompting. She opened herself for him.

Their breath mingled in the pale light. She smiled up at him and reached to pull his face down to her. He allowed himself to be drawn towards her lips.

As she finally reached the all-consuming peak, she prayed that he would take her again later. She wanted nothing more than to spend the whole night in his arms, though one night would never be enough.

In the university courtyard, Li-kah Amanie sat on a low stone slab under the shade of a sinnsey tree dripping with orange flowers. Her head swivelled from side to side in expectation then stopped as she saw Calin and Falvii coming towards her. With only ten metres to go, the pair stepped apart to allow Mikel Piek to be revealed behind them. Li-kah Amanie's reaction was immediate and joyous, running to Piek as he did the same. Their laughter filled the space as they hugged and tried to talk simultaneously. They watched as the normally placid Huthon woman excitedly ran her hands over her missing friend's face as she expressed her amazement.

'I think there's more than just friendship here,' Falvii observed wryly. His grin was boyish.

'I'll admit, I've never seen Huthons so animated,' Calin returned.

'Which proves that love conquers all. Even for Huthons.'

Calin scanned his face and raised an eyebrow. 'Really?'

He shook his head despairingly. 'Oh, Calin, is there not one teeny-tiny romantic bone in your whole body? Not even one?'

She turned to walk away. There was no longer any need to keep tabs on Piek and Amanie's family were now in a safehouse. As for Hasler, he was already under guard and undergoing interrogation. Meanwhile, Piek had told them everything he knew and, when played the recording of Harrie Whitton-Blake's voice, he'd confirmed that this was the woman who had threatened him. Calin recalled how her father's face had drained of colour when he heard this and her mother's mouth had distinctly tightened.

'I knew she was capable of deceit,' Jax had begun, 'but this is reprehensible. How *could* she?'

Surprisingly, her mother had seemed to feel the need to be lenient. 'Perhaps there's an explanation?' She had laid her hand over his reassuringly.

'Unlikely. Harrie's a product of her upbringing. Her father was in military intelligence. She knows how to be devious.'

'Even so,' Linnayen had returned, 'you need to get her side of it before making any judgement. She'll have to be interrogated.'

And she would be. Calin had suggested that she do it. Go to Autabron. *No, better still, have the woman brought to Altan.* She would get a transport organised. Harrie Whitton-Blake could travel under guard. She deserved no better treatment.

Then she saw the angst-ridden look on her father's face. How could he still have feelings for this woman after what she had done? She had betrayed both him and the Autabroni people.

She spun around and looked Falvii straight in the eyes. 'Romantic bones break as easily as all the others. Probably more so.'

'Ouch!' He grimaced and shook his head.

At first she had been pleased that Falvii would be accompanying her back to Altan. They had formed a friendship of sorts on Hutho and, without doubt, he was good company. For sure, the warmth of his smile could melt butter, and she admitted that it had reached into her heart as well. Relentlessly cheerful, he could lift even the spirits of the notoriously morose tamuns, the oh-so-serious priests of the indigenous tribes of Autabron. But since their return to Altan and seeing the way the news of Harrie's deception had hit her father, she questioned again the need for romantic attachment. If love could make fools of good men like her father, and simpering idiots of women like her mother, then she wanted no part of it. Falvii could keep his advances to himself.

Back outside the university grounds, she jumped into her windshifter and looked behind to see if Falvii was following. 'Want a ride back?' she called. He was some twenty paces away, strolling slowly with his hands in his pockets.

'No, thanks, I'll find my own way,' he replied, and turned towards the commercial centre.

She couldn't help but feel slighted. 'Are you sure?' she called to his retreating back. But all she got was a wave.

By the time she got back to the Genara palace, her mood had dropped even further. What was wrong with her? She should be happy for Piek and Amanie's reunion. Why wasn't it enough to dispel her gloom?

'Ah! There you are, sweet girl. We've been waiting for you.' Her grandmother was seated on the end of her bed, twirling a gold thread on the belt of her dress. Calin reflected that the once imperious Li-el

Dacas was looking somehow smaller these days. Instead of the queen she had once been, the dowager Ki-consort was turning into a sweet old lady with a warmth that she had rarely displayed in earlier years.

Calin flopped down onto the pea-green bedspread, making her grandmother bounce. Li-el steadied herself and continued. 'Your mother and father have more news from Autabron – and none of it good.'

Calin yawned and exhaled a deep sigh. 'Why am I not surprised? Apart from finding the missing scientist, all the news seems to be bad these days.'

'Why so glum, child? I thought you were having a good time with young Falvii, who, I must say, is far more tolerable than I had expected.'

Li-el was off and running on what had become her favourite subject ever since she had met them at the transit tower two days ago. Falvii this, Falvii that. It seemed there was little he could do wrong.

'He's such a pleasant young man. I must admit I wasn't convinced by your Aunt Evica's assessment of him. She's so taken with all things Dasnirian, it's hard for her to be objective. But he's actually quite charming. And so intelligent. Those blue eyes and that lovely smile. I'm sure he's already melted a few hearts –'

'Or broken them,' Calin added ungraciously.

'You sound like a teenager. It's unbecoming. Now, come along. Off to your parents.' A little of the old queen had surfaced and Calin knew better than to argue. However tired and gloomy she felt, she would have to follow.

'So what's happened on Autabron?' she asked as Li-el made her way to the bedroom door.

'Oh, that awful Englishwoman has gone and killed Director Jarkoo. Self-defence, she claims. Ridiculous! And your sister … Oh dear …' Li-el shook her head sadly and groaned.

'What's Seti done?'

'She says she's in love.'

'What! With Lieutenant Finn?' She recalled the image of the lieutenant's serious face and warm brown eyes. His maturity and intelligence could be just what her flighty sister needed.

Li-el stared at her, eyes drawn together in confusion. 'Who? No. Who's Lieutenant Finn?'

'Her bodyguard,' Calin replied. 'He was sent to keep an eye on her.'

'Well, he hasn't done a very good job. No indeed.'

'So who's she in love with?' She was getting impatient now. This was interesting news, more so than Harrie Whitton-Blake having killed Avad Jarkoo, although that was startling enough in itself. 'Come on, Grandmother. Who's the man? It *is* a man?'

'Indeed it is. Name of Kalik Denkaun, would-be leader of the Guznon tribe,' she said, rising from the bed.

She passed through the doorway into an ornate hallway, a concoction of gold-plated twisted columns and roseate glass mirrors. Calin jumped up and followed her.

'You know, I've heard nothing good of them. Your grandfather and I met some– oh, let me see, thirty-five years ago now. But I found them a serious, unwelcoming lot. Frosty. Which is odd for such a ridiculously hot planet.'

Li-el was bemoaning the nature of the Guznon people and Autabronis in general and Calin found herself almost smiling when the old woman suddenly stopped dead.

'He's Altani though. At least that's something.'

Calin's mouth dropped open. Now this *was* interesting. How could an Altani be the leader of an indigenous people on another planet? And Seti in love? *There it is, love – making fools of us all again.*

'Come on, Calin! Don't dawdle!'

She picked up the pace. Li-el was already at the marble stairwell that led to her parents' rooms. For an eighty-something-year-old woman, her grandmother was surprising fleet-footed.

Pieter Serekunda stood and shook Finn's hand as the aerporter announcement was made. In the bag beside him were a dozen water samples from the settlement to be tested once back in Zaz. He and Finn had both agreed they had to be taken personally to Kalisa Caspiran and Birkaan by a trustworthy courier, and there was none better than Serekunda himself.

Caspiran and Birkaan had passed on news of the death of Avad Jarkoo and that Harrie Whitton-Blake was being questioned, but so far it looked like a lovers' quarrel gone badly wrong and nothing to do with their investigations. Finn was not convinced.

'We'll see,' Finn had commented to Serekunda. 'I didn't get that she and Jarkoo were together, did you?'

'I'm an ethicist, not a psychologist. Who knows what attracts anyone to anyone else?'

'You can say that again.'

Finn had been barely able to keep the frown off his face for days now since his charge had announced her decision to remain in Beshwuk. Even the amiable Serekunda, a man much given to negotiation and empathy, had tried to make her see sense and return home. But he had hit the same bulwark as Finn. She was in love and she was not going anywhere that Denkaun did not go too.

'Perhaps she'll listen to her mother when she gets here.' Serekunda had commented. 'Though I'm not sure even that will work.'

Finn had concurred. 'It's like she's in a dream. As soon as he walks into the room, she becomes a different person.'

As they now said their farewells, Serekunda came back to the subject. 'Keep a close watch on her, Decker. She'll come to no harm with you here.' He stepped onto the ramp of the aerporter before turning back. 'And look after yourself. See you soon back in Zaz, let's hope.'

Finn nodded. 'Take care, Pieter. Let me know how things go.'

He turned back towards the docking lounge. It was still an hour before the first sunrise but he knew sleep would be impossible now. His mind was churning with thoughts of his charge. He was trapped with her, physically and emotionally, and to make it worse, she loathed the sight of him. She scoffed at his pleas to reconsider her decision. He hoped her mother would be able to work some magic because he sure as hell couldn't.

The aerporter dock was set on a high ledge tucked into a natural bowl of the mountain top, rock walls keeping much of the heat away from the metallic landing platforms. Even so, the force-shield would be employed shortly after the suns rose. If sleep would not come, Finn decided to enjoy the quiet pre-dawn right here in the docking lounge. As the sound of Serekunda's transport finally dissipated and the landing lights dimmed, Finn lay back on a daybed and looked up at the stars with the occasional meteorite flashing past. The constellations were so different here but nonetheless beguiling. The roseate swirl of the stars in the Jarunei Strand could be seen directly above, and off to the south was the bright strand of the Milky Way, towards which lay Earth – home.

Suddenly, a cool breeze on his cheek indicated someone had entered through the dock's panel doors. He sat up and his hand moved down to his ion-laser at his waist as he tensed his body.

'I mean no harm.' It was a woman's voice, a mere whisper in the darkness. 'Lord Finn, I would speak with you.'

The figure stayed by the closed door, a small silhouette shrouded in a deep red hood and cloak.

'Who are you?' Finn asked, hand still hovering over his weapon.

'Someone whose heart is broken. Someone who has been discarded and betrayed.'

Finn was losing patience. Why couldn't anyone here answer a simple question? 'Just tell me your name,' he said.

The woman removed her hood and lifted her chin. 'My name is Wika Dokau. I am the wife of my lord, Kalik, the A'bat.'

Finn's mouth dropped and he struggled to form a response. 'You're *what?*'

'Kalik's wife. I bear his son in my belly.' Her voice was calm and steady.

Finn exhaled hard. 'Holy shit! Is this true?'

Wika reeled back from the curse. 'Of course it's true. Here.' She came closer and offered her belly for him to touch. 'I am growing for him a fine son,' she exclaimed proudly.

'Oh man! Just when I thought things couldn't get worse.'

'I want my Kalik back. Your ganak princess has taken him from me. I'm begging you to take her home. Take her away from here.' At this, the young woman fell to her knees in front of him and held out her hands in supplication, blonde hair tumbling to the ground. She was a beautiful woman – slim, graceful and with a body that would surely please any man. How could Denkaun throw her aside?

'Trust me, Wika, I would if I could. I don't like her being here any more than you do.' He scratched the top of his head. Of course Denkaun would dump this woman when the alternative was a princess and possibly heir to the leadership of the Galactic Union. Why hadn't he seen it before? *Idiot!* 'Thank you for coming to me. I don't suppose the princess knows about you. She may change her mind when she knows the truth.'

'Thank you, Lord Finn. Thank you for your help.'

'I'm not a lord. You don't need –'

Suddenly, the woman grabbed his knees. Finn tried to pull away but her grip was surprisingly strong. She begged once more.

'Please say nothing to Kalik! Or Lady Mira. Or you seal my fate.'

'Which will be?'

She looked up into his eyes then cupped her hands at her throat. Would they really kill her? *Surely not.*

'The A'bat shows no mercy to those who betray him. Remember!'

She leapt up and spun away with a whirl of her cloak. The docking lounge door slid open as she approached, then closed as quickly. Finn took a last look at the stars of this blighted planet and not for the last time cursed the day he'd ever set foot on it.

Chapter Fourteen

Setiyan sipped from the flask at her bedside. Her throat was so dry. Last night had been exhausting, but exciting too. She looked at the shape of the man lying next to her. The silken cream sheet had fallen to below his chest, allowing her to study its rise and fall as he slept. A line of fine blond hairs trailed down towards his waist and, as she well knew, continued lower.

His face in repose was childlike, all the creases softened and smoothed. Like this, he was not the imposing leader of his people, carrying all their cares and responsibilities. He was just a man – her man – and after his words last night, she would always be his too. All the years of training in statecraft and the undertaking of royal duties had dissipated like an early morning mist in the warmth of the sun. She felt reborn. The weight of her heritage was lifted from her slender shoulders and a new, enticing future awaited. A future with him. A future as his wife!

It was only the fear of waking him that stopped her from laughing out loud. Could there be anyone happier on this morning anywhere in the universe? She would marry him and spend every single night of the rest of her life like this – in his arms and in his bed. Her dreams had indeed come blissfully true.

She couldn't wait to share her happiness. Who to tell first? Calin, of course. It would have to be her sister in whom she had always confided everything – well, almost everything. Calin's face would be a picture! But she would be happy for her too. As for Mother and Father ... Seti imagined they would not be pleased at first. But when they got to know Kalik it would be different. *He is a strong, intelligent leader who will be an asset to the Galactic Union.* She would convince them that there could be no better choice for her husband than him.

He stirred. A sudden breath escaped from his lungs and he cleared his throat.

'Good morning, my love,' she whispered into his ear.

A smile crept across his face though his eyes remained closed. He rolled towards her. That was better. Now she could see his full beauty. That perfect square jawline, those full lips and the turned-up eyelashes that any woman would love. She caressed his cheek and planted a soft kiss there.

'Make love to me ... husband.' Her breath tickled his ear but he was still unmoving, eyes closed, a thin smile playing about his mouth.

'Husband ...' She slid her hand down towards his groin but was disappointed to find that her action brought no response.

'Not this morning.' Was this a command? Or was he just teasing her?

He took hold of her hand and brought it up to his mouth. Finally, his eyes opened and focused on her face.

'I have business to attend to.'

Seti's frown deepened. 'Make *me* your business.' There was a hint of the spoilt child in her voice and she instantly regretted it. She did not want him to think badly of her.

'You *are* my business,' he replied and then laughed heartily. 'I have our wedding to plan today.'

She almost collapsed with happiness. She took a large breath into her body and felt she would explode if she did not let it go in a cry of joy. He laughed again.

'Then go! Go! Make plans.' She jumped up from the bed and began racing around the room, gathering his clothes from where they had been hurriedly discarded the night before. 'Come on, Kalik! Go!'

He laughed. 'Steady ... There's time. You will become my wife before the month is out and then ...' He grinned and left the thought hanging. But she knew what he meant. Then they would make love every day! She would touch him and feel his caresses on her body every night. This happiness would last forever.

He took his clothes from her and dressed quickly.

'Go, my love. Do what you must,' Seti commanded, the smile never leaving her lips. 'I shall wait here for your return.'

As soon as he left the room she fell back on the bed, closed her eyes and held herself in an embrace. She yawned deeply and, as she once more saw his face in her mind's eye, she vowed that she would never want for anything more in her life – *ever!*

However anxious Linnayen was to get to Autabron to confront her recalcitrant daughter, she also wanted to meet the Whitton-Blake woman. She wanted to see for herself what hold she had on Jax.

Was she jealous? But she knew how silly that was. Jax had loved her for more than twenty-five years. He had always been devoted to her and, for them, the romance had never faded. True, they were not as passionate as they had been once. But she still found him attractive and desirable. The grey at his temples somehow made him even sexier, and he too seemed to still take pleasure in her body despite the demands that two pregnancies had made on it.

But what was Whitton-Blake like? Duncan McCrae had said that she was an attractive woman with fiery red hair and almond-shaped eyes. He'd remembered her as 'a bit of a stunner', though luckily not his type, he said. Was she still Jax's type? She prayed not. But seeing this woman in the flesh and noting the body language would put her mind at ease. Maybe she would stay on Altan for a few more days until she arrived. Setiyan's latest infatuation could wait a little longer.

She had spoken with Seti the day before and, even though the vidlink was grainy, she could certainly see and hear her enthusiasm for this man. But Linnayen had seen Seti like this before. She remembered the poor young man Seti had met when she went through her charity phase; Laitos was his name. They had met while filming an appeal for funds to set up a new cultural centre for the Latis-Mei community. They had been inseparable for months and she swore he was the love of her life – until she met the incoming Earthan ambassador Arjun Chauvin. Linnayen had met Arjun often as Ki and still felt a twinge of guilt when she saw the sadness in his darkly handsome face. Seti had at first been fascinated by him, his looks – 'smouldering eyes', she had said – and rich velvet voice.

This current flame would pass too. The lieutenant did not know her daughter – at least, not well enough to know that Seti's passions were like a firework, blazing with stunning splendor in the night sky, but the sparks soon faded and the show was over. It was likely that this episode with the charismatic Denkaun would end up a damp squib, like all the others.

Maybe her feelings of discomfort were about the Whitton-Blake woman and nothing to do with Seti's latest fling. She decided she could afford to wait a couple more days before going to Autabron and then she would bring her muddle-headed daughter back home.

The polished stone table bore swirls of ancient fossil creatures, shells and bones and even traces of feathers, hinting at Autabron's far distant watery past. The faces of the city governors and workers' representatives seated around it in the council chamber were lit by harsh midday light filtered through a tinted skylight that spanned half the room. The glare, to Pieter's Earthan eyes, was intense, though the room itself was kept cool by the efficient air conditioning that pervaded all levels of the city. But it was hard not to break out in a sweat knowing the news they had to impart to the stern-looking group.

Sen-Caspiran took the lead, her soft but assured tone breaking the expectant silence. 'Thank you, councillors and representatives, for agreeing to meet with us today. And, of course, our condolences on the death of your director of operations, Mr Jarkoo.' She paused momentarily. 'A serious situation has come to our attention over the course of our investigations. As some of you may know, we were tasked with looking into the disruptions to mining here on Autabron. We have interviewed many employees and examined records and reports going back nearly two years but could find no concrete evidence of wrongdoing. Meanwhile, Princess Setiyan and Doctor Serekunda have spoken to elders from both the Guznon and Gaksi tribes and heard their concerns. But, over these many days, we had uncovered no substantial reasons or motives for the disquiet here. We were about to disband our efforts when news came to us from an unexpected source.'

Caspiran had felt it necessary to lead the Autabronis gently towards their findings and Birkaan agreed. He knew his people. If they just blurted out that their people were being drugged, the councillors and especially the workers' representatives would explode. Birkaan took up the final part of the story.

'A young scientist on Hutho, Mikel Piek, a man who had been reported as missing to the police here, confessed to having supplied large quantities of a drug to a contact in the GKD organisation. With the assistance of Professor Adrik Hasler, who had a laboratory here in Zaz, a total of sixteen barrels of a dangerous drug, urthrengo were sent to Autabron over the past eighteen months. Doctor Piek – who had been threatened with harm to a close friend and her family if he did not cooperate – confessed that he knew what this drug did.'

Several of the panel members stirred in their seats and a murmur went through the group. Others looked to their colleagues, questioning this information. One of the workers' representative could not contain himself.

'Now, wait a minute! What are you saying, Birkaan? That our people are drug addicts?'

Birkaan held up his hands in a gesture of supplication. 'No, no, not at all.'

Caspiran held up a hand to calm the room. 'Please allow my colleague to continue. All will become clear.'

They quietened again and Birkaan took up the concluding episodes. 'The drug causes compliance in people. Even a small quantity will calm a raging animal. It suppresses behavioural extremes and … Well, now we come to Director Jarkoo's part in this. With his help and the bribery of some officials, this drug has been fed into the water supply at all the mine sites. Even here in Zaz itself, though thankfully not also in the outlying settlements.'

He waited for the full import of his words to take effect and, sure enough, the volcano erupted. The men and women rose to their feet, thumping the table and knocking over chairs as voices of outrage tumbled over each other incoherently.

'Councillors!' Caspiran's clear tones cut through the hubbub. 'Please! We must continue.' She waited for the clamour to subside and nearly all to return to their seats. She stood and her clear green eyes swept the room. 'I can assure you that the drug is no longer being fed into the water systems. My colleagues and I, with an executive order from the Ki-consort and with the consent of your Planetary Council and public health department, have seen to that. The conspirators have all been arrested and charges are being prepared. In the meantime, this deliberate control of the emotional health of your people explains so much. It is our belief that the mine workers have not pushed for better pay and conditions because of the effects of the drug. They became pliable.'

The sea of heads nodded and there was a burble of agreement.

Pieter Serekunda stood and took over. 'However, the acts of sabotage have still to be fully explained. It *is* likely, from what the scientist Piek told us, that the urthrengo dosage was wearing off as people were building a tolerance to it. He had been asked to supply more than usual. We don't yet know if this diminishing effect caused one or two workers to break the law or if another agency has been at work. Though what it would profit anyone to blow up processing plants we just don't know. Of course,' he continued, 'there's the matter of the mine's destruction of Euta Sakek. This undoubtedly fuelled anger, and rightly so.'

The men and women in the room were irate, stunned and devastated in equal measure. The grumbles and expressions of anger continued to rumble for some minutes until Caspiran finally brought the gathering to a close. As she stood to leave, she sighed heavily and glanced at Birkaan and Serekunda. They were listening to some of the attendees and nodding their heads. It had been a tough meeting but she observed that not one person had asked about Director Jarkoo's lover, who was even now on her way to Altan for a more intensive interrogation that would hopefully reveal so much more.

Decker Finn spent the best part of the morning following Wika's revelation trying to see Setiyan. He had tried calling both her room and her personal telecommunicator several times but she did not answer, and when he approached her quarters he found guards on the door blocking his entry. His demands regarding why they were there and who had authorised this went unanswered. They directed him to speak to Mira.

She wasn't easy to track down either and it took until the afternoon before she returned to her office on one of the upper levels. She breezed in, still speaking with a female assistant, her hands clasped loosely over her orange robes.

'A thousand apologies, Lieutenant Finn. I was delayed by a meeting of elders. Each must have his complaint heard. Tsk, tsk.' She shook her head as if this was a tiresome duty she faced every day.

A shaft of pale light filtered through the tinted window illuminating carved frescoes of rolling hills, meandering rivers and even trees on the rock walls behind her. Finn was not in a mood to appreciate the fine work or its subject matter. He came straight to the point.

'Shaman Mira, can you tell me why a guard has been placed on the princess's room?'

'Lieutenant Finn. Welcome.' The old woman glanced at her assistant who immediately rose, bowed and left the room. 'Now then,' she continued, 'you want to know why I have asked for your lady to be protected? Simple. She is a most honoured and important guest. We wish no harm to come to her.'

Finn fought to control his anger but he felt his face going red. 'If that is so then why was there no protection on her door when we first arrived?'

'Yes, that was an oversight on my part. My son reprimanded me and I have corrected the mistake. A thousand apologies, Lieutenant Finn.' Her voice remained steady and cool as an iceberg.

He tightened his mouth to hold back the rebuke that itched to be released. 'You realise that I am her bodyguard? I am tasked with protecting her, which I cannot do if I can't see her or speak to her.'

'She won't speak to you? Dear me. But she *is* safe,' the old woman insisted, then continued in a casual tone. 'Indeed, my men are doing your job for you, lieutenant. You could take some time for yourself, perhaps?'

'Thank you. But I want to do my job – *myself*. Can you please order the guards to step aside and let me through. I have important matters to discuss with her.'

'Of course. I will ask our lady princess for a convenient time to meet with you.' Her compliance was delivered with what Finn perceived to be the smile of a snake.

'*Now* is convenient, Shaman Mira. Now.' He planted his feet in front of her desk.

The old woman's smile did not extend to her eyes. 'While you are waiting for her reply, perhaps I could deliver your important matters?'

'No, thank you. I'll wait to speak to my princess myself.'

This was not looking good. All Finn's senses were on edge. They had been here a week now and were already overdue to return to Zaz. He had the distinct feeling that Setiyan Genara was being held prisoner and, if so, there was absolutely nothing he could do about it. Would it be best to back off? He needed to get a message back to Altan – not just about their daughter being guarded from him but also that the object of their daughter's infatuation was a married man. He needed to retreat just enough to give himself room to move.

He forced a small smile. 'Perhaps if you would be so good as to tell her that I'll be right outside her door when she has a moment.'

His concession was delivered with the taste of bile inside his mouth. But it had to be so. If Setiyan could be locked up, so could he. *And one of us needs to be free.*

Harrie had been allowed a free run of the ship on the two-day flight from Autabron to Altan and, although her bruised body limited her movement, she soon discovered that she was never alone. There was always a crew member coincidentally present, whether she was reading in the forward lounge or watching a vidisk on the comms deck. So while she was not officially under arrest, it was obvious that she was under suspicion. As to why she was being brought to Altan, she had been told it was so that her situation could be 'assessed by an impartial authority'. But such diplomatic jargon held no sway with her; she had been raised on it. She knew she could face a trial for manslaughter and the two-day journey to Altan was in fact a blessing, allowing time to polish her story and ensure she had covered all the bases.

In the meantime, there was the delicious thought that she would be seeing Jax again. His tedious run back to his wife almost made her want to give up on him. But a few minutes alone with Jax could give her the lifeline she needed. Even if they didn't believe her self-defence story, Jax would never condemn her. Of that she was certain.

The young man who met her off the spaceracer was extremely handsome, with black hair, clear blue eyes and high cheekbones. Under any other circumstances she would have flirted madly with him, but sadly she had to behave herself. It was entirely possible that her every movement was being watched and the last impression she wanted to give was coquettishness. Falvii Min explained that she was to be taken to rooms in the Genara compound where she would be 'comfortable and safe'. He described her position as a 'guest' of the Genara family, at which she wanted to laugh out loud.

'So I'll be able to explore some of Genkarah's sights? Lovely!' she exclaimed as the young man drove them in a two-man windshifter through the palace gardens.

'Of course,' he replied. 'And I'll be happy to accompany you.'

It was hard to be angry at his diplomatic response when he delivered it with such a smile.

They covered the short distance past trees heavy with pink blossom and down stone-slab pathways lined with delicate ferns until they reached the guest quarters. Harrie had to admit that she would indeed be comfortable here. Double doors slid open to reveal a bright foyer, the rear wall of which was completely translucent. Pink light spilled into the space and made the polished carolite floor glisten. The furnishings were simple in design – no grand flourishes here – but the materials were of the finest quality. The drapes were pearl grey silk and precious kalendarium had been inlaid on the wall panels. To the right she could see a bedroom whose mirrors reflected the view from the outside. Altogether, the apartment was luxurious – such a pleasant change from the utilitarian decor of Autabron.

Her perusal of her surroundings was interrupted by a cough from behind. She turned to see a young red-haired woman standing in the doorway.

'Welcome to Altan, Miss Whitton-Blake. I am Calin Genara.'

Harrie smiled widely. 'Kev's girl, yes? Same eyes.'

'Yes. My father will be here shortly. My mother may also wish to meet you.' Calin's voice was a monotone.

'Your mother?' Harrie nodded and smiled again. 'Looking forward to it.'

'Please let me or Falvii know if you require anything.' Calin indicated the companel by the main door and another at the entrance to the bedroom. She then threw a look at Falvii. 'We wish you good day.'

As the doors slid shut behind them, Harrie went into the bedroom and lay gingerly on the wide expanse of bed. She stretched out her arms and squeezed the crisp white fabric in her hands. So Linnayen Genara wanted to meet her. *That's why I'm here – good old-fashioned jealousy.* Within seconds she had decided exactly what her play would be and she looked forward to the game to come.

Despite their efforts to persuade the council and representatives to consider the news of the water contamination carefully before releasing it to the media, the ensuing leak was no surprise. By the next morning, the news was everywhere. Birkaan had warned that this would be a huge story and his compatriots would likely react with not only anger but also violence. Sure enough, a couple of overseers at the Euta Makaan mine had been attacked that evening and both were now in the medcentre in critical condition. Another group of workers had smashed the doors of the GKD offices in Zaz and sprayed the walls of the building with graffiti attacking the 'ganaks'.

Kalik Denkaun was making the final arrangements for his wedding when the news came through. He had spent yet another evening with Setiyan and had started the day in a good mood. She was such a willing partner and would do almost anything for him. He was looking forward to introducing her to some of his more radical pleasures, but not until after the wedding, of course. Her devotion had to be secure and unwavering.

Mira's idea to put the guards on her door had kept her well isolated – not that she had any desire to leave. His pretty bird was happy in her cage and, as soon as the pregnancy was confirmed, he would be able to relax. No need then to keep on flattering her and pandering to her somewhat insatiable needs. His needs would come first then and he would enjoy seeing the confusion on her simpering face when he whispered in her ear what he wanted her to do. Just the thought of what was to come was enough to excite him.

'Tell me again!' he demanded of the messenger from Zaz, who stood trembling before him.

'The city council released the news yesterday afternoon. The water's been poisoned with some drug – thren-something. It's been going on for months.'

Denkaun knew well the drug, for was he not also using it to make his wife-to-be compliant? 'Urthrengo.' He clenched his right hand into a fist before bringing it down on the tabletop. 'But who has done this? *Who?*'

'They are blaming it on Director Jarkoo, my lord. Although there was also talk of an Earthan woman – a spy – being involved.'

'Jarkoo? But he's Autabroni. Surely one of our own would not do this!' It was unthinkable. How could he poison his own people? To what end?

Denkaun needed time to think. But he also needed to act quickly. As a leader – as the A'bat – he must react appropriately. *A message of disgust, yes. But also a call for reason?* A speech that will sympathise with the miners, many of whom were Guznon, assuring them that those who have committed this horrific betrayal would be punished. *Yes. That sounded right.* It was disingenuous to think that one man could be responsible for such a major crime. There had to be a conspiracy behind all this. The bosses of GKD must have known what was going on.

Perhaps this was the moment. With all the tribe leaders already coming to Beshwuk for the wedding, now was the time to take complete charge of all the mining operations. His people, along with Hanashi's Gaksi and the No'os, could easily remove the GKD managers and take over the running of the mines. *A coup!* With him at the helm and his new wife – the daughter of the Ki – adding legitimacy to his claim. *Of course! This was the time.* Although earlier than he had expected, the A'bat would rise and his planet would finally belong to its rightful owners, along with all the wealth it contained.

Denkaun's thoughts whirled and, as the plan evolved in his mind, he smiled. Jarkoo may have been a shameful traitor to his people but he was going to be the forging of their unity and the making of Kalik Denkaun. The irony was not lost on him.

The messenger stood waiting silently, discomfort and confusion at his lord's pleased reaction clear on his face. Denkaun dismissed him with a wave of his hand and the messenger scurried out of the room. He touched the companel. Mira's face instantly appeared. 'Natar, summon the tribe leaders. Tell those who have not yet set out to come now.'

The old woman nodded. 'Which tribes, my son?'

Denkaun's eyes flashed. 'All of them! Gaksi, No'os, Konkanaw … All of them. The A'bat commands and any who disobey will know my wrath!'

Denkaun stared down at the table in front of him, seeing in his mind's eye a map of all Autabron. His hands floated over the smooth obsidian surface, tracing the imaginary borders of the tribal territories. One by one, he drew them into his grasp, then looked up to the force-shielded window and the sky beyond. It was only a matter of time before he would have the whole Galactic Union in the palm of his hand.

The deep cavern under the Beshwuk mountain settlement where the waters of the Kadis came to the surface was known only to a few, including the Dokau family. Wika knew she would be undisturbed here and sat at the water's edge, weaving her fingers to and fro in the cold, crystal clear water.

The silence was so thick that Wika felt she could reach out and touch it. Each day she had come to this holy place to bathe her growing belly. It had only been a few weeks but Autabroni babies grew fast and strong. In only five or six more months, her boy – and she was sure it was a boy – would be born, and Kalik could not deny his child the right to follow him as leader of the Guznon.

Once Lord Finn had spirited the bitch-princess away, the path would be clear. But there was still the problem of Mira, who was no friend to Wika. The shaman was indeed powerful. She had foretold of many things that had come to pass. The uncommon rains of three years ago that flooded the Gaksi lands, the annual running of the tagirp on which they depended for food, and the quake that had shattered the mountain of Kou'conah. The once mighty peak had clasped so many souls in its terrible molten arms that the people of the No'os tribe would mourn them for a thousand years.

If she were to disobey Mira, or even worse, if she were to defy her, it would likely mean her death. Wika had heard the rumours that she had killed her husband, Lyr Denkau, when he questioned her prophecy about the A'bat and how the people of Autabron would regain control of their planet through his strength. Where was old man Denkau now? Dust of the desert for sure, but not before his lifeless corpse had been seen with a dirk in his back. Mira had mourned, as had they all. But she soon put away her widow's weeds and took up the close fostering of the infant Kalik and for more than twenty years had never left his side.

She scooped a handful of the cool water and allowed it to trickle through her fingers. As it fell in pockmarks on the sandy ground, she shaped the 'w' of her name and the 'k' of her beloved's. Then she stroked her bare belly in ever-widening circles and vowed to her unborn son that she, too, was powerful and would do whatever it took to make him beloved of his father.

It was time to get back. If she returned to her father's home now, she might be able to see Kalik before he returned to the ganak whore. Although she was forbidden his quarters for now, perhaps he could be persuaded to come to her. How she missed him! And how could he be with her when he had his adoring Wika, who was his wife in all but name?

She lifted the hated parab above her head and let it fall over the length of her body before ascending the narrow passageway back towards the city. Her steps matched her mood and she sighed at the humiliation the garment bestowed.

But on entering her father's house she was greeted by pandemonium. Her mother was wailing, her head in her hands, and her sisters were on either side, trying to comfort her and stop her tears. As for her father, his face was even more red than usual. His eyes were black as coal and his body was rigid with anger. Before she even had time to ask what awful calamity had occurred, he grabbed her arm and dragged her across the floor. Dokau threw her down on the hard ground, despite her mother's pleas for him to leave her alone.

'Stupid girl!' he screamed at her. 'Stupid little whore!'

Her mother wailed even louder. 'Leave her alone! This is not her fault! Stop!'

Tears began to sting her eyes. What had caused her father to be so furious? 'Please, Father! What have I done?'

'You know full well, you stupid girl,' he growled. His fist, aimed at her cheek, landed on her ear and she winced with the sharp pain, falling hard onto her knees. 'You have brought disgrace on us. You think you can bring your bastard into our family? Eh? What were you thinking? We'll be humiliated before our neighbours. Such shame!'

Wika looked at her mother's tear-stained face. So her mother had revealed her secret. She supposed it would have had to come out at some time. A swollen belly cannot be hidden for long.

'It's true. I carry the child of the A'bat. And I am proud to do so!'

Her father's shadow loomed over her but she was not afraid. Her held her chin high and glared at the man whose seed had brought her into this world.

'I carry his son who will be your leader!'

Her father scoffed loudly and kicked her buttocks. 'Ha! And how will a bastard become our leader, eh? Tell me that?'

Obviously, her father did not know the extent of her relationship with Kalik. She must tell him. 'How dare you, Father! You pushed me to become his woman, did you not? You told me how it would bring power to our family. And it has! It will ... when we marry.'

Her father's exclamation of rage could have shattered the rock walls. Once more he kicked at her back, knocking the breath from her lungs. 'Marry! You think he will marry you? Stupid girl. He won't marry you. Haven't you heard? No, of course not.'

For the first time, Wika felt confusion. She looked through her tears to her weeping mother, her brow furrowed and head tilted in question. *What has happened?* Instantly, her mother's sobs rang out once more, louder than before.

She turned her bewildered gaze to her father, who stood above her, shaking his head. 'Father. What has happened? Tell me!'

'It was announced today. The A'bat and the ganak princess will marry,' he began, bending down over her, his spittle landing on her cheek. She sucked in a large gulp of air and her eyes widened in disbelief. 'In three days!'

'No. No. No.' Her mouth repeated the word as if it could wash away the truth.

'You think he will marry you now? And what will his new wife say about that?'

Her father's recriminations went on and on, as did her mother's wails, but she heard nothing. A surge of blood gushed through her body, pounding inside her ears and deafening her to everything. *No. No. No. He is mine. Mine!*

She got up slowly, carefully cupping her stomach, with the noise in her head still claiming all her thoughts. She saw her parents and sisters as though they were puppets in a play. Characters moving, arms waving but making no sound. She had to get away from this place. She needed space and time, time to think, time to plan. For if the ganak whore thought she had won she was much mistaken. And if Lord Finn could not fix this problem then she would do it herself.

Chapter Fifteen

Though he had vowed to remain outside Setiyan's room and wait for her to admit him, Finn also needed to contact Jax – or anyone outside of Beshwuk. He hadn't felt so alone since he'd been stranded on the lifeless *Teg-Kanish*, drifting in space, hoping for help to arrive. With Pieter Serekunda back in Zaz-Rakuum and Setiyan sealed behind steel doors, he was isolated and friendless. But worst of all, no one knew of the situation that had so quickly developed. Setiyan's infatuation with Kalik Denkaun was worrying enough. But with her sudden confinement and then Wika Dokau's insistence that she was Denkaun's wife, he envisaged a dark descending spiral that he was powerless to halt. And something in his conversation with Mira was niggling at him, but when he reached for it, it evaporated into the void.

He had waited outside Seti's room for the rest of the afternoon with no result; the door remained closed to him. Now, back in his room, Finn moved to the force-shield viewport and stared out across the expanse of rust-coloured desert. The low hills in the far distance were picked out in shades of red and purple by the low light of the setting suns. His eyes squinted as his thoughts turned and tumbled inside his head. *What's happening here?* His gut churned uncomfortably with an overpowering feeling that he was being kept in the dark, as much a prisoner as his charge had become. He had to do something. Time was running out.

He strode across the room and punched the companel controls on the desk. Lights flashed and the plexi-screen slid up. But when he entered the code for Jax's office in Genkarah, the screen flickered and a message flagged up. *Connection failure. Please try later.* He tried Pieter Serekunda's code, then Caspiran's and Birkaan's. All attempts came back the same. He growled and pushed the screen back into its slot in the desktop. *Useless!* There was no getting away from the facts: both he and Setiyan were now completely isolated. But was it by chance, or had Mira and Denkaun planned this all along?

The more he mulled it over, the clearer it became. *They had been played for fools!* Somehow the shaman and her vile son had manipulated the princess and had now managed to remove her from his protection. He didn't know how this had happened but he knew someone who might. Wika Dokau. All he had to do was find her.

He stepped out into the wide stone hallway. Glow-globes lit the way as he walked towards the main central plaza at the heart of the mountain community. For so late in the day, he was surprised to see this many people still out and about. Groups of men sat at tables playing prijah, the fast-moving game where players push coloured stones in a three-dimensional prism, each trying to fill their side ahead of their opponents. In alcoves around the sides, women stood smiling and talking excitedly to each other while children played at their feet. Finn had never seen Autabronis so animated.

He nodded at the men as he passed through the crowds, though not the women. That would cause all manner of problems as men were not encouraged to communicate with women who were not family. Suddenly, two children ran into his legs, causing him to stumble. They squealed gleefully but quickly jumped up, ready to apologise when they saw their mother bearing down on them.

'A thousand apologies, lord,' she muttered, bowing her head.

'Please, it's nothing,' he replied, grinning at the retreating children. He decided to risk engaging her further. 'Tell me, what's going on? Everyone seems very happy.'

She bowed her head, not daring to meet his eyes and checking to the side to ensure she was not being observed. 'Such happy news, lord.' She glanced up and, seeing his look of confusion, continued. 'The A'bat and the Princess Setiyan. They are to marry.'

His face froze. The woman looked at him curiously, probably expecting to see a smile that matched her own. Instead his eyes wandered across the plaza, taking in each group as the woman moved away.

Then it hit him. Mira had said 'our princess'. *Our.* They had taken possession of Setiyan Genara. But was she a hostage? Or had she gone willingly? How was he to know without speaking to her?

He could hear little but the rush of blood in his ears and his chest ached with the thump of his heart. He had to move – and quickly. He had to get out of this place and get help. On his own, here in Beshwuk, he could do nothing. There was the risk that, as Setiyan's bodyguard, they might feel the need to contain him too.

Then he remembered. The q'ist! One section of it went to Zaz-Rakuum. Mira would hopefully expect him to do as he said and go to Setiyan's room to wait for her. If he left now, though, he could get away before they knew it.

He scanned the plaza for the passageway that led to the lower levels and ran towards it, dodging the groups of women and turning the heads of the men as he went. His sudden burst of speed caused little more than a second's stir before the A'bat's great news refocused the people's attention.

Five minutes later, Finn had made it down to the tunnels where the q'ist platforms were located. He was surprised that here, too, people were milling about, and not just Guznon. He saw blue-robed Gaksi and even a couple of yellow-cloaked Konkanaw. Tribespeople from other parts of the planet were an uncommon sight in any community as their general dislike and distrust of each other kept most tribes from getting too close. What had brought them together today?

His brain buzzed with questions and he shook his head as if the fog of uncertainty would clear. *Of course. The wedding!* But some travellers would have taken a day or two at least to get here. So had this been a plan all along? How could he have been so stupid! For days his instincts had screamed at him that something wasn't right. And now he knew what it was.

A q'ist was due to depart for Zaz in minutes, so he casually mingled with the crowds, smiling and nodding, until he saw his opportunity to jump aboard. As the silver steel doors closed on the tube-like transport and it drew away from Beshwuk, Finn looked back at the fast-retreating platform. He was leaving Seti behind and, though he knew this was the only chance he had of saving her, he couldn't help feeling that he had left her to a grim fate. He only hoped her mother and father would understand and allow him time to explain.

Linnayen stood and stretched her arms overhead. Though she had been unaware of it until now, her muscles had tensed while she studied Harriet Whitton-Blake moving around the garden apartment for the past hour.

The woman looked entirely relaxed and, Linnayen noted, indeed was stylish and beautiful. Once Falvii and Calin left, Whitton-Blake had showered and changed into fresh clothes, then settled down on the sofa to read a book from the pile that had been left for her on the centre table. This lack of even the slightest concern about her predicament was unsettling. Did she not realise that she had been brought here to be interrogated? She must know that she was under suspicion.

Linnayen was about to turn away from the monitor when she saw the woman rise, her discarded book falling to the floor. Jax came into view on the screen and Harrie went to meet him, arms open wide. Linnayen was pleased to see that her husband held up his two hands, stopping her from coming closer. Instantly the woman's arms fell back to her sides and she cocked her head to the side. Linnayen didn't really need to listen to their conversation but the prospect was too enticing.

'Kev! Darling. How sweet of you to bring me to Altan,' she began. Her voice was rich and smooth, a warm honeyed swirl of tones. 'I missed you. Did you miss me?'

Linnayen was gratified that he ignored the question. 'Harrie, you've been brought here to be questioned about the contamination of the water supply on Autabron and your part in the death of Avad Jarkoo. Once you've rested from your journey and had something to eat, you'll be taken for questioning.'

The woman was not deterred in the slightest by his formal tone. 'Of course.' She returned to the sofa and patted the seat next to her for him to sit. 'Come. Sit. Let's catch up. How was your journey home?'

Again, he was not to be deflected. 'I've organised a light meal to be brought here, after which you'll be taken to GU security headquarters. They'll want to know everything. You may be there for some time.'

Harrie rolled her eyes and tutted. 'Tsk, tsk … So formal, sweetie! Not like you.'

Again, her voice was velvet and, as she stretched her neck, she placed a hand there and slid it down to her cleavage. Then there was the way she left her mouth ever-so-slightly open. Linnayen had to admire the way she used her body. She confessed to using these tricks herself with Jax when trying to get him to leave his work and to come to bed.

'Harrie …'

'Yes, darling?'

Linnayen instantly picked up the testiness in his voice.

'Harrie. We are not friends. We were once lovers – nearly three decades ago – but, frankly, you were selfish and inconsiderate then and not much has changed.'

Her body tensed. Her mouth opened in protest. 'Kev! How could _'

'And I very much suspect that you've had a major hand in the drugging of many thousands of innocent people. Though why that should surprise me, I don't know.'

She went to stand up but he stepped nearer to block her. 'No! Don't get up. But understand this. You played me for a fool once and you think that you can do it again. What you don't see is that you're the fool now. You're as insignificant in my life as …' Jax shook his head, searching for an apt comparison, '… as what I had for breakfast this morning.'

Linnayen wanted to cheer and a smile crept across her face.

Harrie lifted her chin defiantly and pursed her lips as Jax turned and made to leave the room. Suddenly, her voice rang out. 'You're wrong! You loved me! You cared.'

Jax stopped. Linnayen saw him slowly shake his head and sigh He did not look back. 'Your food will be here shortly.'

He passed through the open doorway, which slid to a close behind him. Harrie Whitton-Blake sat still for a full thirty seconds before reaching down to retrieve her book. But in that time, Linnayen was able to see a single tear slide down one of her perfect cheeks.

Setiyan pored over the pile of dresses and other garments that Kalik had sent to expand her wardrobe. The little she had brought with her from Altan would never do for a princess of the Guznon, the Aun'bat-to-be, he said, and she needed to dress appropriately. He had instructed a serving girl, a slight young woman with a heart-shaped face and huge dark eyes, to assist the Princess Setiyan with anything that she wished.

'If she is hungry, bring her food, but only food from my kitchen. If she is thirsty, bring her water, but only from my natar's quarters. If she wants anything else, come to me first,' he had said, and his care for her melted Seti's heart.

'What is your name again?' Seti asked the girl.

'Jinau, my lady,' came the shy response.

'Jinau … What do you think of this one?' Seti held up a floor-length green silk gown. It had a black fur trim and the hem was studded with glittering gold beads.

Jinau nodded shyly. 'It is very beautiful, my lady.'

'Yes. But is it right? Does it suit me? I'm not sure of the colour – and the neckline's awfully high.'

Jinau turned back to the pile of clothes spread out on the bed. 'Perhaps …'

'Yes?'

'The red?'

Seti took another look at the carmine gown. She had discarded it earlier, thinking it too brash. But maybe the servant was right. The depth of colour would accentuate her figure, especially if she wore her hair up. The dip in the neckline with its wisps of gold filigree lace would display her long neck and her décolletage and make Kalik hungry for her body. Most Guznon women dressed modestly but those rules did not apply to her. She was, after all, Altani, and of the house of Genara. She need not be bound by those old traditions.

'You're right, Jinau. The red it is.'

She changed into the dress and then asked Jinau to help with her hair.

'I want to sweep it up but leave one or two curls to fall over my shoulders. That would look pretty, don't you think?'

Jinau looked down, fumbling among the makeup on the dressing table for a brush or comb.

'Jinau? What do you think? About my hair?' Seti asked again. Why did the girl not answer? She knew that traditionally, Guznon women were mostly subdued in public and rarely spoke. But here in her rooms she wanted her to be open, and besides, Seti truly needed another opinion. *If only Calin were here. She'd soon let me know!*

'Um …' Jinau began, stumbling over the words before speaking the truth of it. 'Here mostly we wear our hair down.'

'Yes, I know. But …' Seti could not resist smiling to herself as she looked in the mirror. She gathered the fine blonde strands and held them up on top of her head. 'Look! See how much more attractive this looks. You should try it too.' Seti swivelled around in her seat and attempted to style the girl's hair.

Jinau pulled back and instantly grabbed her white-blonde locks with both hands. 'No! I m-mean, no, my lady. That would not be permissible.'

Seti frowned and a look of puzzlement crossed her face. 'Permissible? These are my rooms and I permit you to do anything.'

Jinau's head shook from side to side and her eyes were as wide as saucers. She gulped and steadied her voice. 'Thank you, my lady, but I am happy just to serve you.' The girl dropped her head and looked at the floor.

Seti allowed some seconds of silence to pass before turning back to the mirror. 'Very well,' she sighed.

Obviously, there would be no sisterly camaraderie now. Suddenly a vision of Calin's face pressed itself into her mind and she held her breath, silky red curls and the way her sister's warm green eyes softened when they alighted on her. Seti smiled at the memory. Then came her mother's face, the slight furrow on her brow that was only partly hidden by a strand of black hair.

In the silence that followed as Jinau began brushing her hair, she realised that she had not even told her family of Kalik's proposal. *What was she thinking!* It had not crossed her mind to speak with her mother, or her father, or Calin. *How could that be? How could I have forgotten them? Perhaps Lieutenant Finn has told them? Yes. Of course. He would have let them know. Where is Finn?*

An unexpected wave of nausea swept through her body and she began to sway. She put her hands out to steady herself by gripping the edge of the dressing table.

'Jinau. Stop!'

'My lady, what's wrong?' Jinau cried.

'I feel dizzy.' Seti held herself still and took a gulp of air.

'Some water … I'll bring …' Jinau put down the brush and ran to the bathroom. She returned with a glass of water and placed it into Setiyan's hand, who drank it greedily.

She exhaled and, after a couple more breaths, regained her wits. 'That's better. Just a dizzy spell. Thank you for the water.'

Seti handed the empty glass back to Jinau who gasped and her face suddenly fell. She quickly took up the brush and held it close to her chest. 'More brushing, my lady?'

Setiyan shook her head. 'No. Not now.'

The girl replaced the brush on the dresser and went to return the glass to the bathroom. But Seti called her back. 'Jinau … Find Lieutenant Finn and ask him to come here. I wish to see him.'

The girl's frame stiffened. Taking the glass with her, she nodded her assent and hurriedly left the room.

The q'ist transporter slowed on entry into Zaz and the sudden change in momentum woke Finn from a deep sleep. He stretched out his limbs and yawned deeply.

The journey through the tunnels and caves below ground had taken longer than he expected. Their flight to Beshwuk was only two hours, but the same distance by q'ist had lasted most of the night. He had tried to stay awake, imagining the landscape above. The light of the moon, Aunis, would be shining on the grey plains that lay cold and empty under a million crystalline stars. He reflected that this was the only time on this godforsaken planet when a man could safely stand on its surface and breathe its air. That's what he had missed. In all the days at Beshwuk they had only once stood outside – on the high platform where these barbarous people offered living sacrifices in the hope of rain. *Barbarians!*

With consciousness came the memory of his mission: he had to get a message to Jax and Linnayen on Altan. The princess's crazy idea to marry the insidious Denkaun had to be stopped, and not just because it was madness. Her face swam before him and he recalled the moment they had almost kissed back on the *Teg-Koorym*. Without warning, Denkaun's sneering face followed. Finn emitted a low growl. He pushed the image away and returned to the problem at hand. How Seti's parents were going to get to her now that she was effectively a prisoner was a conundrum. Even if they left Altan immediately, the journey to Autabron took two full days. Then they would have to get to Beshwuk, and Finn suspected that they would not be welcome guests at the wedding.

He had tried his personal communicator direct to Setiyan three or four times last night before he'd fallen asleep. There had been no response. But whether that was due to circumstances of atmospheric interference or something more sinister he had no way of knowing. Now out of the q'ist tunnels and back on the higher levels of the main city, he tried again. *Still nothing.* Though it was early morning and she might still be asleep. *With him next to her?* He couldn't help tormenting himself with the unbidden image. *Stop! Focus!* Now was no time to lose his resolve.

He found Caspiran, Birkaan and Serekunda having breakfast at their hotel and strode up to their table.

'Good lord! Decker!' Serekunda exclaimed on seeing his colleague approach. 'What are you doing here? Is the princess here too?'

Finn's face darkened as he took a seat next to them. 'I wish. I've come to warn Jax and the Ki.'

'About what?' Caspiran asked. 'They already know about the water contamination.'

'Not that. She's marrying him.'

The three faces stared blankly at Finn. Then, one by one, their brows furrowed in confusion. He needed to clarify.

'Big news. Our princess has accepted Denkaun's proposal of marriage.'

'Oh dear lord!' Serekunda stared in disbelief. 'This is madness.'

Normally so calm, Caspiran's voice wavered. 'The princess and the A'bat? How can this be?'

'He monopolised her from the day we arrived,' Serekunda said, 'And he's a strong personality. I can see how she might be charmed.'

Caspiran frowned. 'You say the Ki and Ki-consort are unaware of this?'

'As far as I know, they haven't been informed,' Finn replied.

'We spoke to the Ki-consort last night. He said nothing,' Birkaan supplied.

'This is a real problem. Why didn't you contact the Ki or Kevor Jax yourself?' Caspiran's face was clouded.

Finn frowned. 'I tried to contact both the princess and her parents. All my comms were down – or, more likely, were being blocked.' He shook his head. 'I'm telling you, there's something bad going down here. We've been played. And I think it's been happening since we first arrived.'

Caspiran slowly nodded and sucked in a breath. 'I've felt it, though I couldn't be specific. There have been more disruptions too. The mine at Euta Onjak has been taken over by a group of workers and five supervisors have been killed.'

Finn remembered something else. 'There are tribe leaders going to Beshwuk too. I saw Gaksi and Konkanaw there. If they're there for this wedding, they must've been invited days ago. I'm telling you, this stinks.'

'And how!' Serekunda finished.

Caspiran began pushing her chair back from the table. 'Hang on. There's something else,' Finn began, 'A woman called Wika Dokau claims to be Denkaun's wife. She told me the morning you left, Pieter.'

'Wife? You believe her?'

'I don't know. But she says she's pregnant, too.' Finn's shoulders drooped. 'This whole thing's a mess.'

'So let's get going. I'll contact the Ki from our ship. We've much to do.' Caspiran wiped her mouth with a napkin.

'One other thing,' Finn began. 'The water samples Pieter brought with him from Beshwuk – have they been tested yet?'

Birkaan nodded. 'Yes. All negative, my friend. Whatever's happening to the mine workers, or even here in Zaz, it's not happening there. You've not been affected.'

Finn frowned. He'd hoped there might be an explanation for the princess's unusual behaviour. He'd entertained the idea that she too was being drugged; the effects of urthrengo could explain so much. He'd just have to accept that she truly was smitten with the odious Denkaun. It was a bitter pill and he must swallow it – for now.

Denkaun's grin could not get any wider. The poisoning of the mines' water supplies had worked so well to his advantage that he could not have planned it any better. The people of Autabron were angry at this abominable treatment at the hands of the hated off-worlders that they were even prepared to overlook hostilities and prejudice that went back centuries. It was as Mira had foretold: he would be the A'bat not just for the Guznon but for all Autabronis. For here they came. One by one, the tribal leaders took their seats at the carved stone table in the grand hall at the centre of the mountain and, one by one, they bowed their heads before him.

'See what honour they do to you, my son,' Mira whispered from over his shoulder, one gnarled hand stroking the pale skin of his upper arm.

The yellow-robed Konkanaw sat hesitantly between the cobalt-clad Gaksi and the No'os, who were distinguished more by their white beards than any coloured clothing. There were other tribes too. Even the insular Graan and the Akshanik – tribes he had never met but whose members comprised over forty percent of the miners in seven different mines – had come. Their anger over the water contamination had put aside all enmity and Denkaun resolved to not let this energy go to waste. Once they were seated and stillness had settled, he stood and raised his arms. All heads turned to him, expectant, hopeful.

'Tribes of Autabron! Children of Lau and Uzno! Friends! For are we not as one today? Are we not gathered as compatriots to be avenged on our mutual enemies?'

He did not need to raise his voice – the central hall with its ornate rock pillars and bronze inlaid transoms was well-endowed acoustically. But his words needed to be powerful to pull them to his banner. As an off-worlder himself, he needed to convince them that their cause was his too.

'The discoveries we have made of this heinous poisoning of our people cannot go unpunished! For too long we have been at the mercy of the ravenous greedy ganaks and I tell you now – we will not suffer this torment one day longer!'

Many heads nodded and the murmurings of assent grew. Hanashi, a solid ally already, thumped the stone tabletop and shouted, 'Not one day more!'

Denkaun's eyes flashed him a smile. 'We will take back what is ours! What has always been ours. We will drive the ganaks from our homeworld. We will drive them into the depths of space – back to the barren planets they came from! I am the warrior of hope. The A'bat. I was born to free our people and I vow to you – I pledge my life to you on this day – that I will lead you to victory! I will lead you to freedom!'

The cheers filled the hall and a fine dust cascaded from the ceiling as the hubbub shook the rock cavern. The tribal leaders stood. They shouted and clapped as Denkaun's words rang out through the fetid air. Only one man remained seated and, as the noise receded like the passing of a sandstorm, he spoke.

'A'bat! A'bat! Hear me!' Vit, leader of the Graan, pounded the table with the pommel of a large, curved dirk.

The others slowly took their seats and some glanced nervously at each other. Vit was not a man to cross. It was common knowledge that he had murdered his predecessor and the man's wife and children too.

'A'bat … This is how you are named? No. I think not.' He spat the words out as he leaned forward. His black eyes did not leave Denkaun's face. '*You* are a ganak! You are *not* one of us. You are not Guznon. Your ancestors have not bled for this land. Your people have not sweated the salt from their bodies in the mines. No! Your people have taken from us. Your people are our enemies.' Vit's words were slow and deliberate. He measured their delivery and, at the last syllable, he rose, knife laid across his broad chest. '*You* are our enemy!

A gasp hung in the air and those who had cheered for Kalik Denkaun a few minutes earlier were now intrigued to see how he the A'bat would handle this challenge.

Denkaun walked and stood before Vit, who towered a head above him. His unflinching ice-blue eyes looked up into Vit's black ones as he spoke. 'It's true. I *was* born of a ganak mother and an unknown father.' His voice was calm and controlled, for he knew his words contained all the power he needed. 'But did you know this, my friend? My mother was the Ko-Makum who willingly gave her life on the Day of Grunkaar twenty-five years ago. And the rains flooded the lands and replenished the waters of our holy Kadis Sakek – because of *my* mother! My family's blood has already been shed to bring life to Autabron, and if I am called on to do the same I will not hesitate! I am as much of this land as any of you and if there is a man here who dares challenge me then come forth now!'

He slammed his fists onto his chest and glared into Vit's eyes until the tall leader of the notoriously aggressive Graan tribe dropped his gaze. There would be no challenge today. Denkaun was secure.

Suddenly a voice rang out. It belonged to Mira.

'A'bat sakek! A'bat sakek!' *Our holy warrior!*

The crowd took up the chant as Denkaun moved to the centre of the hall and slowly eyed each leader in turn, his stare demanding their loyalty.

'A'bat sakek! A'bat sakek!'

Finally, he allowed himself to smile. He raised his arms in salute to them. He was indeed their holy warrior and he would lead them all to victory. All except one. And, as his gaze connected with his natar now leaning against the wall behind his chair, her arms comfortably folded on her chest, they both knew who would not be there in the final days, when the horns of triumph rang through the mountains.

Linnayen tapped her fingers on the armrest of the spaceracer and wondered why they had not taken off already. Jax was still talking to a couple of crew members, old friends with whom he had flown before, laughing amiably and slapping them on the back. How he could be so relaxed was beyond her after the news had come through from Kalisa. *Marrying! What was Seti thinking?* And the man already had a wife. *How could she even contemplate it?* Luckily they would get to Autabron in time to stop it – or so she hoped.

Her eldest daughter had always been the more troublesome of the two and certainly the less predictable. It was Setiyan who needed more persuasion to complete her learning tasks and ceremonial duties, whilst Calin seemed to enjoy these activities and took a genuine interest in them. Surely it should have been the other way around, the older sister setting a good example for the younger. But, without doubt, they were two of the most different children imaginable. Linnayen had hoped that Setiyan would settle down as she grew older and, from the evidence of the last two or three years, it appeared that she was doing so. She had moderated her behaviour and shown great interest in her statecraft studies and attending community events. But now – with this crazy idea to marry a man she hardly knew *and* who was already married – all Linnayen's hopes that her daughter had matured were dashed.

Eventually Jax took his place beside her and signalled to the captain that they were ready to leave.

'About time,' she said testily. 'This is no time for chatting with old friends.'

'Sorry. We were waiting for cargo. Water purification filters, as it happens. Seems they've run out.'

'Ah. Of course.' There were problems on Autabron other than her daughter's impending nuptials.

Jax patted her hand then lifted it and kissed it. 'Try not to worry, love. We'll get there and sort it all out. Seti won't be marrying this

Denkaun – or anyone else, for that matter. At least, not for a long time, and only after a lengthy engagement.'

'I hope you're right. But you know how she is,' came the worried reply.

'Indeed I do. And if she doesn't see sense, I'll carry her out of that mountain kicking and screaming if I have to.'

Jax was over fifty years old but still a strong man. Linnayen was glad that he kept himself healthy and in good shape because she wanted him to live a long time, wanted them to grow old together, something her mother and father had not been able to do due to her father's early death from injuries sustained during the Earthan Wars. Thinking now of her mother, she recalled her insistence that she brook no delay in getting to Setiyan.

'You must go immediately! Only the heavens know what's got into my granddaughter's head. But you must get there and put it right. Bring her home,' Li-el had insisted.

Linnayen was worried about Harriet Whitton-Blake's interrogation but her mother had put her straight on that matter too.

'Don't be ridiculous. Calin and I are just as capable of getting to the truth of that woman's scheming,' she had confirmed. 'Actually, more so.'

Linnayen knew that look. Li-el's mentante abilities were well-honed, as were Calin's. 'Mother,' she began to admonish, then gave up. Li-el would do as she pleased anyway. 'Just be careful.'

'Of course,' Li-el countered, smiling mischievously. 'And anyway, you know Earthans are hard to read – unless they get emotional. My task won't be easy, daughter.'

Unless they get emotional. What was the betting that Li-el would get the Earthan spy worked up, thereby opening the doors to her otherwise closed mind? Well, there was nothing for it now. She had to get to Seti on Autabron as quickly as possible. All comms calls to her had been unsuccessful, just as Lieutenant Finn had reported. Was her daughter being held a captive? A hostage? Or was she there willingly? Only by seeing and speaking to her in person would Linnayen know the truth.

But whatever that truth turned out to be, Setiyan Genara would not be marrying this man any time soon. Of that she was convinced.

Chapter Sixteen

Seti's eyes widened as she took in the horror being unveiled on the vidscreen set in the wall of her bedroom. Behind the beleaguered reporter's head, she could see a crowd of angry people shouting and baying for the blood of the GKD managers. They blew horns and carried placards; some even threw rocks at the office doors, and she flinched when the correspondent suddenly ducked at the sound of what might have been a gunshot. How glad she was to be safe in the Beshwuk settlement, away from all the troubles and close to the arms of the man she loved.

A movement caught her eye and she jumped up from the divan as the door slid open.

'Kalik! My love!'

She crossed the few metres between them easily and he opened his arms to receive her embrace. He laughed as she planted kisses all over his cheeks and neck.

'Oh, I missed you. Why have you left me here all alone?' she complained.

He grinned and held her a little away from him, stroking her fair hair and gazing into her blue eyes. 'Ah, my sweet princess. I wish I could be with you too. But events call me away. You must know that.'

'Mmm, I know,' she replied sadly. 'But I wish it weren't so.'

'These are important days, my love. All the leaders have come – and not only for our wedding. There are decisions we must make.'

He drew her over to the window seat which looked out across the vast Beshwuk plains. Both Lau and Uzno stood oblique in the afternoon sky. In the distance they could see a range of low hills and, before them, a sea of crystalline red dunes, whose volatile currents changed hourly with the fiery dust storms that raged above.

He pulled her down onto his lap. 'Look out there. What do you see?'

She smiled, forcing herself to look away from the face she loved. 'Sand. Rock. Hills.'

'Shall I tell you what I see?'

She nodded.

'I see the future. I see my inheritance. This planet, its people, living as free people. Free to roam their lands. Free to choose their fate.'

'That's as it should for all people,' she concurred. 'But many Autabronis have a good life, my love. I've seen them in the city and here too. They seem happy.' Her voice held the innocence of a child and she stroked his face and kissed his forehead. His muscles stiffened as he patted her hand.

'You have been here for less than a fortnight so I'll forgive your ignorance, my sweet. How are you to know what is in our hearts? How are you to know the yoke of oppression? You who have had so much in your life.' He smiled benevolently and kissed her cheek.

Her returning smile came hesitantly. *Had he called her ignorant?* She couldn't quite work out what he was saying. So often these days, her thoughts were foggy and ephemeral. No sooner had she begun to concentrate on an idea or piece of news than the thought drifted away like a leaf on a summer stream. There was something she wanted to ask him. *What was it? Something about the wedding? No. Finn! That was it.*

'I've just remembered,' she began, her eyes brightening. 'Where is Lieutenant Finn? I've not seen him for such a long time. Can you send him to me?'

'Why, of course! I'm sure he won't be hard to find.' Denkaun caressed her upturned face and lifted her off his knee.

'Oh no! Don't go, Kalik. Stay with me.' Her eyes pleaded and she held out her hands, begging for the scraps of his love.

He took hold of her hands and squeezed them, perhaps a little more firmly than she would have liked.

'There are riots in Zaz-Rakuum and explosions in Aktah. The people are protesting. They're angry. They've been poisoned by the off-worlders … and you want me to stay and kiss your pretty lips.' Though his mouth shaped a smile, it did not reach his steely eyes. 'Such are the thoughts of my sweet princess. I should be honoured, eh?'

'I love you, Kalik. I want to be with you all the time,' she implored.

'And once you are my wife you will be. But for now, I'm needed elsewhere.' He turned and strode towards the door.

'Will you come to me tonight? Please ...' Again, her eyes begged him and she placed a hand over her heart.

He spoke over his shoulder. 'All being well.' The doors slid open and Mira, flanked by two guards, stood on the other side. 'Ah, Natar! Perhaps you could entertain my princess? She is restless this afternoon.'

Mira bowed her head and stepped into the room. The men stayed at the door while she took a seat next to Setiyan. Before Seti could say another word, Denkaun had left and Mira claimed her attention.

'My dear. How are you feeling?' she asked kindly.

Setiyan took a few moments to think about the question. How *was* she feeling? There was something she had asked Kalik to do and now she fought to remember what it was. She shook her head as if to regain her senses. 'Erm ... Odd. Not sure ...'

'Ah ... maybe a walk is in order. Or better still, here, take a sip of water.'

Of course! She was thirsty. No wonder she couldn't think straight. She was dehydrated. She thanked the old woman and accepted the flask, drinking greedily.

'Better?' Mira asked solicitously, patting Seti's hand.

'Yes.'

'I have some good news, my princess.'

Seti's eyes brightened and she gazed hopefully at the old woman.

'Your mother and father are coming to Autabron. They will be at your wedding! Isn't that wonderful?' The wrinkles on Mira's face deepened as her papery skin stretched into a smile and her rheumy eyes glistened with unshed tears. 'I am so happy for you, my dear.'

Mother and Father! Seti felt faint again and swayed in her seat. *Of course!* She still had not spoken to them about her love for Kalik. She must tell them! She had been here for – what was it now? Days? Weeks? She suddenly recalled the sound of her mother's voice, as soft and warm as a spring breeze over the Mayar grain fields. And her smiling peridot eyes, so often, as a child, the last thing she saw as she wandered into sleep. She felt once more her father's strong hugs, and the way he would hold her face in his two hands and kiss her forehead. Instantly, she was aware that her cheeks were wet and there was an unfamiliar lump in her throat.

'Oh, my sweet lady. Such tears of joy! How you do honour to your parents by the giving of your tears. This will please the A'bat greatly,' the old shaman crooned as she patted dry the tears on Seti's face. 'Why, you are already learning our ways. Respect for parents. Dedication to the A'bat. You will make a fine wife for my son. My beautiful Kalik.'

Mira's bony arms encircled the young woman and she pulled her head down onto her chest. The old woman rocked her just as she had done for Kalik when he was a baby.

Seti's tears were soon absorbed by the rough fabric. The rocking motion lulled her and, within minutes, she wondered why she was crying. But the thoughts would have to wait. She suddenly felt tired and all she could hear was the rhythmic pounding of blood inside her head. She yawned and blinked to clear away the fog that had descended yet again. The pull of sleep was too strong. Before she knew what was happening, she felt herself being lifted through the air by strong arms and laid down on the divan.

'Rest, lady. Sweet dreams.'

Mira lay a coverlet over her and gave a nod of dismissal to the two guards. She allowed herself a smile of triumph.

'Miss Whitton-Blake! How interesting to finally meet you and ... My goodness! How extremely pretty you are. No wonder my son-in-law fell in love with you all those years ago. Such a face must have turned many heads, eh?'

From her viewscreen in the next room, Calin watched the opening exchange. She raised an eyebrow. She had never seen her grandmother like this before – simultaneously flattering and disarming– and it was both amusing and disconcerting. They did not know how the Earthan would react. She and Li-el had talked about a strategy before Harrie was brought to them: Li-el would be the one to get the woman fired up and Calin would tap into her thoughts. So she hardly expected her grandmother to be this enthusiastic, almost gushing, in front of the woman.

Harrie was equally nonplussed at this reception in a non-descript meeting room on the eleventh floor of the Galactic Union's security headquarters. After two days of doing nothing, she was bored out of her mind and on the point of making a complaint to the Earthan ambassador's office that she was being held against her will when the summons came. Her surprise at meeting the dowager Ki-consort was written all over her face. Harrie had expected interrogation, but here was courtesy and informality.

The compliment from the older woman needed acknowledgement. 'Very kind. Thank you.'

'No, no, my dear. All true. You are a picture of loveliness. You would have been hard for any man to resist.'

The corner of Harrie's mouth twitched. 'You flatter me too much,' she replied.

'You think?' Li-el's crafty smile was matched by a look of good cheer in her eyes. 'I think not enough. I think your look, your style and your manner are worthy of high praise, for they are your tools of your trade, are they not?'

Harrie's frown lasted no more than a second, but it was enough for Calin to pick up the hint of annoyance.

'Tools, as you put it, I was born with. Can't be helped.' She shrugged.

'Oh, how wrong you are, my dear. I, too, was endowed with a noble family and exceptional beauty – though you'd hardly know it now, eh?' Li-el laughed warmly. 'I was also very proud and, some might say, arrogant. But I think you'd agree with me that a deep sense of our own importance – our standing in society – comes with the position. Not so?'

Harrie frowned again. Where was this leading? 'I don't understand.'

Li-el scoffed at the remark. 'Come, come. You are no ingenue. Women of our rank – born into the job, you might say – like my daughter, Linnayen. We know very well what will be demanded of us. I imagine your father had expectations of you, given the work he does. Women like you must be very useful in the intelligence game. I mean, I don't suppose he would have been too impressed if you'd wanted to be, say, a gardener, or a cook.' Li-el chuckled and slapped her hands on her knees, as if pleased with her own joke.

Harrie shifted in her seat and shrugged. 'Women like me?'

Li-el's dark green eyes glittered. 'Yes. People who are prepared to subjugate their dislikes in order to get the job done. Or get ahead.'

Harrie's face tightened imperceptibly. 'What are you suggesting? If it's that I had sex with Avad Jarkoo to get information then you're right. He was a boor and an oaf.' She smiled contemptuously.

'With Director Jarkoo? No, dear,' Li-el replied in a honeyed voice. 'With my son-in-law.'

'What!' Harrie frowned. 'Absolutely not!'

'Really? My dear girl, he was the son of one of the most powerful men on Earth. Don't tell me that didn't cross your mind. Or your father's.'

'No! I loved Kev.'

'Well, yes, I suppose it helped that he was very handsome. Your father picked well for you.' Li-el's saw that her words niggled and stung.

'Wrong! We met by chance. Pa wasn't involved.' Harrie suddenly jumped up and strode to the window. The building was set atop one of the highest hills in Genkarah and she stared out at the city's gleaming spires and wooded gardens below.

'Though he must have been devasted when you cheated on young Kevor. I believe Jax found you with another man? *And* you were high on drugs! Your father's plans were dashed. Was he terribly angry with you?'

Li-el was relentless. Using the woman's relationship with her father was a neat trick. Calin was impressed. Her grandmother sat calmly in a gilded chair while out of her mouth spilled poisonous assumptions and outright lies. Or were they? The way the Earthan woman reacted, maybe Li-el had uncovered the truth after all. Either way, it didn't matter. Harriet Whitton-Blake was opening up nicely and Calin could see and feel her every emotion.

'My father had nothing to do with it –'

'So he supported your behaviour?' Li-el interjected.

'Well, of course he was upset! So was I,' Harrie snapped back, swivelling to face the older woman, hands on her hips.

'How long did it take for you to win back your father's trust? What did you have to do to earn that?' Li-el's face was impassive but

Calin could tell by the straightening of her back that her grandmother was going in for the kill. 'Who did he put in your way next? Ah, yes, it was the head of the Enviro Agency. Luther someone … Wasn't he a little old for you? He'd be in his nineties by now.'

Harrie's mouth was a straight line and her grey eyes stared at the woven swirls of the carpeted floor.

'Tell me, did you have sex with *everyone* your father told you to? Isn't that, as you Earthans would say, the equivalent of prostituting one's own daughter? I doubt your mother would have approved, had she lived.' Li-el's eyes were as narrowed as a shawk-lion's before it devoured its prey. She even went so far as to lick her lips. 'Such a terrible accident, the overdose. Was it suicide or misadventure? What did your father tell you?'

In the next room, Calin felt the surge of anger and frustration rising inside the Earthan. Li-el had rattled her severely. Whitton-Blake's thoughts screamed and spun. They were a morass of seething desperation as she reflected on all the men and women she had manipulated over the last twenty-five years. And why bring up her mother's death? Harrie had been only ten years old. But then, Anthony's new partner, her stepmother, Livia, had moved into their city apartment by the time she turned eleven.

Had Harrie been used by the only other man she loved and respected? Such introspection was confronting and hurtful. Also, she had been left here on Altan without any support from Covert-7 or her father, even though she had called him as Jarkoo's life slipped away. Someone would have to answer to her when she got home!

Harrie came back to stand over the old woman, glaring down at the still composed Li-el as she spat the words at her. 'I know what you're trying to do. Seeds of doubt. Won't work.'

But now was the time to see the truth of Whitton-Blake's involvement in the plots on Autabron. Li-el turned towards more recent events.

'Forgive me. I've upset you. And I'm sure that your feelings for my son-in-law were true.' She leaned across and patted the arm of the chair next to her. Harrie took a second to consider the invitation to sit before accepting. She smoothed the folds of her dress and took a breath before the old woman continued. 'He was a devilishly good-looking young man, wasn't he? Not like that awful Jarkoo. Whatever possessed you to take *him* as your lover? When you might have had Jax?'

There it was! Calin had her now. All her defences were down and she saw clear into the Earthan's consciousness. Harrie Whitton-Blake had loathed Jarkoo. Would never have gone with him but for her father's plan. The thoughts came tumbling forth like a mountain stream in full spate. The poisoning of the water on Autabron was Anthony Whitton-Blake's idea! But he had been commissioned by someone else … Natesha? Someone from Millien Incorporated, the major shareholder of GKD – the mine owners! Now it was falling into place. Harriet Whitton-Blake was not enlisted to *spy* on Avad Jarkoo. She was sent to Autabron to recruit him in her father's plot. But more … She had murdered him – with a poison-tipped knife. It wasn't hard now to see that Millien's revenues had been the driver. They wanted compliant workers who cost less, thereby increasing the company's profits. It was all about money! All about stripping the planet of its riches at the least cost.

But Calin had seen something else, too, and was glad that her mother had left for Autabron and did not have to witness it. There was no doubt that the Earthan woman was unquestionably still in love with Jax.

Li-el gripped the arms of the chair and rose unsteadily. She looked down at the redhead's upturned, expectant face.

'Well, my dear, what an interesting chat we've had. Perhaps we'll meet again.'

Li-el began to walk towards the door when Harrie's voice stopped her. 'Wait! What about the interrogation? I thought I was going to be questioned.'

Li-el met her gaze and nodded slowly. 'Quite so. Well, I must be off. An appointment with my dressmaker.' Her smile was beatific and she gave a fond, disinterested wave as she left the room.

Calin watched as the woman's head dropped into her hands. Whitton-Blake had done despicable things, behaved unconscionably, and yet Calin could feel nothing but pity for her.

There had been no turning back once her father had struck her with such force. Wika had always known he could be violent – hadn't she seen the bruises on her mother's arms and neck? But this was a new level of fury. There was no reasoning with him. She had tried to explain that she was still Kalik's favourite. But he did not even allow her time to take a breath.

Finally, his energy spent, he stormed off, leaving Wika, her mother and her sisters alone. Her mother still wailed and, when she saw the damage to her daughter's body, wept even more tears. Her apologies rang in the empty air as one by one the young women tried to comfort her.

'This is not your fault, Mother. Please don't cry,' Wika pleaded. 'I am still in my lord's favour. All will be well.'

One of her sisters rounded on her. 'How can you say that, Wika? He is taking the ganak to wife!'

Wika tried again to explain while she dabbed the cut on her ear. 'You don't understand. I am his first choice. I am his wife in all but name. I carry his son!'

Her sisters shook their heads and her mother stroked her face. 'No, child. She is a princess. She will always outrank you. Even if the A'bat takes you back into his chamber, she will be the one to sit at his right hand. She will be the one to carry his heir.'

'Not my bastard? That is what you think?' Her face reddened and her voice became thick. 'You are all wrong. She will never bear his child. I will see to it!'

With that, she took her parab from the rack near the doorway and fixed her bag across her shoulders. She turned back in the open doorway and gazed at their shocked faces. 'Goodbye, Mother and my sisters. Think well of me.'

From a high window carved into the rock wall, the early morning rays of the twin suns shot into Mira's private sanctum. The old woman watched the motes of dust as they danced and dived, tracing their random pathways with a gnarly index finger. In the few minutes remaining to her of tranquillity before the business of the day would begin, she sat on the end of her bed and allowed her thoughts to coalesce.

The drug was working well on the princess. It had been a mere eight days since Setiyan had arrived and she was now completely in their thrall. Although the water contamination issue had come out sooner than Mira had wanted, even that was working to Kalik's advantage. Jarkoo would have had to be killed at some point anyway. But thanks to the Earthan spy-whore, the job had been done for them.

Now all she and Kalik needed to do was to seal the allegiance of the tribes and put their own people into positions of power. The GKD's security forces and city police were no match for the tribes and she estimated that soon all mine sites would be taken by the newly formed People's Legion of Autabron. It had been Kalik's idea to start stockpiling weapons two years earlier and, good son that he was, he had shared his plans with her. Of course, she could not reciprocate over the water poisoning. He might have baulked at that as being a step too far. Even now, she felt he did not need to know of her arrangement with Jarkoo. But, when she looked back on their achievements, it was obvious that the mine workers would have had to be subdued. After all, GKD and the other mine owners had to be lulled into believing all was well. They could not suspect rebellion was being fomented under their very noses or the coup would have failed.

No, indeed. Things were working out nicely. Autabron would be under PLA control within the week with Kalik at its helm, and the silly young princess would be his. More importantly, she would provide the heir to the dynasty that was being forged in these very days.

And it could only be her. Mira smiled, recalling the time twenty-six years ago when the Ko-Makum had revealed the truth of her twin brother's misdeed. Navarr thought his sister knew nothing of his rape of the drugged Linnayen Genara while she had been captive in the ruined fortress. But Balisel Navarr had watched through a grille in the heavy wooden door of the cell, all the while fighting to curb her jealousy. The Ko-Makum had cried as she recounted her tale to Mira, begging her to keep it secret – and she had. But then, seven years ago, Mira had seen the image of Princess Setiyan of Altan on a vidscreen. It was like seeing the Ko-Makum come back to life. There was no doubting the girl's heritage and there was no longer any obstacle to the fulfilment of the prophecy made so many hundreds of years ago by the Witch of Rakuum. History was being made and she, Mira Denkaun, mother of the A'bat, was at its heart.

She stretched her arms up over her head and rotated her neck, releasing all tension. A new day had dawned in Beshwuk and she laughed out loud.

When she got to Zaz-Rakuum, Wika began to worry if she had done the right thing. The place was in uproar and there were security guards everywhere. People milled about, their eyes furtive. Parents were hurrying their children into homes as she passed. Men shouted across balustrades to each other, some angry, others cheering. The veyors moving up and down the levels were packed with people, and every one of them held an armed security guard. She took a fortifying breath before stepping onto the next veyor heading for the surface and, from behind the concealing mesh of the parab's hood, she screwed up her eyes, scanning the carriage for danger. She had never seen such chaos and decided to risk asking a young woman what was going on.

'Didn't you hear, sister? The People's Legion of Autabron has taken over the city. This morning, our people stood up to the ganak-lickers in the council and kicked them out. Rejoice! We are free!'

Wika smiled hesitantly. The woman's zealotry was overwhelming.

'Sister? Are you not pleased?' The woman's voice was short and terse.

Wika nodded quickly. 'Oh, yes. It is wonderful!'

'And all thanks to our glorious A'bat!' the woman added.

At hearing the word, others in the veyor took up the chant. 'A'bat! A'bat!' Wika looked around, smiling all the while as she joined the call with them. If only they knew that he was her husband and the father of the child she carried. The veyor came to a stop at the third level down from the surface. Wika turned to the woman again.

'Sister, please, is this the level for the hotels?' The woman looked askance at her. On seeing her frown, Wika added, 'I am tasked to meet my cousin and bring her home to Beshwuk.'

At the mention of the Guznon heartland, the home of their glorious leader, the woman's eyes opened wide and she smiled warmly. 'Of course, sister. All the hotels are that way. I bid you good day and a safe journey home.'

Wika nodded her thanks and set off in the direction she had indicated. Though Lieutenant Finn was still in Beshwuk, she knew he and the ganak whore had come with another man named Serekunda. If she could find him, he surely would help her. She could not understand why the lieutenant had not done something. He had looked shocked when she told him of her position and he swore to help. But that was three days ago now and nothing had changed. Perhaps he had lied. Perhaps he was as bad as all the other off-worlders.

As luck would have it, she tracked Serekunda down almost immediately. The concierge at the second hotel confirmed that Doctor Serekunda and his party were guests and he sent a message to let the doctor know he had a visitor. The hotel lobby was a haven of peace and calm amid the mayhem outside and Wika was glad to wait on the silk-covered lounges. She had not realised how tired she was and closed her eyes for a moment. She had barely slept on the q'ist the night before from the throbbing pain of her injuries.

The next thing she knew, someone was shaking her shoulder and speaking her name.

'Wika. Wika! Wake up.'

The voice was familiar and, as the fog of sleep cleared, she saw that she had slid down on the couch and the lieutenant was kneeling in front of her.

'Oh! Forgive me, Lord Finn.'

Finn caught a bemused look from Serekunda, who had raised his eyebrows. Finn shrugged and grinned before returning to the confused woman.

'What brings you here, Wika?' Finn asked. 'Here, let me help you.' He stretched out a hand, which she accepted with a sudden gasp. 'Whoa! Are you all right?'

She nodded quickly. 'Thank you. I am well.' Then realisation hit her. 'But *you*? Why are you here?'

Finn shook his head sadly. 'It's a long story. Suffice to say my services were no longer wanted.'

'More like impossible to carry out.' Serekunda completed the explanation for him then smiled down at the young woman and held out a hand. 'Hello. My name is Pieter Serekunda. You asked for me?'

'Sir, I did.' She swallowed. The dark-skinned man towered over her. He was as tall as most Autabroni men but nowhere near as intimidating. He took a chair next to the lounge, poured some water into a glass and handed it to her.

'I thought my Lord Finn had deserted me and I came to seek your help,' she said.

'I actually began looking for you before I ended up back here. I wanted your help to uncover the truth,' Finn said. 'Something strange has been happening.'

Serekunda saw the confusion in the woman's eyes. 'Decker was blocked from seeing the princess by Mira's guards. And all his attempts to get messages out of Beshwuk failed – we think deliberately.'

At the mention of the shaman's name, Wika snorted her contempt. 'Mira! She is behind all this.'

'Tell us. What do you know?' Finn pleaded. 'What the heck's going on?'

Wika studied the two faces, both so expectant and kind. Would they be angry with her when they knew the extent of Mira's deceit? *But why would they be?* She had no part in it. All she wanted was to have her beloved by her side and give him a beautiful son.

'The prophecy … Mira's prophecy.' Her voice was barely more than a whisper. Both men frowned. They obviously did not know about it. She swallowed and gathered strength as she spoke. 'She foresees the future. She has told for many years that a day would come when the son of the twins would lead our people to freedom. The son of the twins would become the A'bat, our warrior of hope. But more. That he would birth generations of warrior-leaders – of royal blood – and that they will make the waters of Autabron flow again. Mira says your princess is needed to fulfil the prophecy.'

Finn's eyes widened as he looked at Serekunda's equally amazed face. 'What the … You're telling me the shaman planned this? That Setiyan would fall for Denkaun? You can't *make* people fall in love.'

Serekunda butted in. 'Wait – the son of the twins? What twins?'

At this, Wika looked over her shoulder. There was no one other than the concierge in the foyer but she lowered her voice all the same. 'Kalik's mother was a twin. The Ko-Makum, "little witch" in our language. She sacrificed herself on the Day of Grunkaar. He was only a baby then, but my father saw it all, how the Ko-Makum gave her life to the rays of Lau and Uzno. And he knew the story.'

Finn's brows drew together. 'What story?'

Her voice dropped even lower and the men had to pull closer to her. 'That the father of the Ko-Makum's baby was her own twin brother. Kalik is the son of the twins. And so he has become the A'bat and he is leading our people to freedom. It's all coming true. But be warned, Mira is powerful.'

Serekunda and Finn grimaced at each other. That a brother and sister had had a child was taboo on Earth.

'Let me get this straight. You're saying that that freak, Denkaun, his parents were twins and that he needs the princess to get pregnant to fulfil this crazy old woman's prophecy?'

Wika's face reddened. *How dare this ganak speak so!* 'Freak? He is my husband and I love him! You promised to get your princess to leave. But you have done nothing!' She stood up but Serekunda took her hand.

'Trust us, Wika. We want the same thing. Her mother and father will be here tomorrow and they will speak sense to her. She will be made to give him up. Now, if you have nowhere else to go, please stay here with us. The city is not safe right now and you must allow us to look after you,' Serekunda offered solicitously.

Wika could not believe the kind words of the dark man. She had little experience of off-worlders and had been told how horrible and greedy they were. But this man was gentle.

'Pieter's right. You can't go back out there. All hell's breaking loose and I reckon there'll be worse tomorrow.'

Lord Finn, too, was showing nothing but thoughtfulness. Maybe she would give these ganaks another chance to rid her of the troublesome princess-bitch. One more day would not hurt. And, after all, she was so tired.

As the two men led her to their rooms, the yells and cries from outside seemed to be getting louder. Lord Finn was right. These were unsettling times. But with her beautiful Kalik soon returned to her she would raise their many children and help him to govern wisely. These were Wika Dokau's happy thoughts as she drifted off to sleep on the soft bed they had given her.

The news was scratchy and intermittent but it was clear that things were happening so fast on Autabron that reporters were finding it hard to keep up. The communications officer looked up from an array of controls to Jax and Linnayen. 'Sorry to report, sir, my lady, but the situation is getting worse. Our agents report outbreaks of violence in at least six centres.'

Jax looked into his wife's eyes. Her concern matched his own. They had left Altan thinking to persuade a recalcitrant daughter to come home. Now, only an hour away from landing, they seemed to be on a rescue mission in the middle of an uprising. Although for now the Beshwuk settlement appeared to be stable, there was no way of knowing if that were true or how long it might last. All efforts to contact Seti had proved futile, and Linnayen had to consider that this was deliberate. Was her daughter being held hostage? Even if she didn't realise it?

'And Zaz-Rakuum?' Jax asked of the young officer.

She looked down at a screen. 'There were clashes with security guards last night but it's quiet now. The heaviest fighting has moved to the mines at Onjak and Makaan. We should be clear to land at the Zaz dock within the hour.'

Jax nodded his thanks and he and Linnayen moved away to the bridge's viewport.

'I can't believe this has deteriorated so quickly. In less than forty-eight hours, a sensible, stable government has been turned out and replaced by a bunch of crazed madmen.' Jax shook his head. 'And our daughter is stuck in the middle of it!' He took Linnayen's hand and kissed it lightly.

'I can't work out if she's actually in love with this man or if she's being held against her will,' she said, frowning.

Linnayen eyes scanned the scene below. The russet planet almost filled the portal and she could clearly see the mountains that encompassed most of the central equatorial belt. As ever, there were no clouds, though she could make out a thin milky veil in the atmosphere over both polar regions. These were the lands of the renowned, normally peaceful Gaksi and No'os tribes, considered to be the more fortunate for they at least enjoyed occasional rains.

Jax spoke quietly. 'It's not the prettiest of planets, is it?'

'But it *is* the richest. Everyone wants a piece of it, and that's what's caused this mess,' she replied sagely.

Li-el and Calin's report that Harriet Whitton-Blake had been working under the command of Covert-7 and her father at the instigation of GKD's major shareholding company, Millien Incorporated, had come as no surprise. It was all about greed. Since the Earthans had joined the Galactic Union twenty-five years earlier, its companies had not been slow to extract the original four planets' resources. She and Jax had sat in on many meetings listening to the requests – sometimes demands – for leases to develop natural resources. It had been a constant struggle to maintain the balance between those who sought more industrialisation and those who wanted to preserve what they saw as precious ecosystems. Linnayen was largely in favour of the conservators, but she knew it was a balancing act. People had to work and the market demanded goods. So there had been times when she had reluctantly given approval for projects that in her heart and in a perfect universe she never would have.

Looking at the barren planet below, it was hard to imagine that anyone had a great love or regard for it. As Jax said, it was not a pretty place. But even it was special to the people of Autabron and what the Earthans had done here was reprehensible. The Whitton-Blake woman, her father and the Millien company would be charged for their crimes, including that of murder. Justice would be done. She only hoped they would have a chance to begin delivering it before the indigenous people of Autabron destroyed everything they had worked so hard to achieve.

Jax laid an arm across her shoulder and pulled her in to him. She rested her head on his chest. These might be the last moments of peace they would get for many days.

'You know,' Jax began, 'you never told me why you didn't question Harrie in person.'

Linnayen smiled and looked up. A little teasing might lighten the mood. 'Oh, you mean that old woman you told me about? The one who'd lost her looks?'

She felt his laughter. 'That's the one,' he said.

She pulled away and looked him in the eye. 'I actually felt sorry for her. She's beautiful. She's intelligent. She's had every advantage in life and yet … I felt pity. She hasn't got what I've got – you.'

Jax bent to kiss her lips. 'And you'll always have me.'

A short siren pierced the silence, signifying that the vessel was coming into orbit. They would be landing within minutes. As they took their seats, Linnayen reached across and held her husband's warm hand. The look they shared was one of hope mixed with anxiety. Who knew what they would find down on the surface of the troubled planet?

'Don't worry. We'll bring her home. I promise.' Jax's voice was calm and meant to soothe her fears, but Linnayen couldn't help thinking that not all promises can be kept. *Let this not be one of them.*

Chapter Seventeen

Jinau was more than relieved to know that the A'bat and Mira had not discovered her breach of the rules. Surely, if they had known that she had given water from the tap to the princess she would have been removed from her post, and very likely severely punished. Although she had not seen his anger, she had heard tales that the A'bat could be fearsome, sometimes violent. As for Lady Mira, just the memory of her cold eyes was enough to send shivers through the girl's limbs.

But Jinau was worried all the same. The princess seemed strange to her. When she had first started serving upon her a week ago, she had been bright and cheerful. She had often been kind to Jinau, almost sisterly, which was odd. Jinau had been told that ganaks were evil and callous and greedy. But here was a princess – a lady of great rank, no less – behaving with consideration and friendliness.

As the days went by, though, the princess's good humour seemed to dip and lessen, as though the shadow of Aunis had passed over her and not moved on its way. Often, in the midst of speaking, she would suddenly stop and shake her head, as though to flick away an irritating insect. Jinau noticed also that she sometimes got up as though to leave the room but would stop at the door and turn back. The look in her eyes was one of confusion as though she could not remember where she was going or what she had intended to do.

Then there was her sickness – sometimes two or three times a day she would ask drowsily for a bowl to catch the contents of her stomach. But she was barely eating anything. Surely this could not be healthy? The only time she brightened was when the A'bat came to see her. At first she would jump up and drop whatever she was doing to rush to him. But in these last couple of days she had not even risen from her chair, though Jinau could see the willingness to do so in her sad blue eyes. She would hardly make a happy bride looking like this!

Jinau asked her mother what she should do. Her mother was a wise woman who had knowledge of illness from her work at the medcentre. Jinau faithfully related the princess's symptoms and behaviour. Her mother smiled and raised an eyebrow. She explained to Jinau that the princess must be pregnant and that this was nothing to be alarmed about. However, she warned her not to say anything. They could be wrong! And it was the prerogative of the father to announce his wife's gravidity. Jinau's mother recommended that she keep good watch of the princess and that she would give her a hearty soup, full of goodness, to take to her every day. But did she dare? Surely the A'bat would not mind his child receiving the health benefits of her mother's soup? And even if the princess were not pregnant, what harm could good food do when her spirits were so low?

'Here, lady. Take a little more soup.' Jinau held the spoon to Setiyan's open mouth. The princess supped greedily.

'Mmm. Delicious.'

'My mother will be pleased that you like her soup.'

Setiyan took another spoonful, then another. She brought up a thin hand to bring the bowl closer and spilled a little on the skirt of her dress.

Jinau smiled. 'Soon you will be strong enough to take the bowl. But for now, my lady, please let me. It will save me washing your clothes.'

Jinau was amazed at herself. She had never said so many words in her lady's presence before. What was happening to her? Her mother chided her for being shy and her brother often teased her about her muteness. But in less than a week and under the kind gaze of the princess, she had opened her heart. She had begun to feel genuine friendship for this foreigner.

Setiyan finished the soup and, for the first time in days, Jinau saw a pink glow in her cheeks and a sparkle in her eyes.

'Thank you, Jinau. And thank your mother for me.'

'I will but …' She was hesitant to raise it but her and her mother's safety were at stake. 'Please don't tell the A'bat or Lady Mira. I am ordered to bring you food and drink only from their kitchens.'

Jinau's dark eyes were huge under her worried brow. Setiyan smiled her compliance, then yawned. 'Oh … I think I need a nap, Jinau.'

The girl jumped up and helped Seti to her bed. She then closed the force-shield drapes and the room was plunged into near-darkness. Before she left the princess to rest, she swept up the empty bowl and washed it, happy that now, even if the princess spewed every morsel the A'bat and Mira provided, she would get at least one healthy meal every day.

Though the landing at the Zaz-Rakuum dock was smooth, there was no doubt of the disruption and heightened activity in the place once Linnayen and Jax got into the transit foyer. Vidscreens showed the latest fires and fighting at various mine sites, with footage of officials and security guards barking orders. Even so, the head of the city council and acting Galactic Union agent, a tall Graan tribeswoman named Svikar Kaletin, braved the melee to meet Jax and Linnayen and their personal guards.

'Lord, lady, honoured guests. I am so sorry to give you such welcome as this. Riot and affray at every turn!'

'Councillor Kaletin, we fully understand. These are troubling times,' Jax replied.

Kaletin bowed her head, then continued. 'I can assure you of your safety, though. I have ordered a detail of our guards to accompany you for as long as you need. They are our best people.'

'Thank you,' Linnayen replied. 'But first we need to speak with our team. Can you take us to them?

'Indeed. Follow me.'

It took only a few minutes to reach Finn, Serekunda and the others at their hotel. As they entered the room, Caspiran and Birkaan had their heads together over some papers while Finn and Serekunda were standing, deep in conversation. The Autabroni woman – Wika Dokau, Linnayen presumed – sat in the corner chewing the nail of her index finger. On their approach, she jumped up and gasped, as though the breath had been sucked from her body. The woman was obviously under some stress. Jax placed a hand on her arm.

'Steady!' Jax said, guiding her back to her seat.

'Why don't we all sit down?' suggested Linnayen, turning to the others.

Each took a seat around a low wooden table whilst Pieter Serekunda brought a jug and some glasses.

Linnayen opened the discussion. 'I cannot tell you how concerned we are at the events here. Not only for our daughter but also for the upheaval caused by the contamination of the public water supply.'

'Do we know who is responsible?' Birkaan growled. He had family who lived in Zaz and other communities on Autabron and his anger was palpable.

Jax gazed into the man's eyes and answered honestly. 'We do. Harriet Whitton-Blake acted with Avad Jarkoo under the instruction of the Earthan intelligence agency Covert-7. It, in turn, was co-opted by GKD's major shareholder, Millien Incorporated.'

Linnayen continued. 'Millien's motive was to reduce wage costs by creating a malleable workforce – one that would not seek wage rises and would work longer hours without complaint.'

'And it worked for nearly two years! They'll pay for this,' Birkaan warned.

'Indeed they will,' Jax confirmed. 'Arrest warrants have been drawn up, including for murder and corporate homicide. We have since discovered that there might be up to ten deaths from drinking the contaminated water.'

'In the meantime,' Pieter Serekunda reflected, 'we have the problem of the civil unrest this business has unleashed and the rise of Kalik Denkaun. He seems to be the leader of the People's Legion of Autabron.'

Finn leaned forward, elbows on his knees and eyes scanning the gathering. 'The PLA. You saw the graffiti on your way in?' Hastily written slogans in support of the rebel force had been painted on the steel doors and rock walls of the second and third levels below ground. At nods from Jax and Linnayen, he continued. 'They must have been planning this for months. Suddenly everyone has weapons, and I saw for myself the tribal leaders arriving at Beshwuk days ago before all this kicked off. I thought it was for the wedding. But now …'

'You're not so sure,' Linnayen concluded. 'As for my daughter, how was she when you left her, Lieutenant Finn?'

He squirmed in his seat. 'Honestly? I can't really say. In the last twenty-four hours that I was there, I wasn't allowed to see her and she wasn't answering my calls. I went to Mira, Denkaun's so-called mother, to complain.' He clenched his teeth. 'That woman's toxic, I swear.'

'This is true!' Wika exclaimed, finding courage to contribute to the discussion. 'Lady Mira is wicked! Evil. She keeps Kalik from me.'

'It's more than that,' Serekunda added. 'Wika here told us that she is the source of a prophecy. That the so-called "son of the twins" shall be their saviour. Their A'bat.'

Jax scoffed. 'Their warrior of hope? I don't think so!'

'He *is* the A'bat, lord! He is the son of the twins.' Wika could not contain herself.

Linnayen shuddered. The mention of twins brought back unhappy thoughts of Navarr and his sister. Twenty-six years earlier, in the hunt for the traitorous Balisel Navarr, they had uncovered anecdotal evidence of an unhealthy relationship between the pair. Remembering the distasteful aspects of Durroc Navarr's character, she had not been surprised at that information. And here again, all these years later, a similar story of a repugnant liaison had unfolded.

Her eyes blazed under her dark brows. 'And this is the man my daughter professes to love? May the heavens help us.' She sighed and looked to Jax for support.

'I'm sorry I left her there,' Finn began his apology, feeling the need to explain. 'Once I couldn't get any communications out, I felt there was no other choice. That last conversation with Mira ... She called her "our princess". Like they'd taken possession of her.'

Jax frowned. 'So you think she's a prisoner?'

Finn's eyes were dark. 'Yes ... But I don't think she's aware of it.'

There was silence for a few moments before Linnayen spoke. 'This man, Denkaun – he must be made aware that this wedding demands official sanction. A princess of the Union must be married before the representatives of the five planets, otherwise the union is invalid. Under this proviso, the ceremony must take place here, in Zaz-Rakuum, the only place where GU personnel from all planets are available. He must be ordered to bring her here.'

Jax concurred. 'This will confirm her status too – prisoner or free agent.'

'And if he says no?' asked Finn.

'Then we need to find a way to get her out of there,' Jax concluded.

Linnayen poured some water into a glass and sipped at it while gathering her thoughts. As the voices around her exchanged views and options, she fought hard to concentrate. What if this Denkaun could not be persuaded to bring Seti to Zaz? How could they get her out of Beshwuk? The mountain was a fortress, a maze of tunnels and caverns. Even if they could find her quarters, how could they be sure she was still there? Then there was the problem of getting to the mountain settlement. If they went openly in an aerporter, Denkaun would easily have time and opportunity to keep them at bay or for his guards to overwhelm them. That ran the risk of them, too, becoming his hostages. *No, an open approach would not work.* So could they lull him into believing they came in good faith? As happy participants at their daughter's wedding?

Suddenly, she had it. A strategy that could work. But it would take nerve and help from the Guznon woman, help that Linnayen hoped she would be willing to give.

The invitation to take a midday meal with Lady Mira was unexpected. Vit was not unaware of the shaman's unwavering loyalty to her adopted son. Indeed, he admired her commitment. If only he could believe it was well-placed. Denkaun presented a charismatic figure and it appeared that he had roused the tribes to a unity that had not been seen in many centuries, if ever. But still, he was not of Autabron. He was an off-worlder and his heritage was almost completely unknown. Apart from the mother, the Ko-Makum who had been sacrificed – for no one ever willingly sat in the chair – they knew nothing of him. Mira said he was the son of the twins. If so, who was the man's father? Mira must know. But why did she not tell them? Why keep it a secret?

On reflection, this was the prime reason for Vit to accept the shaman's invitation. Perhaps she would take him into her confidence and give him the proof he needed to be sure of Denkaun and their cause. And such a cause! They had waited for so long to take back their planet and its riches. How had it happened that the ganaks from Altan and Hutho and, latterly, Earth had been allowed to rape their world? If Denkaun had by his mere presence managed to bring the tribes together then maybe his heritage was not so important. Maybe Vit of the Graan could submit to him and become a loyal follower.

'Come, Lord Vit! I welcome you. You are my honoured guest.' As she spoke, the old woman came towards him holding out her wrinkled hands, ready to take his own.

He glanced at the fine furnishings of the private sanctum. The rock walls were draped with heavy gilt brocade between columns of rose marble. In the centre of the room was a polished table of bronzed wood from the ksarpi tree – a priceless item to have had brought to Beshwuk – with matching chairs whose backrests had been hand-carved with scenes of flowing rivers. The old woman lived well. Even the food on the table – so much of it! – looked exotic and delicious.

'My great thanks, Lady Mira. The honour is surely mine,' he replied as he was shown to a seat at the table by an attendant.

'It warms my heart that you were able to find time to visit me,' Mira opened. 'In these wondrous days, all our leaders are so busy preparing their men for the fight ahead.'

'My people have been ready for weeks, lady.' What was she implying? The Graan got the call along with all the other tribes. The destruction of Euta Sakek three months earlier had been swiftly followed by messages to all the tribes to have their weapons ready. He hadn't known then who the A'bat was. If he had, he might not have heeded such a call to arms.

'Indeed. And for this the A'bat is grateful. You have put your trust in him, despite your misgivings.'

'I speak as I see. Your son is not of our homeworld. How can I be sure he is, as you say, our warrior, the son of the twins?'

Mira's laugh was a cackle. 'Ah, Vit! I've not seen you for many years. But you have not changed. Always questioning, eh?'

She sat at his left and continued to smile as two attendants moved forward to pour wine for them. Mira lifted her cup and held it towards Vit in a gesture of comradeship.

'Long life to you, my old friend!'

'And years of health to you.'

They drank and, as soon as the cups were returned to the table, the attendants refilled them. Instantly, Mira dismissed the men who silently left the chamber.

'Lady Mira. My question? Your answer?' Vit was not going to be diverted by this old woman. He knew of her tricks. He'd heard the rumours about the sudden death of her husband.

'Of course, Vit. And as I tell you the tale, please partake of this delicious roulade.' She handed him a small plate on which sat a roll of creamed bika cheese covered in ground yok-nuts and herbs. 'There are some wafers too. Oh, and don't forget the wine. It comes from Earth, would you believe.'

Vit helped himself to a glass of the dark red liquid as Mira began her story.

'You can be sure he is the A'bat because his nativity fulfils the prophecy. Let me explain. Some twenty-six years ago, Lyr and I came across an Altani woman in Zaz. She was a fugitive, looking for a place to hide. But what was she running from? Lyr was ready to leave her in the dirt of the street, but I saw her belly. You know me, Vit – how could I leave the poor child in such a state?'

He knew her all right. Knew that she was arrogant and merciless. He covered his scoff with a clearing of his throat.

Mira smiled and continued. 'There was something about her. Her hair was as fair as any Autabroni's and her eyes were the clearest, palest blue I had ever seen. Then I recalled that the eyes of the great Ko-Makum of Rundak, who gave her life on the Day of Grunkaar three centuries ago, were also the colour of water. Surely this woman, this off-worlder, was the reincarnation of our heroic ancestor – and here she was, with child!' Mira sipped a little water. 'Lyr and I brought her home with us here to Beshwuk. I have to say that she was not the easiest of guests. Unlike her namesake, she lacked humility and there was not a skerrick of humanity in her! But as her belly grew, we learned to endure her and discovered her secrets. She was wealthy, for one. She had stolen much money from her employers ... GKD, no less! But she was wanted by the Union's police for her part in the kidnapping of the Ki of Altan. You remember that, Vit? Vit?'

Her dining companion's head had dropped and Mira tapped his hand to regain his attention. He pulled himself upright with a start.

'My apologies. Please go on.'

'The kidnapping of the young Ki, Linnayen Genara? You remember? Yes, well, it was this ganak woman's brother, Durroc Navarr, and she who orchestrated it. The brother had been the Ki's paramour but she forsook him for her new husband, Kevor Jax. Navarr, in his anger, decided to have the Ki secretly kidnapped and then heroically rescue her from an old castle, assuming that she would then love him again and he would rule the Galactic Union at her side. Ridiculous! And I told the little witch that. She became angry, then tearful. I confess I had not expected such emotion from her. I believe she truly loved her twin. Vit ... Lord Vit?'

Once again, the man's head was drooping. The Earthan wine was strong, but surely her tale was not soporific enough to send him to sleep. She must hurry to the climax of her story. She tapped his hand once more and he regained his position.

'Take some water, Lord Vit. It will refresh you.'

He sipped from the cup and gestured lazily for her to recommence the tale.

'Alas, her brother was killed in the so-called rescue. But to continue – for here is the essence of the tale – she knew that her brother had raped the kidnapped Ki in her cell. Yes! Can you imagine? Did she fight back though? Of course not, for she had been drugged, just as you have been, Lord Vit. Indeed, I doubt she even knew what was happening to her or that he had impregnated her. Navarr's powerful seed blossomed into the beautiful young princess we see today. Now isn't that a tale, Lord Vit? Have you understood the import of this? My son, Kalik, and the Princess Seityan are brother and sister. Their children will continue the bloodline of the twins. Now tell me he is not the A'bat!'

Mira finished her story with a flourish and drained her cup of water. She took back the plate with the roulade and helped herself to a slice, enjoying the melting cheese on her tongue. Next to her, Vit had slumped forward onto the table, his wineglass spilled and a piece of wafer fallen from his lifeless hand. The old woman licked the remnants of the food from her fingers and glanced down at the back of Vit's head.

'Well, of course, you can't, can you? So you will never again gainsay the A'bat, Lord Vit. Your people will mourn your terrible loss. Who knew your heart was so weak? Kalik and I will be heartbroken. So sad.'

She stood and threw back her chair from the table before letting out a howl of anguish. As the servants rushed back in, they saw the shaman inconsolable in her grief, holding her head in her hands, wailing at the sudden and terrible collapse of her old friend.

Jax held his wife's face in his hands and kissed her mouth.

'Be careful, my love. Don't take any chances,' he cautioned. His midnight blue eyes drank in her beautiful face. If all went well, he would be seeing her again within the next forty-eight hours, if not sooner. But they both knew that the times were unpredictable at best.

'Don't worry. Either way, one of us will return with our daughter,' she assured him.

Behind them, Decker Finn heaved his backpack on and strapped a curved steel dirk into the waistband of his tunic, as won by all tribesmen, covering the whole with a russet cloak. Once the hood was up, and given his height, he would pass as an Autabroni, provided no one saw too much of his face.

Wika had helped them both with their costumes. Linnayen would travel as a tamun, a holy woman. Her white kirtle with its flame-red cummerbund under a woven dark brown surcoat and hood would confirm her rank to any prying eyes. Her skin and hair colouring were unusual, yes, but Wika was confident that none would dare question a tamun on her way to officiate at the wedding of the A'bat.

Their q'ist would leave within an hour and get them to Beshwuk by the evening. From there, Wika would hide them until she could gain access to Setiyan's quarters. She was sure her mother or sisters would know who had been tasked with the care of the princess. Wika could then instruct this person to let the princess receive the holy woman for purification, the traditional ceremony every off-worlder must undergo before marriage to a child of Autabron.

Meanwhile, Jax, Pieter Serekunda and Rutak Birkaan would travel in the dark before dawn by aerporter to Beshwuk, taking a troop of armed guards with them. Their job was to invite Kalik Denkaun and the princess to accompany them back to Zaz-Rakuum for the ceremony which, even now, was being arranged by Kalisa Caspiran and the other Galactic Union ambassadors. If Denkaun tried to delay, or insist the wedding take place in Beshwuk, this would surely indicate his dark intentions. On the other hand, his compliance might actually prove that the man was genuine about his love for Setiyan.

One of the two plans to get to Setiyan must work, and Linnayen was convinced that once she spoke to her daughter she could make her see sense. If this man really was the love of her life then there was no reason they could not be married and live happily on Altan – after a short engagement.

With their disguises in place and their farewells made, Linnayen, Finn and Wika set off to the veyor that would descend to the q'ist transit level. Dressed as they were, they turned few heads as they passed. Overheard snatches of conversation told them that the taking of the two mines by PLA forces was the main topic of interest, followed by questions about how the city's council would respond to new leadership.

Linnayen was impressed by the q'ist. She had heard of the underground transit system and expected something less sophisticated, but it was comfortable and the journey smooth as the bullet-shaped carriages sped through the opaque tubes. They had a long journey ahead of them and she wanted to find out more about the settlement and Wika's story, so after some light conversation Linnayen judged it time to dig a little deeper.

'Tell me about your family, Wika. You must miss them.'

Her dark eyes widened at the Ki's interest. She cleared her throat and began hesitantly. 'I live – lived with my father, mother and two older sisters. They are fine seamstresses and my father is renowned for his metalwork. He is a famed artisan. He made the hilt of the dirk my husband carries, you know.'

'Is that how you met? You and Kalik? Through your father?'

Wika's face showed only the slightest discomfort at the question. 'My father took me to Kalik a year ago. He liked me very well.' Wika's head dropped shyly. 'He said I was beautiful.'

Linnayen smiled. 'He's right. You are.'

This was the first time she'd seen the young woman relax. Here was a topic she wanted to talk about – her love for her husband. They certainly had that much in common.

'He chose me nearly every night, you know. No other woman has been so favoured.'

Linnayen glanced across at Finn to see if he had heard Wika's words. He raised an eyebrow.

'He had other partners before you?' Linnayen probed.

'He is the A'bat, lady. He has other women, of course.'

As Linnayen's attempted to rein in her shock, Finn spoke gently.

'This is common practice, my lady. Many men of rank here have more than one wife,' he explained.

'Of course … I knew that. I just didn't think …'

'That it would apply to the princess?' Finn finished. Nor did he, and nor did he want it to – now or ever.

'But I am his first wife!' Wika exclaimed.

Finn frowned. 'So when did you marry the A'bat? How long ago?'

Wika's eyes darkened. 'You don't believe me! I tell you, I am more his wife than the ganak –' Realising the offence in her words, she slapped a hand over her mouth. 'Oh! My apologies, lady. It's true, I did not have a ceremony, but I pledged myself to him and he said he was betrothed to me in return. In our culture, this is marriage. We are heart-sworn.'

The silence was palpable. It was a full minute before Linnayen felt she could speak and Finn's head dropped to his chest.

'So,' she began, struggling to collect her thoughts, 'your ... husband is legally free to marry.'

The tears welled in Linnayen's eyes and she placed a hand over her mouth. She was already worried about her daughter's plight but now it was hard to contain her panic.

Finn, too, realised the new situation. He had hoped Wika's claim would be enough to stymie Denkaun's plans when the princess was made aware. But this was now a phantom obstacle, a hurdle that had dissolved into nothing. They were back where they had started.

Wika looked across to her companions, who were suddenly silent. 'Lady? Lord Finn?'

Linnayen just shook her head and turned away. The words would not come. Finn met the Autabroni woman's questioning eyes with a shrug and a half-hearted smile. With no legal block to this appalling marriage, it might be even harder to persuade Setiyan to give up her paramour. He wondered if the pain in Linnayen Genara's heart matched his own. He felt sure it must.

Chapter Eighteen

Jax had had a fitful sleep. Thoughts of Setiyan and his beloved Linnayen and the danger in which they found themselves prodded at him mercilessly. He kept torturing himself with recriminations. What if he had not sent Setiyan to Autabron? What if he had chosen Calin instead? *She* would never have fallen for this awful man – not Calin. No, it had to be Seti, his hot-headed wild child who had captured his heart from the minute she was born. True, he had not yet met this Kalik Denkaun, but Serekunda had given a poor report on him. He warned that Denkaun saw himself as some kind of messiah, a saviour of his people, and that kind of thinking was always dangerous. Then there was the prospect that Seti would want to live on Autabron and he knew that he would not be able to bear that. No. When he had said he would drag her out of this God-awful place, he meant it. Whatever it took.

With two hours to go before dawn, Birkaan came to wake him for the flight to the Beshwuk settlement but found Jax already dressed.

'Good morning, lord. Ready to go?'

'I am. And Pieter?'

'We'll collect him on the way to the dock,' Birkaan confirmed. 'Captain Zenak and our guards have already embarked.'

With Serekunda in tow, Jax briefed them on the message he had received last night from Linnayen and Finn. They had arrived in Beshwuk and Wika had taken them to her father's workshop where they would be safe until the morning. He also informed them of Wika's news, that she was not officially married to Denkaun. Birkaan explained that in Guznon culture, though, to be heart-sworn was as good as married. So the woman had not been lying and, given her physical condition, they should be understanding. Jax agreed. But the thought that his daughter could be one of many wives was disturbing and distasteful.

'I just don't see how she would allow that,' he bemoaned. 'I know my daughter. She's a proud woman. I can't see her taking second place to anyone.'

Serekunda sighed. 'Maybe she's unaware – of Wika Dokau and the marriage customs of the Guznon.'

'Or maybe she thinks they don't apply to her?' Birkaan posited.

They settled into their seats for the night journey to Beshwuk and soon the aerporter was flying quietly through the dark sky. Despite all his concerns, he managed to get an hour of sleep before the pilot announced that they would be landing shortly. From the viewport, Jax could see the grey silhouette of the mountains creeping nearer. The first rays of a rising Lau picked out the highest peaks, which towered like golden spires above the dark plains below. This was the rock fortress that held his daughter, and somewhere within its maze of caverns and tunnels his beloved firstborn would be waking and hopefully happy to greet the father she had not seen in over two weeks.

He was to be disappointed though. When they stepped onto the ramp at the Beshwuk dock, followed by the Union security team of Captain Zenak and some ten armed guards, only the shaman, Mira, with a group of officials, was present.

'Greetings, great lord. You are welcome in our hearts. The A'bat sends his warmest wishes to you and your party and bids you come join him to break your fast.' She bowed and clasped her hands together in the traditional greeting. It was all very reverential but, given Jax's rank as the Ki-consort, the sending of a mere shaman and not even one city elder verged on insult. Serekunda and Birkaan, standing a little behind Jax, looked at each other with raised eyebrows.

'Thank you, lady. But first I wish to see my daughter.' Jax's tone, whilst pleasant, was firm.

The old woman nodded. 'Of course. I understand. A father's love …'

'Indeed,' he shot back icily. 'So take me to her now … please.'

Mira's eyes darkened and a muscle twitched at the corner of her mouth. 'I believe she will be at breakfast.'

'Then proceed.' He flicked a hand at the shaman, whose body stiffened as she turned.

Serekunda and Birkaan had not often seen Jax use his status. This morning, though, and with so much at stake, all affability was shed.

They followed behind Mira down a winding tunnel to a painted hall whose shielded viewport looked out over the slowly lightening Beshwuk Plain. The hall contained a large circular table of polished slate around which ornate chairs upholstered in crimson velvet were placed. Kalik Denkaun was seated at the largest of the chairs. Setiyan was nowhere to be seen.

Jax fixed his eyes on the fair-haired man, who stood a little too slowly on Jax's approach. The man's features were well-defined and symmetrical, his chest broad and his height matched any Autabroni. He supposed that women might find him attractive. But to be so soon in love? None of Seti's past crushes and affairs had blossomed so quickly. He could only hope that her descent from this pinnacle of passion would be as fast as her ascent.

'My lord, Kevor Jax. Welcome to my home.' Denkaun's smooth tones filled the space between them.

'Thank you, Lord Denkaun. But where is my daughter?'

The blond man smiled and shrugged. 'Ah! My lovely princess. She's not an early riser.'

'Agreed. I've woken my daughter up many times. So take me to her – as I have already requested of your shaman.'

Denkaun's eyes flicked to Mira and in them Jax saw what he needed to know. If Seti knew her father was arriving – no matter the hour of day or night – she would have been there. There was a conspiracy here and he was glad they had brought their own troops.

'Natar, please send a messenger to rouse my Setiyan,' Denkaun commanded.

Jax jumped in again. 'No need. Just take me there.' He couldn't put his finger on it but there was something about the man's voice which made him even more uneasy than he already was.

Mira did not move. She seemed fixed to the spot, waiting for a signal as to which of these men would take the lead. Denkaun took some seconds before gesturing his acquiescence to Mira with a wave of his hand.

'Of course. Breakfast can wait. Natar, would you lead the way?'

She beckoned for Jax and his people to follow them. Jax asked Serekunda and Birkaan to remain with his guards for now while he continued with the captain.

245

Once out of the hall, they passed through another tunnel and descended a couple of levels in a vatortube. Two guards in leather armour stood at the entrance to a room and Denkaun ordered them to open the door as they approached.

Inside the darkened chamber, Jax could make out a shape under rumpled covers on the huge bed. Jax moved towards it and bent to pick up a bedsheet that had fallen to the floor. He sat on the edge of the bed and beckoned a glow-globe to hover close by. Seti's golden hair had tumbled over her face and her exhaled breath lifted a strand or two. She was, as ever, his beautiful child. He swept the hair away from her face and shook her shoulder gently.

'Come, sweetheart. Time to wake up. Come now.'

He bent over her and kissed her forehead. She stirred and gave a short moan but her eyes remained closed. He tried again to rouse her. 'Come, Seti. Wake up.'

'My princess sleeps like a newborn babe.'

Jax stiffened at the syrupy voice. She was not 'his' princess. Not yet and, with luck, she never would be. Jax shook her again, more vigorously this time, and finally she opened her eyes and took a deep breath before yawning.

'Mmm ... Morning, Pa.' Her words were slurred, still laden with sleep.

'Morning, plinka,' he replied.

She smiled, blinking, then came fully awake. 'Pa! Oh, Pa!'

'I thought you'd be awake to welcome me.' He bent and kissed her cheek. 'Instead I find you still in bed.'

'I didn't know,' she replied innocently, gazing into the eyes she knew so well.

'Well, here I am. Ready for breakfast.'

'I'm not hungry,' she sighed. 'Still tired.' Once more she yawned and her eyelids began to descend over her bleary eyes.

'Seti. Come on. Stay awake!' Jax was beginning to worry. He had seen her many times in the morning after a party or event, but this seemed different. This lethargy was close to unconsciousness.

'Mmm ... Need sleep.' Her eyelids fell like steel shutters.

'Seti! Wake up.' There was no doubting her lassitude. As she sank back into the pillows, Jax looked over his shoulder to Denkaun.

'This is not normal for my daughter. What's been happening here?'

Denkaun shook his head. 'I assure you, lord, this is how she is every morning. It is only just past first dawn, after all.'

Jax frowned. 'And why was she not told I was coming here? You've known for days that the Ki and I were on our way to Autabron.'

Mira stepped forward. 'Great lord, our lady princess was informed but she just forgot that you would be here *this* morning. That is all.'

He could barely contain his anger. These two were obviously hiding something but were slick enough to cover it. He gazed down at Seti, who had already drifted back into sleep. 'I'm telling you, this is not normal behaviour for my daughter, who, by the way, is not *your* princess.'

He stood up. Though not quite as tall as Denkaun, his maturity lent him a greater authority. He took Denkaun's arm and pulled him to one side of the room, away from the interfering shaman. 'A'bat – is that how you are addressed?' He received no response so continued. 'I will be taking my daughter back to Zaz-Rakuum this evening. I invite you to join us where we can continue the preparations for your wedding. My wife, your Ki, has already begun to gather the Union representatives to bear witness, which, as you must know, is mandatory for a marriage of such high status.'

'Yes, but I was hoping for a simpler ceremony. We are uncomplicated people here.'

'But this was communicated to you when you were informed of our visit.'

'It was,' Denkaun conceded, 'however, given the turmoil in the city and with all the tribal leaders gathered here already, we felt that a change of location was warranted. Perhaps the Union personnel can be brought to Beshwuk?'

There it was again. Something in the man's voice and the way he phrased his words. Denkaun could make himself sound sensitive and yet domineering at the same time. It reminded him of something – or someone. Jax was having none of it.

'No. The ceremony will take place in Zaz-Rakuum as befits a princess of Altan.' He walked away from Denkaun and returned to Seti's bedside.

Mira spoke. 'Great lord, please come to break your fast while we wait for our ... for the princess to wake.'

His eyes were fixed on Seti's sleeping form, her breathing deep and regular. He thought for a moment. It was time to soften his demeanour. He did not want to alert the old woman or Denkaun to his plan. Linnayen and Finn would need time to get to Seti and it was now his job to provide it.

'Very well. But bring her to me the minute she's up.' He stood and turned to Denkaun. 'In the meantime, I'll get to know my future son-in-law. Lead the way.'

Dokau's workshop had proved to be a warm space in which to spend the night. But neither of them was used to sleeping on a hard floor. So it was no surprise for Finn to find Linnayen already awake by first dawn and rubbing her stiff limbs as the message came through from Jax that he had seen Seti.

Linnayen Genara had surprised him. All he knew of these people was that they led a shielded, pampered life in royal palaces, yet here she faced discomfort and danger with no thought for her own safety. He had always believed that leadership meant having both the ability and willingness to do whatever you asked of those under your command, and he saw those qualities in both this woman and her husband. It gave him confidence that one of them would retrieve the princess, though he hoped it would be his and Linnayen's efforts that would prove successful, if only to gain a kind of redemption. It still pained him that he had abandoned her, even though he had little choice.

Suddenly, the panel door slid open and Wika Dokau closed it smartly behind her after checking over her shoulder. She handed them a small piece of warm kiska each, fresh from her mother's oven, she explained, and as they munched the tasty bread, she told them her news.

'Thankfully, my father has been sent to Hiresh in the Gaksi lands to deliver weapons,' she began, her eyes wide with relief.

Finn frowned. 'What sort of weapons?'

The woman shrugged. 'I presume blades he has forged here.'

'And what of your mother?' Linnayen asked.

'She and my sisters are making the gowns for the princess and her retinue for the wedding ceremony ... pah!' Wika's anger surfaced.

Linnayen soothed her. 'I'm sure they would have little choice in the matter. But what else did you find out?'

Wika took a deep breath and continued. 'The princess is still in the same rooms as before. She is being attended by a young woman of the Akika family, Jinau. I know her.'

'She'll help us?' This was Finn.

'If her love for the princess is greater than her fear of Lady Mira, then yes.'

Linnayen swallowed the last of the bread and took a long draught from her water flask. 'Then let's get going. My husband is keeping Denkaun occupied at breakfast, but who knows for how long.'

In less than a minute they were on their way. Few people were about at this early hour so they made rapid progress, and, with Linnayen dressed as a holy tamun and Finn in his hooded cloak as her guard, those who were around quickly stepped aside, bowing their heads. They hurried through the tunnels, vatortubes and passageways, ever upward towards Seti's rooms on the higher levels. Finally they reached the corridor leading to Seti's chamber and Linnayen took the lead. But, once level with the two armed guards, Wika steadied her breathing and stepped up.

'Good morrow, sirs. My lady, the holy Ra-Makum, is here to perform the blessing of purification on our beloved Aun'bat. Permit entry.' Wika put her hands together in the universal sign of supplication and bowed her head.

The guards seemed unimpressed by Wika's calm dignity. One looked to the other, his face a grim mask.

'We have not been advised of the Ra-Makum's visit, sister. We cannot –'

'Do you dare question my authority?' Linnayen's voice pierced the air, quiet but imperial. 'I come by order of the A'bat himself. Stand aside!'

At a hurried nod to each other, reluctantly the guards parted, and the door slid open on Linnayen's approach.

They moved briskly into the room. A young woman laying out clothes on the back of a sofa jumped back, startled at the intrusion.

'Do not be alarmed, cousin,' Wika said, walking to her with palms open to show they meant no harm. 'I bring the holy tamun to our princess.'

Jinau's brows met in confusion as she looked from Wika to the holy woman and then to the large man behind them.

'Child, I am here by command of the A'bat. The princess must be purified.' Linnayen spoke softly. 'Will you take me to her?'

'Holy lady, I was not told.'

'No, I imagine not.' Linnayen waved away the Jinau's concerns and smiled. 'The princess?'

Jinau swallowed nervously and bit her lower lip. 'Follow me, lady,' she said and led Linnayen and Wika to the bedroom while Finn stayed alert by the door.

Seti, still in her nightgown, sat on the edge of her bed staring into space. She turned her head slowly only when she became aware of the people coming closer towards her. Blinking, a slow smile began to take shape on her lips.

'Mother? Is that you?'

Even her speech was paced in slow motion and Linnayen flew to kneel in front of her. 'Seti, my sweet. How are you?'

She clasped her daughter's hands and covered them in kisses.

'I am well, Ma. I am well.'

The smile was fixed on her face; it was the look of a beatific statue. Linnayen could see no light in her eyes. She looked like a stunned witaq, the little mountain deer, unknowingly caught in the hunter's sights. Linnayen had not expected this. Had she been mesmerised? Or drugged? Something was terribly wrong here and the need to save her daughter became urgent.

'Come, Seti, my little one. Come with me.'

As she stood, she raised an unresisting Seti up and indicated to Wika to fetch something to cover her. Wika scanned the room for a cloak and saw one hanging in an alcove nearby. She went to retrieve it but Jinau stayed her arm.

'What are you doing, sister?'

Wika tried to smile reassuringly. 'The princess must be purified in the holy waters of Kadis Sakek, Jinau. The holy tamun is here to guide her and perform the ceremony.'

Jinau's brow furrowed. 'But ... she called her mother ...'

Wika laid the cloak around Seti's shoulders. 'Of course. *Holy* mother, who has come to take her for purification.'

'Child, we cannot delay,' Linnayen said gravely. 'This must be done before Lau and Uzno have completed three dances around our homeworld before the wedding can take place.'

Jinau's mouth opened as if to object. But instead, she nodded shortly. 'Of course, holy mother. I have been ordered not to leave her side, however. I must come with you.' She gathered a cloak for herself.

Seti had offered no resistance and, as the women neared Finn, he almost gasped at the sight of her. This was not the buoyant princess he had last seen only days ago. Her cheeks were sallow, her hair had lost all sheen and her eyes were glassy, as though she was drunk. When they reached Finn, the princess looked straight through him. There was no doubt that Setiyan was in trouble.

As they passed through the doorway, the guards instantly stiffened and one stepped forward to detain them. Linnayen held up a hand and lifted her chin, her clear green eyes drilling into theirs. She spoke in a deep voice. 'Brothers, I am taking the princess to the waters of Kadis Sakek. We shall return within the hour.'

'But, holy mother, our orders –'

The look of fire that Linnayen fixed on the outspoken guard stopped him and the second guard nudged his partner firmly.

'My apologies, holy mother,' the first guard said. 'I will escort you.'

Linnayen nodded her assent. This was not the time to argue and she had no doubt that between her and Finn, the man could be easily incapacitated later.

'Very well,' she acknowledged before turning to Wika. 'My servant will lead us.'

Wika turned, followed by Linnayen. Finn and Jinau were next with the amenable Setiyan between them and the guard followed. Finn noticed Seti's occasional missteps and motioned for Jinau to hold her arm. The settlement was stirring, with people outside workshops busy packing palletrons with clothing, foodstuffs and other accoutrements, supplies presumably for the rebel forces fighting in the mine sites across the planet. The passing of a small group with an armed guard at the rear hardly warranted their notice, and within fifteen minutes or so they had reached the lowest levels of the mountain's core. With only a few more steps and one more turn of the passageway they arrived at the quiet corner of the great underground lake of Kadis Sakek. They stopped and took a few moments to survey the placid waters stretching away before them. A few glow-globes danced over the surface, lighting the scene.

The guard moved in front of them and Linnayen heard him exhale a long breath in wonder at the scene. She considered that it was the last he would take while conscious as she plunged a fine needle into his neck. The drug would knock him out for a couple of hours and, hopefully, by the time he awoke they would be far away.

Falvii Min had not expected that reconnecting with his delightful and beautiful cousin Calin would lead to such fine adventure. After escorting her to Altan, he had fully expected to be sent back to Hutho to take up his teaching post at the academy. However, Calin's grandmother, the imperious Lady Li-el Dacas, the dowager Ki-consort, had insisted that he seek a sabbatical from his duties. She had a special mission for him, she said, a mission that only he, a Dasnirian, could be trusted to undertake. The fact that he got to spend more time with Calin was a lure he could not refuse.

He had to admit that the woman had got under his skin like no other. He only had to look at her and his breath came a little faster and he could swear his heart skipped a beat. She so often had a studious look; whatever she was taken with was all-important and the outside world hardly existed. When she pushed untidy strands of auburn hair behind her ears he couldn't help but imagine his hands loosening those curls and kissing those ears. But then, when she finally noticed her surroundings and the people around her, her face softened. Her emerald-green eyes glowed and the corners of her mouth relaxed in a contented smile.

He had watched her like this a hundred times on their flight to Autabron, as she pored over the maps of the underground warrens of the planet, nodding to herself and making notes. Which was just as well, because he would need her navigation skills.

Their landing site on Autabron had been determined by the landscape. Docking at Zaz, or anywhere else, for that matter, while the planet was in such turmoil, was a non-starter. Besides, the need for secrecy was paramount. Jax and Linnayen had been specific. He and Calin were to set out from Altan after the royal delegation with the troops and specialised gear they would need for the support mission, though Jax had expressed the hope that it would not come to that.

Only Calin knew where they would be going. She ran through the mission with him as soon as they left Altan orbit a few hours behind her parents, including the equipment. He was more than familiar with submersibles. When you came from a planet that was ninety percent water, there was little you did not know about travelling on it or under it.

The plan seemed sound but Falvii could see that Calin was worried. The more they knew about Seti's situation on Autabron, the more cause they had for concern. Linnayen had connected with her as they were landing to say they had reached Beshwuk and taken Setiyan to one of the dozen or so ingresses of the vast underground waterway of Kadis Sakek. Once she and Falvii were underway in the submersible, her mother would activate a tracking beacon to lead them to her location. Similarly, the spaceracer would emit a signal to help them find their way back – hopefully with Setiyan in tow.

One thing that worried Calin, she had confessed, was Seti's state of mind. Both she and Linnayen had tried to connect with her using their mentante abilities once they had arrived on Autabron, but she could not be reached. There was, as Calin put it, some kind of fog around her mind that she could not penetrate, and her mother had said that Seti had hardly spoken a word, other than to say how happy she was and how lovely that her mother had come for the wedding. Without doubt, it sounded to Falvii that Seti was not herself, and the sooner they got her home the better.

The breakfast that had been prepared for Jax and his party was indeed a feast, but it was hard to put his daughter's lethargy out of his mind, despite Denkaun and Mira's sudden show of deference. Before them were freshly baked kiska rolls, spiced tagirp roe, smoked kilimaj rashers and an array of fruits that Jax had not expected to find so far from the city.

'Lord Kevor Jax, we hope you find these humble offerings to your taste,' Mira intoned as she led them to their seats around the huge slate table where some five or six Guznon elder men and women were already seated.

'Thank you. I'm sure we will enjoy this feast.' The discomfort he felt after seeing Seti was still with him. He was sure she had been either drugged or hypnotised, although he didn't imagine the latter would be easy. Seti's mentante abilities, though not as well-developed as her mother's or sister's, were still there, and she would surely be alert to any form of mind control.

He looked across to the shielded viewport, now significantly brighter than when they had been in this hall thirty minutes earlier. The second sun, Uzno, had risen above the horizon and the temperature outside would now be hot enough to drain a human body of all its moisture in under four hours. Even here, in the hall, the temperature had risen by a couple of degrees, and the only one of his party who looked comfortable with this was Rutak Birkaan. He smiled happily as he engaged Denkaun and another of the Guznon elders in conversation.

'I've been a representative on the Union Council for nearly three years now,' Birkaan was telling them, 'and this is the first chance I've had to get home. I am, of course, very happy, though the times are troubling.'

'You are on Altan most of the time then?' This was Denkaun.

'Yes. Council gatherings occur monthly. It allows little time to come home.'

'And you have family here?' the elder asked.

'I do. My mother, two sisters, four nieces and a nephew.' Birkaan reeled off the tally proudly.

'Only one male child in a swarm of women!' the elder sneered. 'I hope your own seed proves more fruitful.'

Birkaan looked askance at the elder.

Denkaun spoke. 'Tuqar is perhaps overly proud of his own three sons and wishes the same happiness for you, friend Birkaan.'

Jax, though on the edge of the group, had heard enough of the conversation to contribute. 'Trust me, Elder Tuqar, daughters are a blessing too – most of the time.'

Denkaun met Jax's steel gaze. 'Your daughter is indeed a blessing to me,' he affirmed and then placed his right hand on his chest. 'For she has stolen my heart.'

He smiles like a snake, thought Jax. It was time to up the stakes. 'Has she? I rather think *you* are the thief, don't you?'

Denkaun cleared his throat. 'Her love for me is given freely, my lord. I needed to take nothing.'

'I fear love has robbed her of her good sense, though,' Jax persisted. 'I'll be frank, Denkaun. I would rather she take more time to get to know you. Why not a period of engagement? Maybe back on your homeworld of Altan?'

The younger man shifted in his seat and forced a smile. 'If only that could be so. As the A'bat of my people, I cannot leave.'

'But they're not your people. You're Altani, aren't you?'

'This is the place of my birth.' Denkaun's face was a stone wall. 'This is my home.'

'As is Altan for my daughter,' Jax countered. 'I know what it's like. I left my home on Earth for a life with Linnayen and I'd do it again in a heartbeat. But marriage is about compromise as well as love. Setiyan would be sacrificing everything she knows and loves for a life with you. Would you do the same for her?'

Denkaun's eyes narrowed almost to slits. 'Her place is with me, wherever that may be. I am sure we will visit all the other planets in time, after our child is born.'

Jax's breath stopped. He had to turn his gaze away from Denkaun for a moment to hide his confusion and building anger. 'Are you telling me that my daughter is pregnant?'

Denkaun nodded. 'I believe the gods have smiled on our union already. All the more reason to marry soon, my lord. I trust you understand.'

It felt like a chess match and Jax's next move – the only one he could think of right now – was to counter with a smile. 'I do indeed. And what happy news.' Jax glanced up at Serekunda and Birkaan and then checked the time. To be on the safe side, he would drag out this breakfast a while longer.

He turned to Denkaun with a bright smile. 'Then I shall be a grandfather! Wonderful!'

For nearly an hour Finn had kept guard by the cavern's narrow entrance. Linnayen, Seti and Jinau sat on the stone floor while Wika kept watch across the motionless dark water. The body of the guard lay still.

The drug would hold until Calin and Falvii arrived but there was more if needed.

'Ma, I can't wait for you to meet Kalik. You will love him.' Seti smiled and patted her mother's hand. She seemed unaware that they were sitting in the dirt in the bowels of a mountain with no apparent purpose.

'Perhaps I will. You have known him such a short time, though,' Linnayen replied.

'I feel as though I have known him forever.' Seti sighed and hugged herself, closing her eyes as she did so. On hearing these words, Wika spat on the dirt floor.

Linnayen turned to Jinau. All this time the young woman had sat silently, her eyes wide and a look of concern on her face. She had long since realised that this grand lady was no holy tamun but the princess's actual mother.

'I'm sorry to have deceived you, Jinau. I hope you understand. My daughter isn't behaving normally. Not as we know her to. We think there's something wrong with her.'

Jinau lowered her head. The tears began to well in the her eyes. 'I have tried my best to take care of her, great lady. I am so sorry … Please forgive me.'

'Oh! Please don't cry. None of this is your fault.' Linnayen stroked the girl's hair and wiped her tears with the edge of her dress, but still they fell from her dark eyes.

'I did my duty, I swear to you. I only forgot about the water one time. Please don't tell the A'bat.'

Linnayen's eyes flashed up to Finn. 'You're not in trouble, Jinau, and I will not tell the A'bat anything. What's that about the water?'

Jinau sniffed and wiped her eyes with the backs of her hands. 'I gave her a cup of water from the tap, not the flask. But I swear it was only once! All other times I used the flask.' Then her face fell. 'Oh, and some soup from my mother. The princess was unwell. Please, I beg you, don't tell Lady Mira!'

Finn's came over and kneeled by Jinau, lifting her chin up to look at him. 'I don't understand. What was wrong with the water?'

Jinau shook her head and her eyes were puzzled. 'Nothing, lord. But the A'bat ordered me to give her water only from the flask and all her food must come from Lady Mira. I should not have disobeyed. I am so sorry. Please don't tell!'

Finn and Linnayen sighed simultaneously. 'That explains everything,' Linnayen said before turning back to the cowering young woman. 'Jinau. Look at me. You have done the princess a great service. Do you understand? You've helped her.'

Jinau's eyes flicked anxiously from one to the other.

'You might just have saved her life,' Finn concluded with a smile.

At that moment, Wika called out that she could see lights in the water. Linnayen breathed a sigh of relief. They would at least be able to get Setiyan away from this awful place. But what about Jinau? She feared Denkaun and Mira would not treat her kindly.

The slim submersible docked alongside the shallow beach and the opaque roof of the metallic hull slid back to reveal Calin and Falvii. With a sigh of relief, Calin climbed out of her seat and walked through the shallow water towards them. Linnayen led the still smiling Seti to the sub where, on seeing Calin, she flung her arms around her neck.

'Sister! You've come too. How wonderful. I can't wait for you to meet my love.' Her voice was dull and slow and breathy in a way Calin had never known her usually animated older sister to be.

Over Seti's shoulder, Calin looked at her mother. As their minds connected, Calin learned all she needed to know about Seti's condition. She squeezed her sister tighter to her.

Linnayen nodded to Falvii Min, who sat at the controls of the tube-like craft. 'Thank you for doing this, Falvii.'

He gave a broad grin. 'Wouldn't have missed it for the world.'

'I'm guessing my mother signed you up for this?'

He laughed out loud. 'The Lady Li-el is a force to be reckoned with and I can't wait to thank her.'

For what felt like the first time in days, Linnayen grinned. Her sister had been right. Falvii was a man with many fine qualities.

'Take Jinau with you,' Linnayen said, and she gently pushed the young woman towards the craft. There was only enough room for two more and the plan had been for Linnayen and Setiyan to take the seats. 'She will not be safe here now.'

Jinau stopped and looked back. 'But my mother ... I can't ...'

'I'll make sure she's all right.' This was Finn. Then, seeing concern on Calin's face, he reassured her also. 'We'll find our way out. No problem.'

Linnayen nodded and sent a thought to her anxious daughter. *I'll be safe with him. Go. You know what to do.*

With their passengers safety stowed, Falvii closed the roof and veered away back towards one of the underwater shafts. Within a minute, the lights had faded and the surface of the lake was still and dark once more.

Linnayen turned to Finn and Wika. The morning was passing quickly and she was sure that Seti's disappearance would soon be discovered if it hadn't been already. For Jax and his party, high up inside the mountain, she feared that events were about to become more dangerous. She and Finn needed to be ready to help in whatever way they could.

Chapter Nineteen

Denkaun scowled. The Ki-consort had surely dragged out the breakfast conversation long enough. The older man had rambled on about the duties Denkaun would need to be instructed in as a son in the royal household: the committees, the opening ceremonies, the sporting events and the patronages he would have to embrace. It all sounded tedious in the extreme. But there would be no need for all that once he was in control. When he became Ki then he would decide what his duties would be, and if his royal relations did not approve, well, there was a way to resolve that problem.

He threw a sharp glance at his natar. She too was getting anxious and wanted to move the day along. But, once again, the Ki-consort interrupted his thoughts.

'So, Denkaun, you see that no matter the troubles, the ceremony must be performed in Zaz-Rakuum. And there'll have to be a ratification in Genkarah, too, before the marriage is legalised. We've quite a schedule ahead of us.' He quaffed the remains of his drink and sighed happily.

All through the preceding hour, Denkaun had insisted that the wedding ceremony should take place in Beshwuk. He explained his worry of the possibility of violence in Zaz with its marauding rebels. This would endanger his princess. Surely Lord Kevor Jax could see that? He even added that in Setiyan's condition it would be foolish to move her at this time. But the older man would not budge and Denkaun began to think that he might have to accede to the Ki-consort's demands.

'Now then, I should think my daughter will be up and about by now,' he proclaimed, rising to his feet. 'Shall we see?'

Wika set a rapid pace as she led Linnayen and Finn back up through the passageways and staircases to her father's workshop. They had left the unconscious guard by the subterranean lake. But once the sedative wore off – and it would all too soon – he would wake and sound the alarm. She bad Linnayen and Finn to take refuge in the workshop while she went to find out what Denkaun's reaction to the loss of his princess was, if he was aware yet.

'Wika.' Linnayen held her arm as she turned to leave. 'You don't have to go.'

'I will return with news, my lady.' Her eyes glittered in the dim light of the glow-globe.

Linnayen nodded. 'Thank you for your help. But be careful.' Her eyes went to Wika's stomach and she placed a hand on the small bulge.

The woman's mouth was firm. 'I will, lady. Have no fear.'

Finn sealed the door behind her, his features grim as he spoke. 'I'm not sure about this. Can we trust her? There's something strange.'

Linnayen raised an eyebrow. 'The madness of love? I see it too. But she's valuable to us right now.'

'Maybe. But I won't be happy until we know the Ki-consort and the others are airborne and heading back to Zaz.'

'With us on board, too, hopefully,' Linnayen finished. She stood and rolled back her shoulders before settling herself on the stone floor. She had not realised how tight her muscles had become over the last two hours. 'We'll know soon enough, even if Wika fails to return.'

He nodded and sat on the floor next to her, his knees pulled up.

Linnayen looked sideways at him. 'Tell me, lieutenant, was she very different from the last time you saw her?'

A dark look crossed his face. 'Setiyan? I mean, the princess,' he spluttered. 'I'll say! I mean, she was … Well, she's normally a woman who knows her own mind.'

Linnayen laughed. 'You have a gift for understatement, lieutenant. You can say it. She's a firecracker … usually.'

His eyes were suddenly warm and a smile spread across his face. 'I hate to say it but it'll be good to have her back.'

'Back home. Where she belongs.' Linnayen yawned and rubbed her eyes. 'Let's get some rest. This isn't over yet.'

There was no doubt about it. Calin's study of the subterranean waterways had proved very useful as the submersible pushed on through the crystal waters, and Falvii's knowledge and instincts on their journey through the waters of Kadis Sakek were indispensable. He had an in-built sense for the flow of the water and its depth, which, due to its clarity, was often hard to judge. Occasionally, as they passed close to jutting rock ledges, Calin and Jinau would tense and cringe. But Falvii just laughed and kept a firm hand on the helm to steer them smartly around all obstacles.

Jinau's eyes widened in wonder as they passed through a world of watery halls, with sunken columns of smooth rock. Sometimes they surfaced in a lake with a roof that appeared like a sky of diamond shards from glow-worms she never even knew existed. As for Setiyan, her smile seemed to be a permanent fixture and, though her eyes were open, to Calin it seemed that she saw virtually nothing. Once when they chanced upon a huge silver tagirp swimming lazily in front of their bow, they all gasped with surprise, but not Setiyan, who remained as mute as a statue, albeit a happy one.

Finally, shafts of natural light pierced the water and lit the way ahead.

Falvii turned in his seat with a grin on his face. 'Here we are, ladies. My but that was fun.'

'So glad one of us enjoyed it,' Calin uttered with a tight smile.

The Dasnirian looked over his shoulder and winked at Jinau, who still sat wide-eyed and open-mouthed at the adventure into which she had unwittingly been swept. She smiled as the vessel surfaced into an open cavern and the top hatch slid back. Above was a circle of harsh blue sky, but the high dark walls of the sinkhole kept them in shadow below ground.

Directly ahead lay a pebbly beach where they disembarked. For Jinau, almost as impressive as the sight of the sleek aerporter and the somewhat larger spaceracer on the beach was the statuesque woman – as grand as the Ki herself – who stood waiting to greet them. Jinau gently led the placid Setiyan forward and bowed respectfully.

'Greetings. I'm told you have attended our Princess Setiyan most carefully.' Kalisa Caspiran glanced at Calin, acknowledging the update she had transmitted via their mutual mentante abilities. 'Come.' She gestured for Jinau and Setiyan to enter the cool metallic interior of the gleaming aerporter where some half a dozen uniformed guards stood ready to welcome them.

Jinau could not speak. So much had happened in these last couple of hours and she had seen things she could never have imagined. She could do nothing more than bow again before gratefully taking a seat on a bench in the main cabin of the vessel.

Calin had already connected with Kalisa Caspiran to tell her of the partial success of their mission. Yes, they had brought back Setiyan, but her mother had remained, and she would trust that Lieutenant Finn would either find a way out for them or get her mother to Jax's party. Meanwhile, they would need to stay with the aerporter and keep hidden inside the capacious sinkhole until they received word from Linnayen or Jax. With both her parents still inside the Guznon stronghold, the rescue mission was imminent and they must be prepared.

It was mid-morning before the message came back that the princess was not in her quarters. Denkaun had insisted on sending for her, rather than lead her father there again, because it was fitting that she come to him. She would have to get used to obeying his commands, after all. Indeed, Denkaun was surprised that she had not been raised to be more dutiful – both to her father and to all men. No matter. All that would change in time. Setiyan would find life with her husband a calm and peaceful haven where she would need to do little but attend to his physical needs and raise their children. Meanwhile, once her parents were retired – or removed – he would take charge of the Galactic Union Council, and his son by the princess would inherit after him. The dynasty had begun to be forged and the future looked assured.

Already the PLA rebels had seized control of all but two mines. The speed of their rebellion was gratifying. The tribes had been let loose and they would be given their head until he, the A'bat, called them back into line with promises of a great and glorious future. Finally, they would be given the wealth they deserved and the power to control the flow of ore and gases. These resources belonged to them and a new way of life, without the interfering ganaks, would be heralded.

Such visions kept his mind engaged while the Ki-consort and his party continued their dreary talk, going on and on about the various protocols that would need to be followed both before the wedding ceremony and after.

'I'm sorry, Lord A'bat.' The voice of the messenger shook him from his thoughts. 'The Princess Setiyan has been taken for purification by the holy mother tamun.'

His brows drew together and he glared at the man, who immediately looked to the ground. 'Purification?' He glanced across to Mira. Was this her doing? But by the confusion on her face he assumed that she was as much in the dark as he was.

'Yes, lord. In the waters of Kadis Sakek.'

'A tamun?'

Mira rose quickly from her seat and came to his side. 'I gave no such orders.'

'Purification? Does she need this?' Denkaun asked of his natar.

'As a ga – as an off-worlder, yes. She must be cleansed before the ceremony can take place. But …' Mira confirmed.

Jax spoke. 'So where *is* my daughter?'

Denkaun's look of annoyance lasted no more than a second before he replied smoothly. 'It is a custom she must follow. We shall wait for her in her rooms.' He turned to Mira and whispered urgently. 'Natar, find her.'

He stood and pushed back his chair forcefully, signalling to a handful of red-robed armed men to come to him. Jax got up ready to follow, as did Serekunda, Birkaan and the Union troops.

Denkaun shook his head dismissively. 'Your men can stay here. She may be a princess, but her rooms cannot accommodate us all.'

With a friendly smile, he gestured for Jax to go with him. Whatever nonsense Setiyan and the interfering tamun was up to would soon be sorted out.

All was quiet in the Dokau workshop. Finn remained on the floor with his eyes closed while Linnayen was stretching her hamstrings by flexing her feet against the back wall. Suddenly she stopped and spoke her thoughts out loud.

'The servant, Jinau – she said her mother made soup for Setiyan. We have to help.'

Linnayen did not need to finish the thought for Finn. 'We can find her. The family name is Akika.'

He jumped up and searched the companel on the wall near the doorway. A Na'jin Akika was listed on level five. Finn was confident he knew the way and, after adjusting their robes and pulling up their hoods, they quickly left the workshop.

The passages were much busier now. People were rushing with heads down carrying bundles, calling out orders and yelling greetings to each other. And all around them was news about the rebellion.

'Our men have got Pikaa!'

'Untakeo's been taken, thanks be to the A'bat!'

Linnayen grimaced under her cowl. There would be a new regime to deal with when all this was over, and such rapid change nearly always spelled trouble for the stability of the Union. She was not looking forward to the weeks and months of wrangling and political infighting that was to come. But, she consoled herself, they had faced troubles in the past, and if she and the other Union planets stood firm, this too would be resolved. They could not afford to lose access to the resources of this rich planet, with its precious ore and gases that were used in all things from the building of spacecraft to the production of medicines.

At the humble Akika dwelling, Jinau's mother was cooking a large batch of feir stew. She welcomed the two imposing strangers in and explained it was for the men at the front.

Finn quickly introduced himself and turned to bring Linnayen forward. Instead, the woman reached up and pushed back a fold of his hood.

'My Lord Finn! Is that you? My Jinau speaks so well of you, lord. Though she said you have been away for many days. Where did you go? Oh, no matter. And now you catch me cooking for our men! And my poor kitchen all a-messed. Oh, forgive me, lord.'

The small, plump woman wiped her hands furiously on her stained apron before dipping a curtsy. 'And forgive me also, holy lady. I am so honoured by your visit. Wait while I find you a seat and fetch you a flask.' She looked over their shoulders to see what furniture she might have and, seeing nothing uncluttered, frowned as she scratched her chin.

Linnayen smiled and held out her hand to still the woman's worrying. 'Please, Sister Akika. We've no time to sit. Indeed, we've come to take you away, and most urgently.'

264

Her face contorted in confusion. 'Is it my Jinau? What's she done? Oh, holy lady! What's wrong?'

Finn walked behind her and turned off the flame under the stew. 'Jinau's done nothing wrong. Quite the opposite. Both you and she have done the princess a great service. But Kalik Denkaun will not thank you for it.'

'Oh, you mustn't call him that. He's the A'bat now,' she remonstrated.

Linnayen took the woman's hands in her own. 'Good mother, no matter his title. He will be angry with you and Jinau for having fed my daughter. She was unwell – made deliberately so by your A'bat. But you and Jinau saved her from even greater sickness.'

The older woman pulled back from Linnayen, the confusion in her eyes now replaced with alarm. 'Your daughter? The princess?'

'That's right.' Finn's voice shook with urgency. 'This is the Ki of Altan, Lady Linnayen Genara, and you must do what she says.' He would brook no further delay. 'Mother Akika, you must come with us now. We have Jinau away from here in safety but your life is in danger.'

As Finn helped the panicked woman pack her duffel with anything she valued, clothes, trinkets, mementoes and the like, Linnayen contacted Calin, flashing a mental image of Na'jin Akika. She asked her to arrange for the old woman to be met in Zaz and looked after. The chances were that she would not be returning to Beshwuk at any time in the near future.

Linnayen checked the passageway outside and they left once more, walking quickly past the milling crowds, descending stairwells and tunnels to the levels of the q'ist transport. The transit hall was filled with orange-robed men loading supplies from a dozen hovering palletrons onto a q'ist, which was to depart for Zaz-Rakuum.

'Looks like we're just in time,' Finn said. 'Quickly, mother. Get on board or there'll be no space for you.'

The small woman looked anxiously at the crowded compartment. A single bench seat remained adjacent to the door. She placed her bag onto it and faced Linnayen and Finn, her eyes questioning.

'Sister Akika, remember: you'll be met in Zaz by Councillor Kaletin, who knows to expect you,' said Linnayen with a gentle smile. 'She'll look after you.'

'Great lady, I must trust you, yet I am afraid.'

'You'll soon be safe – as your daughter already is.' She again took her hands in her own and kissed them. Instantly, tears welled in the other woman's eyes. A klaxon horn rang out through the transit hall and the door between the women slowly closed. Finn raised a hand in farewell and watched the transporter glide away.

'That's one less thing to worry about. Let's find the Ki-consort and get the hell out of here.'

He turned and held out a protective arm to lead Linnayen away but she was standing stock-still, an expression on her face that sent a shiver of alarm through him.

'What? What's wrong?'

Linnayen could not speak. Her eyes were glassy and her breath came in short gasps. Finn placed a hand on her shoulder to wake her from the stupor that seemed to have descended on her.

'No. No. No …' The wail was soft and all-consuming.

'My lady?'

Her head fell to her chest and she would have collapsed had Finn not sensed the weakness in her limbs and lifted her clean off the ground. He wove a way through the men and sat her down on a low rock plinth at the side of the transit hall.

'Here. Drink.' He offered her water from his flask but she did not see it. All colour had drained from her face. Finn was at a loss but he knew that they could not stay here. They were drawing attention from one of the burly overseers who was rounding up the men to leave the hall.

'Come. We must go!'

He pulled her to her feet and, nodding to the overseer, pulled her towards a passage. Whatever had come over the Ki would have to wait.

Jax sat on the end of Setiyan's bed. It had been remade and his fingers played over the pattern of leaves woven into the deep green coverlet. He sighed loudly and was about to ask Denkaun again where his daughter was when the door opened and Wika Dokau entered. Her eyes were fixed on Denkaun and she seemed taller than when Jax had last seen her. She did not seem to see him and, Jax thought, given the poor woman's state of mind, that was just as well.

Denkaun glanced up at her but did not move from the window seat. 'What are you doing here, Wika? Go away.' He waved a dismissive hand but she continued, then kneeled before him.

'My lord, my love …'

At these words, Denkaun looked at her sharply.

'You're waiting for your ganak princess?' Wika asked him.

The smugness of her tone overlaid the insult, and if Denkaun had not heard it, Jax certainly did. It was time to ensure the Guznon woman's loyalties lay in the right place. He hoped they could be sure of her. 'What did you say, young woman? Are you referring to my daughter?'

Wika turned in surprise to see the Ki-consort. 'Ah, great lord, forgive me.'

'Wika, be gone,' Denkaun said, annoyed. 'This is not the time or the –'

'But it is, my love,' she interrupted. 'Now is the time and this is the place. For your princess is gone!'

'What?' Denkaun pushed her away and she sprawled back onto the richly textured carpet. 'What do you mean?'

Jax stood and walked over to offer a hand for her to rise just as Mira burst into the room.

'Wika Dokau, leave this place! Now!' She bent over the woman and would have struck her.

Denkaun jumped up and placed his arm in front of his natar. 'No! Wika, what are you saying?'

Jax helped her to stand. 'Please, tell us what you know. Where is my daughter?'

Wika laughed as she stood and caressed her belly. 'Oh, great lord, she is long gone from this place. Taken into the waters of Kadis Sakek!' There was madness in her voice.

Jax's face fell and he stumbled back towards the bed, confident that his show of distress appeared real enough. Denkaun grabbed the young woman's arm and dragged her to him, his face dark as the sandstorms that spun across the Beshwuk plains and, Jax feared, as dangerous.

'Tell me! Where is she?'

She struggled in his grasp and winced with pain but her face was triumphant. Her eyes glittered as she spat back at him. 'Her mother came for her! She was spirited away in a vessel that swam through the waters of Kadis Sakek to who knows where. And who cares where! She is gone and we can be together again, my lord, my love.'

For a few moments, Denkaun held her as she struggled to caress his face. Then his lips drew back in a snarl and he threw the woman back down onto the floor. He raised his foot to kick her but checked himself when he saw her hand go to protect her belly. His head lifted and he turned slowly to stare at Jax, his gaze colder than ice.

'Cleverly done, my lord.' He strode towards the door to call for guards when Wika cried out again.

'Wait! The mother is still here! I can tell you where.'

Jax's mouth tightened. Linnayen was supposed to leave with Setiyan. What had gone wrong? And now this woman who they had helped was about to betray Linnayen.

Denkaun kneeled beside Wika and held her face in an iron grip. 'And where is the lady?'

Her response was to slide closer to him and stroke his face. 'But only love me, lord, and I will tell you everything.'

'Love you?' He shook his head and laughed. 'Sweetheart, of course. And I'll love you better when you tell me where the Ki is hiding.'

'No, Wika! We helped you!' Jax reached out a hand to connect with the crazed woman, but his plea fell on deaf ears.

Wika gloried in telling him everything that had happened since she met Decker Finn and, later, Linnayen, Jax and their group in Zaz the day before. Finally, she reached the part where she told of her father's workshop where the Ki's was hiding.

Denkaun's reaction was immediate. He threw a look at Mira who simultaneously called to the guards outside. As the door slid open, he spoke to the nearest of the armed men. 'You four, with me. The rest, take the Ki-consort to the high cells along with the rest of his party. Be sure to remove all their weapons and communicators.'

Mira made to hurry away but Denkaun held her arm in a tight grip. 'I'll close the city, my son. She will not escape.'

He released her and spun around, glaring angrily at Jax, whose smile was derisive as a guard moved towards him. 'Don't be too quick to mock, lord. I'll give the Union the choice of who to save: their Ki and her useless husband – or their princess.'

He stormed from the room and, whilst Jax felt some sympathy for the obviously deranged young woman on the floor, his last thoughts as he was led away were for his wife and the desperate need to warn her.

In the aerporter, under Falvii's cheerful grin, Setiyan had begun to recognise that her circumstances had changed. Her Min cousin was indeed a most amiable companion and she wondered if he should be asked to attend her beloved at the wedding. That smile would work wonders on her at times sullen lord. Yes, it was true. Sometimes Kalik was a little short-tempered – never with her, of course. But she had seen a servant or two cringe from time to time.

Calin offered her water. *My goodness! I'll explode if I have any more.* Jinau, too, stayed right by her side. *A good and faithful girl.* She had a vague memory of having seen her mother. *Where was she now?* Calin might know.

'Where's Mother? Did she go back to the palace?'

Calin leaned across the aisle and took her sister's hands. 'Something like that. How are you feeling, sister?'

'Oh, fine!' *Yes, fine. What did I just ask?* She yawned and stretched her neck. 'Where's Kalik? I can't wait for you to meet him. You'll love him too.'

'I'm sure I will.' Calin glanced at Falvii, then stroked her face. 'Close your eyes, Seti,' she ordered. 'Now, describe your Kalik to me.'

Setiyan's grin spread across her face. 'Oh, I like this game. Let me see …' Her head fell back against the wall as she tried to visualise his beautiful face. There he was. That strong square jaw, the full rose lips, the crystalline blue eyes and almost white-blond hair. A vision of perfect manhood.

Seeing what she saw, Calin had to agree that he was indeed an extremely handsome man. No wonder her sister had been attracted to him. His looks were perfectly symmetrical and, when Seti pictured him smiling, it was hard not to be charmed.

Calin tried a deeper link with Seti but she could get nothing but thoughts of Kalik Denkaun and, more embarrassingly, their lovemaking. It had been enough, though, to contact Linnayen and show her what she had seen inside her sister's muddled mind. She could not have known the effect it would have on her mother.

All the way back up the levels to the Dokau workshop, Finn became more concerned about the Ki. She acted as though she had been stung by something and her mind was not focused. Given their situation, this was worrying. He needed her to have all her wits about her, especially as they might need to spring into action at a moment's notice.

He heard the commotion before he saw anything. The sound of wood being smashed and metal clanging signified trouble ahead, and it was coming from the direction of Dokau's place. A young boy ran past and Finn called to him while still supporting the Ki.

'Hey! What's going on up there?'

The lad came back a few steps and gabbled quickly. 'Soldiers, lord, smashing up old Dokau's.'

The boy darted off as Finn nodded his thanks. Obviously Wika had betrayed them. Given the woman's state of mind, he was not surprised. They would have to find a new hiding place.

He took Linnayen's arm and guided her to the next stairway rising up to a higher level, only two away from Seti's rooms. At first it seemed like a crazy idea. But logically, it might be the one place in the whole mountain Denkaun would not search. Seti's rooms were also defensible, there being only one way in and a window that, if necessary, could be de-shielded for a climb down the cliff-face. He remembered also the small closet where they could hide for the time being.

Sure enough, the passage to Seti's rooms was empty and the door slid open on their approach. Once inside, Linnayen straightened and walked through the foyer area and into the bedroom, where she stood at the end of the bed and stared at it.

'My lady? We should hide.'

She seemed not to hear him but allowed him to take her arm and lead her towards a small room tucked away behind the bedhead.

'We should be safe here.' Finn sat her down on a teal silk-covered stool and pulled a thick velvet curtain across the doorway. 'Some water?'

He offered her a flask but she shook her head before finally speaking.

'I'm sorry, lieutenant. I received news – an image, actually – of this Denkaun. From my daughter Calin. She connected with Setiyan.'

'Then the drug's wearing off?'

Linnayen nodded. 'Perhaps. I hope so. But ...'

'What? Denkaun?'

'Yes. I never got a good look before.'

Finn's brows drew together. 'Sorry? Am I missing something?'

'It's just ... he reminds me of someone, from a long time ago. Someone cruel.'

Finn harrumphed. 'Well, that figures.'

'The likeness is uncanny.'

Once more, Linnayen retreated into her thoughts as Finn settled down on the soft padded floor. His Ki seemed to have regained her wits a little and this was as good a time as any to rest.

Questions reeled inside her brain. Could he be Navarr's son? With his twin sister? We never found Balisel. Could she have ended up on Autabron? And what about Seti? Could she ...? No! No!

She recalled the dreams – no, nightmares – she had had over the years. They had plagued her, the visions of Navarr's face swirling grotesquely above her. His twisted laughter echoing in her ears, then soft heated whispers and the sounds of metal chains on stone flagstones. In her nightmares she could feel his hot breath on her face and she was once more in the ruined fortress of Guyvar Neref back on Earth.

Had Navarr been there? It was so hard to remember. For two days she had been in a drugged stupor after they had taken her. Anything could have happened. *Was he there?*

The still of the small chamber was broken by a sudden excoriating gasp. Finn sat up in surprise.

'What the ...'

Barely conscious of the worried bodyguard beside her, Linnayen felt the tears streaming down her face. *It was true! They weren't nightmares. They were memories!* She sobbed as though her heart would break, now certain that what she had seen so often in her sleep was no fantasy.

Chapter Twenty

The afternoon air funnelling through the single high window of the cell was blisteringly hot. Birkaan was full of advice for Pieter, Jax and the contingent of guards on how to cope with the brutal conditions.

'Stay still. Already the suns are low. And sip slowly,' he cautioned, passing around a leather flask.

The guards – seven men and three women – did as they were told. In truth, there was little else they could do since being rounded up and incarcerated nearly five hours earlier.

Denkaun had made it clear to them and to Svikar Kaletin, the city leader in Zaz, that if Princess Setiyan Genara was not returned to him in Beshwuk before the first sun's rise then her father and his whole party would be taken to the high platform on the top of the mountain, the Sill of Makum, to face their fate. Kaletin, a member of the Graan tribe, knew only too well what that fate would be once the twin suns breached the horizon. But whether the A'bat would carry out his threat was something she could not decide alone. If only her tribe leader, Vit, had not died so suddenly in Beshwuk, for his advice was always sound. Even so, the A'bat's message had been communicated to both the representatives of the Galactic Union and Sen-Caspiran, and between them they must find a solution to this terrible development.

Jax licked his parched lips and looked up at the window to see if the light was finally fading. They had been left water but no food. Not that he could have stomached any. The thought that Linnayen was still somewhere in Beshwuk, even with Lieutenant Finn to protect her, was deeply worrying. He drummed his fingers in the dirt in frustration.

Birkaan looked sideways at him under heavy eyelids, the sweat beading on his brow. 'Don't worry, my friend.' He gave a half smile. 'It could be worse. He could have put us in here this morning, in which case half of us would already be dead.'

Serekunda laughed. 'But the water would last longer.'

Jax couldn't help but smile at their efforts to humour him.

'Help will come,' Serekunda said, 'and I'm sure we will be saved from a fiery death.' He smiled at Jax reassuringly.

Fiery death. The words triggered a memory of Navarr all those years ago when he had been swallowed up by a fire-twister during the earthquake at Guyvar Neref. Denkaun had a likeness to Navarr. *Dear lord!* Could he be his son? *And the mother? Navarr's twin sister?* He grimaced as the pieces fell into place. *Even the voice was the same.*

The thick wooden cell door creaked open and Denkaun appeared, backed by a posse of guards. All Jax wanted was to place his hands around the man's neck, but Serekunda sensed his anger and placed a hand on his arm. 'Save your strength.'

Denkaun scanned the sweat-stained faces of the men and women seated around the edges of the compartment. He raised a hand and fanned his face.

'Warm in here,' he said over his shoulder to his guards. 'They look cooked already!' The men behind him grinned.

Denkaun crossed the floor and smiled down at Jax. 'I bring good news, dear father-in-law. There will indeed be a wedding between your beautiful daughter and myself. Tomorrow morning, in fact. The Union has agreed to release her back to me at first dawn. My natar, Lady Mira, is preparing the hall even as we speak.'

He laughed and placed his hands at his waist as he bent down to whisper into Jax's ear. 'And I shall take my pleasure of her whenever I want. She loves what I do to her, you know.'

Jax flushed red and his muscles tightened, ready to spring up at the evil being that loomed over him. It was only the touch again of both Serekunda's and now Birkaan's hands on his arms that held him in check.

Denkaun returned to the doorway and, without turning around, spoke again. 'Make the most of the time that's left to you, for Lau's next ascent may be your last.'

A deep voice broke the silence and Jinau opened her eyes to see the black-haired man talking to Princess Calin.

'You look awful!'

Calin looked up at Falvii with a glare that would kill a bika without a spear. 'Thanks. Not!'

'I mean, you're tired. Get some sleep. We've a short night ahead of us. There's a bunk back there – only big enough for one, I'm afraid.' He smiled at his joke.

She sighed. 'Oh, Falvii, stop it. It doesn't work on me.'

'What?' Now he looked wounded.

'The charm. The lines. Though I'm sure there are plenty of women they do work on. Save it for them.'

'Maybe I should. But I think you'd be jealous.' He strolled away laughing before she could respond.

From her corner seat in the main hold, Jinau watched the lovely princess and the handsome man with the sea-blue eyes. These fine, strong people. So free, so happy. No woman in Beshwuk would be allowed to talk to a young man like that and a man would be risking a beating from her father if he spoke thus to a woman. The events of this day had quite overwhelmed her. They said that she had saved the Aun'bat, that she was a hero. But she did not see how that could be. Then they had swum through the sacred waters like the mighty tagirp, passing through dark caverns and along swirling rivers. And now, here they were, still tucked inside the huge sinkhole and safe inside the belly of a glossy aerporter, where all the walls were smooth and clean. *No rock dust! If only Mother could see this. Mother ...*

'Are you all right, Jinau?' Calin's voice cut through her thoughts and she looked up through a veil of tears. 'You're upset. What is it?'

'My apologies, lady. I was thinking of my mother.'

Calin smiled and sat next to the girl. 'She's arrived in Zaz. She's safe.'

'Yes. But ... Our home. Our friends. Nothing will be the same after this.' The girl sighed sorrowfully.

'It's possible. But, Jinau, you must know what a great service you've done.' Calin took the girl's two hands and kissed them. 'Once this crisis is over you may well be able to go home – if you still want to – and you'll soon see your mother again, I promise.'

Jinau's smile returned slowly as she sniffed back her tears. A Union trooper entered the cabin and summoned them all to join the briefing on the bridge. Sen-Caspiran had news of the hostage exchange. Denkaun had demanded the return of the Princess Setiyan for her father and his troops. He had also ordered how it would happen. They had been given a time and place but they all needed to be armed and prepared for any eventuality. Once the captain of the guard finished his portion of the briefing and demonstrated the many weapons they had at their disposal, Caspiran advised them all to get some sleep before their mission would begin.

Falvii came over and sat next to Jinau, a reassuring smile on his face. 'All a bit much, eh?' He patted her hand and glanced over at the guns. 'Don't worry. We won't have to use them.'

'Have *you* used such weapons before?'

'Occasionally. My Uncle Tariik was a trained weapons expert. He made sure we knew what we were doing.'

Lord Falvii sounded so confident that it gave her hope. He stood and gestured for her to join him at the table where an array of small arms was laid out. She ran her hand lightly over them.

'Here. This would be best for you.' He handed her a short-barrelled metallic pistol. 'Keep it tucked in your waistband and leave this safety switch on until you need to use it. Personal protection only, okay?'

Her brow furrowed as he reeled off the many properties of the weapon and showed her the simplicity of its use.

'It fires explosive haligon pellets. Deadly in close quarters. Nice and light.'

Her eyes were the size of saucers as he placed the weapon in her trembling hands.

'Best to use both hands, though. But don't worry, Jinau. Chances are we won't have to use any of these if Caspiran's plan goes as expected,' he said, indicating the spread of weaponry on the table.

'He's right,' said Calin, coming over to join them. 'Kalisa and I have been in contact with my mother, and if there's one person who can turn the tables on Kalik Denkaun, it's her.'

Falvii raised an admiring eyebrow and turned his smile on Jinau. 'I can believe it. This is a family of amazing women.'

Calin poked her elbow into Falvii's ribs, shook her head despairingly and walked away.

'I think she really likes me,' he croaked to Jinau, who did not even try to suppress her giggle.

Linnayen guessed that it was close to midnight when she heard a sound coming from the bedroom. She had managed a couple of hours sleep earlier, just after connecting with Calin and Kalisa Caspiran to go over their plans; the gift of mentantism at a time like this was invaluable. Then it had been Finn's turn to rest. He lay curled on the soft carpet next to her, oblivious to the singing now coming from the next room. She nudged him gently and put a hand over his mouth to warn him to be quiet as his eyes snapped open.

The woman's voice was soft and low, crooning what sounded like a lullaby. The fabric of a muslin dress hanging next to Linnayen's head moved in a sudden draught, presumably caused by the opening of a door. A woman's sharp voice broke the peace of the lullaby.

'What are you doing here, Wika? Get out!'

'No. This is my place now.'

'Don't be ridiculous! This is the ganak's room and she is coming back in the morning.'

Linnayen bristled at the use of the derogatory term for her precious daughter. Whoever this woman was, she would pay for her disrespect.

'No! She cannot have him! He is mine!'

'Fool! He is not yours and never was.' The woman spat the words.

'I carry his seed!' Wika's voice rose ever higher.

'You … and her. And maybe a dozen more.'

'No! You lie! He is mine.'

'Listen,' the other woman hissed, 'it matters not that you bear his child. Hers is the only offspring that matters, for she is his sister, you fool!'

Linnayen heard Wika gasp as she tried to stifle her own.

The woman's vitriol was unstoppable. 'You are nothing, Wika Dokau. Go back to your stupid, simpering mother. And your ambitious father, who sought only to further himself by peddling his daughter. You are nothing but a whore! Do you hear me? Whore! Get out!'

The words were delivered with pure venom. Wika snarled back at the woman and next came the sound of a smack and a yelp, the word 'whore' repeated with each further slap. Linnayen looked to Finn in alarm. Should they help Wika Dokau? Finn frowned and lifted a hand to urge caution.

They heard a sloughing sound and then a sudden silence descended. Had Wika been rendered unconscious? Then, muffled groans were followed by a sharp exhalation of breath.

'A whore with a blade, lady.'

Linnayen looked to Finn who exhaled through pursed lips. It was Wika.

They heard her spit in disgust. 'He is mine! Mine!'

Linnayen and Finn stared at each other, not daring to breathe as Wika recommenced her lullaby. The sound faded away and they realised that the woman had left the room. Finn looked through the crack between the curtain and the wall behind the bedhead. There was little to be seen from this angle. He opened the curtain a fraction more and in the reflection of a burnished wall mirror Linnayen could see a crumpled shape and an expanding pool of thick ruby blood staining the fibres of a woven rug.

Finn pulled back and signalled for Linnayen to keep quiet while he left the antechamber. She watched as he crept along the side of the bed before returning soundlessly to their hiding place. He relayed the news to Linnayen.

'It's the shaman, Mira. If she's found here, they'll search these rooms.'

'Can we hide her?' Linnayen asked.

He nodded. They would have to be quick. The blood was cooling and becoming viscous, but so far, all of it was on the rug. They wrapped the body in the thick rug and carried it awkwardly to a long linen chest in the antechamber that was mostly empty. A blood-spattered bedspread quickly joined Mira in the trunk and they settled back down to wait out the last hours.

In the quiet dark, Linnayen reflected that whatever her earlier betrayal, Wika Dokau had removed one of their enemies. So how could she not be thankful to the poor woman? She just hoped Wika would find peace for herself and her unborn child.

The heat had long since been replaced by the cold of night and Jax and his group huddled close to keep warm. No one had slept much so it was easy enough to rouse his men and women. They had only another thirty minutes or so until Lau began to crest the horizon. The hostage exchange was minutes away and Jax found it hard to contain his anxiety. It was crucial that he keep calm. His daughter's life depended on it.

Their comms devices had been taken when they were locked up by Denkaun, but their jailers were unaware that they had other means to communicate. Never had Jax been more happy that his wife and a few other Altanis had mentante abilities, because one of his team, Ensign Harr, had shared their location with both Kalisa Caspiran, on board the aerporter at the sinkhole, and with Linnayen, who remained hidden in Beshwuk with Finn. Within minutes, all three groups would converge on the Sill of Makum for the expected handover – Setiyan for Jax and his people. So when the doors of the cell were suddenly wrenched open, it was no surprise to any of them. They were ready to move.

Denkaun followed the group as his armed guards pushed them along the passage. Glow-globes overhead gave some light in the thick darkness as they marched, but it was hard not to stumble. At the rear of the column, Jax turned to sight Denkaun, a sneer on the man's face that Jax itched to remove – permanently.

Finally, the group reached a wide doorway cut into the rock at the back wall of a flat platform some forty metres wide and thirty deep. The entrance had none of the intricate carvings of the lower levels. This was a passageway that had been hacked out in prehistory and was wide enough to allow four abreast. From what Jax knew of this place, the Sill of Makum was an ancient gathering place dominated by a marble chair on a wide plinth in its centre where human sacrifice had been commonplace. He hoped it would not be so today.

The aerporter hovered in front of the rock ledge, its thirty-metre silhouette taking up nearly the whole width of the platform. There was a soft whirr from its engines while lights from its port side lit the ground on which they stood, casting the white stone of the sacrificial chair into sharp relief. Above the vessel, the night sky was still filled with a million sparkling points of starlight. But already a rosy glow touched the horizon, warning of the impending sunrise. The aerporter's hatch remained closed and silence dropped like a curtain upon the scene for a full minute before the voice of Kalisa Caspiran filled the air.

'Lord A'bat! Your summons has been answered. Release the Ki-consort and his people.'

Denkaun's reply was immediate. 'Not until you release my princess. Show her to me!'

A metal panel of the aerporter slid to one side and a wide, cross-hatched ramp extended some five metres to bridge the gap between vessel and the rock shelf, below which a chasm dropped away for a thousand metres. At the top of the ramp stood Setiyan, her gaze fixed on Denkaun. She was flanked by Falvii and Calin, who held her arms as she struggled to free herself.

Jax reeled as he witnessed his daughter's desperation to get back to her lover. She called across to him. 'Kalik! I'm here! Come for me!'

Caspiran moved to stand in front of her, arms splayed to either side preventing any forward movement. Her firm voice filled the space. 'The men and women first. You may hold the Ki-consort until we exchange.'

Denkaun raised one eyebrow and scanned his captives. He shrugged and signalled to his men to release Serekunda, Birkaan and the others, who quickly and quietly moved up the ramp leading into the vessel. But he kept a firm hold on Jax.

'Thank you, Lord A'bat.' Caspiran glanced over her shoulder to Calin and nodded. She stood to one side as Falvii and Calin led the reanimated Setiyan towards the man she still so desired.

As soon as her feet touched the stone shelf, Setiyan broke free and ran towards Denkaun. At the same moment, Jax shrugged off the two men holding him and walked towards the ramp, staring dolefully as his beloved eldest daughter rushed past him to drape herself over Denkaun. The drugs were clearly still playing their part, but how would she feel about this vile man once they wore off? And were they affecting the child that he had said grew already inside her?

The pink glow of early dawn formed a backdrop to the sleek metallic lines of the aerporter as Denkaun's men raised their arms in salutes and cheers, slapping each other on the back for the success of their warrior of hope. The A'bat had led them to another victory. Denkaun's grin was wide and mocking as he pulled Setiyan into his arms, laughing as he looked to where Jax still stood one foot on the platform and the other on the ramp.

In their celebration, none of the Guznon had noticed two figures emerge from the shadow of the craggy arch that led from inside the mountain to the Sill of Makum. Crouching low and taking advantage of the shadows at the rear of the platform, Linnayen and Finn made their way along the left-hand edge of the rock wall as it curved towards a metre-high boulder close to the lip of the sill. The original plan was that Finn would have been here with the tranquiliser gun on his own, hidden and waiting for a clear shot at Setiyan. But seeing Linnayen now tucked behind the bodyguard made Jax's heart beat even faster at the possibilities for this revised strategy to all go terribly wrong. His eyes had flicked to his right for a mere second. It was the slightest of gestures but Denkaun noticed the movement. He cocked his head and, with a look of puzzlement, stood up straight as he pushed Setiyan away.

Now Seti was a little clear of Denkaun, that small movement gave Finn the angle he needed. He took careful aim and shot a micro-dart into Seti's upper arm. She began to swoon and her knees buckled as she sank to the dusty ground.

Denkaun glanced at her quickly then swivelled his head from side to side, reaching for his weapon. At the same time, Jax ran the few metres from the ramp to the crumpled form of his daughter. The men on either side of Denkaun looked to each other, their confusion evident at the princess's collapse. They began to raise their weapons. Just as Jax managed to cover Setiyan's body with his own, Denkaun screeched in sudden pain. Jax looked over his shoulder and saw Falvii standing at the top of the ramp taking aim again at Denkaun, as the latter's ion-laser dropped heavily to the ground from what remained of his hand.

Either side of Falvii, from their raised position on the ramp, the Union guards quickly formed a double-row attack, firing at Denkaun's men from behind translucent shields while Linnayen and Finn took out men on the left flank of the Guznon huddle from the cover of the boulder. Even so, Jax was terribly exposed where he lay, desperately protecting his daughter. The hovering aerporter's ramp was only three or four metres away but it would have been foolish to make a run for it.

Within seconds the group of red-robed Guznons had instinctively retreated towards the back wall of the rock shelf, taking fire from both the front and the left and returning it in a hail of red flame. Even so, outnumbered and outgunned, Jax could see they had already lost some six or seven men, dead or wounded, their blood and splintered body-parts staining the dirt of the ground around him. Under a barrage of green fire from the Union guns, two of the Guznon guard grabbed Denkaun and dragged him behind the sacrificial chair as shots sent stone flakes zapping through the air. But he did not go easily and snarled furiously at being so restrained.

'Kill him, you cowards!' Denkaun pushed a man forward to take a shot at the prone form of Jax. But as soon as the man poked his head out from behind the side of the chair, a spit of green flame split the side of his head open.

Between the Union troops on the ramp and Linnayen and Finn on the left, Denkaun and his men were pinned, their only protection the massive stone chair between them and the aerporter.

For a few seconds, a salvo of shots continued between the Guznon and the Union troops until Jax, still atop the unconscious Setiyan, felt the vibration of pounding feet as some dozen of his guards, shields raised, passed by to form a barricade between him and the remaining Guznon. Four splintered off to give cover to Finn and Linnayen, who emerged from the boulder and ran the short distance to the hovering vessel, collecting Jax and the unconscious Seti on the way. As they climbed the ramp with the troops' shields protecting their rear, Falvii and Calin made room for them to pass through into the safety of the aerporter. With Seti safely stowed on board, Jax hung back and turned to see that Denkaun and his remaining guards were now pinned down behind the chair's wide span. Their situation was hopeless. He only hoped Denkaun would realise it.

Suddenly the voice of Kalisa Caspiran broke though the noise. She stood behind a shield at the top of the ramp, her arm raised, open-palmed. She signalled to the troops to cease fire.

'Kalik Denkaun! Stand down and save your men!'

Jax stood with Finn a pace behind her, both still panting from their exertions. 'If he's a man of honour, he'll concede.'

Finn shook his head. 'Don't hold your breath.'

Seconds passed, the sky behind the aerporter's silhouette turning pale peach as the huge stone chair began to take on a rose hue. Lau would soon be above the horizon and they would have to seal the doors and be on their way.

Caspiran, her hands now clasped in plea, offered Denkaun one last chance. 'Kalik Denkaun! I say again, stand down and be taken into custody. I promise you a fair hearing.'

Jax tensed at the promise but instantly felt Finn's hand on his arm. However hateful, the laws of the Union must prevail. More seconds passed and still nothing.

Caspiran had been about to raise her arm to resume the attack when Jax called to her.

'Wait!' He caught a movement at the craggy entrance to the sill. The rock dust stirred, its crystals catching the early morning glow. There was the sound of metal scraping on rock.

'Stand down? Surrender?' Denkaun's voice bellowed in the warming atmosphere. He stepped out from behind the chair and Jax could see an oozing bloody stump where his left hand had been. Denkaun kept it across his chest as he threw back his head and laughed. 'I'll see you all in hell before I'll submit!'

He lifted his uninjured arm and, roaring his hatred, punched the air. The signal given, his men ran back towards the passageway's entrance to heave a fully primed rakonium-cannon the rest of the way out onto the sill. While the Guznon guards struggled to heft its metal carriage around the marble chair to position the gun for firing, Jax and Finn knew they only had seconds to get away. At such close range, the aerporter would be pulverised. A choice had to be made – and fast. Even if they closed the doors and got away now, the cannon could take them out mid-air.

'Damn it!' Jax yelled, as Denkaun moved to get behind the controls of the cannon. Both Finn and Falvii raised their weapons, ready to take a shot at Denkaun.

'Stop!' The command came from Linnayen, who stepped forward gripping a qasar-mortar firmly to her chest. She turned the barrel towards Denkaun and, with one touch of the trigger, a bolt of blue fire shot across the ten-metre space and obliterated the cannon in a deafening explosion. The shock wave from the blast rocked them all where they stood and Jax quickly grabbed Linnayen's arm to keep her upright. Chunks of hot metal shrapnel blasted upwards and outwards, but their shields protected them from the worst of the impact.

Through the clouds of brown dust, Jax saw another three or four Guznon guards on the ground, what was left of their bodies a bloody mess. It was hard to imagine that anyone standing close by the cannon could have survived. But where was Denkaun?

As they waited for the air to clear, Linnayen nudged Jax's arm, indicating a point close to the end of the metal ramp. Denkaun lay face-down, his head pointing away from them, a metre-long spear of dull metal pinning his left leg to the platform. They watched in horror as he rolled himself over, the action wrenching the metal spear out of the rock floor. With his right arm he took hold of the shrapnel and pulled it out through the flesh of his leg. His screams – seemingly more of anger than pain – vibrated in the dusty air. Jax was transfixed as Denkaun dragged his broken body towards what remained of the sacrificial chair, gouging a path through the rock shards and twisted metal.

Denkaun turned and leaned against the foot of the stone chair, fixing his eyes first on Jax, then on Linnayen. Without breaking his gaze, Denkaun spat on the ground, his chest heaving as he yelled to them. 'You think it's over? You can't stop what has begun!'

Jax was pulled out of the horrifying moment by the commotion behind him as their troops retreated into the main cabin, stowing their weapons and taking their seats. Beside Jax, Calin took her mother's arm to draw her away from the doorway, beyond which they could see the rocky ceiling of the platform now glowing a fiery orange from the rays of the first sun's rise. Their departure was imminent and urgent. There was no hope of arresting Denkaun now.

'Come, Mother. We have to go.' Calin led Linnayen to a seat in the row behind the pilots and Jax tore himself away from Denkaun's face twisted with hate to follow. As he dropped heavily beside her, the haunted look in Linnayen's eyes faded a little when he took her hand and kissed it.

The metal door clamped shut with a hiss of air and instantly the aerporter dropped away into the chasm below the Sill of Makum, making for the protection of the sinkhole to wait for the cool of evening before the flight back to Zaz. As the vessel swung in a dive away from the mountain of Beshwuk, Jax looked over his shoulder. Falvii, Calin and the troops were sharing water flasks, smiling and relieved that the fight was over and they were all safe, bar a few flesh wounds. His eyes went to the only discordant sound in the cabin – Setiyan. She was moaning and crying, pleading with Finn to take her back. He in return said nothing, but held her firmly in his arms, stroking her tousled hair and pulling loose strands away from her tear-stained cheeks. But Jax was not the only one to see the soft kiss the bodyguard planted on his daughter's forehead. His eyes caught Calin's and they shared a knowing smile.

No one saw the last minutes of Kalik Denkaun's existence, just as no one had witnessed the last minutes of his mother's life twenty-five years earlier. The remaining few Guznon guards had retreated into the safety of the stone passageway, not now knowing or caring if their revered A'bat was still alive. For within a minute Lau would fully top the horizon and, within another ten, Uzno, its twin, would join it. But as his tortured body was slowly devoured in their heat, Kalik Denkaun, the A'bat of Guznon found comfort. He knew that his legacy would live on. The prophecy would be fulfilled.

Epilogue

J inau wondered if she would ever get used to a single sun rising over the snow-tipped peaks of the Ksas Mountains. She marvelled at the way the frozen caps emerged from the colourless grey mist of pre-dawn to pink, then peach and, finally, a rich rosy cream. She and her mother, Na'jin, made a point of rising before dawn every day purely for these moments before they began their work in the Genara household, Jinau to get the nursery ready and Na'jin to crush the cuya fruits for breakfast. The Princess Setiyan was most particular about having fresh juice every morning, though Lord Finn would accept whatever fare he was handed.

She smiled at the thought of Lord Finn, who had been so kind to her after their adventure on Autabron nearly eighteen months ago now. He and the princess had made sure she and her mother were looked after and gave them a delightful chalet within the Genkarah palace grounds in which to live. He had said it was the least they could do after her help in looking after the princess while she had been the A'bat's prisoner.

As she tidied the toy shelf, she grinned, recalling the way Lord Finn and Princess Setiyan looked at each other. It warmed her heart. She remembered how he had nursed the poor princess on the spaceracer back to Altan. Her delirium had lasted for nearly a week and she would sometimes cry out in her sleep for Kalik Denkaun. Each time, Lord Finn had calmed her and held her and spoken soft words until she quieted. Even the lady's mother and sister could not work such magic! And when they tried, she pushed them away reaching only for Lord Finn. But then, thought Jinau, who could resist those warm brown eyes? Eyes that would melt the ice caps atop those far mountains.

She giggled, remembering the time when she accidentally walked in on them one day about three weeks after they had arrived back on Altan. They were in such a deep embrace, just standing in the middle of the princess's bedroom, that they didn't hear her come in at all. She had stood looking at them, dazed with the beauty of the lovers caught in a sunbeam, and it wasn't until she coughed that they pulled apart, like two teenagers caught up to mischief.

'Oh! Jinau … That wasn't what it … I mean …'

'No! It wasn't … He means … Er … Yes.'

She had grinned and began humming a bright tune she had picked up since being on Altan, sweeping through the room to the closet where she deposited the fresh laundry. When she passed back through the bedroom again she noticed that they were once more smiling at each other, unaware of her presence. The princess was wrapped in Lord Finn's arms and Jinau saw her take his face and kiss him with such passion that she could not help but blush.

The day was moving on and already the little princess was awake and gurgling in her cot. She pulled her toes to into her mouth where her dribbly gums clamped onto them. On seeing her nursemaid, she quickly let them go and stretched out her arms to be picked up.

'And how do those toes taste today?' Jinau laughed, picking up the baby and enclosing her in a warm hug. 'Oh! You smell, Vivee! We cannot take you to your mama like that.'

She busied herself with the changing the baby and dressing her in a simple shift, all the while chatting and laughing with her. The delicately woven dress laid out on the table would not be needed until later at the naming ceremony. For the daughter of such a horrible man as the A'bat, little Princess Viveen was delightful. She had the fair hair of both parents, but the blue eyes of her first few weeks of life had already changed to a forest green that was so like her grandmother's. This baby had charmed them all and brought such happiness from so dark a time.

As for her homeworld, Jinau was grateful to be away from all its troubles. The riots and protests had continued for many weeks after the death of the A'bat. A juggernaut had been released by his and Mira's machinations, and many innocent people had been caught up in a frenzied few months of panic and violence. But now, with the Ki and the Ki-consort's intervention, calm had been restored. The mines had reopened and both the pay and living conditions for the workers had been much improved. So maybe something good had come out of all the mess after all, Jinau reasoned. And the poisoners who had started it all? The daughter had been sent packing back to Earth, where the Ki-consort had insisted that she and her father be tried for murder, as well as the GKD bosses. They had been found guilty and imprisoned. Jinau could not understand such greed. Surely a warm home, a full belly and family were all anyone needed?

The door opened and cries of delight pierced the air.

'Vivee, you're awake! Come to Mama! Oh, I missed you, my heart's love.'

Instantly, the baby's eyes searched over Jinau's shoulder for the source of the noise and she squealed happily. Seti, still in her nightclothes, scooped up her daughter and smothered her with kisses then twirled her in the air. There could be no sweeter sound than the eruption of laughter that came from little Viveen.

'Thank you, Jinau. Oh, I see you've got everything ready. Well done.'

'I shall come back when it is time,' Jinau replied, and, with a little pat on the baby's head, she left the room just as the Lady Calin entered. They exchanged a greeting before Calin stepped up to her sister, arms up and ready to receive the baby.

'My turn! I need hugs too.'

Seti happily handed Vivee over. 'What a smile! And all for your Aunty Calin. Lucky Aunty Calin!' Setiyan smiled and added, 'Lucky me. And lucky Decker, too.'

'That goes for all of us.' Calin moved to the window before turning back to face her sister with a sad smile. 'I'm going to miss you – and Vivee.'

Calin kissed the baby on the nose, deftly missing the baby's attempt to return the gesture with an excess of drool. Moving away from the warming sunlight, Calin handed the baby back to Seti, who sat on the sofa at the end of the bed.

'It's only for a few months,' Seti assured her. 'And you know you'll love teaching. You'll have Falvii to keep you company too. That'll be fun.'

'That's down to Grandmother getting me a post at the same academy as him.' Calin flopped onto the sofa next to her sister, who was bouncing the baby on her knees, helping Vivee to stand up. 'Why can't she leave it alone?'

Seti raised an eyebrow. 'Because if it were left to you, Falvii would be waiting until he had wrinkles and grey hair. Although maybe he wouldn't. There *are* plenty of other women out there.'

Calin couldn't hide the worry in her eyes.

Seti continued, 'Oh, really, Calin! Just give in. He's meant for you. He adores you. Marry him and be happy.'

'Just like you and Decker.'

At the mention of Decker's name, Setiyan blushed and her eyes glowed. It was true. He made her heart sing. And who would have thought it? But once the urthrengo had left her body and she began to think clearly again, it was only his face she longed to see and his kisses she wanted to feel on her lips. Oh, and such kisses! Kisses that melted away all thoughts of Kalik Denkaun. Kisses that made her head spin and her heart beat faster than she thought possible.

'Speaking of,' Setiyan countered, 'it's time to hand over this little princess to her papa and grandpa so I can get dressed. Come on, Aunty Calin. Let's go!'

Seti bounced up, sweeping the baby with her and she headed for the door at such a pace that she nearly collided with Linnayen as she entered the room.

'Seti! How many times have I told you? Don't run holding the baby. What if you drop her?'

'But I won't,' came the confident retort. Behind her, Calin shrugged and smiled.

'You say that, but ...'

'Don't worry, Ma. I have it all under control. Now, step aside. This baby needs her poppas.'

Linnayen sighed and shook her head. 'They're in the dining room having breakfast.' She moved to one side, allowing Seti and the baby to pass by. Her eyes lingered on the baby as Seti bounced down the wide marble staircase, a gurgling Vivee jogging merrily in her arms.

She placed a restraining hand on Calin's arm. 'Have you got a minute?'

Calin nodded and tucked a stray tendril of hair behind her ear as she and Linnayen walked back into the bedroom. Calin moved to the open window and took a deep breath as Linnayen spoke.

'Should I tell her? I feel I should.'

Calin frowned. 'What's brought this on?'

'It's always on my mind. I just worry.' Linnayen sank down onto the couch.

'No, Ma! She doesn't need to know.'

'But what if ...' She trailed off despondently.

Calin glared at her. 'No. It would crush her. She feels bad enough already.'

'Yes, but nothing was her fault. She was drugged, just as I was.'

'What good would it do? She's happy. More importantly, Vivee's healthy. Let it be.'

Calin was right. Linnayen knew it. The chances were that there would never be a need for Setiyan to know her true heritage. Or for Viveen to know hers. Why would there be with such a devoted father and husband as Decker Finn, and the strength of the Genara family to support and cherish them?

Linnayen smiled and took her daughter's arm as they descended the stairs to join the rest of the family for breakfast.

The red-skinned woman stretched lazily before pushing back the silken sheets. She had slept well in Vexar's soft bed. Her ebony eyes took in the lavishly furnished room, the gold-embroidered tapestries decorating the stone walls and the heavy claw-foot couch on which he had first taken her many months ago, vowing that she was his heart's desire and that she would be his. And childbirth had not robbed her of beauty or voluptuousness. Indeed, it had only enhanced it, and Vexar took much pleasure in tracing her curves with his long fingers. As the new leader of the Graan tribe following Vit's untimely death, he was well-placed to look after the widow of the A'bat, as her status demanded. She had presented herself to him, kneeled before him as she had once done for his predecessor, her beloved Kalik, and, when she lifted her dark eyes to his, he licked his lips. She had found a home.

Vexar was a good lover, kind and gentle. Considerate of her wishes. But he was not her Kalik. There was no fire, no urgency in their lovemaking, none of the delicious pain that she had once craved. It was bearable, though, and Vexar was a good father to her little Jikaal. Her boy was growing so tall and strong, just like his father, who had died a martyr on the Sill of Makum. The agony of losing him still tore at her heart and, without doubt, she would raise his son to know his father's story and who had led him to his death. Indeed, if he knew nothing else, he would know that.

Penn Adams

GLOSSARY OF TERMS

PEOPLE

Adrik Hasler	A professor of biogenics at the university in Genkarah
Avad Jarkoo	Head of the GKD mine on Autabron
Calin Genara	Daughter of Linnayen and Jax, younger sister of Setiyan
Decker Finn	First officer, *Teg-Kanish*
Duncan McCrae	An actor, Jax's oldest friend
Evica Genara-Min	Linnayen's older sister, married to Tariik Min, now living on Dasnir
Falvii Min	The son of Tariik Min's older brother, Odar, cousin by marriage to the Genara sisters
Hanashi	The leader of the Gaksi tribe on Autabron
Harriet Whitton-Blake	An operative for the Earthan secret service, Covert-7
Jinau Akika	Personal maidservant to Setiyan
Kalik Denkaun	Son of Altani twins Durroc and Balisel Navarr, adopted son of Lyr and Mira Denkau, leader of the Guznon tribe on Autabron
Kalisa Caspiran	A member of the Galactic Union Council and cousin to Linnayen
Kevor Jax Bashir	Ki-consort to Linnayen Genara, father of Setiyan and Calin Genara-Jax
Li-el Dacas	Mother of Linnayen and Evica Genara
Li-kah Amanie	A scientist working with Prof Hasler
Linnayen Genara	The Ki of Altan, married to Kevor Jax, mother to Setiyan and Calin
Mikel Piek	A scientist, formerly worked with Adrik Hasler, friend of Dr Amanie

Mira Denkau	Widow of Lyr Denkau and Kalik's foster mother, a shaman of the Guznon people with the ability to foresee the future
Na'jin Akika	Mother to Jinau Akika
Natesha Koskinen	Chief officer of Millien Inc. a multi-planetary mining consortium
Navarr, Durroc and Balisel	Twin brother and sister, the parents of Kalik Denkaun (both deceased)
Nen	Maidservant to Linnayen Genara
Pieter Serekunda	Head of the Galactic Union's Eco-ethics Council
Rutak Birkaan	The Galactic Union's Industry secretary
Setiyan Genara	Daughter of Linnayen and Jax, older sister of Calin
Svikar Kaletin	Leader of the city council in Zaz-Rakuum, a member of the Graan tribe
Vit	Leader of the Graan tribe on Autabron
Wika Dokau	Concubine to Kalik Denkaun
Yenshar Genara	The former Ki of Altan, Linnayen's father, died when Linnayen was twenty years old (deceased)

PLACES

Adnat'olak	A hidden oasis near the southern polar region of Autabron. The name means 'heavenly spring'
Altan	One of the five planets in the Galactic Union, an Earth-like planet with mountains, steppe plains, forests and oceans
Aunis	Autabron's only moon
Autabron	One of the five planets in the Galactic Union, largely hot desert but with low scrubland plains near the poles, rich in many minerals
Beshwuk Highlands	A range of mountains on Autabron, riddled with caves and tunnels, largely carved by the Guznon tribespeople
Beshwuk settlement	The central community of the Guznon tribe, a thriving city carved into and below one of

	the largest mountains of the Beshwuk Highlands
Camdru Hills	A range of low gritstone hills on Autabron
Cavern of Gunda	A holy place inside the mountain that forms part of the Beshwuk settlement, home to the Guznon people of Autabron
Dasnir	One of the five planets in the Galactic Union, a watery world where nearly ninety percent of the surface is ocean
Earth	The most recent member of the five planets comprising the Galactic Union
Esor Valley	A famous wine-growing region on the planet Hutho
Euta Makaan	A large bergussian ore processing plant on Autabron
Euta Sakek	A 2000-year-old richly carved underground hall of worship, sacred to the Guznon people of Autabron; translates as 'holy place'
Genkarah	One of the largest cities on Altan, ancestral home of the Genara and Dacas families
Guyvar Neref	A ruined thirteenth-century fortress in north-east Anatolia on Earth
Hiresh	The main town of the Gaksi tribe on Autabron
Hutho	One of the five planets of the Galactic Union, a planet of forests, mountains and rivers
Jarunei Strand	An arm of the Milky Way
Kadis Sakek	A huge underground waterway comprising lakes and rivers, sacred to the people of Autabron; translates as 'holy waters'
Ksas Mountains	A chain of mountains on Altan with peaks reaching up to ten kilometres above sea level
Lau	One of the twin suns of Autabron
Rakuumna Spaceport	A busy spaceport on Autabron
Silbaraz-Re	Largest city on the planet Altan

Sill of Makum	A large rock platform at the top of the Beshwuk mountain settlement upon which sits a sacrificial chair
Te'kaan	A large bergussian ore mine on Autabron
Utieku River	One of the largest rivers on the planet Hutho, famous for its waterfalls and rapids
Uzno	The second of the twin suns of Autabron
Xaca	An abandoned village in the rainforest on Hutho
Zaz-Rakuum	An underground city, home mainly to miners and processing plant workers on Autabron

THINGS

A'bat	Translates from the Guznon as 'warrior of hope', honorary title given to Kalik Denkaun
A'batau	In Guznon, is the female for 'warrior of hope'
aerporter	An aircraft used on Autabron for transporting cargo and passengers
Akshanik (the)	One of the native tribes of Autabron
ambicinite	A pale blue mineral found only on Altan, used mainly as a veneer for furniture
Aun'bat	An honorary title in the Guznon language meaning 'daughter of hope'
belika	A small, purple-feathered bird, native to Altan, famous for its skill in mimicry
bergu	The molten state of pure bergussian
bergussian	A metallic ore mined on Autabron, used in the production of alloys, essential for building spacecraft
bika	Plant-eating, soft-hoofed animal living in herds in the arctic zones of Autabron
carolite	A rose-tinted marble found only on Altan, mostly used for flooring
clikon	A handheld device for activating electronic equipment

Covert-7	An Earth-based intelligence agency, also known as C-7
cuja	A tasty fruit that grows on the foothills of the Ksas
deego tree	Known as the 'screaming tree', a shrub with spiral-shaped flowers that close with a squealing noise when touched
dej-net	A fine mesh positioned to capture morning dew on Autabron
dirratin gas	Found primarily on Altan and Hutho, used as a propellant in fuel systems of interplanetary craft
D'nongra tribe	The D'nongra people live a traditional life in the trees of the deep forests of Hutho
entaki bush	Native to Altan, and with gold-coloured leaves, the entaki is grown as a decorative house plant
feir	A protein-rich fungus that grows in the caves of Autabron
fre-gath	A drug used on Altan to lift mood
Galactic Union	The name given to the combined political entity of the former Earthan UDN and the Union of Planets, now comprising the five planets of Altan, Autabron, Dasnir, Earth and Hutho
Gaksi (the)	A tribe of native people on Autabron whose territory covers the northern polar region
ganak	A derogatory term used by Autabronis to describe people from another planet, especially Altanis and, more recently, Earthans
Graan (the)	A tribe on Autabron
Grunkaar, Day of	A time on Autabron when the seers estimate that rains will fall, usually occurs only once a year
Guznon	One of the original, indigenous tribes of Autabron

holomask	A holographic device used to project an altered image onto a person's face
Horn of Gurkat	A ceremonial horn of bergussian used by the Guznon people in religious ceremonies
ion-laser	A handheld laser that fires an ionised particle beam
jekarion gas	A gas found in the atmosphere of Altan, which has the property of refracting light in the red wavelength, responsible for the rose-coloured skies of Altan
Jensa-Kadenx	An inter-planetary space-liner
kalendarium	An opaline crystal mineral mainly used to decorate buildings, found only on Altan
kaypak	A species of monkey found in the rainforests of Hutho with a comical red beard
kareek	A small dog-like animal with scaly skin, very loyal, kept as a domestic pet on Altan
kek	The monetary unit of all the five Galactic Union planets
Ki and Ki-consort	The Ki is the highest-ranking secular individual of the planet Altan, male or female. The title which has 'royal' status is attained through birthright and training, but incumbents can be resigned by vote of the Altan Council
kipr'aa	A small fish that shoals in the shallow waters of lakes on Altan
kiska bread	An unleavened flatbread made by the indigenous people of Autabron
klik	A measure of distance in the Union, a little under a kilometre
Ko-Kura	'Little infidel' in the Guznon dialect on Autabron
Ko-Makum	Means 'little witch' in the language of the Guznon people
kooruk	A strong Autabroni liquor made from the pulp of feir fungus

Konkanaw (the)	One of the half dozen native tribes on Autabron
ksarpi tree	Species of dark-wood tree on Hutho that grows to an average one hundred metres tall over its usual lifespan of 700 years
Latis-Mei	A race of indigenous people on the planet, Altan
larka	A tree native to the planet, Hutho, the bark of which emits a fragrant oil used in many perfumes
mawkaan	A faith doctor of the Guznon tribe
mentante	A trait, usually passed on genetically, that allows for the reading of minds, a higher form of telepathy
natar	Name given to a female adoptive mother, means 'beloved of the child' (Autobroni)
No'os (the)	Another of the native tribes of Autabron
off-worlder	The generic name given to natives of another planet
Opponetix	A violent video game played on Autabron where the first player to kill ten victims by ten different methods is the winner
pakiran	A tent-like structure made from the hides of the bika, traditional home of the Gaksi tribe on Autabron
palletron	A hovering pallet used to transport heavy objects
parab	A full-body covering worn by the excluded men and women of the Guznon tribe as a punishment. In effect, they are 'seen' not to exist
plinka	A colourful species of night-moth, found in the forests of Hutho
prijah	Game where players move coloured stones in a three-dimensional prism, each trying to fill their side ahead of their opponents
psytro-ions	Rare ion particles found in deep space with a gravitational force

psytro-ion stream	An unusual cosmonic phenomenon where super-charged ion particles align themselves in the same plane and can penetrate metal
qasar-mortars	A mobile qasar-pulse mortar with a range of 500 metres, suitable in open-area field combat
reviv	Short for 'revivitator', a combined defibrillator and respirator
rhonium-mortar	A short-range mortar that fires 5mm rhonium shells
rilo pine trees	A type of coniferous tree found on Altan with distinctive blue needles and sweet nuts which are used in pastries
sauconium	An explosive compound
Sen	Title denoting honour acquired through service to the community
sivakaan	The juice of the sivaka, a succulent found in the polar regions of Autabron
srif	A high-protein seagrass, found in the shallower waters of Dasnir
stukka	A spice native to Autabron, used to flavour most foods
tagirp	A native fish species found in the underground waters of Autabron
tamun	Tamuns are the holy men and women of the tribes of Autabron
Teg-Kanish	A spaceracer, smaller spacecraft designed for short-haul journeys between the original four planets
Teg-Koorym	A spaceracer
turgex	A compound of turellium and sulphur used as an explosive in mining operations
urthrengo	A powerful behaviour-modifying drug, developed on Hutho
veyor	The public transit system in the underground city of Zaz-Rakuum, a walk-

	on/walk-off driverless tram that rides up and down spiral tracks
windshifter	The name given to a small one- or two-person air-car used widely on all Galactic Union planets
witaq	A small deer found in many mountain ranges on Altan
xelex cannon	A powerful mortar gun which fires xelex cartridges over a distance of up to five kilometres
yargon	A pain-killing drug

ACKNOWLEDGEMENTS

The support and encouragement of my family, friends and professional colleagues has been so wonderful and, without doubt, kept me enthused to produce this sequel to my first book, *The Malign Alliance*. Although the physical constraints of a certain pandemic helped, for what else was there to do in 2020 but write a book?

Yet again, Simone Ford has been an amazing editor and has polished my rough diamond into a dead-set sparkler. Her advice on how best to present the characters and tweak the storylines to make them perfect was just superlative and as for what she does with my grammar… Just know, it's more than good. Thank you, Simone. As for Belinda Holley, words cannot express my gratitude for your encouragement and your eagle-eye for detail. She even enlisted her beautiful daughters, Izzy and Gabsy, into the Holley proof-reading clan extraordinaire. Thanks girls!

Rob Williams has produced yet another stunning cover. I had so many compliments about his work on my first book that I would have been a complete idiot not to go with him again (and, yes, he's still 'stuck' in South Korea, but ever cheerful and working hard). Thanks, Rob.

As for my advance readers and local supporters here in Australia, in the US and the UK… Wow! Thank you, Lyn Crossley, Wendy Jeffery, Sue Marcucci, Sharon Edwards, Peter Elzer, Benita Morris, Jen Thompson, Ian and Michele P-G, Fiona and the Serendipity crew, Susan Hood and Angela Robinsen. Your reviews and advice were so helpful and I hope you'll do the same when the next book comes out.

To my much-loved daughter, Caroline, my beautiful grand-daughters, Chloe and Amelia, and my super son-in-law, Jesse – thank you for being there and keeping me strong, well-fed and wrapped in warm hugs.

Finally, thanks to all my lovely Facebook Friends and Followers without whose support I probably wouldn't have sold half as many books. Thanks go beyond words.

ABOUT THE AUTHOR

Penn Adams is a writer of science fiction romance and adventure as well as stage plays.

Her first book is *The Malign Alliance* in which a proud alien queen devises a controversial plan to end the war with Earth. But her passion for an unsuitable man threatens more than just the peace treaty. This is the first of a trilogy in the Malign Series and the second book is *The Malign Legacy*. The third book, *The Malign Paradox*, will be released in 2022.

Penn has written two full-length stage plays, *Autumn Song* (2014), a rich family drama about guilt and redemption, and *Companion Planting* (2018), a farcical comedy about the residents of a retirement village taking over the filming of a television reality show. Both plays were performed by community theatre groups in northern New South Wales and garnered much acclaim.

Originally from London, Penn now lives in the paradise of northern New South Wales encircled by rainforests, beaches and the glorious Pacific Ocean.

BOOK THREE of the

MALIGN SERIES

The watery planet, Dasnir, stands in danger of an alien force determined to subjugate its people and claim its riches. The Galactic Union's forces must act quickly to avert disaster. But the Genara family's leadership is under threat from a rival house and internal bickering looks set to lead to catastrophe. Will the people of Dasnir be abandoned in their hour of need? Or will an uneasy alliance between a Genara princess and the son of a hated enemy finally save both the planet and the whole Union?

Follow the story in *The Malign Paradox* out in 2022.

www.pennadams.com

https://www.facebook.com/pennadamsauthor/?ref=py_c

Leave a review

I hope you have enjoyed reading *The Malign Legacy* and I thank you for choosing it. Maybe you read its predecessor, *The Malign Alliance*? Please do 'follow' me on Facebook for all the news about further books in this series and other works.

If you're intrigued by the universe I've had such fun creating in these books, do please leave a comment or a review on your favourite platform, such as Goodreads. Writers thrive on knowing how their work is received – it enthuses us to do better so that we can continue to make your reading choices entertaining and satisfying.

Penn Adams

www.ingramcontent.com/pod-product-compliance
Lightning Source LLC
Chambersburg PA
CBHW030531120726
47904CB00005B/1723